The Swithen: Book Two

The Sons of Constance

By Scott Telek

This book is dedicated to my father,
Andrew Stanley Telek.

Praise for *Book 1: Our Man on Earth*

The Swithen series is an exciting new addition to modern Arthurian fiction... **Our Man on Earth** *shows that getting at the meat of the individual [Arthurian] stories brings them to life in new and rewarding ways. Too often, Arthurian characters become stick figures in modern retellings, but that is far from the case here.*

Telek doesn't shy away from the supernatural but makes it feel real. I don't want to spoil the plot... But I do want to say is how very powerful the end of the novel is. The conversations between [Merlin] and his mother on [his moral character] are the culmination of the book and bring the story to a powerful close... I only wished it was longer.
    – Tyler Tichelaar, Author "Children of Arthur"

The whole thing is different than the "King Arthur fiction" you know. This is a very personal story, and one of the cool things about it is that you just get involved with the characters, and then you realize that THAT is MERLIN. So it makes you come at the characters in a new way... Rather than the typical magic and sweep of history and all that, this just shows them as real people.
    – Robert C., Amazon Review

Praise for *Book 2: The Sons of Constance*

What is fascinating about the novel is not the plot, but the psychology of the characters as the chain of events unfolds. If you weren't fascinated by how Telek depicted Merlin in the first novel, I guarantee you will be here.

Merlin is the star of the novel, although the depiction of the three kings who precede Arthur are, in my opinion, Telek's triumph simply because they have been sketchy and not fully detailed in most Arthurian works to date.

Vortigern has always been a rather undeveloped figure in Arthurian legend, but here he comes to life as a fully-rounded individual. Telek has created the most real and sympathetic version of Vortigern to date.
– Tyler Tichelaar, Author "Children of Arthur

Praise for *Book 3: The Void Place*

"What sets the book apart is the complex interplay amongst all the characters and the way their high-stakes situations play out against each other. A lot of secondary characters get great parts here which makes the entire thing a complex tapestry of interwoven storylines. Foremost is Uther's best friend, Ulfius, who knows he is doing wrong in helping the king, but is forced to go along against his will. Then there's Igraine's two girls (one of whom will grow to be the famous Morgan le Fay) who are caught in the middle and stand to be unwitting victims (plus, the ten-year-old future sorceress Morgan is a hoot!). It all just keeps turning and twisting until you arrive at THAT ending.

By the end, we have the baby Arthur, making all three books the lead-up to all that we know is to come—although these books prove that there's a LOT of engrossing new life that can be breathed into these old legends. If you make it through this book, you will be hooked for the series. It leaves you in a spot where the story is poised to explode, which gives the exciting feeling that as gripping as this series has been, it's just getting started."
– Judy K.J., Amazon Review

Table of Contents

In Previous Books

Our Man on Earth: The Swithen Book 1

Taking the example of Jesus Christ, only 400 years earlier, the devil
wants to create a mortal man on Earth. He will allow that person to see
all events of the past in order to lead people into temptation. A young
woman, Meylinde, finds a shadow falls over her house, and her family
mysteriously dies one after another, as the demon draws closer to her.
A holy man, Blaise, hints that a demon may be targeting her. Despite
Meylinde's fortitude, and Blaise's support, she is impregnated by the
demon.

At that time, an illegitimate child bears a judgment of death by burning.
Blaise suggests that Meylinde be locked in a tower until the child is
born. Her faith is sorely tested, as once the child is born, she will die.
The infant is a monstrous devil upon birth, but Blaise baptizes it
immediately, and he becomes human. He is able to keep his knowledge
of the past and ability to shape-shift, and to this, God adds the ability to
see the events of the future. Meylinde names him *Merlin*.

The power of the child's mind grows exponentially. At one year old, he
is able to defend his mother at the trial for her life, and wield his
knowledge of all things to enact his will for the first time. Merlin then
announces that he has realized his purpose on Earth: to effect the
complete transformation of Britain through the creation of a king—
named Arthur.

Returning Characters

Merlin. Child of a demon but baptized at birth. Given the ability to see
all events of the past by the devil, and the ability to see the future by
God, as well as the freedom to choose his own path. Since Merlin sees

the events of humankind across centuries, it is difficult for him to care about any one person.

Meylinde. Merlin's mother. Her faithfulness and strength won Merlin from the devil's influence, and she is very influential on his sense of right and wrong.

Blaise. The holy hermit who helped Meylinde during her ordeal, he is her friend and Merlin's partner and human advisor.

Rossa. One of the midwives who accompanied Meylinde in the tower that she formed a bond with.

In Coming Books

Book 2: The Sons of Constance – YOU ARE HERE
Merlin serves three kings while setting the pieces in place that will result in Arthur's birth.

Book 3: The Void Place - Available Now
Uther, Igraine and the birth of Arthur.

Book 4:
Arthur's childhood, from infancy until he encounters a certain sword in a certain stone.

Book 5:
Arthur is put into training with Ulfius and Bretel until he is coroneted as king.

Book 6:
Arthur must wage war on those who dispute the reign of a teenage king, and receives Excalibur.

Book 7:
Arthur forms the Knights of the Round Table, meets Guinevere and begins constructing Camelot.

Book 8:

Arthur marries Guinevere and his knights depart on three mystic adventures.

Book 9:

The childhood of Lancelot in the Lady of the Lake's hidden matriarchal society.

Book 10:

The adventures of Balin le Savage and Sir Gawain and the Green Knight.

Book 11:

Morgan Le Fay makes a daring attempt to destroy Arthur and claim his throne.

Book 12:

Lancelot joins King Arthur's court and embarks on the adventure of the Dolorous Guard.

Book 13:

Lancelot is torn between love for Guinevere, King Arthur's wife, and fellow warrior Galehaut, the Lord of the Distant Isles.

Book 14:

A mysterious new knight, Beaumains, is entrusted with a crucial adventure.

Book 15:

Lancelot becomes ensnared in an affair that results in the birth of Galahad.

Book 16:

Lancelot wanders insane as Gawain searches to bring him back and heal the court.

Book 17:

Over the course of one day, mysterious adventures unfold and the quest for the Holy Grail is enjoined.

Book 18:

The knights depart to seek the Holy Grail while Arthur and Guinevere's marriage is in ruins.

Book 19:

The knights encounter death, destruction and despair as they seek the Holy Grail.

Book 20:
The few remaining knights stumble back to Camelot as three knights encounter the Grail.

Book 21:
Lancelot is drawn into a relationship that leaves Guinevere furious, and another woman dead.

Book 22:
When Guinevere is kidnapped, Lancelot departs to save her while Arthur's jealous rage grows.

Book 23:
When Guinevere's affair is finally exposed, the kingdom collapses and the aged Arthur goes to war.

Book 24:
The distraction of the war allows Arthur's bastard son Mordred to launch a hostile takeover.

Book 25:
The death of Arthur.

Keep updated on new books and insights about the series at theswithen.com.

Sources

The mission of **The Swithen** is to honor the original Arthurian legend by maintaining strict fidelity to the source material, while fleshing out characters and scenes to make the thoughts and emotions of the characters clear to modern readers.

In short, *nothing about the original legend can be changed.* We can only expand, add and enhance characters and scenes. The challenge of **The Swithen** is to create a plausible psychology and unifying storyline that will slot seamlessly into the existing legend, with changes only permissible when there are conflicting sources.

This novel is adapted from *The History of the Kings of Britain,* by Geoffery of Monmouth, of approximately 1150 A.D., "The Story of Merlin" from the *Lancelot-Grail (Vulgate Cycle),* written between 1215 and 1235 A.D. and the *Prose Merlin* of approximately 1450 A.D.

Please share your opinion of this book with others

Please take the time to share your honest opinion about this book in a review online, to your friends and family, and on social media. I am an independent author, without the support that other authors receive, and your honest review or comment is tremendously influential, incredibly helpful, and greatly appreciated. Thank you for taking the time to share your honest opinions.

Part One
THE FIRST KING

The room was dark and cramped, reached at the bottom of a dark stone stairway that was not moist, as so many underground stairways are, but instead cool and dry to the point of creating raspy noises as one's sleeves brushed against the close stones of the corridor. The torch illuminated the wooden door into the bottom chamber, thirty feet underneath the ground, where the cleric Arledge was headed. As he entered, the air changed once more, to a desert heat, created by the other torches in the circular room, which hung a few feet apart across the perimeter of the upper wall. The floor was bare earth, and the six other clerics sat, as appointed, on wooden benches in a circle, illuminated by the pulsing amber light of the torches, which created a skein of moving shadows and occasional creeping line of black smoke that wafted over the stones of the ceiling to turn sharply upward upon reaching the small hole in the center of the roof.

"Were any of you seen in coming here?" asked Arledge, eyes moving around the circle to see each of the assembled clerics shaking his head in turn. It was imperative that this meeting take place without knowledge of the king.

Arledge sat at the seventh bench, completing the circle. With a last look around the room, and finding only the expectant faces of the other clerics focused on him, he began. "I have met with each of you individually, so that you could speak to me about the visions you have seen, without the possible corruption of hearing each other," he said. "And it seems that each of you has told me one thing—for each of you has seen the same thing—and that each of you has hidden one thing from me."

The clerics said nothing, but the way their backs stiffened, the audible intake of breath, and the way their eyes darted to steal glances at the others, told that the man's words had struck them.

"Tell us what we said to you and what we hid from you," said Rylan, another of the king's seers.

Arledge held the man's gaze for a long moment, then let his eyes fall to the reddish dirt of the floor. "None of us has had any thoughts at all about what we were asked to give advice on, which is why King Vortiger's tower cannot stand. None of us saw anything about the tower whatsoever, no matter what ritual we performed in which to see. The matter of the tower is completely obscure to us."

The eyes of the gathered clerics were kept lowered to the ground, but some were seen nodding in silent agreement that despite their best efforts, the matter for which the king had sent forth to gather them, the greatest seers in the land, had left them all completely confounded.

"What you of all did see, and there is not one of you that did not see it," Arledge lifted his finger and gestured around the circle, "was a boy, seven years of age, born without a father, but conceived of a woman."

This brought their eyes up, first to look at Arledge, then to quickly search the faces of their companions.

"And no matter how you asked, and performed rituals to gain information on why the tower will not hold, all you could see was this boy," Arledge continued. "And each of you told me that you saw nothing more," he said, "nor did I myself see anything more."

Silence reigned as each of the gathered men sat quietly. The puttering flame of one of the torches was the only sound in the underground room.

"But each of you has also seen one other thing, that none of you told me about. And I know this, because I have seen it as plainly as any of you." His graven eyes searched the faces of the assembled clerics, but each of them was staring downward at the floor, still hands resting clasped in their laps.

"There is not one of us who did not see clearly that he will die because of this boy," he said.

No word was said, but all reacted. There was the quiet sound of mouths opening in shock, the hush of muffled gasps, as the men drew

12

back, their hands coming out of their laps, or lifting to cover their mouths thoughtfully. Their eyes darted around to look at the others, yet all were afraid to speak, or would not interrupt Arledge until they were bidden to respond.

Arledge stood. "But I will tell you what I think we can do," he said, "since we know about this so long before when our deaths are foretold to come." He spoke as he began to pace slowly just outside the circle of men. "We will agree on one thing, and all of us must agree on it. We will say that the king's tower cannot stand, and never will, unless that boy is killed, and his blood is mixed with the mortar in the foundation." He stopped and looked about the now-upturned faces of the astonished men. He saw the signs of clever, self-interested thinking, but he did not see any signs of disagreement. "And we will say that if the king does this, if the blood of this fatherless boy is put into the mortar of the foundation, then the tower will stand, and be good and strong forever."

"What happens when we put the blood of the boy in the tower, and it still does not stand?" asked one of the clerics.

"We will handle that when we come to it," Arledge said.

"At least we are still alive to handle it," said another, "since the boy will have been killed then."

Rylan raised his hand, and spoke when the leader indicated him. "But how will we find this boy?" he asked.

"The king himself will send men to look for him, after we have told him of his importance to his tower," Arledge replied, "for you well know that he wants nothing more keenly in this world than that tower."

"With enemies mounting as swiftly as his, he does well to plan a strong fortress to protect himself in," said one.

"And his pagan queen," was heard another.

"Here is what we'll do," continued Arledge. "Each of us will speak to the king separately, and act as though we had never met about it or compared our visions in advance." His pointing finger found each of them in turn. "And we will all, using our own words, and our own voices, say the same thing; that we have each seen this boy, and that his blood is the only thing that can make his tower stand." He brought his hands together. "Hearing the same thing from all of us separately, he will be sure to believe it."

All nodded, and each thought on how he would say on this to the king, and in what words. None spoke aloud, for they did not want to influence the words of their companions, or have their own borrowed.

"But what if the boy should appeal to the king?" said Rylan. "Or say something to someone that would create sympathy for him, or turn people toward his welfare? He is only seven."

Arledge was ready for this question. "We will convince the king that the child, being fatherless, is in league with evil spirits, which is why his blood contains magical properties. Because of this, we'll order those who go out looking for him to kill him at first sight, and bring back only his blood."

There was heard an all-round sound of agreement, and all men nodded that this was an excellent plan.

"That will make the boy harmless," said one cleric, "and silent."

"And also lighter to carry," added another.

And the sound of raspy laughter was heard echoing off the rough stone walls.

-2-

Blaise walked by the door and saw Merlin inside. He was working on a drawing. Something round, a circle with several concentric circles, one that contained a pattern of twisting vines, and a center section with what looked like ripples in a pool.

The boy was now seven years old, and looked indistinguishable from any other boy of his age. He had a covering of light brown hair that spilled over his head in unruly waves, and his body was lean and athletic, honed by his constant rambles throughout the countryside and tireless exploration of natural things. He had never lost his intense manner or ability for extreme concentration.

"Blaise, I am happy to see you," he said, and looked up. "The time is coming soon when you will need to move to Northumberland, so I suggest that you make yourself ready."

The older man entered the room and approached the table. "It is coming time for me to move," he repeated. "I have been expecting this a long while. Does that also mean that you will be leaving this town?"

"Yes," said Merlin. "Men will soon be coming to take me away. But I am glad you are here, for I have wanted to ask you some questions." Merlin finished the work he was doing, blew the excess charcoal off of it and showed it to Blaise. "What do you think?"

The older man looked with curiosity at what Merlin had created. He did not understand what it was, but this was not new, for the majority of the matters that Merlin interested himself in were largely beyond his comprehension. "It's pretty," he said. "What is it?" He had learned to be careful to keep his hands away, for Merlin was always very irate when one of his creations had been touched or altered in any way.

"It's a table," said Merlin.

"Oh," said the hermit. He had not known that the boy was taking an interest in furniture, but nothing surprised him anymore. "Is this part of your little project?"

"Yes, and so are my questions," said Merlin. "Please come sit in the sun so we can discuss them."

The two of them moved over to sit in seats near the window, where the afternoon sun streamed in upon the older man's face. Merlin settled himself in the chair opposite.

"What is it, do you think," asked the child, "that creates a man's character?"

The old man considered. "I suppose there are many things," he said. "A mixture of what physical things he is born with, such as are inherited from his parents, but also what happens to him in his life, with his parents and other people he meets." Blaise thought a bit more, as the child stared intently at his face, and finally decided he had no more to add. "I suppose it is a combination of all of these things."

"I have been thinking on how my mother won me from the influence of the devil who had fathered me," said Merlin. "It was because of her goodness, and her observance to our Lord's will that even within the womb, I was able to know of the existence of God and to begin to see my way toward him, which your having me baptized completed, once I entered into this world."

"Yes," said the hermit. "And what have you thought on it? Well, actually," he interrupted himself, "first let me say that you represent a very special circumstance, and it is unwise to extrapolate from yourself and compare that to the upbringing of ordinary people."

"Well said," mused the child, "and understood. But," Merlin went on, "consider. As for my mother, there is her physical makeup, yes. There is her decent upbringing of me, yes. And there is in me both the physical makeup of my mother and also the semi-physical, semi-spiritual makeup of my father. But I was thinking specifically of her will, and of her goodness," Merlin said, and here he raised his finger in the air, "and more importantly, of her *wish* to be good."

Blaise looked out the window and stroked his beard as he thought about this. "Do you think her wish to be good had a great effect on you?" he asked.

"Well, that is what I wonder," said the child, picking up a nearby book and flipping through it absently, for Merlin's mind was usually going so fast he found it uninteresting to concentrate on just one thing at a time. "I wonder how much of an effect it has to be within the womb of someone, and soaked, as you might say, in their thoughts, and hopes, and dreams, and wishes," said Merlin. "And from the father. Do all of his thoughts and dreams and wishes also travel through the sticky milk he produces to create a child?"

The old man's eyes widened, as he still could not get used to talking of fully adult matters with a seven-year-old boy.

"It is impossible for me to say," said Blaise. "There is so much that goes into the making of a person. And most people simply do it, without specific effort to create a certain person, except I suppose for," and here he paused, searching for words, "for a generalized wish that their child to be healthy and decent, and such a person that will live out a good and worthy life."

"Exactly," said the child, "that is where it is difficult, for I am looking to create a very specific person, that will do very specific things. And will need to have a very, very specific character if he is to stand up to all that he must face." He flipped through several pages in the book and tossed it aside. "I guess part of it will be a grand experiment," he said, "but I have come to think that perhaps the desires of our parents can, and do, very much influence the desires and dreams of their offspring."

"Is this... also part of your little project?" asked the older man.

"Yes, my little project," said Merlin. "And we will see how my experiment works out, for the child I have in mind will spend no time with either of his birth parents, and therefore cannot pick up on their wishes and dreams through time spent with them."

"And why is that?" asked the hermit.

"Well, I am also coming to wonder if a great individual must arise from an anomaly of birth, such as we saw with Jesu Christ, and then with the next great marvel to walk on this earth," he said, "by which, of course, I mean myself."

The older man said nothing, and his face betrayed no flicker of thought, for he had long been accustomed to Merlin's extravagant statements regarding his own wondrousness.

"Do you think it is evil to use other beings for your own ends?" the child asked.

The old man thought. "I suppose it is," he said. "Especially if you are deceiving them, and do not make them aware that they are acting out a part for you, or moving toward a goal that has been decided not by them, but by you."

This interested the child, and he looked up. "So you think it is acceptable if I let them know?"

"Well, I suppose it is very highly dependent on the circumstances," said the hermit, and waited, but it soon became apparent that Merlin was not going to tell him the circumstances. "The important thing is that you not be deceitful, and that you not lead them falsely toward an unfortunate end which they would not otherwise come to themselves."

"A-ha!" said the child, and then he put his finger to his lips and sat in thought for several moments. "But now you get to the essence of what I am asking. What if they might come to an unfortunate end, but their suffering will bring much goodness—goodness for many thousands of people, far outweighing the sufferings of two—would that then be worth it?"

"It sounds," said Blaise, thoughtfully stroking his beard, "when I hear you say that the goodness will outweigh their suffering, that you have already made up your mind."

"That is not true, or I would not be asking," said the child, mildly vexed. "I value your opinion greatly, for you are a very learned and holy man. I also value the opinion of my mother, who is a very just and moral woman." He thought for a moment, and his finger tapped restlessly on his knee.

"Now think on it this way," he said. "Mankind holds himself superior to animals, and for this reason he justifies forcing animals to perform toward his own ends, and cares little for the labor of those animals when they suffer for completing his designs. I am something more than a man, and hold part of my heritage from a being that is superior to men, and for this reason I myself am superior to mortal man."

"The old tale," said Blaise.

Merlin pulled up short. "I did not make it this way," he said.

"No," Blaise said. "But oft do you speak on it."

The child glared at him pointedly. "Does this," Merlin said, a sharpness in his voice, "in the like way, make it acceptable for me to use man as my animals to carry out my will, which," he said firmly, "as we know, is one with the will of God."

Blaise chuckled. "Does God know that?" he asked.

Merlin did not see the humor, and spoke in an even tone. "Everything that I do is with the intention of bringing the people of this country closer to God, for their own salvation and better ends."

18

"I understand," Blaise said, chuckling and reaching out to stroke the boy's head, which he pulled away from. The old man thought. "It is true that mankind uses animals for his purpose, but I suppose even so, a good man is kind and respectful to his animals, cares for their needs, and does not use them in a way that would be harmful to them. And it is evil for man to use an animal cruelly, even if we accept that animals are inferior to him, for he should show respect and kindness for all of God's creations."

"I knew you would say that," said the child, and slipped off his chair to walk in circles around the room. "What if," he said, and raised his finger, "what if the animals did something that was harmful to themselves, but it was through their own decision?"

The older man stood and slowly walked over to lean against the wall opposite where Merlin was pacing. "But it sounds like what we are talking about will not be their own decision," he said.

"Well," said Merlin, tilting his head back and forth, "does it matter if they have made the decisions they do through being gently prodded in one or another direction?" He glanced quickly up at the hermit's face. "Or based on certain information that they have been given? They are still making their own decision."

"Well, it seems like it is not fully their decision if you have prodded them in one way or another to do it. Or supplied such information, or only certain information, that you knew would result in their making a specific decision."

Merlin crossed his arms. "Does it matter if this prodding that we speak of was several layers removed, and of such great gentleness and subtlety that they never knew with whom it originated, and did in fact, for all intents and purposes, make their own decision?"

Blaise seemed confused. "Can you be more specific?"

Merlin shook his head.

"It may not be wrong in a court of law," said the older man, "and it may not be something for which anyone can directly to be blamed, but if you, in your heart, know that you influenced them to act in a certain way..." Blaise considered, "you may never be discovered, and may never be blamed, but you will have to decide for yourself if you can live with the consequences of what you have done to those people."

"There are many things that I must live with," said Merlin. "This has been a very fruitful discussion and I thank you for your frank answers."

Blaise hung still. "I have the funny feeling I have just given you permission for something I'm not sure I would approve of," said the older man.

"Isn't life funny that way?" asked Merlin.

Blaise looked down at the circular drawing and tried to imagine it as a table. "I didn't know you had taken up interest in designing furniture," he said. "Is this something that you plan to have made?"

"It is indeed," said Merlin. "The making of it is very far off, and the path there is quite a winding one, although we stand at the very beginning of it! At this moment, seven clerics to the king are advising him to send messengers after me, with instructions to kill me. Those are the men who will come for me that I have told you about."

"Messengers from the king—*King Vortiger?*" Blaise's mouth dropped open. "Why, he is well known to be a bloody and ruthless tyrant! I hope you are not messing with something that is much bigger than you—remember you are but seven years old, Merlin! And these men are on their way this minute to kill you?" He raised his open palm to his forehead. "Does that not worry you?"

Merlin shrugged, squinting at his drawing. "Why would it?" he asked.

-3-

At that time, rule of the fledgling country was still very much in question. The pagan Romans had kept Britain as part of their empire, but had left the country approximately fifty years before. When they left, the land was essentially up for grabs, and its inhabitants were constantly busy defending against invaders from foreign lands. But the Britons were not wealthy and not organized, which had allowed them to be overrun by the rich and regimented Romans, and put them at a grievous disadvantage in the face of their new invaders. Mostly they were besieged by the Saxons, who came from Germanic countries, and saw the opportunity for easy expansion of their territories in Britain, while the country was disorganized and its leadership weak.

The people who lived in Britain were of Celtic heritage, and the king of the land at that time was named Constance. He had three sons, Maine, Pendragon, and Uther. He also had amongst his retinue a trusted servant named Vortiger. When Constance died of old age, Maine was elected to be king, being the eldest of the three brothers, and Vortiger became his seneschal; the one who is entrusted to take care of official affairs. Maine was only seventeen when he became king. Pendragon was thirteen, and Uther eleven, at that time.

Vortiger, who was a large, imposing and handsomely bearded king, with long black hair, and who often wore robes and mantles of the richest red, wanted power for himself and resented that the weak Maine, who was inexperienced and never prepared to be as ruthless as he was, held the throne. He began a series of sly and cunning manipulations that found the love of the people accruing gradually to him and draining away from Maine, until the point that people were coming to him for advice and wishing for his rule, rather than that of their own king. They said to him "Vortiger, we may as well have no king, for he is so young as to be worthless as a leader. Please, let you be our king, govern and protect us, for there is no one but you who could rule us at this time."

Maine, who had observed his father but had very little experience with warfare, was unable to keep out the Saxon invaders, who made great strides in taking over British towns and strongholds during his reign. The people saw their country being slowly, gradually taken from them, and for this reason, they cried out to Vortiger for leadership.

"There is no way I can govern you as long as my lord is alive," said Vortiger. "You know that very well. If it happened that he died, and then you came to me and wanted me to be your king, I would gladly do so," he said, looking each man carefully in the eye. "But as long as Maine lives, I cannot—and must not—rule you." He smiled. "For that would be treason."

These men listened and understood what they thought Vortiger was saying: if they truly wanted it, they should kill Maine so that Vortiger could then become their king. At that time, there were many who trusted Vortiger and vehemently claimed that he had the best intent for the British people in mind, and would never, ever suggest that anyone murder the king, but there were others who said that he had delivered a coded message. He outwardly showed respect and deference for the king, while clearly implying that they should kill him.

The men decided, and acted. Twelve were chosen, and they came upon the young Maine in his private chamber, where each of them stabbed him once. He died immediately.

At that time the brothers Pendragon and Uther were only boys, and the man who looked after them realized that since Vortiger had his own lord killed, the moment he was king, he would have the boys killed as well. For no matter how despotic Vortiger might be, he knew full well that the kingdom's power was earned by Constance, and rule of the country was his sons' birthright, and should by all rights be theirs.

Their guardian took the boys to Brittany in order to protect them from the murderous king, where they were trained as knights and taught to rule, with the intent that they would one day return to challenge Vortiger and lay claim to their land. Uther was younger and had less patience to learn the discipline needed for ruling, but it mattered little, for he was an excellent fighter and excelled in strength, and, as his older brother was next in line for the throne, it was assumed that he could be his support while Pendragon took on the burden of leadership.

Vortiger was chosen and proclaimed king. After his crowning, the twelve who had killed King Maine came to him, hoping to join his retinue. When Vortiger saw them, he gave no indication of ever having seen or spoken to them before, and was aghast when they told him that they had killed Maine. He ordered them taken prisoner and said to them, in front of all his advisors, "You unworthy men have provided your own judgment and condemnation by admitting that you killed your own king! And now you come to me for approval, and to sit at my side? I know as well as I sit here that you would do the same to me if you could, but I am not so foolish as to trust the likes of you."

The twelve were aghast. One of them stepped forward and said "Sir, we did it because we thought your rule would be best for us, and you would love us for it."

But Vortiger stood firmly, hands on hips, and said so that all of his advisors could hear: "I will show you clearly how I love people like you."

He had all twelve of them taken and each tied to the tail of a horse. They were then dragged behind for so long that little was left.

But these twelve were of noble stock, and had many wealthy and honorable family and kinsmen who were shocked and appalled at how the king had treated their brothers and sons. They came to the king and said "You shamed us mightily when you killed our brothers and friends so unworthily. Therefore we will never serve you willingly."

Vortiger grew angry at these words and said that if they did not mend their tongues, they too would die in the same unworthy way.

And one of them, a father of one of the men who Vortiger had killed, and a wealthy baron and very important man in his own right, stepped forward, holding up a damning finger, and shaking in his place with incandescent rage.

"King Vortiger," he said, "threaten us as much as you will, but I say one thing to you; as long as we have one friend left on earth, you will have war." He moved his hands powerfully apart, and said, "From this moment, we break our faith with you. You are not our lord, and you do not hold this land lawfully, for you have taken it wrongly from the sons of Constance, who should have inherited it naturally after the death of their brother. And hear this now," he said, pointing directly at the king, "you can be sure that you will die the same death that you gave our kinsman."

Then these people made war on Vortiger, and he used the money and resources he could have used to prop up the struggling country to pay knights to provide his defense. After a number of skirmishes, he was able to drive his opponents out of the country. But as he did so, not only did the common people of the land see the sore way he treated his own subjects, but many men and women came away with stories of the king and his men behaving dishonorably toward them, and from then on he was widely derided as a tyrant.

Vortiger, running out of British men to protect him, was forced to align himself with the invading Saxons, offering them the promise of land and status in his country in return. He became the ally of a prominent leader of the Saxons, Hengist, who was more ruthless and fearsome than any of the others. Together, they rained brutality and violence on the people who opposed Vortiger, until they were either dead or remained silent. At that time, Hengist told Vortiger that his own people sorely hated him, and played on him night and day with the threat that his people posed to him, directing him with cunning into even greater alliance with the Saxons—for truly, Hengist saw the opportunity to solidify Saxon control over the fertile land, and some thought it obvious that his ultimate goal was to have Vortiger killed and thus complete the Saxon overthrow of the country.

To this end, Hengist persuaded Vortiger to take his daughter, Rowena, as his wife. She was a Pagan, and all Christians grieved at the wedding, for because of her, Vortiger abandoned his religious belief, and ceased funding and support for all the land's Christian churches.

Thus did the original British people fear that their hold on their own country lay in great peril, and they faced the imminent threat of becoming prisoners in the very land in which they were born. Their only hope, they cried in greater and greater desperation, lay with the return of the sons of Constance.

Vortiger knew well that he was hated by the people, and also knew that, as long as they remained alive, he would live with the threat that one day the sons of Constance would return to lay claim to their rightful inheritance. And he was wise to fear them, for if they returned, he would face not only the two brothers and their armies, but the might of all the people who would be inspired by their return to rise up and reclaim the land that was theirs.

And though he never made public show, in his heart Vortiger knew with great certainty that he had committed a grievous wrong, and that by all rights he should be condemned by God and all the creatures of the earth. Nevertheless, there was reason—good reason—to think that he might, after all, just end up getting away with it, and ransom the country without facing the slightest consequence.

His plan to do this was to build a tower so big, so strong and so impregnable that he need not fear anyone. He sent for all his master masons, ordered huge amounts of limestone and mortar, and began building the tower on Dinas Emrys, which offered natural defenses in its steep, rocky sides, and would allow him a view of all coming to attack him. But when the tower had been built up to twenty or so feet above the ground, it came crashing down in a tumbling wave of masonry and stone. The same thing happened again, three or four times.

When Vortiger saw that his tower could not stand, he became very distraught, and sent throughout the land for the best builders, and best architects, and best workmen, but still, nothing could be done to make his tower stand. And all were greatly amazed, and unable to tell him why the tower would not hold, for there was no logical reason why it should not.

When the ideas of all of the building experts had been exhausted, the pagan Hengist suggested that he reach out to the great clerics of the land; those who commune with spirits and can see things that normal men cannot. Thus he sent out to gather all the learned clerics in the land and he found seven who were the best in the country. And among those seven, there was not one of them who did not believe that he was the master of the others.

The clerics did all that they could, and tried every one of their methods of precognition, but they could not see a single thing about why the tower would not stand. Instead they saw just one thing, and they saw it again and again. It had nothing to do with the tower—and it terrified them. So they asked for nine more days, and went on their way to perform their own rituals. When they returned, each of them spoke separately to the king and told him that they had clearly seen a fatherless boy, who was in league with the devil, and that, in order to redress the balance away from the devil and toward man, the only thing that would make the tower stand is the blood of that boy. They said that if this boy's blood were mixed with the mortar holding the tower together, then it would stand and, fortified by the magical properties of the boy's blood, be even more powerful than any normal tower could possibly be.

The king came before the gathered clerics and said "It is a great amazement, for you have all said the same thing, and yet each of you says it in his own way."

The clerics looked at each other in astonishment and said to him "Please my lord, tell us what it is."

The King told them that they had all reported about a fatherless boy, seven years of age, and each of them feigned great wonderment. The king asked of them "Can it be true that a man was born without a biological father?"

And Arledge, who was pushing himself into a leadership role by making himself most visible to the king, answered and said "We have never heard it said of anyone, except this boy, but we can assure you that he was born fatherless and he is seven years of age. He is the only one of his kind in this country, and because of this, when you put his blood in the foundation of your tower, it will surely stand without fail, and last for many years."

Vortiger barely had to think before he said, "I will send messengers to fetch this boy and bring him here." He smiled as he thought about meeting such a wondrous boy. "It will be fascinating to see what a boy born without a father is like."

"Please, sir," said Arledge, "for your own safety, it would be great danger to you if you were to speak to—or even see—the boy, for he is the vessel of the devil and his powers of persuasion are very strong." He raised his hand beneath his chin, as though he had an idea. "We advise that you have the messengers kill him immediately upon determining that he is the one, and simply bring back his blood." He nodded, and

26

looked at the king as though to inspire fortitude. "That way, your tower will surely stand, but you would not be put in mortal peril."

Vortiger regarded the cleric with restrained respect, for he had learned never to give a servant the impression that they had pleased him completely, then looked around at the other seers. "Do all of you agree on this?"

They all nodded quite vigorously.

He let his gaze fall on each of them in turn, then, with a glance at Arledge, said "Then let it be so," and walked off.

Twelve messengers were found, and the king had them swear on saint's relics that the one who found the boy first would kill him at once and bring back his blood, and that not one of them was to return until the fatherless boy was found.

-4-

Merlin found his mother downstairs in her front room. She had turned her house into a place of service to the church, and she and Rossa, whom she had befriended while she was held prisoner in the tower, had created a place in which troubled girls could stay and receive instruction while working through what bothered them, and until they could be set once more on the path that led toward a good end. Blaise had also moved into the large house, having given up his hermitage out near the forest.

"Mother, I must speak with you," the boy said.

She gave him a peculiar look, curious about the unusualness of his statement as well as the tone in which he said it. "Of course," she said automatically, and went over to shut the door that they might be alone. "What is it?" she asked once she was seated comfortably.

Merlin stepped out to stand in front of her and put out his hand, which she took. "Mother, the time has come when I will be going away," he said. "In a few days, men will come looking for me, and will want to take me back to their king. From that time I will serve as adviser to kings, and will be very busy—and tremendously important—for the rest of my life." He curled her arm up and put her hand between both of his. "But I will always have time to come visit you and to receive my remedy as you have helped me with." He smiled and kissed her hand. "And I will not go before I have received your leave to do so."

Merlin—and his mother—had learned that he suffers from periods in which he cannot be around people, a remnant from the fact that he is half demon, although baptized and won to the service of the Lord. During these times, he retreats to his mother, who has the ability to calm and soothe him, and care for him when he can not be around people, for if he were left unchecked he would do harm to people. Together they even agreed to bar off a section of his room, that he could be shut into during these times.

Meylinde raised her hand and used it to push the child's hair out of his eyes, and then to caress the side of his face, as her eyes took on a sad and loving look. "Since before you were born I knew this day would come, that one so extraordinary would be called away to render service to people far more important than any you will find in this town." She smiled and her eyes blinked slowly. "I am not so clever as to think I could ever keep you here. Therefore, go with my blessing, and I will be happy to see you whenever you choose to return. Furthermore, your room and chamber will always be empty and ready for you whenever you choose to fill them."

"I thank you, mother," said the boy, "that will be great comfort to me, knowing that you are here." He let go her hand and placed his fingers on her arm. "I should let you know also that Blaise will be moving away from here and taking up residence in Northumberland, for it is time for him to continue writing his book in a place where he can be in the solitude of the forest and uninhabited mountains and draw on their power."

"Oh," Meylinde said and drew back. She had not anticipated this, and the first traces of tears came to her eyes. "Is it necessary that Blaise must also go?" she said.

28

"Yes, I am afraid he must, mother. He has done all that he can here, and it is time for him to be in a place where he can have the solitude to continue his holy learning."

She nodded and thought silently for a long moment. "Is it possible that I could go with him?" she asked. "I could keep house and take care of him, as though he were a father."

"I would not recommend that," said the boy. "Northumberland is a very wild and dangerous place, filled with many places that no one has yet been, and even those who live there find it very rough and perilous. I think that you would be much more comfortable staying here, where you have already done so much excellent work, and you and Rossa can continue to be a benefit to the women of this town."

She nodded and leaned back in her chair, letting her hands slip away from him. Her head moved slightly to the side, and her gaze strayed longingly out at the late afternoon light of the street outside. "I see," she said sadly. "I will miss Blaise very greatly," she said, "and you," and here she reached forward once more to take his hand.

Her eyes drifted away again and she sat, looking out the window for a long minute, as her child stood by her knees, holding her hand, gazing expectantly up at her face. At last she drew in her breath and sighed, then said "Why don't you go prepare the places for dinner? And let me think on this a little while in private."

"Yes, mother," the child said, and moved away towards the door, opening it.

When he looked back she had stood and was over by the window, the small shears in her hands. Her eyes had taken on a distant look as her limbs moved automatically, pruning the excess from the plants, mind clearly miles away.

A few days later, Merlin was sitting on a large stone near the open field at the entrance to their town. It was a bright, sunny, beautiful day and several of the children in town were at play in that field, while their parents were away at work and they were left with the day to amuse themselves.

Merlin sat alone, for he had never had noticed any children of his own age, as they were far too unintelligent to provide any amusement or diversion for him, and he had enough company with his mother, Rossa and Blaise. As well as the procession of women that came through his mother's house for various periods of time. Not only did he find children unintelligent, their petty squabbles with one another, moronic tests of strength and prowess, and worst of all, their slimy noses and phlegmy coughs left him completely repulsed.

This was the day when the messengers would come to this town, and he knew they were quite near and in fact—there they were! He saw them immediately upon their striding up the path, and he had to scramble to think of something to get their attention. Some way for someone else to identify him as fatherless, for Merlin was always canny about what must be found out by someone else, as opposed to what he could tell people directly, in terms of which way it was most to be believed.

He scooted forward and dropped off the stone, where his feet had not been able to touch the ground, and walked towards the approaching messengers, sizing them each up individually as he walked. Between him and the messengers were a few different boys playing together, two of whom Merlin disliked intensely for their cruelty to each other, and torturing of animals, and although he disliked one of them more than the other, he knew the one he liked a bit better was a hothead and blabbermouth, which made him more suited to Merlin's purpose just then.

Merlin slowed his approach, for there would be no sense in having the boy shout out were he not in earshot of the approaching messengers. During this time, he cast about and picked up a fairly thick stick. A few moments later, as the strange men were about ten feet from this boy, Merlin came up to him, raised the stick and whacked the boy hard, flat on the forehead.

"Owww! What did you do that for?" cried the child. "You idiot! Why don't you go away? No one wants a freak boy with no father around here! No one even wants to see a freak who doesn't have a father!" Then he gave up and went back to playing.

Merlin has simply walked away after striking the boy, throwing the stick down, and retreated to the rock he had been sitting on to watch the messengers as they came to him.

The messengers stopped the young boy that Merlin had hit, who had a pretty good pink one on the noggin there, and asked about what the child had said. One of them was in front, and dropped down to one knee to talk to the boy. He was a fine young man with black curly hair and eyes that were attentive. Behind him stood a taller, blonder man, and two other messengers, one with a thick neck and the other nondescript.

"Why did you say that about the boy who struck you?" Mark, the one with the black hair, asked.

"He's the boy of a woman who never knew who made him, and he's never had a father, and he's a freak. And no one likes him, and no one wants him around, ever." He sniffled. "And he smells."

Mark wrinkled his nose at the repellent child, but forced a smile and gave a pat, then stood and turned to the others. "It sounds like that may be the boy we are looking for," he said, and all of them nodded in agreement. Each reached inside his tunic and let their hands wrap securely around the knives tucked into their belts, and they tried to steel themselves to the point where they could kill.

Then they raised their eyes, and saw the small boy there, his light brown curly hair blowing wildly in the wind, and their ability to murder was drained within them. This boy was going to kill them? They were supposed to murder this boy? In plain sight? But then they thought: 'We have heard that he is the emissary of the devil, and is so dangerous we must not allow him to speak to us,' and they once more reared into defensive murderousness. Then Merlin plopped himself down off the rock, and strode right up to them, a broad smile on his face, his limbs moving in a cheerful and animated march.

The men froze, hands on knives.

"Hello!" Merlin said. "I am the one you are looking for, the one you have sworn to kill, to take my blood back to King Vortiger."

The messengers were struck dumbfounded. The boy stood there as before, a broad smile on his face, hand shielding the sunlight from his eyes and hair blowing around like before, as he seemed to watch their discomfort with amusement.

Mark could say nothing, and stood with his arms out, unable to think clearly, only aware of how helpless and silly he must look. One of the messengers from behind, the one with the thick neck, had to take the initiative to speak, and could merely shout "Who was it told you that?" Mark would have hoped to have handled the situation more smoothly, but at this point he had no better suggestions.

The boy smiled openly as before. "I know for a fact that you have come here to kill me," he said.

Then it struck the messengers, with a creeping chill, the completely adult and assured way in which the child spoke, which added to the strangeness of his words. Mark turned away from him to have a private word with the other messengers, but then whirled about almost immediately, afraid to let the child out of his sight for fear that he might vanish. Or attack.

"What do we do?" Mark asked the others.

"Kill him?" said Birley, the blond messenger.

"We are obligated to kill him and bring back his blood," said another. "That is all we are to do, not talk to him," he said, a hint of desperation in his voice. "They told us specifically *not* to talk to him."

"And that talking to him is so dangerous, we are to kill him here so that he might not talk to the king," said the fourth. "That is—that shows how dangerous he is."

"Clearly his words bring deception and can poison the mind," said Birley.

"I say we do it and get back right swiftly," the thick-necked one said.

"It seems…" Mark deliberated, his face troubled by thought. "He told us our purpose immediately upon coming here, he knew what we were coming here for—and he couldn't possible have known that. And we found this boy, this one wonder in the world, the moment we were in the yard, and he came right up to us." Mark shook his head. "He has incredible abilities, and… it seems a shame to kill him."

"But that is why," said Birley. "This is probably the *exact* reason why they told us to kill him on sight, and not speak with him."

"His words can deceive and trouble the mind—it is happening with you," the fourth messenger said. They all went quiet and turned to look at the boy, who was watching all of them eagerly, a great smile on his face.

They turned back to confer with each other. "But if he is… if he is a wondrous seer, it would be a shame to destroy that," said Mark, "and rid the world of something incredible. Perhaps they were hoping to silence him."

"Maybe he drives people mad with his words," said another, his mouth dropping open. "I've heard there are wizards that can do that."

"I've heard of wizards that are hundreds of years old," said Mark, "but not of ones as small and young as that kid there."

"This is probably why we had to kill him straight away and he cannot be in the presence of King Vortiger," Birley said, "Because if he were—"

Mark turned. The child stood still and watched them with amused interest, but remained distant, about eight feet away. Just far enough that they could not grab or otherwise touch him, for as wise as Merlin is, his body can be killed just as easily as anyone's. The wide, beaming smile remained on his face as he watched the flummoxed messengers.

"We would like to ask you some questions," said Mark. "Would you come with us somewhere where we can speak privately?"

"I will go nowhere with you until you have given me your oath not to kill me," said the child, smiling as before.

Mark stood, frozen, unsure what to do. "We're not supposed to ask him questions, we are supposed to kill him," tersely whispered the blond messenger. Mark looked at the frozen smile on the child's face, while the boy's blue eyes stared directly into his.

"I know perfectly well why King Vortiger's tower will not stand," said Merlin.

Mark's mouth dropped open. The heads of the other messengers whipped around to look at him.

"And if you all swear an oath not to kill me, I will go with you to speak to your king, and explain to him why his tower will not stand, and what he must do to make it hold." He smiled. "I am the only one that can tell him this, and if you bring me back, instead of killing me, you will have rewards for having sense enough to disobey your orders."

Mark turned back to the messengers that were with him. "This boy tells us wonders," he said, "and whoever killed him would be committing a grievous sin." He looked back once more at the small boy there, who looked otherwise so plain and unremarkable. Mark's dark, intelligent eyes were drawn tight, as he thought on what was best to do. "I would rather break my oath than to kill him," he said at last.

Before any of the other messengers could say a word, Mark turned once more to face the child. Merlin spoke first.

"You will come take lodging where my mother lives," said Merlin, "and we will depart tomorrow. I could not go with you without my mother's leave, or that of the holy man who lives in her house."

-6-

Vortiger sat in the bedroom of the castle that would have to do until he was able to build his tower to his specifications. He had moved

34

the owner of it into the guest quarters until he had decided of his own volition to vacate. It was stone, it was fortified, it had much to recommend it, but he would feel better when his tower at Dinas Emrys was finished. Then he would be in a place built specifically for serious defense, as the smallish hilltop, accessed only by quite steep rocky ground, would make it quite difficult for any siege machines to be wheeled next to it, and attackers pushed off balance could easily go tumbling down the hill. It also offered a view of anyone descending the higher mountains all around, so essentially, it was perfect, and he could rest easily, protected there. A perfect place for a tyrant to withstand an uprising.

Tyrant. That one was the word that stuck the most, and, from his side, seemed the most ludicrous. How he had gone from well-liked, well-trusted seneschal to tyrant in just a few years was a wonder, even to him. The truth is that he never wanted to be in the place he was now. He had never sought it, never intended it, and God knew he did not want it. Well, okay, he did want it, and did seek it—but only for a short time, until he realized what it really meant, what it really entailed… and what atrocities he had to engage in to keep it. But by then it was impossible to back out—he was trapped. Was it possible to be an accidental king? That's what he was.

He had served gratefully and with excellent service his lord Constance, who was a wise, just, and worthy leader. What a great king! And how happy Vortiger was then, happy to be in his place, seeking no position above it. Then Constance died, and his son Maine, then just seventeen, was coroneted as king. We are all familiar with the children of wealthy and powerful parents, who consider gaining responsibility, and patiently learning the numerous steps involved in having a position of power too tedious to spend their precious, hormone-driven youth on, and expect generous praise for any time spent in study or learning. That described Constance's three boys perfectly, for as much as he was a great ruler, he was ridiculously indulgent with the boys—who had lost their mother at a young age—and many were the times Vortiger would have to paste on a smile as he attempted to interest the king in the affairs of his kingdom while the boys chased each other around the table with wooden swords. So when Constance died and Maine was made king, you can imagine the gall of being an adult made responsible to a leader who was barely past puberty—in body, although certainly not in mind.

To say that Maine had not absorbed the valiance or leadership of his father would be a very charitable understatement. He was not good at war, he was not good at peace, he was not good at diplomacy, he was not good at maintaining good relationships amongst the barons of his lands. He wasn't really good at anything. And it makes sense, he was young and completely inexperienced. At least he had had some time to stand by his father's side and observe, even with disinterest, which is more than could be said for the two younger brothers, who were too busy stuffing their faces, stealing swords from knights and in Uther's case, playing cruel tricks on Vortiger's prized wolfhound to take any interest in the responsibilities of kingship.

What Maine did have a going for him was his great good looks, his large welcoming eyes and vast smile, which, regardless of what any of us might think about it, did much more to make the populace of the country feel happy and secure than any policy or promise of protection that Vortiger could have made them. Maine just *had it.* He had what it takes. Whatever it takes for the common people to like you and feel like you were governing them fairly and that you knew what you were doing and everything was under control—that is what Maine had. Vortiger was approaching his late thirties then, had always been large and imposing, and had a face that rested in an expression that looked like he was angry, while Maine was young, fresh-faced and enthusiastic, which, Vortiger soon found, mattered much more to the morons populating the small towns than any actual ability to handle the decisions of leadership. Not to mention that he was the son of the beloved former king, which made the people of the land weep sentimental tears, regardless of whether he could rule an ant farm, let alone a country.

At the time Vortiger was seneschal to the king—the one who arranged his affairs of state—and things were easy then. He made things happen, he got things done behind-the-scenes, he became the one that the barons and knights could go to for answers and to find out, in a concrete way, what they were expected to do. Not like Maine could do this. For God's sake, he could barely stay attentive through a meeting, and had no idea what life was like for anyone who was not the king's son.

Still, regardless of how frustrating the overgrown boy leader had been, that was probably the best time, when Maine was in control and Vortiger could just go along doing what he did best. And in retrospect, probably he should have just stayed there. Not probably, definitely. In retrospect. Then he could help out and contribute, but none of it was really up to him, and thus none of it was his fault. So he enjoyed a level of responsibility, and respectability, but without having everything ultimately depend on him.

So eventually the knights and barons, and people of the castle, started to realize that Maine didn't have the answers, and Vortiger did. Not the common people, who only cared whether their town was in the path of a battle of not, but the leaders, those who actually had to make things happen, started to realize that Maine couldn't really make tough decisions, and Vortiger could. That Vortiger is the one to go to if you are looking for a change, or for direction, where Maine just dithered and lost himself in confusion. Is it his fault that people eventually started to see him as the competent one? He *was* the competent one! He could hardly be blamed if others began to realize it.

Then, as people told him so, and as he began to see how much he was doing, yet how much credit Maine was getting, it was not a complicated stretch of thinking for him to believe that maybe he *would* be better as the leader. And, from his place running the show but still a servant of the king, it was not difficult to think how he really *ought* to be the king himself. How much easier it would be for him—and how much better for the country—and how much more he was suited to it.

Looking back, he had no idea how absolutely unsuited he was.

One thing that he had to tell people, one piece of hard-won wisdom that he could offer—but which mattered little now that he was a "tyrant" and no one wanted to hear his side—is that history is often decided by the smallest things. The day the barons came to him, asking for him as their king, he had just come from a meeting with Maine on several pressing matters of state, but where he could make no progress, because he kept having to break to explain basic concepts of government to the king. The meeting ended when his wolfhound emitted a squealing yelp from the far corner of the room—and Uther emerged from there, a moment later, eyes cast downward, vicious smirk on his face. At least Constance would force the boy to make a po-faced apology, but not Maine, who actually laughed when he learned what the boy was doing. Vortiger had left the meeting shaking with rage—and *that* is when the barons came to him.

So he said what was true—he could not take over as king while Maine was alive. It was only on the second utterance that he began to see a different meaning to his words, but even then, he had no idea they could possibly take him seriously. Did he mean it? Did he want Maine dead? In that moment, you'd better believe that he did. Would he have later? Would he still have suggested it had he been more level headed? Had he been able to calm himself and think clearly?

We'll never know.

He spent that night holed up in his chamber, hiding away, afraid, while also madly excited, to hear word that they might actually have done it. He could not stand to be around people that night and waited in his chamber, although he had to be sure that guards and other people knew he was inside, so that he would later have their alibi during the hour in which Maine was killed. He remembered being so nervous he could not eat, alternating between being wracked with guilt that someone might kill Maine—who he did genuinely like, as one likes a puppy—and his greedy excitement at the thought of someone coming to his door, telling him that the leader was dead, and it was all only matter of time before he himself was king.

Then it happened. And all of a sudden everyone looked to him for answers, and it was his responsibility to find them, or be considered a failure. That was when the attacks of breathlessness started. Moments where his heart would threaten to burst out of his chest and he could barely catch his breath, and his brain would freeze in panic. Panic at what was expected of him and all the eyes that were on him, constantly.

Not to mention never, ever having a moment to himself, when his moments of solitude had been some of his most important time spent when he was just a part of the retinue. Not only that, but, for someone who prized honesty and directness in his friendships and associations, to suddenly be surrounded by people who only pretended friendship because they wanted money, wanted him to pass their law or build their road, or even—and these were the ones he found most vile—didn't want a thing, except to be next to the most powerful person, to assuage their simple-minded vanity. No, perhaps he should have just remained the seneschal, and governed in practice while Maine received all the credit. For no one wants to see the seneschal fall. But everyone, even if they are your dearest and closest companions, wants to see the king fall.

As for overstepping the line that separated a fearsome king from a tyrant... well, who knows. Part of it came from his inability to suffer fools. And then there was his temper. If someone was stealing from him, or insulting him by resisting his laws or taxes, there were times he got so angry he *wanted* to see them killed. Now, he could arrange it. It was shocking at first—and satisfying—to see someone pulled apart by four horses, but very rapidly, he grew used to it. And the people needed to understand that this was no joke, he was making a future for that country, even if it was under the rule of the Saxons, and if they opposed him, it's not that they would receive a fine, or go into the dungeon for a while, *they would die.* It was the only way to get them to stop drinking for a moment and take him seriously.

When the men who had killed the king had come to him, what was he supposed to do? He had to make a big example, had to show the people how aghast he was that their precious Maine was killed, and he was sure this first act would go over big. How wrong he was. In retrospect, that one order lay behind every one of his subsequent problems. Because of that, he had to go to war with the kinsmen of those he had killed—the fact that they had killed the king was easily enough forgotten, apparently—and because of that, he had to accept Saxon help and ally himself with Hengist. And because of that, he ended up married to Hengist's daughter, Rowena.

Now he was in the awkward position of having to defend the Saxons, who were, of a class, much more prone to violence and barbarity than the average British person. So now every pack of soldiers who raided a home for food suddenly became his responsibility, and his fault. And let's just say that raiding a home for food was among their more palatable crimes. Yet Vortiger was usually forced to rule against the British, whatever the circumstances. What he got with Rowena was a beautiful wife and the promise of enough Saxon knights to lay final claim to the country and ensure his own safety. But in the eyes of the people, he was a British king, welcoming an invading force to take over his beautiful land. As far as they were concerned, he was handing their country over to the Saxons. That was also the reality, although in practice the promise of additional Saxon knights had remained, thus far, just that; a promise.

Vortiger harbored serious suspicions that the additional troops were coming. Rather, he knew that they were coming—anyone with any sense could see that the Saxons would one day conquer that land completely. What he began to doubt is whether they would come before he was dead. Because the British people were rising up—Hengist himself told him that they hated him—and with the long rumored return of Uther and Pendragon… it was probable, it was actually likely, if he had to think about it, that Hengist would wait until Vortiger was out of the way before making a serious push to rule that land. Logically, why wouldn't he? Why defeat a country just for someone else to be king? Not the Hengist he knew.

So why did Vortiger go along with him? Because he had no choice. He had so alienated his countrymen that they had abandoned him, and his only friends were invaders, who ultimately had no use for him. He was in, too far in, and there was no way out. But maybe Hengist actually was bringing the troops. Maybe they would arrive and he would preside over the Saxon defeat over the Britons. He would be happy to hand rule of the country over to Hengist then, and step back into the role of assistant. He would have to tell Hengist that—perhaps it would change any plans he might be making. Short of that, he didn't see any possible way out. The sons of Constance would make their glorious return, and he might be able to withstand them in his tower until the troops arrived—assuming he could ever get it to stand—or slay them as they made landfall if the Saxon troops arrived first. But think and think as he might, he did not see any way that he would live if the Saxon reinforcements did not arrive.

Most painfully, not in any circumstance of living but against his ease, mind and sanity, was the fact that, in his heart—for Vortiger did have a heart, despite what the common people said—he knew that he had done wrong. He had an idea, and he saw his chance and he took it boldly—as you are supposed to do—but he did it in a heat, and looking back, he knew with the most appalling clarity that he had acted against nature. If he had done what was right, he would have found the patience and kindness to teach Maine to lead, and would have counseled him, and protected him and his brothers. He knew that he had the power he used to seize the country because of Constance, and Maine, and the alliances that they had forged before him, not through any doing of his own. And maybe Maine would have driven the country into ruin, and maybe the Saxons would still have conquered, but it would have been an honest defeat, and he wouldn't have damned himself through actions that can never be forgiven. He could have been a Saxon prisoner with a clean heart, and nothing to despise himself over.

So yes, he had damned himself. Now the only question left was whether this would remain a knife in his side, a private pain and endless, joyless life that would have him growing old, bitter and withered in his soul, or if he would actually die for it.

What numbing, painful anxiety that was. During the few moments when he was alone, say lying in bed with his wife, waiting for sleep, it seemed that it was time to panic, time to resort to emergency measures, but he could never think of what they should be, or what he could do, other than what he was doing. He was a powerful king, but there was nothing he could do—except wait for the future. The only hope he could see was those troops, and the tower to protect him until they got there. In every other direction, only the steady, implacable approach of death.

7

Merlin brought the messengers to the shelter that his mother had created and where Blaise now made his home. When they entered, Merlin gave orders to give the four men a warm welcome and make sure that they had every comfort they could desire, for they would be leaving early in the morning and needed to be rested and well fed. Plus he took pride in the hospitality and graciousness he would offer them, knowing it would serve him well when they made their the report to the king.

"Blaise, please join us, and gather my mother too," the child said. "I would like the both of you to hear this, for here are the men I told you were looking for me, and have come to kill me." Every time the child said this, it made Mark wince a bit in embarrassment. Merlin's mother led them into a room where they could sit comfortably and talk, but not be disturbed by the work of the other women as they went about their business.

Merlin addressed the messengers and he said "I will tell my mother and this good man what I believe is the situation that has brought you here, and you will tell them whether it is true or not." Merlin squinted one eye, "and I want you to know that if you lie, I will know it."

"We will not lie to you," said Mark, who cocked his head swiftly. "If you don't lie to us."

"That will not be a problem," replied Merlin. Then he turned to Blaise and his mother. "These men come at the request of King Vortiger," he said, "who wants to build a tower in order to protect himself, but each time when it gets to twenty feet or so, the tower cannot stand and everything that has been finished crumbles down."

The child went on. "The king has summoned the most powerful clerics in the land, but not one of them could figure it out. So they asked for more time, and they resorted to their most powerful magic in order to get an answer. They saw nothing about the tower—but they did see that I had been born, and it seemed to them that I could hurt them. In fact, each of them saw that they would die because of me. And so they arranged to have me killed."

Meylinde raised her hands in silent frustration, and Blaise was also staring wide-eyed at the child, but he raised his hand for them to wait.

"The clerics told the king that his tower will stand if some of my blood were put into the mortar of it, and they advised these men here to bring him my blood," Merlin gestured toward the messengers, "after killing me immediately on sight."

"Well, Merlin, that's awful," said his mother.

"It truly does not seem like a good group of people for you to be intermingling with," said Blaise. "Are you sure you want to...."

"Let me say on," said the child.

Blaise threw up his hands, while his mother simply shook her head.

Mark had raised his hand and was waiting for Merlin to address him. "We had not been told any of this," he said, "about the deceit in order to have you killed, and that the clerics saw their own deaths because of you."

"No, of course not," said Merlin. "The king himself does not know. They want you simply to kill me without questioning why, and to prevent me speaking directly to the king."

"You can see why they wouldn't want him speaking to the king," said Birley. "He knows more than these 'best clerics in the land.'"

Merlin bowed before the man. "Flattery," he said, "will indeed win you my affection. But let me finish my tale. King Vortiger chose twelve messengers and these four came together and decided to search on together. This morning they came to the big field where other children were playing ball, and I knew that they were looking for me, so I struck one of the boys—"

Meylinde sighed in exasperation. "Merlin," she said, "I have asked you not to strike the other children."

"Because I knew for certain that he would say the worst thing he could about me," Merlin said, eye on his mother, "which is that I was born fatherless." Merlin turned to the messengers. "Now, please tell the good man and my mother if I have spoken the truth."

"Yes, he has told the truth in everything he said, although I do not know how he should know any of these things," said Mark, gazing in puzzlement at Merlin. "And he did not lie to you, even in a single word."

"Yes," said Blaise, "Merlin is a very special boy and will be most wise," he eyed Merlin with annoyance, "if he lives long enough." The old man then looked at the messengers with a sad eye. "And it would be great shame," he said, "if you killed him."

"Sir, we would sooner be perjured all our days than kill him," said the thick-necked one, who had been moved by the knowledge Merlin displayed. "He seems to know all truth, and he himself should know whether I am lying or not."

"I do know," said Merlin, smiling and gesturing generously toward the man who had just defended him, "and I know for truth that you no longer wish to kill me. Come, have a nice meal and let us prepare for our journey tomorrow."

That night they had good wine and fortifying food and music from Merlin's mother and several of the other holy women. And Merlin stayed to talk and get to know some of the messengers, and he liked Mark particularly well. He was a goodhearted and honest man who was tickled to be in the presence of the special boy and was not afraid to show his wonder, and gratitude. He also treated Merlin's mother well, which earned him the love of the young wizard.

The next morning they all gathered in the large dining hall and had their breakfast. And Meylinde had prepared a special pack for Merlin, with an apple and some snacks and a few special things that he liked, and remembrances of her, that would keep her alive in his heart while he went on his adventures. And Merlin gave her a special embrace and kissed her and told her not to worry, and that she would be seeing him often, for he could foresee great frustrations ahead.

Blaise also got a sad and somewhat bewildered look in his eye— for unlike Meylinde, he now was tasked with uprooting and moving to a wild and untamed region—but Merlin told him to have good cheer, for he too would be visiting the wise man several times, and he knew that Blaise would have a full heart in ways he could not then envision, when he took his place in Northumberland and be in a lovely enchanted place, where he and Merlin could work on their book in solitude.

They went outside and prepared their horses, and as they did, Mark took Merlin aside and said, "Merlin, I want you to know that we were not aware that we had been ordered to kill you in order to prevent the death of the clerics. And that we were rubes in their deceit just as you should have been the victim of it. In this way we were being used against our will, and I want you to know, before we ride, that now that our eyes have been cleared, I could never wish to harm you."

"Mark, I know that you speak the truth, for I can see your heart. And I want you to know that I, too, will speak favorably of you and all the messengers to the king, and intervene on your behalf if he is unhappy that you have not carried out his orders."

Mark smiled warmly and lowered his eyes in bashfulness, and Merlin could see that he was true-hearted and faithful. "I would appreciate that very much," said Mark, "for I fear that we will be in great jeopardy if the clerics get to us before we can speak with the king alone."

He then made sure that everyone was ready to go and made a last inspection of his horse, then bid adieu to Meylinde and Blaise standing at the door of the nunnery. "Would you like to ride with me on my horse?" asked Mark.

"Yes, I would," said Merlin. "That way we can talk as we ride, and I can hear all about your youth in Wales, and your family, and how you came to serve the king."

And as Merlin's horse was ambling off, he turned back once to see Meylinde, standing alone, arms crossed before her, waiting and watching in the receding distance.

8

Vortiger was hearing his briefings. Normally kings hear them during the day, but, he couldn't even remember how it happened, they ended up going later, and later, being postponed, until now they came just after supper, just before he usually took to his apartments, or entertained guests and allies. The irony was, it all started from a few days, not long ago, when he didn't want to hear the briefings—it was little but a series of news reports that carried the general theme: The People Are Gradually Turning Against You. These people had to be jailed when they refused to pay their tariffs. These people attacked his men when they marched across their fields (he had those ones publicly killed). This piece of graffiti went up here, saying that he was a tyrant, that everyone wanted him dead. This piece of graffiti was spotted there, praying that Constance's sons would return and reclaim their birthright. This carriage was attacked. Those messengers were captured, these ones deserted.

But after a few days, then weeks, of putting the briefings off until later in the day, now they happened just before he retired from official business for the night, which carried the unexpected consequence of causing that to be all he thought about all night. He thought to change it, move it back to the morning, but by then it had come to take on the air of a daily penance. Like a punishment he had to endure as part of his daily routine, in order to gain another day. Another day of wondering when it would all come crashing down. It certainly would soon, if this child couldn't get his tower to stand, and the armies Hengist promised didn't arrive soon. His own men were thinning fast—mostly through desertions.

He sat by the fire, head forward to the flames, but eyes cast to the side, at his wife, Rowena, not looking at his advisors as they stood to the side and behind them. For God's sake, he had more than enough of looking at them all day. He was beginning to loathe the sight of some of them. Or all of them. As they droned on, Rowena sat near the wall across the room, laughing and talking with her group of handmaidens and knights who were devoted to her. All of them were Saxons. He had thought that she might assimilate to the local ways, and they would be the land's foremost couple, a shining example of a country shared by the original Celtic Britons and the Saxons, a dazzling amalgam of both cultures. And he hoped that the people would love her, and it would help to ease their hatred of him. But no, she kept all her old customs, kept her pagan beliefs, and her severe hair and makeup, ate only Saxon food and associated only with her Saxon retinue, which she brought with her, and the Saxon knights she had known beforehand, or had come to know. The British knights in his court, she was polite enough to, but one never saw her talking to them, and never saw them with her, chatting amiably in the hall.

How could she be chatting quite so amiably, he wondered, when the days of their kingdom were counting down with unceasing swiftness? Was she not growing increasingly terrified, as he was? Perhaps she was simply better at hiding it, with that mysterious Saxon lightheartedness that allowed for no show of anything but nonchalance. Was she worried? Or was she not at all concerned?

Or, perhaps, she knew something he didn't.

Abruptly he turned to his advisors. "How long do we have?" he asked.

They were startled by his sudden turn of attention. "Uh, before what, sir?" one asked.

Vortiger closed his eyes with the quiet resignation of contempt. He reached behind his shoulder, and drew all of his hair over to one side, where he began twisting it and squeezing it in his fist. "How long do we have," he clarified, "before an actual outbreak?" he said. "Before a rebellion."

"Oh sir," Brantius said, "we could easily quash a rebellion."

Vortiger held his breath for a short moment, but did not again close his eyes. A man could go insane if he gave into all the contempt he felt for the morons that surrounded him. "But in your opinion," he said slowly, "given all that you have read of these incidents, and what you hear of the turning talk," and then he tried again, enunciating every word, "how long, do you estimate, it will be before we see an actual, outright, organized rebellion?"

"Oh, *organized?*" scoffed Brantius.

"There seems to be nothing, as of yet, that we can't keep down, sir," said Roldan, another of his advisors. "And certainly nothing organized. So far. I would say that you're set for the year, at least. Barring—" But then he stopped talking.

Vortiger raised his eyebrow, and turned his head. "Barring?" he asked.

Roldan smiled a frightened smile, his lips pulled back, stiff like on a shrunken head, and he shook his head, as though he didn't understand what he was being asked.

"Barring?" Vortiger asked again.

Now Sir Brantius made a show of impatiently looking toward Roldan, as though vexed, impatient and curious what he might say.

"Barring the return of Constance's sons," said Roldan.

"Oh, those boys," said Brantius, with a flick of his hand.

Vortiger's head turned once more to the fire.

"The people are—well, from what I hear—they're quite sentimental over those boys, sir," said Roldan. "Your outlook seems to be quite good, sir, for at least the year ahead that we can see from here. Barring," there, he said it again, "anything that might unite them."

"Those pimply-faced boys couldn't command a rock to sit still," said Brantius.

Roldan's eyes narrowed at his rival. "They wouldn't need to," he said, "as much as the people love them, and are prepared to fight for them."

Vortiger suddenly stood. Both advisors reared back at his always-unexpected height. His eyes looked on them both wearily, from within their dark sockets, and with a slow, almost pained movement of his hand, he waved them away. They started moving toward the door immediately.

"I'd love to have a moment to talk with you about some of my ideas for favors you could do for the people, sir," Brantius said. "If you were to free up just some of, even the cheapest things—"

"Tomorrow," said the king. "I am tired." He continued advancing on the men, causing them to slightly quicken their pace toward the door. "And what we need to think on, what you both should be thinking on," he said, "are ways to get more money from the people, not giving things away."

Even Brantius gasped, and he was the most shameless of suck-ups. Roldan opened his mouth too, but he was too wise to say anything, and in a short moment, both of them had been shooed out the door. Vortiger continued past it, to where Rowena sat with her servants and admirers.

He loomed over the group, in his regal scarlet robe, making his height and width impressive, especially when he placed his arms akimbo and stood tall. He said nothing, just waited at the perimeter of the group, as the knights leapt to their feet and the handmaidens kept their heads demurely down. His wife was laughing at the joke of one of the knights, who was no longer laughing, but standing and awaiting word from the king.

Vortiger ignored them all, his gaze directed down at the queen as she let the laughter continue until it died out naturally, chuckled to herself a bit more, then slowly raised her head, her eyes closed as she savored the laugh, as the king waited. At last her eyes opened, lazily, and she gazed up into his. "Yes, my lord?" she asked tonelessly.

It had long seemed as though his very presence annoyed her. Perhaps it was merely her gruff Saxon ways.

"My darling," he said, equally tonelessly, "have we any indication of when your father might arrive?"

"My lord," she said, lightly laughing in a mocking way, "how should I know?"

He hated when she was snide with him in front of the others. He could see their mocking smiles, which they thought they were cleverly concealing, from the corner of his eye.

"You have more contact with him than I, my sweet," he said.

"It takes eight hours to ride here," she said. "If he left at his normal early hour, he should be here any time now." She looked at him with wide eyes, as though to ask whether he had any other idiotic questions.

The king nodded. "Thank you, my dear," he said. As he walked away, he heard the muffled explosion of repressed laughter, one of her fawning servants. He did not look back. There was no point. This was life now. Whenever someone laughed, part of him wondered if it was at him.

He strode with heavy, slow gait back across the room and settled once more in front of the fire, receiving a drink on the way from one of the servants who stood against the wall. Always there, always watching. Blank faces. Saying nothing, but talking behind his back.

He watched the flames, and the movement, as of a wandering spirit, of the glow within the burning logs. The time passed. The drink worked in his brain. His thoughts covered great terrain, the Britons, the Saxons, the growing sentiment against him, and what he could possibly do about it. But it all came back to the tower. He must get that tower built. Then, when Hengist arrived with his army of hardy additional Saxons, he could either put down any uprisings before they started and finally, at Hengist's side, begin the real transforming of the country. Or, alternately, he could hole up in the tower to withstand any rebellion, then, when Hengist's army arrived, put it down, and the outcome was the same. He *had* to have that tower.

In time there was a commotion heard, and soon the door opened, and in walked Hengist. He was tall, not as tall as Vortiger, but tall, with a broad, strong chest, sharp nose and a grand mustache that came to points that stuck downward from his face, like spikes. He was fearsome, it was sure, although his age had reduced the physical threat he was able to inspire. He was twenty years older than Vortiger, and a leader for that much longer, which surely played into the air of paternal condescension the king sometimes perceived from him. But Vortiger was losing track of the various shades of condescension, irony, smarm, attitude or distancing he was receiving—or imagining?—from everyone but those who had the most to lose.

50

The Saxon leader stopped and greeted his daughter, while the maidens and knights around her made great excitement over his presence, then they all streamed out, and Hengist, bringing his heavy eyes up to regard Vortiger with a resigned tolerance, put on a smile and strode across the room to greet the king.

"Vortiger," he said, with that deep, slightly nasal and insinuating voice he had, "I hope you have been keeping well."

"I have, sir," he said, "I hope your journey was safe and free from incident."

They made pleasantries. Vortiger indicated the chair across from him, in front of the fire.

"When can we have the pleasure of expecting your army?" asked Vortiger.

"Soon, soon," said Hengist. "When will you be able to raise this tower?"

There it was; the brush off, and shift to another topic. It was always that way. One of the skills Hengist had picked up in his years of leadership was the ability to wrench conversations in any direction he pleased.

"Soon, soon," he said, throwing the Saxon's evasion back at him. "All I hear is the conflict the Britons are having with the ways of your Saxons."

"*My* Saxons?" Hengist pointed to himself.

"Different ways of eating, different ways with the maidens, when your own maidens aren't taking over homes and kitchens, and the religious conflicts," he shook his head in exasperation. "And anyone who doesn't like a Saxon blames me for allowing them into this country. If I had your army here—"

"My Saxons are the future people of this land," said Hengist, still stuck on the last point.

"When they arrive," replied the king, "perhaps they will be. My advisors speak in terms of the time we have until there is a rebellion. As you can imagine," he took on a more accommodating tone, "I, and all around me, would feel better knowing we had an army of strong Saxon men to enforce the peace."

"And so you shall," Hengist smiled. "But it takes time to build a force, to find the best men, outfit them, supply them weapons," he said, "and ship them here," he added with emphasis. "It takes time," he looked at the king significantly, "and expense."

Vortiger's face dropped. "Well, I suggest you cast into your other sources for money," he said. "I am being bled dry by building and rebuilding this tower, I have nothing left." He turned his gaze to the fire. "And advisors telling me to give money to the people to quell the coming uprisings."

"Let them be quelled by a spear in the neck," replied Hengist. He stood and held his cup out for more drink. The servant flew over, filled it, and vanished. "But what is it with this tower? What keeps going wrong with it?"

"Damn if I knew," Vortiger said, raising his hands to the side of his head, indicating it was driving him mad. "God damn it if I knew. We have messengers out, scouring the countryside right now," he said. "They will bring back the blood of a boy, a fatherless boy, and mixing it with the mortar will apparently make it hold."

Hengist settled one arm onto the back of his chair, and gawped at Vortiger. "A boy?" he asked. "Blood in the mortar? What is this supposed to do?"

"This is the advice the of clerics *you* recommended," Vortiger said.

"I recommended clerics, not any that would recommend something so…" he waved his hand around in the air.

"They *all* saw this boy," Vortiger said, standing also. He would not let the Saxon tower over him. "I spoke to them all separately, and they all said the same thing. It's bizarre, but—that's what clerics do!" He too settled his arms on the back of his chair. "And I would do anything to get this tower built." He shook his head in exhaustion. "Having it will change everything." He quickly looked up at Hengist, and corrected himself: "And your army."

A smile took hold under the Saxon's mustache. "Oh, they are coming, you be sure of it," he said, striding over to place a huge hand on

Vortiger's shoulder. "You just get this tower built, and you'll see," he said, "we'll have a gorgeous, fertile new country to divide between us."

-9-

The messengers rode for one day and then another. They had many companions on the road, for it was the middle of summer and the air was mild and many people were out traveling from one town to another, or visiting the markets of larger towns to get the supplies that they needed. Merlin enjoyed listening to the stories of all of the messengers and how they had come to serve King Vortiger, hearing their own individual impressions of the king (although it was always very difficult to get anyone to be honest about a reigning king), and what they hoped to do with their lives. He liked each of them very much, but he liked Mark the best, so Merlin stayed close to him. And in time Merlin also told them his own story, and how his mother had gone to trial for his birth, for she would not lie and say that there was a father and thus falsely implicate someone who was innocent. And he told them the amazing story of how she was eventually freed.

On the third day, they passed through a market town and on the way out came upon a peasant on the road who had bought a pair of new shoes and the leather to repair them when he wore a hole into them, for he planned to go on a pilgrimage. After he had gone off a few paces, Merlin began to laugh, and Mark asked him why he was laughing.

"Because of that peasant who plans to go on his pilgrimage," said Merlin. "The truth is he will die before he gets home, and he will never even get to put on his new shoes, let alone embark on his pilgrimage."

This struck the messengers as very odd, so they decided that they would split up then, and two of them would take the high road and follow the peasant, and meet up with the other two later, who would follow the more straight road. But the two who had separated from them had not gone but a few paces after that before they saw the peasant lying dead in the road. When they returned, they talked to the other messengers apart from Merlin, where he could not hear them.

"What did you find?" asked Mark.

"The man was dead exactly as he said."

"Which was a shock, as he seemed hale and hardy when we met him."

Mark shook his head in wonderment when he heard this and looked over to where Merlin was amusing himself by looking at all the life that lived within a stone wall. One of the other messengers spoke and said "Our clerics don't know what they're saying when they order this boy to be killed, for he is the wisest in the land."

"And," Mark said, "I would rather be killed myself then kill him, for he is truly a wonder, and belongs in the world."

And when he looked back over at the wall, Merlin was smiling at him, and when the boy rejoined them, he thanked them heartily for what they said.

"What have we said that you should thank us for?" asked Mark.

And Merlin repeated to them precisely what they had said, and he thanked them very kindly and said he would trust them implicitly.

Then the messengers shook their heads, saying that there is nothing they could say or think that the boy does not already know about.

Within a few days more they rode into King Vortiger's kingdom. And as they did, they went through a town and saw a procession of people taking a child to be buried. They were all about the body, men and women wailing bitterly, and when Merlin saw the sorrow, and the priests and the clerks chanting and carrying the body to be buried, he once more stopped and began to laugh.

"Why are you laughing now?" asked Mark.

"I am laughing for the great wonder that I see," the child's said. "Do you see the father over there who is mourning, and the priest who is chanting?"

"Yes, of course," the messengers said.

"I am laughing because is the priest who ought to be crying, and the other man should be singing. For the child is actually the priest's son, and yet it is the man who is not his father who is mourning and making such dole over him. That is why it seems to me a great wonder."

"How can we find out the truth of this?" asked Mark.

"That's easy," said the boy. "Go to the woman who is mourning and ask her why she is weeping. She will tell you that her son is dead, and you should answer her: 'I know as well as you do with that this is not your husband's son, but the son of the priest who is over there.'"

When this was accomplished, they did exactly as Merlin said, and when she heard it, she was very much afraid and said to them, "My lords, by God's mercy I know that I cannot hide from you, so I will admit the whole truth. It is just as you have said, but for God's sake, but take pity on me, do not tell my husband, for he would kill me."

And the messengers were astonished and turned to look at Merlin and saw him where he was intently delighted by a hill of ants.

"This boy is the greatest seer that has ever lived," said Mark. "And I will be dead before I hear of anyone killing him."

-10-

They rode until they were a day's journey from where Vortiger was. When they stopped that night, the messengers asked Merlin to advise them on what they should say to the king, because they had disobeyed him and not killed Merlin as soon as they found out that he was fatherless—which is the one thing they had pledged to do.

Merlin smiled at each of them, for he knew that they were taking a great risk for him, and so he said to them "If you will do as I advise, you will face no trouble. Go to King Vortiger and tell him that you have found me, and the truth about how I know things that no one could know." He raised his finger, and pointed it to emphasize his words. "And inform him that I alone can tell him truly why his tower falls down, and what he can do to make it stand. And I will also explain why the clerics wanted to have me killed." Merlin paced in front of them, then gestured toward the town. "Leave me nearby, where you can get me when it suits you, but where I may be kept safe, for some of the other messengers may come upon me, or indeed some of the clerics—who have a very deep and very good reason to keep me from the king." Merlin stopped to consider all that he had said, then nodded. "When you have done all of this, and told the king all that I have advised you to, you may feel safe doing whatever the king orders you to."

So they wrapped Merlin up in Mark's sleeping blanket so he would not be noticed, and Mark took him to his own house and let him be trusted to the care of his mother. "I will very willingly speak to your mother and father," said Merlin, eyes excited and smiling at the simple woman, "for I would like to know how they raised such a fine boy of such stout heart and true faithfulness."

At this Mark could not help but keep his face from growing red and hot, for he had long adjusted to having a less prestigious job than the knights and barons he was always in contact with, and the goodness he tried to keep in mind every day was often overlooked.

Then the messengers left and rode back to the castle, and let everyone know that they had returned, with news for the king. As they were being brought into the hall where the king was, Arledge, head of the clerics, intercepted them first, and stopped Mark with a firm hand on his chest, asking "Have you not found the boy? Why do you not bear his blood?"

"We will see the King and report on our news there," said Mark, feeling an implied threat from the head cleric.

"Have you not killed him?" said the cleric. "Those were very clearly your orders."

"We have not killed the boy, for he claims to be able to tell the king why his tower will not stand," he said, and forced himself to boldly look the cleric in the eye. "Which is what we all want."

"You have not killed him!" said Arledge, reeling. "Can't you see the boy is lying to you to save his own life? Idiot! You have disobeyed direct orders, and will suffer very grievously for your acts."

"That is for the king to decide," said Mark.

Arledge reared up in shock, then came back with force. "And who exactly do you think is the king's adviser?" he asked. "The orders you were sent forth on originated with me, for I have much influence over the king. And your punishment will also be decided by me," he said, "for the king does exactly as I say in these matters. Now where is the boy?" he asked

"He is just back there in the other room," Mark said.

Arledge had already pushed past him, followed soon by the rest of the other clerics, their haste telling Mark everything he needed to know about their fear of the child. The messengers scurried quickly forward to enter the room where the king stood, before the clerics could realize that the boy was nowhere about.

The king saw them and broke away immediately to come greet them, for he was very eager to be able to make progress on his tower. He said "My faithful messengers! You have returned. Have you done your mission?"

"We have done, sir, the best we could," said Mark, "which may not be exactly what you expect." He raised his hand to quell the immediate disappointment. "But if you will listen to us, you will find out how to make your tower stand."

The king looked at them with surprise and a bit of annoyance, but he held his tongue as they told him everything just as it happened. In the middle of their speech, Arledge and the rest of the clerics charged boldly into the room, and had to calm themselves swiftly when they saw that the messengers were, at that that moment, talking directly to the king. Arledge shot Mark a furious look of scorn as he stood out to the side and folded his hands before them. The clerics felt it incumbent to project an attitude of calm and patience, such as would befit those with an acquaintance with the events of the future, something Arledge's hot temper often made difficult for him.

"It is true that we found Merlin, although he could have very easily eluded us if he wanted to," said Mark. "But he comes to you willing to help."

"Who is this Merlin?" said the king. "This is the boy who was born fatherless? Whose blood you were to have brought me?"

"He is the very one," said Mark, "and you can be sure that he is the wisest and best seer who was ever in the world, except for God."

At this Arledge's face went white, for he did not know that Merlin was a seer. That part had been hidden from him. It was not only that he claimed, according to what he heard, to have better insight about the king's tower, and thus would present competition for the king's favor, but... he had already gotten inside the minds of he and the other clerics. Who knew what he could manipulate anyone into? You could see the thoughts swirling furiously in his brain as he attempted to process what he was hearing, interrupted every now and then by him looking up to stare daggers over the shoulder of the king at Mark and the rest of the messengers.

"Sir," continued Mark, "Merlin told us many things that he could not have known, including that he knew we had been ordered to kill him and bring back his blood. And he told us other wonders, very great ones, each of which has come true exactly as he said." Mark shook his head in wonder. "And he told us, without our having told him why we had come, that the clerics you have employed know nothing about why your tower keeps falling."

Vortiger turned at this, and looked at the assembled clerics with an icy eye that made their stomachs drop, then said as he turned back to Mark, "Yes, I truly believe that they know nothing about my tower."

"Yes sir," Mark said to him, unable to look past him at the clerics, "It honestly seems that they know nothing at all. But Merlin promises to tell you exactly how to make your tower stand, and since that is the true goal of all this," Mark forced himself to raise his eyes to meet the king's, who loomed over him most imposing, "we made the decision to preserve him in order to save your tower." Then he lowered his eyes humbly. "I apologize for disobeying your orders, and if we were wrong, sir," Mark swallowed, "you may take our lives. But I hope that we have done as you would have liked."

The king held him under his fearsome gaze, then nodded. "You have made the correct decision, which is for the tower to hold." He sighed. "I need more men with the sense to put the larger purpose ahead of blindly following orders. Bring this Merlin to me."

"Sir," said Mark, "he will meet you on the hilltop, where he may tell you straightaway what is preventing the tower from standing."

"This afternoon at the hour of nones," said the king.

He gave a nod to all of the messengers, who had each held themselves reserved despite the relief that flooded them, and with a whirl of his grand red robes, was out of the room, followed by his close advisors, walking past the gathered clerics without a glance.

When he saw this, that the king would not return his placid, smiling gaze, Arledge turned to the messengers with a tight face of fury. He strode directly to Mark and spoke through clenched teeth.

"This little folly of yours will cost you dearly," he said.

Mark looked the head cleric directly in the eye. "You will be dead soon," he said.

As the color drained at once from Arledge's face, he and the other messengers filed past him without a word.

-11-

When Mark returned home, he found Merlin on a bench right next to his mother, head tilted up as she animatedly told him the story about when Mark was his age and was repeatedly thrown in the sewage ditch by the older boys. When Mark entered, both the seer and his mother glanced up at him with great affection, and Merlin climbed off the bench and walked directly up to Mark. "You have vouched for me with your life," he said, warmly taking Mark's hand.

Mark smiled, then sat down himself, for he was dizzy when he thought about it. "I hope you can do what you claim you can," he said.

"Have no fear of that," Merlin said, with a wave of his hand.

That afternoon, they were on the hill of Dinas Emrys, the cold, wet wind whipping their hair around as they climbed toward the large figure of Vortiger, who watched the boy approaching with hands on hips, his robe held out by his arms and creating the impression of a very large, fearsome ruler.

The place that Vortiger had chosen for his tower was a high rocky hilltop covered here and there by patches of thick bushes and hardy grass, seeming to cling tenaciously to the firm rock. Below, the large lake of Llyn Dinas, farms and fields in the valley, and all around, higher mountains that surrounded the site of the future tower and gave a solid sense of security. It was obvious that any invading force would have a very difficult time scaling the steep hill, and siege engines could not possibly be brought near to assail the structure.

The day was wet and raw with the clouds so low they seemed to brush over the hilltop where the men were gathered. The king stood amidst the foundations of the tower and surrounding buildings that had been attempted before. Now it was nothing but a pile of rocks fallen into a vague circle of dark gray, almost black stones, darkened by the moisture in the air. Around them, strewn all over the hillside, were scattered stones from the towers that had collapsed in the past.

The clerics made one group, standing between the messengers and Vortiger, who could be seen gathered with his advisers at the top of the hill. Merlin drank in his first actual sight of the king, not the shadow image in his mind, and saw that he was truly a large, imposing presence, made still more impressive by his massive scarlet robes. He did indeed live up to the image of a tyrant, and radiated a fearsome power, even at that distance.

Arledge saw Mark and the boy approaching and broke off from the group to stride with great, efficient purpose for them. He extended his hand and walked with great authority, saying loudly "This is the boy? I will take him now, so you don't cause further embarrassment in front of the king."

The young boy pointed directly at him, large smile beaming from beneath his tousled hair. "I will not go with you," said Merlin. "You are the one who wanted to kill me."

And the two of them walked by, leaving the shaken Arledge standing there, hands held before his chest in a concerned and unsteady stance. The king saw them and came away from his group to approach them as they ascended.

Merlin showed a great smile as he left Mark to approach the king and he held out his hand, saying "King Vortiger! You are a great and impressive king!"

"And greetings to you, Merlin," said Vortiger, a curious smile on his face as he examined the slight, unimpressive boy. "I have heard much of your fantastic abilities, and great effort was expended in finding you."

"Yes, you ordered these messengers to search across the country until they found me," he said, gesturing toward the messengers, "on the advice of these wise clerics," and here he turned and gestured toward the group of assembled clerics, who had scurried quickly closer to hear what he had to say. "You wish to know why this tower will not stand, and why it falls down each time after growing to twenty or so feet in height. These men," he gestured toward the clerics, who each stood at rigid readiness for whatever the boy might say, "told you that the blood of a fatherless boy, if put into the foundation, would cause your tower to stand." Merlin indicated the clerics with a sweeping gesture of his hand, and then turned once more to face the king.

"But they lied," he said.

"In truth they have no idea why your tower will not stand. But each of them saw that he would come to his death because of me. That is why they lied to you and told you to have me killed," Merlin said. "Not to help your tower, for even if my blood were mixed with the mortar, it would not have stood any better than before. They told you this simply to forestall their own deaths."

The king looked up sharply at the clerics. He had not surmised this angle on the matter, and did not like being used and made a fool of.

His scornful gaze settled most on Arledge, and his cringing manner and downcast eyes told the king that what the boy said was true.

"But if they had said that the tower will stand due to all that I see and know, they would have said the truth," Merlin said. "And if you promise to do to them what they wanted to do to me," he cast a clever eye over the gathered seers, "then I will tell you why the tower will not stand."

The clerics looked up quickly. Their faces were ashen and gaunt and Arledge's eyes widened, while still standing still and trying to appear composed before the king, as he put together what he had just heard. Some could be seen swallowing, others staring with hollow eyes at the ground, but all tried to maintain his still composure as they stood before the king.

"Did he just say—" whispered one.

"Yes!" hissed Arledge.

The king passed an appraising eye across the gathered clerics, who were not known men of his, but ones he had assembled for intelligence about why the tower would not stand, and none of them had been of any use to him. He then turned away and said to Merlin "If you show me why my tower keeps collapsing, and how to get it to stand," he waved his hand dismissively, "I will do what you wish with these clerics."

A small gasp escaped Arledge's lips, like the hollow sound of a pebble hitting the side of a well on the way down, and his face seemed to grow even more ashen still.

"These are not men you want to have in your court," said Merlin, "for they were not trying to help you, but only to save their own lives. And any tower you would have built on their advice, my blood in the mortar or not, would have only fallen down again. Ask them yourself if this is not true," Merlin said, taking hold of the king's hand and gesturing to the clerics with the other, "for they would never be so bold as to lie to you in front of me."

The king strode directly to the clerics and asked them whether what he had heard was the truth.

"Sir," Arledge said, whining through his shallow breath, "God forgive our sins, but yes, he tells you the truth. But we don't understand how he knows these things. We ask you," he lowered his eyes in supplication, "please let us live long enough to find out whether or not the tower will stand through his sight."

Merlin spoke boldly and said to them, "You will not die until you see why the tower falls down."

Arledge bowed his head in thanks, then all held still for a moment, because Merlin had given an order before the king could speak. The king said nothing, but smiled slightly in amusement at the brashness of the boy. Arledge opened his mouth as though to answer, but thought better of it and quietly retreated a few steps backward.

"You do not want these men, because they are not true in service to you and your wishes," said Merlin to the king, waving his hand dismissively. "These messengers, however, have acted with bravery, honor and stout heart, with complete obedience to your will." And here he led the king over to where the messengers stood. They found it hard to meet the king's eye and stood humbly before him, gazes lowered to the ground.

"They were brave enough to disobey your direct orders so that they could fulfill your wishes, and took great risk upon themselves to do it. This man in particular, Mark, has shown great courage and is a stout-hearted and faithful man. His family is in servitude, as are three of the four others. You should buy their freedom and give them an allowance that they may serve you more closely in your court, for these are the kind of faithful men a king requires around him."

The king stood before them, regal and upright with hands on his hips and looked over the young men appraisingly. He nodded and said "I will do as you advise, and bring these four into closer service with me," then raised a finger, and lowered it toward Merlin's face, "if you can tell me how to make my tower stand."

Mark looked up momentarily at the expression of the king, such that Merlin could see the gratitude on his face, and when he could no longer keep the king's gaze, bashfully looked at the ground, unable to suppress a smile.

"That I can do easily," Merlin said. "Let me tell you right away the reason that your tower will not stand," and with this he grabbed the king's hand and drew him, the child leading the man, up towards the top of the hill, each stepping carefully on the wet rock. "And if I lie in even one word," he said, "you may have me destroyed."

Merlin led the king into the circle created by the fallen bricks of the previous towers. The messengers and the clerics followed, as well as the king's advisers, and they all fanned out within the enclosed space of the stone circle. When they were all ready, and looking expectantly at him, Merlin began.

"Do you know what is underneath this rock?" he asked. "There is a great pool of water. And at the bottom of that great pool, there are two enormous stones. And beneath those two stones are two sleeping dragons."

The mouths of the clerics fell open. None of them had ever seen anything like that. The king's eyes flared open slightly, and took on a quick fiery look, then he was able to compose his face again.

"Neither of these dragons can see a thing, but each of them can feel the presence of the other, and they are very big," continued Merlin. "When they feel the water upset above them, because of your tower, they become uncomfortable and turn over, causing the pool above to make such a great uproar that whatever is built on it must fall down."

At this he turned directly to the king and gestured to the ground. "Break through this rock and see how it is for yourself," he said, "and if it is not exactly as I have told you, then you may have me burned to death. But if you do find it, you will burn the clerics to death instead," he gestured toward them, "and help the messengers."

Vortiger was looking with eyes afire toward the stone beneath him, as though he could see right through it to the pool beneath. "If what you tell me is true," he said, "I will follow all of your advice, and also hold you to be the greatest seer in the land."

"But if you find that it is so, then let the messengers go free and buy their freedom." Merlin gestured towards the clerics without looking at them, "and let the clerics be proved guilty, for they knew nothing of any of this, and tried to deceive you through their feeble wiles."

64

Vortiger was still gazing at the ground, but now his mind was clearly working, his shrewd wisdom returned, and he brought his hand up under his chin as he thought. "When I see the pool and the stones, and the dragons beneath them," he said, "then I will burn the clerics, and reward the messengers." He raised his eyes to meet Merlin's. "For, impressive as your abilities have been, all I have had so far are words."

Merlin bowed to him. "Very wise, king," he said, and gestured to the ground. "The sooner you start digging, the sooner you will see that I am right." Then he turned his back and dismissed the king, walking over to stand near Mark.

-12-

So the king ordered his men to set to work clearing land and stones away from the spot on which he wanted his tower. And it was only a week or so until one day while they were working, the rock beneath them gave way, and they ran quickly as the stone below them began to crack away in great chunks. They lost several pieces of their best equipment, as they fell down into the hole, and great splashes of water began to fly up out of the hilltop. Then they could stand to the side and see the great water that was beneath the earth there, and when the sun shone, you could see clear to the bottom, covered in stones that had no moss or vegetation, through water that was crystal clear and of an unsurpassing clarity. And at the lowest center point of that pool within the hill, there could be no mistaking two enormous flat stones, lying next to each other. Then even the workers marveled at Merlin's gifts of sight, for he had seen something that no man could ever have seen.

Then the king said to his advisers, "Very wise indeed is this child who knew that this pool was under the ground." His advisors had to agree, and began to have worry about Merlin, this new advisor who came out of nowhere, and represented a dangerous new element, for there is no one around a king—especially one as volatile as Vortiger—who is not in danger of being replaced and cast out. Sir Brantius tried to ask the king what he knew of this child seer, and if he was sure that his intentions were the preservation of the king, but the king had seen his pool, and could see nothing but his tower.

The king called Merlin to him and said, smiling for the first time in months, and friendly, almost affectionate, with the boy. "You have told the truth, for the pool has been found. But I don't know yet about the two dragons beneath the rocks."

Merlin smiled broadly and touched him warmly on the arm. "How can you know it if you haven't seen it?" he asked.

The king asked him how he could get rid of the water.

"Break holes in the rocks further down the hill, so that the water will drain away," Merlin said. "This will expose the two rocks that cover the slumbering dragons."

The king said it would be done the next day.

That night, when the land was still and silent and all were slumbering, Dinas Emrys was asleep and vacant, its exposed rock glowing under the strong bluish white moonlight, the smooth undulating surface broken by the smashed-in section where they had broken through to the pool, rather like an egg that had been bashed in at one place with the heel of a spoon.

The great hole in the hill was dark, but if you could hover above it, you could see the rocks of the bottom sitting silently under the bright moonlight, so clear was the water that was contained within that hill. And if you were hovering above, you might have seen a corridor open up in the air, and a small boy step out, then ascend the rest of the hill to stand on the verge of the void.

Merlin looked down. The water was so absolutely still, and so clear, you might not have been able to tell that there was any water in the hole at all, were the reflection of the cracked hole edge and the sky, brightened by moon, not visible on the surface, like an illusionary onion skin floating halfway down into the chamber. Merlin noted that the level of the water had significantly decreased from when they first

66

opened it. The people of town had been there earlier, collecting this water for their medicines and drinking, for their stews and to soak into their fields and to feed their elderly and their babies, and well they should; water of this purity would hardly ever again be found in the earth, and once it was gone, it would never again appear for any of the ages going forward.

Merlin looked down at the water, and had an impulse, but restrained himself. It wasn't fitting... but then, what was? Who said anything was fitting for him? No one had placed any rules on him, except he himself, and there was nothing to say that, being alive, he was not allowed to simply enjoy himself as any creature that walks on this earth can do. He was, in fact, away from his mother for the first time in his life. Was it seemly? Who knew—and who would know? No one was there. It was still many hours until the dawn. And again, Merlin thought, dammit, I'm here on earth and I deserve to enjoy myself just as much as any human would.

He let his clothes drop beside him, and dove, naked, into the pool.

The water was cold, so cold, but that thrilled him. It felt so absolutely pure and soft, like the air of a cool night breeze, or the cold sleeve of a silk shirt, as it passed over his skin. The boy descended, almost to the great stones that covered the dragons, then slowly arced upward, and came straight up until he broke the surface. Above him, darkness broken by the huge jagged hole in the roof of the hill, and the moon a thick crescent within it. Gently moving wavy lines of reflected moonlight danced along the interior stone that covered the cavernous space.

Merlin leaned back and floated in the water, feeling its blessed purity. It was so beautiful. He really needed to simply enjoy himself more. He had driven himself to use every moment he had, to learn necromancy, to learn everything of astrology, and any and all rituals that could be of use to him—but remained within the realm of white magic—and he rarely allowed himself the time to just be here, on God's creation, and enjoy the gifts that he gave humans, but that he, too, was entitled to take pleasure in. He didn't have to be just an observer. And, as he learned while he was in that water, the experience of enjoyment had its own lessons, and was not wasted time, but every bit as necessary to the mind and soul as touch, or sleep.

Before he left that place he would fill forty-eight large urns with the water, and, through his craft, send them to where Blaise would be in Northumberland, and where it would be safely kept until he needed it for his purposes. But for now, he let it simply soak into his skin, feeling that the very essence of the water was entering him through the skin, filling him, bringing his body what it had always wanted, but never had.

He sank down into it, and whirled his arms so that he tumbled end over end. He dove down to the bottom, and touched the dragon's stone, then came up to the surface and flopped onto his back, creating a great splash which echoed with a lovely rushing tone throughout the cavern. He threw the water at his face, and felt its coolness slide off of his cheeks and nose. He blew out all the air that was within him, and let his body sink toward the bottom, until he needed oxygen and rushed once more to the surface. It was moments like that which made him feel most human, something as simple as needing air, and when he did, he felt less alone. For as you know, he was the only creature of his kind on the entire planet.

Enjoying himself—he was all for it. He began to think of a way he could let Blaise enjoy it, too. The old man would go nuts for a bath in this, thought Merlin. And then he thought of his mother, and what wonders the water might do for her, too. There were too many uses for the water, and too little of it. Maybe he would take all of it. It really shouldn't go to waste. But then he thought, no, the people of the land surrounding should be able to take advantage of it. So he would encourage them to, when it was released from the hill. Gather it for themselves. Whatever was left.

-13-

So it was done, and the crystal clear water leaked in great gushes from the holes that were cut into the rock near the pool's foot, and many people of the town came around with buckets and urns as they could manage and gathered some of that water as it rushed out of the rock and cascaded down the hill. Then at the bottom of the pool could clearly be seen the two extremely large flat stones lying one next to another.

These stones, and the dragons beneath them, were put there by Lludd, an earlier king of Britain, who trapped them there decades earlier in order to rid Britain of the plague caused by the dreadful scream that came each May Day, and caused all women in the land to miscarry. This tale is a confirmed history of that land, and you can read it, the tale of *Lludd and Llefelys,* in the book of stories known as **The Mabinogion.**

The king was informed that the pool had been drained, and he wanted to go see the two stones himself. He went there with Merlin, and his advisors who were always at his side, and the clerics went too, although they remained mostly meek and silent these days.

Along the way, Sir Brantius, a portly and pompous knight, peppered Merlin with questions which were spoken in an effusive tone of respect, but all had an undertone of suspicion. It was this tone that irked Merlin, for it assumed that he was so simple he wouldn't have the sense to realize that the man was grilling him. His conversation was also notably held in the king's hearing, so that the ruler might note how loyal and protective Brantius was.

"How do you know the things that you know?" asked Brantius as they climbed the hill, looking down at Merlin with an air of detached amusement.

"My knowledge of the past comes from the devil who sired me," said Merlin. "My knowledge of the future was given to me by God when the devil lost his hold on me."

The advisor gave a dismissive chuckle. "And why should the king listen to a seer whose powers spring from the devil?" asked Brantius.

"Well, the main reason is that I know so much more than you," said Merlin, looking directly up at the man.

Sir Brantius laughed pompously, as though somehow the joke was his. "You may find yourself surprised at what I know," he said, nodding judiciously.

"Indeed, I would be quite surprised if you were found to know anything," said Merlin, and stepped ahead, taking the king's hand and speaking very submissively. "Sire," he said, "must I tolerate the inquisition of your lackeys?"

"Leave off, Brantius," the king shouted back, not looking over his shoulder.

The advisor stopped in his tracks for a moment, then hurried on, focusing hot hatred on the little boy ambling along at the side of the king. That ridiculous upstart had been in the court for just over a week, and now he held the hand of the king like a beloved child, while devoted advisors who has been in the king's service for years were treated like part of the scenery. Brantius decided then and there to drive a fat wedge between those two, or see his own place near the king be displaced even further away.

The group came to the edge of the chasm where they could see the two great stones. One entire side of the rock that contained the pool had caved in once the water had run out, so Merlin and the king stood on the high ridge overlooking what looked like a massive scoop taken out of the hillside. Pools of the clear water still lay down in the rocky bottom of the crater.

Merlin held the king's hand and pointed down at the two stones at the bottom of the drained pool, and said "Do you see those two great rocks?" he asked.

"Yes," said the king.

"Beneath these two rocks are the two great dragons, each fast asleep," said Merlin. "These dragons won't move before they catch the other's scent. But wit you well, the moment they smell each other, they will fight until one of them is dead." Then Merlin raised his face to the king. "In their fight and eventual victory, there is contained great meaning, for those who know how to see it."

"And," the king said to Merlin, "will you tell me which one will be defeated?"

"I will, in private, before three of your closest advisers," replied Merlin. "I will tell you before the fight which one of the dragons will win, so that once the fight is over, you will know that I have said the truth."

"And will you tell me the meaning?" asked Vortiger.

"That I will tell you after you have seen that I am right about which one is victorious," replied Merlin.

The king's eyes turned away, downward, to reflect in thought for a moment, and his face was serious. But he agreed, so he returned to his castle and brought Merlin before three of his closest and most trusted advisers. Sir Brantius was not among them, and ended up standing like a fool outside the closed door, his enmity beginning to focus entirely around this Merlin, who had so easily captivated the king's full attention.

Merlin cast his eye around the three men chosen by the king. "These three liegemen of yours," he asked the king, "are they in your confidence?"

King Vortiger replied "Yes, more than anyone else I know of."

"And I can say in front of them what you ask of me?"

The king answered "Yes, indeed."

"Then you should know," said Merlin, "that the red dragon will be killed by the white dragon. He will have a great deal of struggle and pain before he kills him, but kill the red dragon he indeed will. His victory will have very great meaning for he who can perceive it, but I will not tell you more until after you see that I am correct," Merlin finished.

"Let us now arrange a day to move the stones and let the dragons clash at each other," said the child, having to look up to meet the gaze of the men seated around him. "And be sure to have your greatest men around to witness, and all of the people of the surrounding countryside, for they will see a marvel of great astonishment that they will remember all of their days, and will become a legend of this place for all eternity."

-14-

Then Dinas Emrys had a great dark gouge in the side of its undulating armor-gray exposure of ancient rocks, where the men had opened up the earth to find the pool. That now drained away, in the great chamber that was left in one side of the hill and visible at the bottom, were the two enormous rocks.

Workmen waited in the great depression that had once been the bottom of the pool, with horses and ropes ready to pull the rocks away. Hundreds of villagers from the surrounding towns had massed upon the lower end and sides of the hill surrounding the vast hole, and still more could be seen on the distant hills and down in the valley. Merlin had advised the king to stand on the upper rim of the hole and gather all of his barons, advisers and liegemen, plus the clerics, there as well. He told them that place would keep them safest and afford them the greatest view of the battle. You can be sure that none of them gave any contest to this suggestion of Merlin's, regardless of how they estimated his prophetic power. The advisors who had heard Merlin's prediction about which dragon would win were closest at his side, to see if the child's words were true. The king strode, along that ridge, before the rest of his gathered barons and liegemen and told them everything Merlin had predicted up until then, and how each thing he said had come true. And he told them now that Merlin had predicted that there would be two dragons, a red and a white one, resting under the two stones they saw before them.

As this happened, Merlin stood, a broad and slightly spooky smile on his face. He had his arms crossed before him and his tousled hair whipped around in the wind of the blustery day, looking for every intent like just another mischievous village boy. The men found him quite out of place and his presence a bit unnerving. Merlin watched as the gathered men's eyes darted to him as the king delivered his words, wondering that this seemingly simple child had predicted all of these great events. Brantius was not the only one who expressed mistrust or condescending dismissal. For his part, Merlin enjoyed their looks, and chuckled internally as he saw their disbelief, meanwhile lazily poking through their histories and futures to see which among them were good and honest men, and which were disloyal or self-serving.

A light cover of gray clouds was sealed over them and the day was windy but not wet. The king, for some reason, had eschewed the normal attire of deep scarlet that he so often appareled himself in, and now wore a grand mantle of very light cream, one could almost say white. When he had finished telling his important men of Merlin's predictions, he turned towards the boy and said "Now Merlin, as you wish."

The child came forward, smiling upward toward the king, and took him by the hand. He led him toward the center of the group at the apex of the hill, surrounded by his clerics and closest advisers, the space of most honor and most fitting for a king. The king stood with his legs wide and hands upon his hips as he looked down over the great hole, and all the townspeople gathered on the hills around. Beyond that, he could see the hills and the great valley leading up to the site, and behind him rose an even greater mountain, framing him in monumentality to all the people who stood below. If Merlin were to tell him that the white dragon represented his power and might, and that all of this were to be a great signifier of his strength over the country, he knew that this day would be considered one of great importance that all men would speak of for centuries into the future.

Of course, Merlin hadn't yet told him what the victory of the white dragon would mean. Yet Vortiger sensed that it wouldn't turn out to be good for him. At this, he felt a shrinking in his heart, and for a slight wavering moment, he thought he might tip forward into the abyss, and land between the two great stones. But it passed in a moment, and he was able to draw a deep breath and raise his head regally while he calmed the trembling of his organs inside.

Merlin gestured to him and the king raised his hand to give the signal to the men below to draw the stones aside.

The horses below were led forward, the ropes grew to tautness, and all stood still for a moment as they pulled apart at the greatest tension, then issued a low rumbling as first one, then the other stone, began sliding. The two stones moved slowly away from each other, the grinding of their weight on the earth and rocks beneath them causing a dull roar to echo within the hollow that had been carved from the hill. Soon great holes were seen underneath where the rocks had been.

Standing from the king's perspective, looking down, within the hole on the right, the light that was cast in as the stone drew back fell on what first appeared to be a large white boulder, with golden highlights of crusty yellow growing in its crevices. All on the hill took in their breath as the stone was finally clear, and they could see what looked like a white boulder that seemed to be about ten feet in height and fifteen in length.

The king stared at it, surprised to see a stone where a dragon had been predicted, but then his eyes followed the yellowish veins and the lustrous ceramic white look of the stone, and suddenly he could see that it was not a stone at all, but a tightly coiled and sleeping reptile of immense size. It had tucked its head under its tail and both were coiled tightly around its body. The men all around gasped when they seemed to realize at once what it was, and many took an involuntary step back.

As the left stone was drawn back, it too showed a hollow chamber, and within, a second stone, only this time all knew better than to think it was simply a rock. As the covering stone drew back and the light fell on the sleeping beast, it revealed a shiny surface of the deepest red. Rather than the ancient and encrusted quality that the white dragon displayed, this one seemed clean and sleek, and more like a beautifully-carved piece of lacquer than anything living. It too had its head tucked within its folds, and no one could see the movement of breath. Then there was a loud crash as a rope pulling the second stone snapped, causing the suddenly-released horses to topple forward, and the stone to crash down, only half-drawn back over the hollow.

For a long moment the king gazed down without speaking, not only because he had never seen such a marvelous thing with his own eyes, but because all of it was unfolding exactly as predicted by the young boy. And he had, he thought with a suddenly stiffening heart, good reason to think that the outcome of the event he was about to see would be inextricably tied to his own. His breath came in slowly and very deeply.

"Now you will absolve the messengers," said Merlin in a pleasant voice, "and you will promote and do service to them as I have advised."

"I will do as you say," said the king.

The boy brought his hands together and bowed to the king in thanks. "Then the dragons will be awakened at your command," said Merlin.

The king waited a long moment, looking down on the scene, before raising his right hand and gesturing down toward the workmen there. One of them had been selected, and others of his group could be seen clapping him on the back in encouragement as he stepped forward. He walked nimbly among the rocks along the bottom of the hole carved out of the hillside and approached the edge of the chasm of that contained the white dragon. He held a large rock balanced upward in the palm of his hand and, looking back once to ensure a path to get away, turned and set his shoulders, facing the white dragon.

The young man crouched, sending one leg back for support as he lowered his arm, then leaned forward and threw the rock as hard as he could at the flank of the sleeping dragon. He then turned and ran as fast as his legs could carry him until he had once more reached his comrades, who all began running away to the far side of the chasm.

The rock hit the side of the dragon with a deep and resounding thud, then fell away to land on the floor of the chasm. For a long time, nothing happened, and all who could see stared at that white mound with anxious breath, eyes trained steadily to detect any movement.

First there was nothing, then a swelling, as the entire hump grew larger and held for a moment, and when it started to deflate a deep rumbling growl was heard, low and aggravated, like a long and weary sigh. Then the great lump shifted this way, the crunching of earth heard from beneath it, then it shifted in the opposite direction, and quickly the lines of the beast began to unfurl. And suddenly a head was lifted high out of the hole, on a long, sinuous white neck.

It blinked its eyes a few times, then focused, saw the men on the hill and its head whirled around to see the people all around, surrounding it. Then it closed its eyes languidly and tipped its head back, stretching its long neck this way and that, for dragons are not greatly afraid of men.

The beast then arched its back and raised up on its legs, like a cat, and now its large tail uncoiled and rose up out of the pit, stretching back twenty feet and moving in strange whirls as it stretched out the kinks in its body. It lifted its head and sniffed at the air, its nostrils visibly expanding and long tongue reaching out to curl in the air, then it turned and reached up to claw itself upward out of the pit. The earth along the whole side collapsed beneath its weight, and it flailed clumsily for a few seconds before finding purchase and dragging its heavy body up out of the hole, on the side away from the king.

The townspeople standing lower on the hill, far below the king, could thus far see nothing but the lower ridge of the chasm in the hill. Now suddenly the head of the white dragon appeared, and a great cry rose up, while all of them stepped quickly five paces back. Soon the body of the dragon followed as it climbed up over the ridge. Its head was held low, moving slowly back and forth and it stepped forward, eyeing the people gathered all around, its nostrils quivering as it sniffed their scents.

Behind the creature, a man on the other side ran and hurled a stone at the red dragon. It bounced and ran down the creature's side, which was suddenly struck by an involuntary tremor. Then a pause, and then the great red mass shifted to the side, unfurled quickly and its head was seen to rise up out of the pit, bright yellow eyes darting up, left and right. Then its head whipped around to see the people behind it, and the lumbering form of the white dragon. It gave not much thought to the men, but at the sight of the other dragon, its nostrils could be seen working quickly and a long forked tongue slipped out of its mouth. The red dragon tried to raise itself, but couldn't entirely, due to the stone still half over the hole, and when it felt itself hemmed in, it gave a great shriek that was like a horse's whinny, but deeper and richer, which put a chill into the hearts of all that had gathered around. At the sound, the white dragon turned its head and saw the red dragon, drawing up close behind.

The red dragon's body drew back, then surged forward, trying to force itself out of the hole. Then its front claws came up and started scratching at the side of the hole with great rapidity, as a dog does while digging in the dirt. Huge clods of earth came crashing down, and then the dragon once more forced itself up, lifting the side of the huge rock with the lump of its body, and finally slipping out to crawl in an ungainly way up and out of the hole, until finally it was free, and the massive stone behind it fell back into place with a resounding boom.

When it was free, all people gathered around took a step back, for none of them could have predicted how huge the animal would be. If the white dragon was thirty-five feet stretched from nose to tail, the red dragon must have been fifty feet. And although in the intervening years we have come to regard dragons as sometimes cute, helpful, friendly and perhaps even cuddlesome, these beasts were nothing but ferocious wild animals, and while everyone wanted to see them, no one wanted to be closer than they had to be.

The red dragon dragged itself up to the ridge next to where the white one was and unfurled its immense wings, stretching them up in the air. Looking from below, people on the hillside could see the light of the sky shining through, and red veins crossing the thin flesh. Furling its wings once more and blinking its eyes, the animal took a look at the people all gathered around, then turned its attention to the white dragon. Both animals regarded each other for a moment, then put their noses right together. Their eyes narrowed as their nostrils could be seen rapidly undulating, tongues pushing out and then retreating.

Then their noses moved back further along their necks, and both lost all interest in the humans as their noses slid along their haunches and all over each other's backs, like a pair of greeting dogs. A strange rhythmic whooshing sound was in the air, the sound of the sniffing beasts, their tongues darting out periodically. The creatures smelled all around and finally their long necks curled and angled low as their faces went up under each other's hind legs, toward their most scented parts. Then both animals froze in place and one could hear the long breath as they took in each other's scent.

Suddenly the two beasts sprang away from each other, placing twenty feet between them at a single jump. Luckily no one was trampled by their feet, but their tails swung out wildly, causing several on the steeper side, behind the white dragon, to be knocked off their feet and go bouncing down the hill. Those on the side of the red dragon ducked as its tail swing overhead, except for two men and a woman who were sent reeling. A horse was also struck full on the side and sent flying through the air, its legs spinning wildly and long neck spiraling around before coming down to bounce ungracefully down the hill.

Now people on all sides stepped back even further, or found places of less precarious purchase on the hill, as the two animals arched necks up tall while keeping their heads low to the ground. Their cheeks came up over their enormous teeth and each issued a hissing sound accompanied by a low guttural rumbling from their throats, which could be seen to quiver with the noises they were making. The hissing and flicking of tongues continued as they circled one another, the red one coming lower down the hill, causing the spectators to move back even further when its long tail swung among them, knocking one woman off her feet and onto one of the large tower stones laying about.

Suddenly the red dragon sprang forward with its mouth open, but the white dragon moved aside quickly and got in a good bite in the red one's neck. The red dragon, however, was so powerful that it dislodged the white one with a flick of its neck, then reared up quickly and smashed its open jaw down on the ridge of the white dragon's back, pressing it down to the ground. The white dragon's legs kicked out beneath it. As it did, a high bellowing screech came out of the animal that sent chills through everyone who heard it, like nails on a chalkboard. The white dragon's head whipped around as it was trapped there, until its mouth clamped onto the red dragon's rear leg, pulling it and causing it to let go its grip. When it did, red blood began cascading down in rivulets along the white scales.

The white dragon scampered under the neck of the larger red one and whipped its tail around to bash the red one's head downward into the earth. When the red beast's head was down, the white one leapt upon its back and began mashing its head down repeatedly, biting the red dragon's flank each time. The red dragon arched its neck back and grabbed the white animal where its neck met its body, then yanked the entire beast off with a fantastic snap of its neck. The white dragon was momentarily on its back with its belly exposed, and the red one stepped right up to place its foreclaw on the soft belly of the white beast, mashing its head down repeatedly, causing red blood to once more leak across the white scales. The white dragon screeched in agony and its neck and tail thrashed around violently, beating down on the ground with great booming thuds as the red dragon tore at its throat.

Brantius stepped up close behind the king. "It would seem certain that the red one is going to win," he said. The king said nothing, and Merlin could not be bothered to look back.

Indeed all of the people gathered around thought it was sure that the red dragon would win, for its size was almost twice that of the white one.

While still on its back and shrieking wildly, the white dragon drew up its hind legs and began rapidly slashing with its claws at the underbelly of the red dragon with strikes so rapid its legs made a blur. A gash appeared there, but it was hard to see the blood of the red dragon against the already scarlet color of its scales. It withstood the attack until suddenly the white dragon's claws pulled a bit of pinkish gut out of the red beast, and a high-pitched screech echoed from the surrounding mountains. As the red one jumped off and to the side, the white one slipped from under it and with a quick twisting of its entire body, righted itself and stepped away into a defensive posture.

The creatures opened their mouths to roar at each other, then the white one caught the red in the neck, just behind the head, and in a moment, both animals had twisted up and intertwined, wings flapping out wildly as they lost balance and tumbled one over another. Neither was on its feet and their legs flailed in the air as they became one solid mass of dragon, sometimes coming to a complete standstill as each strained against the other, then erupting once more in violent thrashing.

Then the ground gave way beneath them, sending a wave of dirt and rocks cascading down the hill, and with their thrashing movements, the creatures began tumbling over each other down the hill. The crowd of people assembled there turned and started running, but it was too late for many of them as the dragons rolled swiftly down the hill and right over many people who could not escape. Later, thirty-two were found to have been killed, and twice as many injured. The beasts separated as they continued rolling down the hill, and the white one was able to get a purchase higher than the red, who finally came to a stop several feet below. It didn't take more than a second to right itself, however, and with an angry screech that rent the air, it lowered its head in rage and charged back up the hill.

The white dragon was visibly weakened, and one of its eyes could not open fully. The blood that flowed from its wounds now made patches of the beast appear a light pink, with only a few streaks of white showing through. Its long forked tongue hung from its mouth and its breathing was a horrible wheezing sound. The red dragon, also worse for wear but in nowhere near as bad shape, charged up the hill and clamped its mouth on the flank just above the white dragon's foreleg, pushing the white beast five feet up the hill with the force of its attack.

Others of the king's advisors drew closer to him and were making noises of excitement that the red dragon might prove victorious. "It looks like the red one is sure to win," said one who had been present at Merlin's prediction, clapping the king on the shoulder.

80

"Looks like you might have missed the mark on this one, Merlin!" he said jovially.

The child turned and gave him a wide toothy smile with big enlarged eyes that was so creepy the man froze in place and turned quickly away. The seer returned to watching the dragons without a word. The king said nothing, looked at no one, only wishing he could be alone.

The red dragon's neck tensed with power, jerked its head back, and jerked again, ripping the white dragon's entire foreleg off, tearing a strip of flesh that went up the beast's flank in a garish red triangle toward its bony ridge. The red dragon whipped its head around, some observers thought with a flourish of triumph, and the severed leg went flying end over end to land somewhere in the valley below. The bone is still in a pub somewhere in Wales. At this, a gasp rose up from the gathered people, for it seemed certain now that the red dragon would be victorious. Seeming to feel this himself, the red dragon lifted its head high and made a series of barks that echoed across the hill and throughout the valley. Meanwhile, the white dragon tried to pull itself backward, away and out from under the larger beast.

The red dragon lowered its head slowly, now taking its time, as the white dragon dragged itself slowly back, blood leaving a scarlet stain on the hill under where it had been. Its eyes were drowsing now and it was greatly weakened. The red dragon seemed to take a vicious delight in the suffering of its enemy and a guttural snarl emerged from its throat as it slowly stalked forward.

The white dragon brought its head directly back into its body, causing its neck to get shorter and much thicker, closed its eyes completely and it began making strange rhythmic guttural sounds that came in time with hacking pulses of its neck, as though it were about to vomit. Then the people thought that the white dragon was surely dying, for its eyes had closed to small slits, and it seemed to take no care at all for the approaching red dragon.

Stepping directly up to the prone body of the wounded animal, the red dragon's head began to rise regally up on its long neck, mouth salivating and dripping long strands of drool as it opened its mouth to deliver the death strike. But the neck of the white dragon suddenly thrust forward and clamped its mouth directly on the breast of the red dragon at the base of its neck. The flesh of its neck expanded and pulsed rapidly forward, while the guttural throbbing sound grew faster until it reached a fever pitch.

Then was heard a sound like no other, and suddenly flame spewed outward from the lips of the white dragon where it was clamped to the breast of the red one. The vicious expression of the red beast suddenly changed to one of agony and it gave a shriek that increased in pitch and intensity as its short front legs tried to claw frantically at the head of the white dragon, but its eyes were clamped tightly shut and neck stiffened, ready to hold on until the end. The red dragon's head whipped around rapidly like an injured snake, then swiftly came down to clamp its jaws on the rear flank of the white beast. For a moment it lifted the entire body of the white dragon off the ground as the red creature tried to pull it straight back off its body, but the white dragon's jaws were clamped tight, flames still shooting out ten feet or more from where its mouth was joined to the red beast's chest.

Finally the white dragon's grip slackened and it was thrown violently away, trailing a line of flame that quickly dissipated into the air. Once it was free, the red dragon stumbled and fell back, sliding about fifteen feet down the hill as its head, neck and tail thrashed around wildly, striking the ground and creating huge brown gashes where it struck grassy patches. The spot on its breast where the white dragon had held glowed with a yellow molten fire, and many were interested to have the legend proved true, that dragon scales retain heat, just like iron.

The white dragon used the last of its strength to push itself on its hind legs, like a frog pushing its body forward, using the downward slope of the hill to bring it slowly closer. Its neck was still short and squat, eyes half closed, and it was again making the eerie thrumming sound that had preceded the fire.

The red dragon continued flailing and screeching while the stored fire from its superheated scales cooked its insides. Its neck and tail whipped around violently, often bashing its own head down on the rock as it was senseless with pain, while the white dragon, eyes closed to slits, edged closer. As it did, its neck grew even thicker and the rhythmic convulsions of its flesh began again.

The red dragon saw it and started to crawl away, but the white opened its great mouth and burst forward with a jet of flame that hit the red one along its seared chest and spread over the rest of its exposed underbelly. The legs of the red dragon now appeared as black appendages flailing about from inside a whirling cyclone of flame. Its screams filled the air of the diminishing afternoon so loudly that it seemed to be the only sound in the world at that time.

Then the white dragon trained the jet of flame onto the glowing section of the red dragon's chest and kept it there until the scales glowed even hotter, and, with a sudden pop and whoosh, the animal's chest exploded, shooting out hot organs that arced spinning through the air and came down an all sides with unpleasant squishes. One woman was hit with a bit of scalding liver which burnt one whole side of her face.

The king's advisors all gasped and drew their hands up before their mouths—the end of the red dragon was unexpectedly horrific— but King Vortiger, standing in front of all of them, paid no attention. His eyes watched the entire fight, and its conclusion, with the same solemn grimness. Merlin had not yet told him the meaning of the fight, but he could see that it was clearly quite significant, perhaps in a way that no man alive could truly perceive, and he had the nagging feeling within him that the meaning Merlin would tell him would not be tremendously positive for him. It was not just that he had been, until that day, most often clad in shades of red. It was consistent with the way the world had been slowly, inexorably, closing in on him for the past few months. Ever since Maine had been killed, and then—it was like something was broken in the world, or at least in this country, definitely in his life. The symbolism of the two dragons, buried in eras past, dragged up out of the earth, engaged in a fight to the death... it was right there, and stunned all who watched with an overpowering aura of significance, but not he, nor anyone, could fully work out what it meant. Vortiger only knew what it felt like; That the shadowy figure of death that had been haunting the edges of his vision, drawing ever closer, finally set its skeletal hand on his shoulder.

That was how it felt, but it had not been announced yet, so the king was forced to go on as he had for the past months; pretending that there was some slim chance that everything would work out.

His grim eyes saw something from their corners, and when he looked down, he saw Merlin looking up at him with a placid expression. No guilt, anger or shame, just observing him. But then the child turned away, and Vortiger returned his gaze to the aftermath of the fight.

Once its chest had burst, the red dragon stared at the open hole in its breast with what seemed like shock, then suddenly all support drained out of its neck, and it fell loose to the ground. Its head actually bounced when it landed. Its limbs went limp except for a few dying twitches, and its body deflated as a last sighing breath escaped its mouth.

The white dragon used the last of its energy to open its eyes and watch the death throes of the red beast. Then its weight shifted, and without its forearm to keep it upright, it collapsed forward and slid helplessly a few feet down the hill. The long neck came down gently, but then the head turned over on its side and mouth opened, tongue falling out and laying extended in the dirt. Its eyes were slightly opened slits, and it lay like that until it died sometime overnight. All the rest of that day and until the body was carved up and taken away, all of the people in the nearby towns came to see the fallen beasts, bringing their young boys and girls along, knowing none of them were likely to ever see such a sight again in their lifetimes, for dragon sightings had grown more and more scarce with the wide spreading of humankind.

Now, after the great cacophony of noises that had been made during the fight, silence again fell upon the hill, before the people began to speak once more to each other, move closer to the fallen beasts or gather their things to return to their towns. Others moved in to rescue or aid the ones who had been hurt when the two dragons rolled over them down the hill.

Then men who had drawn near to the king during the fight, and those who had told him that the red one would win, now backed silently away or looked toward the king with expectant faces, trying to find some way to make a positive comment, but there was nothing to say. Within a few moments they had lowered their heads and walked away. Sir Brantius was seen watching the king's back with a pained expression, as though he should be able to think of something to say, something that would prove his worth to the king, but at last he gave up.

As for the king, he stood, hands on hips, looking with grim face down at the sprawled bodies of the two beasts, his stillness and the hard set of his jaw daring anyone to speak with him. He just wanted all of those idiots to go away, but of course they never do, they hover around the king like flies smelling rot, hoping there will be a bite for them. He would have to eventually just turn and walk through them, eyes lowered to the ground, then tolerate their following him like puppies. He sighed and his eyes gazed down at the bodies of the two magnificent beasts. How unbearably sad, he thought, that such noble creatures should be released and die within such a short span. And he did that. He caused it. Another beautiful thing lost to the world because of him. Soon all of the mysteries of the world will be uncovered, he thought, and the like of those fearsome creatures will never again be seen. Then bold kings who take risks and rule by great force of will also would be driven out, to make way for handsome boys who know nothing of rule, or the treachery of people, but have their birthrights and their broad smiles, which is all anyone wants. The king briefly wondered if he would die if he let himself topple forward into the chasm from that height. He saw a movement out of the corner of his eyes and raised his glance enough to see Merlin, standing there, hair whipping in the wind, watching him very intently.

"Now you can build any tower as high as you like," said the boy, "and it could never be so tall that it would collapse."

The king immediately ordered that the tower be started the very next day. The workmen dragged the dragon's carcasses out of the way as best they could, as they had been beset by villagers taking bones and scales as souvenirs—the entire head of the white dragon was gone the next day, and one of the pubs in town claimed to be serving dragon meat for the next month—and began their work, confident this time that it would amount to something. The foundation was built into the chasm where the pool had been, allowing the bricks to be joined directly to the rock, which was expected to create the strongest tower anyone could think of. Along with the steepness of the hill, making any approach to the site an arduous one, it was thought that when completed, it would be the most secure fortified place in existence. Atop the hill, the octagonal tower began to be built, with extremely thick walls and great internal reinforcements, created for the sole purpose of sheltering the king and his men against attack from without.

"Seems rather spacious to house what few people will stand with the king when the time comes," said one of the workmen, who had to be shushed because the king was walking near, inspecting the progress.

Vortiger went back and forth on whether to ask Merlin about what the fight between the two dragons meant. He would think that he had to know, but then he would ask himself why, when it would not help him and might in fact distract him badly from his purpose—if not completely disable him with indecision or melancholy. No, the one thing he knew for sure had to happen was that the tower be built, so that is what he concentrated on.

The paralysis of melancholy, something he had never known before—he was known throughout the land as a decisive man of action—now became a regular occurrence. Many times now as he was in court, and his advisors were going on about this or that, throwing their endless maps in front of him, or going on about the issues of this town or that town, he would allow his attention to drift, and eyes to stare vacantly forward, seeing something distant that no one else could see, and would have to be reminded to grunt in reply to something that had been said, or utter a weary "Make it so as you advise," before drifting off. Many times now Rowena had walked in as he sat near the fire, watching its flames lick upward and destroy the logs below, and had to poke him hard on the shoulder before she could get him to acknowledge her.

Merlin was around, but rarely came near the king. Nor did the king call for him. They seemed to have an unspoken agreement to avoid each other for the time being, as the presence of the child could only bring up uncomfortable questions for the king, and urge the king to ask questions that he wasn't sure he wanted the answer to. One day Merlin was near, while the tower was not yet completed, and the king couldn't bear it, and asked the boy the meaning of the fight between the two dragons.

Merlin regarded the king with eyes that were cautious, but not filled with animosity. "It is a sign of things that are to come," he said. "But if I told you the thing that you ask for," he said, "you would grow very angry."

That was enough, the king was up, hand outstretched, and walking away from Merlin as fast as could appear seemly, without further word. It took him two weeks to drive the implications of that hint, and what it could possibly mean, out of his mind. Now he avoided the young seer even more, which Merlin showed no signs of considering a burden.

Finally the tower was done, the king had his defense against any invaders, and he knew that the time had come. He once more requested that Merlin tell him the meaning of the white dragon's victory. The child looked at him with narrowed eyes, then seemed to conclude something in his mind. "If you assure me that you will not harm me, no matter what I may tell you," said the child, "then I will tell you the significance of the of the white dragon's victory over the red one."

The king said that is what he wanted, and then the child looked at him for such a long time that he grew unnerved, but held his ground, and said nothing. "If you truly wish to know," said Merlin, "gather your council and have the clerics come before me who wanted me to be killed."

All the above parties were gathered in the large hall of the new tower, and Merlin approached the gathered clerics, who had been hanging about the court uselessly in the meantime, as neither the king, nor anyone, wanted their advice.

"Now the king's tower is built, and you have seen the outcome of the dragon's fight and how his tower was finally made to stand," Merlin said.

"Yes," said Arledge, his voice on edge. He said nothing more, but stared at Merlin with wide eyes and stiff manner.

"Therefore it is the time when you must meet your judgment for your plan to have me killed," the child said.

The eyes of most of the clerics were trained on the floor, hands clasped tightly before them, and two of them had wet traces of tears on their faces. "We understand," said Arledge quietly.

"You are very unwise to think that you can traffic in the occult arts without being pure and noble of spirit, because when you do, evil spirits are drawn to you, seeing an easy way to find fools eager to work their plans," Merlin said. "Because of this, what you wanted to see was hidden from you, and what you saw instead was me." The child raised his finger curiously. "But do you know who it was that showed me to you?"

Arledge and the rest of the other clerics looked up cautiously.

"It is the devil who was my father, and who, out of rage that he had lost his hold on me, showed me to you, so that you would complete his bidding and have me murdered."

Arledge's eyes widened, then he looked down quickly, eyes scanning the floor. He had never considered anything like this.

"Thus all of you became servants of the devil without even knowing it," Merlin said, and gave them a moment for this to sink in. "But I will show you how you might not die if you will swear to do as I advise."

Arledge gasped. "We will swear to anything that you say," he said, almost shouting, "for it is clear that you are the greatest seer who has ever lived."

Merlin looked over all of them in order to be sure that they agreed. "You will swear on saint's relics that you will never more work in the occult arts," he said, "and because you have already done it, you must confess to a priest, and remember," he pointed, "that whosoever asks forgiveness for a sin but does not then forsake it *is truly lost.*" He once more scanned the faces of the relieved clerics. "If you will swear to this, I will order the king to remove the promise he made to have you killed."

One of the clerics cried out and his head fell forward, unable to keep himself from crying in relief. The strain suddenly left all of the others too, at about the same time, as their shoulders fell out of tension and great relieved sighs were heard. "We will do exactly as you say!" said Arledge.

Merlin nodded, but then he could see that the king and his advisors waiting for him at the other end of the hall, and he gestured at the clerics as he walked away. "Come, if you would like to hear the meaning of the dragons," he said over his shoulder. The clerics followed not far behind.

Vortiger and his men were gathered near the fireplace, which blazed brightly. "Merlin," said the king, "now my tower is built, due to your wisdom. Now please tell me the meaning of the fight between the two dragons, for," he took in a deep breath and sighed, "I am ready to hear it."

Merlin looked around at the gathered men, and the clerics who had come over to listen, and considered how what he was about to say might go down amongst such a large group, for there were about fifteen in total, including the king, and all of them had reason to flatter the king. But Merlin had warned him, and he chose to have all of those people around. So he began.

"You should know," he said, "that the red dragon symbolizes you," and Merlin gestured. "And the white dragon," he continued, "represents the sons of Constance."

Vortiger did not move, nothing happened at first, while every one of his advisors stared openly at his face. Then his pallor grew pale, and even more pale, while at the same time the rims and undersides of his eyes grew very red and inflamed. He seemed to age five years right in front of them, his face growing more gaunt and shoulders shrinking from their normally fearsome stance, and finally his hands came up, long fingers outstretched, which he placed at the sides of his face as his body crashed forward onto his elbows. One of his advisors, gossiping about it later, said that he crumpled like—well, he did not want to say "tower."

The room was silent. It may as well have been empty, save for the crackling of the fire. "If you wish, I will tell you no more," said Merlin. "Please do not harm me because of it."

A long silence, then the king raised himself. His familiar expression, the one dead to all feeling, the one of the man who was detached to all the pleasure of life, was now back on his face. His eyes remained on the floor, staring grimly, and he took in a great, long breath, during which his shoulders regained their large and full expanse, although seemingly with great effort. He sighed out, and his expression once more went into the abyss, as though the thought of continuing the façade was now too imbecilic, but he fought it back and a moment later, turned his placid face to Merlin and spoke in an even, controlled voice.

"No, tell me the meaning," he said, "and leave out nothing that touches on it."

None of the advisors moved, nor the clerics behind them.

"That the red dragon represents you I have said, and now I will say the reason why," said Merlin, and he moved to stand fully in front of the seated king, his head at face level. "You know with certainty that the sons of King Constance were left without protection after their father's death, and Maine only more than a boy, and if you had acted as an honorable man should, you would have offered them protection and counsel, and defended them over any men on earth."

Tears streamed down the king's face at once, while his expression remained as stone.

"And you also know full well that it is with their landholdings and their liegemen that you won the kingdom. Then, when you saw that the people loved you, you abandoned them, for you thought that they would be defeated by the Saxons. And when the people of the kingdom came to you to say you should take the place of the king, you answered like a coward and said that you could not be king while Maine yet lived, knowing full well they would understand that you wanted him dead. This left the two brothers, but they fled the country, knowing eventually your murderous eye would fall on them. And so you inherited the kingdom against the law of nature," Merlin said, "and you still wrongly hold their birthright."

Vortiger's tears had dried and now he just stared forward, past Merlin and through the advisors and clerics, who stood still as stone and breathed very quietly. The king's face looked as though it was carved from wood.

"Now you have built this tower to protect you against your enemies," said Merlin, pacing before the king as he gestured, "but the tower cannot save you, because there is nothing in you left to save."

Now the king's gaze darted to Merlin's, with a flare of fury, and immediate defeat, then openness, and even affection… because who wouldn't want the friendship of someone who knew one so intimately? Merlin knew the king's most secret thoughts, but it was beyond pointless, because kingship had destroyed him. By wronging the brothers in that way, he had damned himself, and the heavy weight hit him now that no, there was no way he would escape punishment. The tower almost gave him something to do, to while away the ticking tock of time, but in himself, somewhere, he had always known that the matter was settled, and he would one day face his punishment. How was he to enjoy kingship after that? The pleasure curdled and life, because of what he himself had done, became a long slog through a tangling wood, and always alone. Always, always alone. And Merlin knew this about him. If only he had time to talk to Merlin about what that was like—Merlin was the only person who could know, and understand.

Vortiger spoke with low, exhausted voice. "I recognize that you possess the greatest sight of any man in the world," he said to the boy. "Please tell me what I may do in the face of these challenges," he asked, "and please tell me how I will die."

And Merlin looked him directly in the eye. "I am telling you how you will die," he said. "That you will be expelled from the world is the meaning of the white dragon's victory."

Vortiger's eyes lowered to the floor before him. His face was still, as though carved of wood, and ashen gray. "Please tell me, and do not obscure anything," he said.

"You should know that the great red dragon represents your evil heart, and that the beast was so large indicates your immense power. The white dragon represents the birthright of the brothers Pendragon and Uther. The length of the fight stands for the long time you have held their kingdom illegally, and the fire is the truth of their right over this land, which will burn you right up." Merlin stopped and stood full in front of the king, his hands held behind his back. "And so, King Vortiger, I do not believe that there is a tower or stronghold on earth that can protect you from death."

A hush had fallen over the chamber, and it seemed for all intents that Merlin and the king were alone, for every advisor and cleric had never before seen any king being talked to so openly, and were in rapt silence.

Vortiger, strangely, seemed more relaxed than anyone had ever seen him, and leaned forward to ask Merlin; "Where are Pendragon and Uther now?"

Merlin's arm extended behind him and pointed away. "They are across the sea this very minute, gathering a great army to rise against you. They say openly that you had their brother killed, so you can take no refuge in untruth." Now Merlin turned back to face Vortiger fully, the small boy dwarfed by the immense king. "And I tell you in truth that they will land at the port of Winchester one month from today."

"Is there any way," the king asked, "that it can be otherwise?"

"No," said Merlin. "It is not possible that you will not be killed by the sons of Constance, just as the white dragon killed the red one."

The king did not react, and his gaze remained frozen in the air beyond the child.

Merlin stood up straighter and changed his tone. "It is now time for me to leave you," he said, "and you will not see me again." He bowed, said "Great king," made a gesture of respect, and then a corridor opened in the air behind him, extending right through the advisors and clerics. Merlin stepped back into it, it closed again, and he was gone.

-16-

Two weeks later, Vortiger was on top of his tower, looking down across the land. It was sunny, it was May, the hillsides were just then moving from the lush, beautiful green of spring toward the more mature tones of summer, and the breeze up there was wonderfully warm and scented with the many flowers, small and large, blooming across the hills and fields. His arms were folded atop one of the crenels of his tower, his head resting on his arms. It looked so peaceful and lovely out there, he wished he could be down on those hills, just taking a walk, as he used to do. It had been so long since he had simply taken a walk, just looking at all the little plants and flowers, as he used to love to do as a boy. For the past few years he could barely get a moment alone, and that he had to fight for, and he was definitely not allowed to just go take a walk by himself—that was something of the past.

The past two weeks, since Merlin had told him his fate, had been grim ones. What are you supposed to do with your time, when you have a month to live? Everything seemed somehow stupid. Yes, he could go out and try to enjoy himself, drinking, whores, the typical amusements, but even then, what would be most apparent was that he was trying to enjoy himself. He had tried to go out hunting for sport one day, but he was tired of it almost as soon as it began, as he could not suppress the knowledge that it was all a rather desperate attempt to have fun, and ignore the fact that he had only arranged it to give himself some activity to engage in. Not to mention that, at the bottom of it all, he didn't really love hunting. And when you are the king, everything you do involves an entourage of about a hundred. So yes, he could just cancel it, turn around and go home, but then you have all the people who got up early to have the horses and hounds prepared, all the people who prepared meals, all the guests, and guests of guests, all the support staff... he ended up having to go through the entire day of hunting—filled with liegemen and advisors riding up to him with beaming smiles, pretending to have the most fun ever—just so as not to make an even bigger fuss than the hunting had already created.

Then there were his advisors. The clerics had been let go and had scattered back to their various parts of the country. The advisors had all heard what Merlin had said, yet they were mostly ambitious, flattering men who hoped to get ahead, so they said they didn't believe it, or that Merlin would turn out to be wrong, or that there were things he could do to escape his fate. At first he just wanted them to shut up, but in the last few days, Vortiger, who could feel his cares falling away as nothing he had previously been concerned with had much meaning anymore, took to telling them that they would do best to leave him now and go hide out somewhere until the new rulers came along. It was almost funny, because you could see how badly they wanted to go, but they couldn't let themselves desert the king that they served. Vortiger had even told them that he would pay them to go away, but they still wouldn't go. This made him think on it, and on their service to him thus far, even as he ran around the country hiring clerics and doing anything to build his tower, and he pulled each of his advisors aside and gave them great gifts of money, property and armor. They were stunned, and it was pleasing to do, especially since they were so surprised and delighted by it. This started him giving away much of his wealth to his staff and those in his court, and even the people of the towns nearby. It got to the extent that Hengist came to him and asked him to stop it, since the Saxons could use that money and support in the royal coffers, which only made him give away even more of it, beginning the next day.

94

Vortiger had gone the first week after Merlin's revelation to him in a deep and bitter stupor, barely able to tolerate anyone, barely listening to what anyone had to say—all pure idiocy anyway—and dwelling on how his entire life had, through his own machinations, become like some sort of horrible labyrinth in which he had lost himself. It had gone like that, all that week and a half, until, finally, he simply grew tired of it. He was so tired, so damnably tired of everything, and he had been wallowing in grimness and the inevitable tragedy he had arranged for himself anyway, so when Merlin confirmed that the very worst thing he could foresee would indeed come true, it devastated him... until, almost two weeks later, he just got bored with being devastated. It was empty, and unsatisfying. That's when all of the caring, all of the worrying over what would happen, began to simply fall away. He just could not care anymore, and he knew full well that there was no reason to. It wouldn't get him anything. Then, also, the reality that, if he were to enjoy himself again, or do anything fun and worthwhile again in his life, he had two weeks to do it. That's when the people around the king began to be very confused by his sudden change of mood and erratic behavior.

Even now, looking down at the gorgeous May afternoon, a sudden thought hit him, with a wave of yearning to be amongst the blooming flowers and verdant grasses, and Vortiger vowed to ditch his guards and advisors and get down there. He turned slightly to look at where they all were. The advisors were talking amongst themselves, while the guards stood nearby, looking straight ahead. Vortiger turned and moved toward the door that would take him downstairs. The advisors began to move as a result, without even looking over, and the guards also shifted in place, everyone instinctively ready to move when the king moved. It seemed so insane to Vortiger. He hated it from day one, and he was determined to get away from it now.

"Stay here, I'll only be a moment," he said to the advisors, holding out a hand. They looked confused, but he smiled and once more bid them stay. He also said to the guards "I'll just be a moment, stay here."

"We are to guard you wherever you may go, your highness," said one.

"Yes, that's all right," said Vortiger, "I'm telling you to stay here."

"Those are not my orders, my lord," said the guard.

"I am giving you new orders," Vortiger said, and when the guard once more made a face, added "I am ordering you to stay here. I'm just going to relieve myself," he laughed, "I'll be back in a moment."

When the guard looked at him dubiously, he simply opened the door and went through himself. When they didn't immediately follow, he ran.

He was down a few floors before anyone had seen, and it was fun! It was like a game, and he enjoyed figuring out how best to avoid his own guard and staff. His goal now was to get out of the tower unseen, and to get down the hill before anyone came after him.

Rowena would be in her chamber, and he could easily throw his crown and mantle in there, but she would be with attendants, and besides, she herself would send people after him. Anyone in the tower would recognize him. He took off his crown, robe and mantle and threw them down on some bags of grain stacked against the wall of one of the floors. Now he was just in his white shift, but still, how would he get out? He would surely have to cover his face. He threw one of the bags of grain over his shoulder and turned his face toward it while he kept creeping down, floor by floor, sometimes moving quickly by groups of women involved in work, who didn't look up because they did not see the king's robes, or groups of male guards who gave him not another thought. And the heavy sack of grain—how long it had been since he had lifted anything heavy! It felt great, and for the first time in years, he felt alive.

The simple sack of grain was a better disguise than he could have imagined, and before he knew it, Vortiger was down to ground level. He faced far less suspicion down there, where the king rarely went, and headed outside and into the stables, for he knew he could get out easily that way. He didn't want to take a horse, but on the other hand, that would greatly facilitate his getting away from the people who would come looking for him. Actually, it then occurred to him, he made a mistake in telling the guards that he would be right back, for that meant that they would come looking for him fairly soon, after they discovered that he hadn't come back and was nowhere to be found. Suddenly the sack of grain grew too heavy, and he bent to let it fall to the ground. When he raised himself, there was a stable hand there.

"Get lost, did you?" asked the man, who had a round, rosy and friendly face. He was about to speak again when he looked at the king, his eyes narrowed and he leaned in closer. Then he stepped in closer, and squinted once again.

"I am the king," said Vortiger.

"My king!" the man said, and went down on one knee. Vortiger rolled his eyes. "Please stand," he said. Then something occurred to him, and he said "Can you help me?"

"Of course I can, sir, anything you may like." His eyes looked with confusion at the king's attire, but he decided not to comment.

Vortiger wasn't sure how to begin. "I am trying... I just..." he found the words so unfamiliar they were difficult in coming. "Could you help me get out of the tower unattended? I just... I would love to have some time to myself."

The stable hand held still for a moment, then suddenly laughed. "Impossible for a king to get a moment to himself, is it?"

Vortiger now stared back in disbelief, for it had been years since anyone had spoken to him in an unforced, friendly way.

"Yes," he said at last. "It's just—it's a beautiful day, and I just... I want to get out and enjoy it without a hundred guards and advisors around me all the time."

The red-cheeked man nodded. "That's how I feel with my wife's parents living with us!" he said. "Drives me mad, it does. You'd probably have a lot better time of it if I rode out with you, and then I'd leave you alone once we got a safe distance away."

The king let out a laugh that was somewhere between a sigh and a sob, the man's words were such a relief. "That would be wonderful!" he said. "I will see to it that you face no punishment, and that you are amply rewarded."

The man was already preparing a horse. "Ah sir, helping the king is its own reward," he called over his shoulder, "although ensuring I don't get punished, that would be of great help."

"I will make sure," said the king. He couldn't remember the last time he had conversed with someone without him commanding their full attention. It came with an unexpected degree of freedom. "What is your name?" the king asked.

"I am Jerald," he said, turning and extending his hand, which the king shook vigorously. "Do you have a hat?" he asked, then took off his own and extended it. "Let's see how that looks on you."

The king took his hat, a well-worn and greasy affair, and looked into it for a moment. In his royal life, he would never allow such a thing to touch his head, but now, that seemed the exact reason to put it on, which he did a moment later. "What do you think?" he asked.

Jerald regarded him while trying to suppress a smile. "Well, no one will mistake you for the king," he said.

Within a few moments he had two horses ready for riding, had given the king his ratty surcoat to wear, had him put his long hair up into his cap, and they were at the tower gate, where he chatted amiably with the gatekeeper while the king slouched quite unroyally on his horse. Then, before he knew it, both of them were through. They rode out into the sunshine and the wonderful breeze, which filled the king's lungs and caressed his skin the moment they were clear. Oh, the king thought, even if I am only granted this one moment of freedom, this was worth it.

Jerald asked the king where he wanted to go, and in a few minutes they had crossed the shallow river at the base of the hill. There, both dismounted, under the cover of trees that would keep them obscured from the tower above. "Can I keep your hat and surcoat for the day?" asked the king. "I will see that they are returned to you."

"Keep them," said Jerald.

"Thank you very gratefully," said the king, "but I will return them. And when you go back," he continued, "if you say that you did not see me, and that to the best of your knowledge I have not left the tower,

I will see that you not be punished when I am found out," he said. "Which will not be later than tonight."

The stable hand nodded and smiled, shaking the king's hand, and a moment later, to the king's utter surprise, he stepped forward and embraced him briefly. "All that I will do," he said, and jauntily mounted once more on his horse. "Enjoy your day off, king," he said.

Vortiger was momentarily choked up, the man's casual, unforced friendliness was something he had been quite unaccustomed to for some time, and while he wished to say something noble and memorable, he could merely raise his hand and smile, standing there silently, before Jerald spurred his horse, crossed the river and was heading back up the hill. The king watched him recede, then turned, and saw the valley before him.

The hill with his tower was to the left, behind the trees, the river extending just ahead, and farm land, with a distant farm house, several bow-shots off in the distance. He didn't know where he wanted to go first, then realized, with a flooding sense of relief, that he didn't have to choose, and more importantly, there weren't several people staring at him, waiting for him to choose. The revelation made him simply stand and take in a long breath through his nostrils, savoring the smell of the fresh grass and tiny flowers that dotted the sides of the river, and scent of dung that came from the field and distant farm. He stepped forward so that he could be in the sun, but still concealed from the tower by the trees. He closed his eyes and let the bright sunlight warm his face.

Then he opened his eyes and sighed. He couldn't remember the last time he simply had nothing to do, and the feeling took him right back to his boyhood, when he spent several long, uninterrupted hours simply walking through the fields, wondering at the plants and bugs and tiny animals. He had loved it then, and, well, it was amazing how life can take one far away from the things one loves. This made Vortiger turn and gaze upward, toward the tower, partly obscured behind the trees, which did indeed look quite solid and formidable. He almost had to laugh that he had placed all his hopes of protection on that. And now—he was just becoming conscious of how Merlin's prediction had freed him, and allowed him, against anything he could have imagined, to enjoy a few final days of freedom.

He ambled alongside the river, sure to keep his borrowed hat and surcoat on, for surely his own staff would be gazing down from the tower, looking for him. In fact, it would be a much better idea to get out of sight of the tower before he once more dismounted his horse and started to look around. He got right back up on his horse and walked slowly alongside the river, looking down at the rocks and brown silt-covered logs lying under the rushing clear water, or out across the lovely, verdant green field with its bursting new growth, and he was of a sudden suffused with the feeling that it would be a shame if this place went to the Saxons, whom he knew did not appreciate its beauty and rough-edged difficulty. Not to mention that it simply didn't belong to them.

That was his own misperception, shame at his own weakness that he had projected onto the entire country, and he knew that a lot of the damage that had been done, he had allowed to happen. The natural first thought was that he should undo the damage, but soon after followed the knowledge that he need do nothing; the country itself was going to be rid of him. Like a shard of blade left in a muscle, the body would eventually push it out. And with that, counter intuitively, came a strange feeling of freedom, and assurance that things would be put right—even if, as it happened, what was wrong was him.

Once he had gone around the hill and was out of sight of the tower, he rode into an area of untrimmed field and dropped off his horse, walked a few feet along the river, then dropped down to sit in the grass right beside. He reached out and ran his hand through the dense grass, feeling the blades tickle the spaces between his fingers, then pushed his fingertips down between the stems, in toward the ground. As he did, his eyes played over the lichen-covered trunk of a twisted tree that grew alongside the river, a living thing that had become a colony for living things. His lungs drew in the fresh, warm air, filled with thousands of scents, and he was filled with so many overlapping thoughts and impressions that he showed no outward reaction, while inside he was so overcome, his mind was blank. This, the simple fact of

100

nature, was what he had allowed himself to get lost from. As his hand balled and gripped the grass within it, feeling its firm hold on the dirt, he just concentrated on the simplicity of this life, and how it was pure, elemental, at the heart of everything—and how far he had drifted from that. At least he got to have this moment. If he were to burn up now, he would have had this moment.

How lucky he was to have someone come and tell him: your life is ending. Everything you've done is wrong, and you will pay for it. It gave a clarity that he had given up as he sought power. How naïve he had been. He had thought he would seek the kingship—it was so easy and practically offered itself to him, for the mere cost of a murder—but how could he have known that he wouldn't just get power and be happy, but his life would become an endless procession of keeping power, solidifying power, and gradually, without even noticing it slipping away, what he felt now would be lost to him? He turned his hand and ran it over the grass, seeing the blades snap back into place after it had passed and that, just that, seemed to contain more truth about resilience and survival than anything he had learned in the last few years. How fortunate he was to get that final week, to see life once again, instead of sealing himself off from it. Protecting himself, away from life, in a tower. He could have gone to his death never having this experience again, never again having a breath of the afternoon air, seeing and feeling the grass, or wildflowers that bloomed at the riverside. How lucky he was that Merlin told him that he would die.

"Thank you, Merlin," he said out loud.

The king stood, and, leading his horse, ambled along the riverside. His eyes wandered over the hillsides, wondering at all the different kinds of life there and how they all clung tenaciously and struggled together to hold onto the rough, rocky terrain. Then the air, and the sky, and the clear and beautiful water, it all seemed to be parts of a brilliant, perfect machine. Then, instead of trying to process it all and mourning further how he had become divorced from all of it, he simply left off thinking and gave himself to the experience of it. He stepped slowly, at a comfortable pace, letting the sun warm his face, hearing the gentle gurgle of the river, smelling the spring air. Passing a low stone wall, he looked over and was surprised by a young boy, about eight, working there. The boy stood and regarded him.

"Hello," said the king.

"Hello," said the boy.

The king had to remind himself that the boy did not know who he was. At least—he didn't think so? It was difficult for him to truly believe, he felt he showed his kingship as plainly as a disfigurement.

"What are you doing?" said the boy.

"Just walking," said Vortiger. "Enjoying the day. I hope you don't mind."

The boy shrugged. "What do I care?" he said. "From around here?"

The king named a town nearby, not too close.

"Ah," said the kid. "Did you see the dragon fight?"

The question made the king chuckle lightly—he was walking through a different world, and it tickled him with freedom and relief. "No, I didn't," he said. "Did you?"

The boy scrunched his face in anger and looked at the ground. "My pa wouldn't let me," he said. "But we went and saw the bodies later, and that was sure mad. Have you ever seen a dragon?"

"No," Vortiger said. "Was it," he sought for words, "incredible?"

"You bet," said the child. "I was pretty sore I couldn't see them when they were alive, but my mum wouldn't let me near. And people got killed, I guess." His eyes wandered over the attire of the king. "You have funny clothes," he said.

Vortiger laughed, and looked down at himself, the dirty coat, his kingly boots, and saw it all with new eyes. It did look strange. "Yes," he said. "I was... in a rush to get out."

The kid raised his eyebrows, but said nothing, and looked at the wall where he had been working. "Our bitch had pups," he said. "Six of them."

"Ah," said the king, feeling a quick shiver of tears come, and pass, over his face. "How lucky you are."

"Want to see them?" said the boy, squinting at him.

102

There was an impulse to stay away from closer contact with anyone, that he was in disguise, and could be found out, but then today, he was resisting familiar impulses. "Yes," the king said.

The boy led him along the wall, as the king asked him about his work and what all he had to do on the farm, as they made their way toward the house and shacks near to it. Vortiger had the thought to ask the boy what he thought of the king, or what he overheard his parents say, but he stopped himself, for knowing would not help him, and might bring back reality to crack the immersion of this day.

He tied his horse outside and was led into the stables, where the boy's father was tending to the cattle. "Who is this?" said the man.

"I was just passing by," said Vortiger.

"I'm showing him the puppies," said the boy.

"Ah," said the father, and Vortiger realized, to his surprise, that the man was fine with it, and held no hostility, and did not regard him as a threat or unwelcome presence, which made his heart soften within his chest. He also remained cautious and restrained in his movements, watching the face of the man, only to discover, to his dawning amazement, that he wasn't recognized. This set off a long chain of thoughts about how long it had been since he had met someone who didn't come to him with an extensive set of expectations already in place, or approach him from behind several layers of deference and regard—even if they despised him.

He briefly considered asking if he could stay. And then the thought—could he just *run away?* Was it possible to escape? The image of the tower burning without him in it came to mind.

The boy led him into an empty stall and there in the hay, in the corner, was a mother sheepdog, white belly and black backside, with highlights of light brown, surrounded by pups of not much more than a hand-length in size. The boy reached down and picked one up, handing it to him, while the mother lifted her head and regarded him. The boy's father leaned against the end of the stall and watched.

"Oh," said the king, taking the puppy in both hands and lifting it towards his face. "So adorable," he said. The large black eyes of the puppy looked over his face and beyond, head wavering, and before the king knew it, it licked his nose. "Oh!" the king said in surprise.

"Yep, they sure are cute," said the boy's father, "when they're young."

A hundred thousand feelings coursed through the king at once, so much that he concentrated wholly on simply remaining still and not betraying his emotions. The puppy stretched out its head with tongue extended, and, suddenly aware that he did not have several people staring at him, making much out of every movement he made, and parsing it endlessly for what it might mean—the king pressed the puppy to his face. The new fur was soft, and the pup started licking his face immediately. The king wanted to wallow in this simple affection, so long lost to him, but was afraid if he gave into it he would act like a child. He had also, over time, drifted away from even knowing how to act in simple society.

The puppy took a great mouthful of beard in its mouth and tugged. It hurt, but the king laughed. He looked over at the father, expecting to see disapproval on his face, but his eyes were wrinkled with affection, and his face bore a slight smile.

"You can have him if you want," said the boy.

"You'd be doing us a favor," added the boy's father.

Now Vortiger had a hard time keeping tears from his eyes. The puppy stared up at him with its large round eyes, completely focused on him, a mouth full of his beard, in that still waiting period before tugging again. The king thought of the possibility, running away with his puppy, something alive, simple, something that mattered, that didn't know him or what he had done, that didn't care, and had no way of knowing.

He grabbed his own beard and pulled it out of the puppy's mouth, which engendered a short tug of war. Once it was free, the puppy's head leapt forward to begin a barrage of licking. The king held him close and let his face get wet. Then he lowered the animal, regarded it once more, and handed it back to the child.

"I couldn't," he said. "I thank you very much, but…" he smiled first at the boy, then his father, "it wouldn't be fair to him."

The man clapped him on the back as they once more stepped out into the bright sunshine of the day outside. The boy followed. "Can't be weighed down any more than you already are, eh?" said the father.

Vortiger looked down, seeing the mud by the barn, the grass, and the beginning of the stone wall, and felt the sweet breeze once more touch his face.

"I certainly can't be," he said, smiling.

-17-

A month to the day after Merlin had told Vortiger that he must die in his tower, Mark was on the beach at Winchester, where Merlin had told him to be. The other messengers who had gone seeking Merlin were there, too, for he had given them all clear instructions. The air was wet and cold, foggy with low gray clouds, which left the vegetation dark to almost black, and the beach a ruddy tan, where it could be seen beneath the feet of the gathered troops. They stood in rows, the iron of their helmets glinting in the dim light, red surcoats over the dully shining mail of their hauberks, creating a forest of men topped with a layer of sharp upraised spears.

In front of them, the sea was a dark gray, extending not more than a mile out before it was lost to sight in the grayish white of the fog that hung over the ocean. Straight ahead, right where the surface of the sea faded into the background, two large white sails, side by side.

Everyone saw them, the two white rectangles appearing brightly against the dull expense of gray, although not everyone knew exactly what they meant. Mark turned his head and saw King Vortiger atop his horse, standing upon the bluff at the back of the beach, surrounded by his advisors and liegemen, also on horseback. They all looked out toward the two approaching sails, which were so abstract as to appear like a vision. Now was the time for Mark to do what Merlin had told him to do.

"Make ready to face the sons of Constance," he shouted, "for they now return to claim their birthright!" The other messengers were spread out among the soldiers, delivering this message as well, seeming for all intents to rally the spirits of the assembled men to face the approaching enemy. "Make ready," he shouted, "for the sons of Constance have returned!"

"The sons of Constance?" asked one of the soldiers, grabbing his arm as he passed. "Are you speaking of Pendragon and Uther?"

"Yes, that is them," said Mark, pointing at the two approaching sails, and beyond them, where a large complement of additional sails was beginning to appear out of the mist. "They are coming back to fight for the land they claim is their birthright. Make ready to defend yourself!" he said, and moved on. But he could see by the man's face that he was troubled.

The news brought lowered gazes and quiet introspection to that man as he thought on what they were doing. Mark moved among them and spoke loudly, as though to rally spirits, but his words had the opposite effect—not quite by accident—and forced the men who heard to grow heavy and reconsider the spears and shields they held in their hands.

"Constance was my lord before all of this happened," said one man. "I served under Maine during the short time he held reign."

"We have all served under better masters than Vortiger," said another. "And if they are coming back," he looked down and seemed to consider his words, then raised his head resolutely and spoke boldly, "if they are coming back, then I am to serve a better master today."

"Constance was lord to all of us," said another. "It is now time to rally behind his descendants and help them achieve their rightful rule," he said. "If not, this country will go completely to the Saxons, and we'll be second place in our own land."

"Constance was never my lord," said a younger man, "and I have never served under an honorable king. I don't know what that's like. But King Vortiger will lead all of us to our deaths and create the ruin of this realm. If we greet the returning sons with bowed heads and swear fealty, perhaps they will let us serve under them and make up for some of the damage we've allowed to happen."

"And look on their size," said another voice. "They have three times as many men as we. They will easily take us if we don't surrender immediately upon their reaching land."

It was true, for now the other ships had emerged completely from the mist behind the two bright white sails in front, and all on land could see that the brothers came on with a huge force of additional men. As the ships drew closer, there could clearly be seen the colors of Constance hanging on their sails, which several of the men recognized from when he ruled the country. Then the front rows of the soldiers dissolved from their order, and without an announcement or organized movement, the men just began to move in a mass toward the water, where they placed their spears and shields down and threw off their surcoats that showed them with the colors of Vortiger, ready to declare their obedience to their arriving new masters.

Great masses of soldiers deserted Vortiger right in front of him and moved as one to the ocean where they bowed, leaving only a few standing in place, those toward the rear of the beach, nearer to the king. The majority of those would even desert him after he had left. Mark also moved to the front, where Merlin advised him, ready to declare allegiance to the returning sons as soon as they made landing.

Moving toward the crashing line of waves, he knelt in the gravelly sand and waited. He craned his neck to look back and see King Vortiger there along the bluff at the rear of the beach. Mark saw as he looked out to the ocean, although he was too far away to see his facial expressions. He was still looking a moment later, when the king could be seen turning his horse around and leaving the scene. The horses of his advisors turned after him, and soon those few who held with the king left too, heading back toward his tower to hold out against the coming onslaught.

-18-

The most agreed-upon estimates were that the brothers and their armies would be at Vortiger's tower four days after their landing. Merlin had been exactly right, to the day, about when the brothers would return, and Vortiger took some perverse comfort in the knowledge that everything else he predicted would also come true. It had all brought a remarkable change in him that last week, and he enjoyed watching the surprised faces of all who came into contact with him as they found him in a good mood, chatty and forgiving.

On the morning of that fourth day, the enemy army could be seen gathering in the valley beneath the tower, and Vortiger knew that the final day had come. The mood in the tower became hushed, but electric with tension. The few remaining servants, for most of them had left, went about their business with grim, tight faces. On his way through the great hall, Vortiger was surprised to see Rowena still there, an anxious and tight expression on her face, surrounded by her maids, none of whom seemed any happier. He looked at the group in surprise, then strode right over to them.

"My love," he said, smiling, "what are you still doing here? I'm surprised to see that you haven't deserted me yet."

The pained smile on her face was frozen. "Desert you, my lord?" she asked.

He laughed. "No need to pretend," the king said. "I know your father isn't going to let you perish in this tower. Go," he gestured, "have your things brought outside, I know they've been prepared."

One of the maidservant's eyes darted rapidly back and forth between the king and her mistress. The surprised eyes of the queen glanced over to look at her, then back at the king, trying to keep a placid expression on her face. "Master, you think too little of my faithfulness and devotion," she protested.

Vortiger laughed out loud. "Yes," he said, "perhaps I do. But the enemy is just outside," he pointed, "and I don't think they'll leave until this tower has been breached. I plan to be on the battlement, so even if you're long gone, miles away and traveling under the protection of your father's Saxon troops," he trained a merciless smile on her, "I would think that you're right down here, faithful to me right up to the fiery end." He directed a vicious smile at each of the members of her group. "Be sure to serve your queen and ensure her safe passage," he said to the servants. "And your own." Then he walked to the staircase at the other end of the room, and opened the door there. He could see, looking back though the crack beneath the hinges, that the entire group was on its feet the second he was out of sight. He chuckled to himself and continued up to the next floor.

When he reached it, Roldan was there, with a clergyman he had brought from town. Roldan had been present when Merlin had predicted Vortiger's death on this day, which clearly influenced his bringing of the clergyman there, just then. "My lord," he said, arising to approach the king, followed closely by the sympathetic-eyed priest, "I have brought this holy man here to take your confession," he said.

Vortiger's face softened at the offer, and his heart broke for the kindness of both men. It was very considerate and thoughtful, and he appreciated that he was acknowledging what Merlin had said, and watching out for the king's soul. It was very kind, and the king hadn't foreseen this twist, but as he looked on the holy man, a noble feeling came within his chest—a feeling he wished no more to turn away from.

"That is very considerate, Roldan," he said, placing his hand on the advisor's shoulder, and nodding to the priest standing behind, "and I thank you, father, for coming this distance during," he tilted his head to indicate the armies gathering outside, "this time." He looked at them both with smiling eyes as he sighed, and the goodness he saw on their faces expelled any doubt he may have had. "But I cannot."

Both men's mouths fell open.

"But sir!" said Roldan. "You don't want to—" of course, he couldn't say the unpleasant thing, "all of us must be confessed before—" and he experienced that problem again.

The priest was even more astonished, and looked on him with truly gaping eyes, while his words came out in short, dumbfounded gasps. "But— Your soul— You will go to— You will not be allowed in—"

Vortiger's heart was cheered by the agape concern of the men, and he smiled with warm eyes. "That is what I have decided," he said with finality. "I am going to the battlement," he gestured, "and I suggest that both of you get well away before," and here he paused, and his eyes looked slightly away, "before this tower is destroyed."

Then, without looking back, he turned and strode away from the men. He was up the stairs and on the battlement in a moment. He had ordered a man to bring a chair up here that morning, and there it stood, in the middle of the empty octagonal surface. It was quite royal, oversized, of course, with gold-plated wood and red velvet cushions. The sun shone down brilliantly on the armies gathered in the valleys below—the farmer whose puppy he had been offered was sadly having his fields destroyed by the stomping of several knights—and left the hills and mountains glorious arrangements of grass, trees and rock. It was a spectacular vista, all around, and he had to admit that he had been right—this was a fantastic place for a tower!

Now he could look around all he wanted, and for some time he just stood, elbow balanced on one of the crenels and head in hand, marveling at the beauty of the land below. The breeze came very strong, but warm and caressing, across his face, and without a thought he reached up and removed his crown, tossing it down on the wooden boards with a dull bang. He leaned up on his toes to see the people under his rule running out of the tower while they could, and he watched for awhile to see if he could see Rowena, or Roldan and the priest, but he didn't see any of them for sure. He knew for a fact that Hengist would make arrangements to get Rowena out of there—he chuckled with amusement as he thought about the scene the Saxon probably expected to face, with Vortiger demanding that she stay and ride out the siege—so he had no concern on that account. There were still a few of his people streaming out as the armies of the brothers began to scale the hill, and he got involved in watching one or two of them as they made their escape. At one point, he looked down upon the

110

hill, shining brightly in the sun and dotted here and there with tiny bursts of wildflowers, and he was amazed to think that the two dragons had fought right there, right where was so peaceful now. Then later, he sat down in the chair, arranging it so that the wind would come right at him, and he closed his eyes and felt the warm sun on his face as he considered whether the floor beneath him would collapse before or after he burned to death.

Part Two
THE SECOND KING

-19-

Pendragon and Uther stood side by side as they watched the tower burn. The battle was now over, and had not been nearly as long or difficult as they had imagined, for as their ships touched the land, many men came forward and laid down their arms, asking to join their army. They said either that they wanted to help reclaim the country from Saxon rule, that they had turned against the horrible tyrant Vortiger, or had been faithful servants of Constance or Maine, or both of them, and wanted to help the rightful rulers retake the land.

The resisting Saxons, for almost all of those who had resisted their coming had been Saxons, were unable to put up much of a fight, and the brothers didn't have great trouble moving swiftly inland and securing their territories, until they came to the tower. Uther and his friend Ulfius led most of the battle in the valley, what little of it there was, while Pendragon took another group and went straight to the large and imposing tower where they knew Vortiger held. The battle on the open field below the tower had begun in the early afternoon and ended just before sunset, and now they stood, hand in hand in the valley below the great hill, watching in silent awe as the flames leapt from the small slit windows in the sides of the great tower. Pendragon had encountered almost no resistance as he and his men entered the base and set fire to the stores and supports that they had found there. They were able to stay long enough to ensure that the fire was well established before leaving. Now as they looked up, they could see the tower as a large black silhouette against the flickering orange light that reflected off the low overhanging clouds, like an illusory vision in the sky, for with the remnants of the battle and the rushing wind all around, they could hear nothing, just see the massively looming tower. Soon a great tearing sound was heard that filled the entire night, and they didn't know what it was until there was a sudden increase of light atop the black looming mass, and flames whirled a hundred feet high, straight out of the top of the tower, turning and twisting into a great whirling spiral of flame that reached up and burned a hole in the low layer of clouds.

It was a grand, imposing sight, and both of them were almost afraid to speak and ruin the close and intimate moment they shared. Pendragon was twenty-two years old now, but stood a few inches shorter than his brother, who was twenty and the larger, wider and stronger of the two. Both had beards, brown eyes and long brown hair that reached Pendragon's shoulders and down to Uther's shoulder blades, but Pendragon's face was more narrow and rested in an expression of friendliness and confidence, and could express great thoughtfulness, especially when he was listening to someone. Then he would lean forward and set his soulful gaze ahead steadily, letting the person who was speaking know that his words were being attended to quite carefully and that the man was thoughtfully processing all that he said. It was in part because of this that gave all who encountered him great confidence in his ability to lead and govern, as well as the fact that he was a direct descendant of the beloved King Constance, since noble lineage was then much more important as a signifier of character than it is considered today.

His younger brother Uther, at twenty, was the larger, more headstrong and hotheaded of the two. His great chest showed incredible strength, and his fearsomeness in battle was well known. His arms, legs and chest were hairy and virile, and he was known to be a great devotee of leisure, drinking and maidens. He always had one or two ladies writing him letters or seeking to take up some of this time, which he generously allotted, being on the whole less in demand—and less interested in—ruling and official functions than his brother. Where Pendragon could get into hours of speculation about a course of action, turning over this possibility or that, and trying to seek out and address all potential things that could go wrong, Uther usually saw issues with clear rights and wrongs, advantages and drawbacks, and rarely had any trouble making up his mind—or expressing that opinion to Pendragon. Together, with Pendragon assuming the role of king and Uther his closest, most trusted advisor, they made an envious and assured leadership team.

They needed no words as they stood, hands clasped tightly, watching the tower burn. This was an auspicious return to the country they had known, and bode well for their future as rulers, imparting the feeling that their luck had turned, and would now be with them. The night was wild, and knights on horseback could be seen riding here and there, the amber flame of the burning tower reflected in their metallic surfaces, as the sound of pounding hooves filled the air, while behind it all the great roar of the flames filled the night sky with overwhelming thunder.

This is how Pendragon and Uther returned to their land, and they wasted no time in letting it be known throughout the kingdom that they had returned. When the people learned of their arrival, they were overcome with joy and came out to greet and honor them as their rightful lords. Pendragon was made king, and the primary work ahead of him was to wage war on the Saxons whom Vortiger had allowed into their land, and who held onto the castles they had seized with fierce determination. Over the course of the next year, Uther led the sieges on the great castle that Hengist had holed up in, but was unable to make any progress, held in stalemate and trapped in endless small skirmishes that wore away at supplies and morale on both sides.

Pendragon met with his advisors and trusted men, many of whom had been advisors to Vortiger, but had parted from him in the last days and rallied to the side of the brothers. Some of these advisors had been there when Merlin explained to Vortiger about the dragons under the pool inside the hill, and they told him how everything that Merlin had said had come true, and that he was truly the best seer that ever lived.

"But there are other seers whose advice is very valuable," said Sir Brantius, who nearly fell out of his chair with dismay when he heard that the wizard who had wedged himself between him and the former king was now about to be invited to sit at the side of this newest one. "And besides, the advice of men who rely on intelligence, experience and wisdom is of great—and certainly more reliable—assistance than some gifted child whose wisdom comes from the devil!"

"True," said Roldan, who had also found Pendragon's service, "but Merlin knows things that no other man on earth can know, and if you asked him," he said as he turned to the king, "he would surely tell you plainly whether Hengist's castle can be taken, and exactly how to accomplish it, if so."

Brantius opened his mouth and raised his hand to protest, but before he could, the king asked "How do we get in touch with this seer?" Pendragon stood and his fingers pulled at his beard below his chin as his eyes grew deep with ideas of all the advantages that such a powerful sorcerer might afford them. But mostly he could only see the immediate task, which was defeating Hengist and taking his castle.

"I don't know where he is," said Roldan, "but I do know that when anyone talks about him, he is aware of it, and I'm sure he knows very well that we are talking about him right now." He also stood, and began pacing. "And if you wanted to, and you sent for him, he would surely meet your messengers, for I know that he is in this country."

Pendragon smiled, for it seemed that God himself was placing advantages in his path. "I will send for him immediately," he said.

-20-

Since that time when Merlin had left his small town, Blaise had made his way to Northumberland. He was nervous about making the long trip, just he alone in a hired carriage—at least there was a driver and porter with him, should their carriage get stuck—and he had trouble keeping this nervousness from taking over his heart, rendering him unable to read, as he saw the landscape grow more and more wild, and towns and villages fewer and further between. The journey took several days, and by the last day he was struck with the beauty of the wild canyons, waterfalls, expanses of rolling hills and vast areas of unexplored forest he was passing through, while also growing less and less confident that they would find any people where they were headed. The carriage took a long, winding climb up a barely-demarcated road that ascended the side of a high hill, and entered a flat area that jutted out to the side of the slope, filled with huge trees whose thick trunks grew out of a rolling carpet of blue wildflowers. The day was coming to a close and the gloom began to cling to the interior of the trees, when, looking out the window, he caught sight of a distant light. Then he saw a few more, and rounding a curve, the trees and leaves parted to reveal a small cottage, with a charming thatched roof and a few windows standing open, the warm light of lamps glowing from within, built on the edge of that hill and looking down on the immense valley that extended below.

Merlin was there to open the door for him. The cottage contained a large main room, and two smaller rooms, one for each of them. It was bigger than Blaise's hovel on the edge of the forest, but smaller and less comfortable than his place in Meylinde's shelter. Merlin showed Blaise around the place and the surrounding yards, where they could get water, where the best views and most beautiful, secluded spots were, all the while asking about his journey and if he was in good health.

Merlin and Blaise lived comfortably together in that cottage and spent many happy hours there in contemplation and conversation, and working together on Blaise's book, which recounts all of the events that you are hearing and those that you have yet to hear, and which is how we still know today that these events happened in that time.

One day they were coming to the close of working for the day, and Merlin said "Alas, I have to go now, but I will be back before supper time." Then a corridor opened in the air behind him, with two sides and a peaked roof, which extended far beyond the wall of the small chamber. Merlin stepped into it, it closed, and he stepped down onto the forest floor just on the Southern outskirts of Northumberland, where there was a small tavern on the edge of town. The wizard entered, the door creaking loudly as he opened it, and when he closed it behind him, he was in the guise of an old wizened woodsman, looking quite wild and mad, in an old dirty tunic that was worn to shreds. His hair was standing out from the sides of his head, with uncombed beard long and unkempt.

The messengers Pendragon had sent to find him were eating there, as he very well knew, and as they saw him enter they lowered their eyes and avoided his sight. "Don't look—some wild man from the forest," said one to another, while they all went on eating, keeping eyes down.

But it was too late, he stepped right behind them and leaned down over the largest, letting his long beard hang down to tickle the back of the man's neck. "You are not doing the work your lord sent you on very well," he said.

The messenger opposite looked up at him through lowered eyebrows. They didn't want this guy around, and if he was going to insult them, things might have to get unpleasant.

"I know that he has ordered you to find the great seer Merlin," the woodsman said, "and yet here you sit, filling your bellies!"

The other men couldn't help but look up when they heard this. "What do you know about it?" one of them asked.

"Exactly what I have said," the woodsman replied, "but if had been my job to look for him, I would have found him sooner than you."

One of the messengers stood and spoke to him. "Do you know who Merlin is?" he asked. "Have you ever seen him around here?"

"I have seen him, and I know where he lives," said the woodsman, pulling on his disheveled beard. "He knows very well that you are looking for him, but you will never find him unless he is willing to be found," he said, "and even if you did find him, he wouldn't go with you. But you can tell your lord that he will not be able to take the castle he is besieging until Hengist has died."

One of the messengers at the table stood straight up, gazing in wonder at the woodsman, for none of them had mentioned the name of Hengist while they had been in that tavern, or even among themselves for the past few days, and they were amazed to hear it on the woodsman's lips. "What else do you know?" he asked.

"I know that five of the king's advisors told you to look for Merlin, but when you go back, you will find only three, for two have died," the woodsman said. "And tell your lord and the three who remain that if they looked for Merlin in these woods, they would find him. But," and he raised a finger, "if the king himself does not come, he will never find Merlin." Then the wild man of the woods turned, and as he did, he was lost to sight. In the next moment, Merlin was once more at the side of Blaise, and he said "See? I told you I would be back for dinner. Now what are we having?"

-21-

The messengers rode back for many days until they came to the place where the king had his army, their tents arranged in a clearing among the trees and stones of the forest near the castle stronghold where Hengist was holed up with his remaining Saxons. Pendragon saw the messengers as they rode in among the tents, and moved right away, reaching them as they were dismounting their horses.

"Did you find who you went to look for?" he asked.

"Yes and no," said the lead messenger, "but something very strange happened to us. Gather those who advised you about the seer, for they will be better able to understand our news, and we will tell you everything."

The men required were gathered in the king's pavilion, and the messengers told of the strange words of the woodsman, and asked after the king's advisors, saying that the woodsman said that they would find two of them had died.

"They are indeed dead," said one of them. "One in a raid and the other to illness."

The king heard this and stared intently at the messengers, pulling on his thick beard. His mind was afire with the advantages a great seer could offer him in driving off the Saxon holdouts.

"The woodsman also told us," said the lead messenger, "That the king would not succeed in taking the castle until Hengist was dead."

King Pendragon stood, eyes lighting up at this. "He knew about Hengist?"

"He named him," said one of the messengers, "without our first mentioning him."

The other messengers nodded.

The king hung still, visibly thinking for a moment, then his arm came up quickly in a gesture of triumph. He turned away and was a moment in private reverie, before he once more faced them and said, "I *must* know this Merlin."

Sir Brantius stepped forward and began "My lord, he tells us words we would like to hear, but this is someone we do not know—" He was ignored.

"Sir," said Roldan, "I believe it must truly be Merlin himself who said these things. Only he could have known about the two who have died, and none but Merlin would be so bold as to mention Hengist's death."

"He said that if you wish to know him," the messenger told the king, "you yourself should come to Northumberland."

Pendragon stepped right by Brantius' upraised finger, somehow enchanted that this seer already knew he was looking for him. He thought, somehow, that this man, out there, knew him already. And he had the hint that, in some small way, some distant shred of feeling, he knew Merlin, too. With his eyes focused thoughtfully and the slightest, tickled smile on his face, he raised a hand to summon some footmen. "I will ride out tomorrow morning for Northumberland," he said, and they went away immediately to prepare his horses. "The friendship of this Merlin could be the making of us."

The next day, the king rode out with several of his best men, leaving Uther in charge of the siege against Hengist. In a few days he made camp on the edge of the great Northumberland forest. One of the

120

king's knights was out hunting for their meal that night when he came upon a very frail and misshapen old man tending a herd of cattle.

"Greetings, worthy knight," the old man said.

"As to you," said the knight, who did not want to be distracted from his hunt. "Fine day and luck with your herd," he said, already spurring his horse to be on his way.

"Oh, they're not mine," said the old man. "They belong to a man who employs me," he said to the retreating knight. "He told me that the king would come looking for him in the woods today."

Hearing this, the knight stopped. He pulled on his reins and turned, ambling back to the old man. "It is true that the king is looking to speak with someone in these woods," said the knight. "Can you say on this man who employs you?"

"Oh, I could say things to the king that I could not say to you," responded the old shepherd.

"Then come with me," laughed the knight. "I will take you where he is."

The old man put his thin arms on his hips and scoffed. "What kind of shepherd would I be then? Besides," he said, and waved his bony hand as he began to walk away, "I have no need of the king. But if the king were to come to me, I would tell him right away where to find the man he seeks."

"Then I will bring him to you," said the knight, and spurred his horse away.

When the king heard all of this, he rose at once from his seat and said "Let us go to him immediately."

They found the old shepherd deep in the woody shades of the forest, and the knight pointed him out to the king. Pendragon's eyes fell upon the weak-looking old man, and wondered if this could possibly be the one he was seeking.

"Noble king," said the withered old man, "you honor me with your presence. I know for truth that you seek Merlin, but you'll never find him until he himself wills it. But if you were to take residence in the town which is very near to here, he would come and speak with you."

The king checked an impulse of impatience, for he had hoped to have spoken to Merlin that day, but he made a show of gratefulness and the wizard noticed, and was pleased. "How do I know that you are advising me truly?" the king asked in a gentle tone.

"It is foolishness to heed bad advice," said the old man, "therefore, if you do not believe me, do nothing. But wit you well, I give you advice of more value than you could get from anyone else."

The king smiled, and looked in pleased wonderment at the old man, for he had just begun to notice a certain amused twinkle about the shepherd's wrinkled eyes, that accorded with the pleasant, tickled feeling he got when he thought about Merlin.

"Then," he said, with an amused smile, "I will believe you," and he spurred his horse away.

-22-

Uther stood, near the outskirts of the tents, away from most of his men. The night was breezy and fair, with a rich blue sky of stars such as we could not believe, for no one alive now has ever seen a sky so clear as they were then. The surrounding trees and distant hilltops made silhouettes against the endless blue, with the castle where Hengist and his armies were holed up forming a massive shadow looming over all, lit here and there by distant torches. That, and the fires scattered among the tents made the place, despite being a necessity of war, quite beautiful. There was a quiet peace over the entire encampment, with the far-away sounds of a few men singing as the sparks of the fires floated up into the sky, all of it quite serene and magical. It brought Uther's mind around to a maiden he had known in Brittany where he and his brother had hid out during Vortiger's reign.

He knew his mind should be ever on war, but how could it? That was always Uther's problem; keeping his mind off the maidens. He was known as a dog for it. With such a beautiful evening, he could not help but want to spend it with the lovely one he thought of, to point out to her the magical sight of the sparks floating up into the silent trees, whose low boughs were illuminated by flickering firelight. He was so tired of the endless fighting, which had gone on for months now with not one day's relief, that when he had a quiet moment to let his mind drift to more pleasant matters, he felt he deserved it. Worse still, he had no idea when he might see her again. In fact, there were no plans at all, and she was back there, across the sea—and married. They had enjoyed a brief, hot affair, the deception involved in which somehow made it that much more exciting. There were things he'd wished he had told her. Things that, in thinking of her, he had realized only after leaving that he would wish that she knew. If only he could have even a word from her... but that was impossible.

"Fearsome Uther!" rang a loud voice at his side, and he turned to see a small, frail old man, clad in a peasant's robe, with a face so shriveled and wrinkled, he was amazed that such a booming voice had issued from it. The old man raised a hand and gestured to the night sky, saying "The night is peaceful and quiet, and it hides Hengist as he moves through this very camp, intending to take your life!"

Uther looked at the old man, and it took a second for him to register what he had just heard. Jarred, he straightened suddenly. "Hengist is here?" he asked. "Who are you?"

"That matters not," said the man. "What matters is that you be on your guard, and carry arms—and armor! He comes to slay you in your tent!"

Uther stared, mouth agape, at the man. "What—who are you? What are you doing in the middle of this camp?"

The old man raised his arm, and a bony, gnarled hand emerged from his robe, with finger pointed directly at Uther. "There's no time to waste on questions of no importance. Hengist is on the edges of your camp, stealing in to meet you. Greet him well!"

Then the old peasant turned suddenly and was lost in the night before Uther could think to say a word more. He stood in the silence left in his wake, and thought on what he should do. It was too bizarre, what the man said. And how should he know the name of Hengist? How should he have any information about where Hengist was? He looked after where the man had disappeared to, then turned away to once more overlook the campsite, shaking his head in wonderment. Who were these people you came across when camping in these strange, small towns? It was hard to imagine anything so dire happening on such a quiet, peaceful night, and his mind returned once more to thoughts of that lovely woman he had left behind.

Yet... what a perfect night to steal into a camp and kill a leader, unnoticed and undercover? It was a devious plan, and audacious. Perfect in its simplicity. No armies, no battle, just slip in and take out the leader, leaving the army adrift. Uther thought on it further. Diabolical! If he were killed, it would take days before Pendragon was back, during which time his army could be heavily diminished, if not outright destroyed, especially if surprised and leaderless. His men were smart, all self-sufficient knights, but he had seen even great men lose focus without a leader, and groups of knights with no coordinated plan were easily enough separated and picked off. Uther scratched his beard as he looked back toward where the man had disappeared. It was too strange to believe, and yet—perhaps exactly so strange that he *should* believe it? There was no harm in donning his armor. And none in arming himself. And maybe even finding a perch from which he could observe his own pavilion.

He was already moving toward the tents that housed the armor while still only half convinced.

He stole in, with a finger over his lips to the man sitting guard, and emerged a moment later in hauberk, strapping a sword around himself and carrying a long dagger, with a blade of about eight inches, and helmet in his hand.

"Something afoot?" asked the guard there.

"Just being sure," said Uther. "Stay here, think nothing of it." In a moment he had moved off into the night.

As he walked, Uther's nerves came out of relaxation and into the heightened awareness and coiled nerves that come with battle. His step quickened and became more stealthy as he picked his way through the

124

tents toward his pavilion, beginning to orient himself toward spotting threats. His eyes avoided looking directly at any of the fires, so he could retain his ability to see in the darkness.

As he approached, he searched for some way to get up high, so that he could have a view of his pavilion and all that approached. That is, without making himself obvious, sticking up above the line of all the tents like a fool. There was a tree nearby, but it wasn't very large and he might be obvious to anyone looking at it, but he took the risk. Hengist, were he coming, would be too focused on finding his pavilion and picking his way among the tents unnoticed. Uther climbed up and took a seat in the lowest branch that could support him. He looked down, and almost laughed. The iron rings of the hauberk shone brightly in the firelight, but he hoped that Hengist would be too occupied to notice. He was far enough away from the pavilion, anyway.

He sat long enough in that tree that he started to feel like an idiot. The encampment was as quiet as ever, most of the men lying asleep to refresh themselves for another round of besieging Hengist's stronghold the next day. A small group of drinkers were heard singing in the distance, over on the far edge of the camp. Uther's mind started to drift to how the small man could possibly have wandered that far into the camp unnoticed, and what he or anyone might have to gain by having him armed and waiting at his own tent, when his eyes caught something moving in the darkness. Uther gripped the tree tighter and stared out into the darkness when he saw the movement again, and— yes, it was a man!

The figure was clad entirely in black and moved about the tents to avoid the light of the fires. He moved with stealth, waiting now as two men passed, crossing just behind them, standing momentarily on a stone, looking about for the pavilion, then stepping down without a sound and moving swiftly across several rows and turning rightward. He drew ever closer to Uther's pavilion. There was something in his hand. It flashed once in the light of the torches and fires. A dagger.

A light tingling surged up Uther's body, the feeling akin to delight that often came with battle, and with a silent motion he swung his leg up over the branch and dropped to the ground with a thud. He was

125

hardly upright before he stepped steadily around to the side of the nearby tents, plotting out a circular route to intercept the intruder. Where should he meet him, among the tents? Outside his pavilion? In the pavilion? His mind clicked through each different scenario, with its varied advantages and drawbacks.

Uther drew his dagger as he walked, and as adrenaline surged through his limbs he began to feel his strides becoming sleeker, more purposeful, and his movements drew into greater efficiency as his mind calmed into the eerie heightened focus he felt with anticipation of close combat. He came to a tent just across from his pavilion, and suddenly deciding that this was the perfect spot, donned his helmet and crouched down at its side.

The movement of his quickened blood, as he crouched still and waiting, created a low rhythmic thrushing sound in his ears.

He did not have to wait more than a moment before the figure in black rounded the side of his pavilion, looked quickly to be sure he wasn't spotted, then slipped soundlessly inside. Uther, incongruously, felt tickled. The old man was right! He must have done something to earn the favor of this man, and as Uther stood to his full height, he felt the power of having great advantage. He thought of taking his hood down, as he wanted Hengist to know at once who it was, but the old man had warned him to be defended, so he would have to forego that satisfaction.

Uther stood, legs planted far apart, a few feet just in front of his own pavilion. And he waited. He heard rusting inside, objects falling over, then a silence, and in his mind's eye he saw the assassin inside, realizing that the one he came to kill wasn't there. That his plan was foiled, and he was now stuck in the very center of the enemy camp. It almost made Uther laugh, but not as much as when, a moment later, he saw the sight of Hengist's head, emerging from his pavilion then stopping, eyes widening and pallor fading to white, as he beheld the massive knight standing before him.

"Hengist!" said Uther, although he had only seen him at a distance on the battlefield. He made a welcoming gesture with his hands, one swinging the long blade of his dagger. "How good of you to visit!"

The Saxon stood still as a cobra, eyes fixed on the helmet of the knight opposite him. His reddened eyes made the light blue at their center shine brighter, the colors made more vivid as the blood drained from his face. His eyes darted left, then right, but there was nowhere he could go. To retreat into the pavilion, slit it, and run out the back? But Uther would sound the alarm and he would be overcome. His face became shiny as a layer of sweat emerged, and strange lumps appeared in his face as he set his jaw, the knowledge that his plan had collapsed crushing in on him with horrible force.

Now the wild thoughts came. Throw a lamp at the knight? Trip him and try to run—or steal a horse? The knight stood, simply watching, as all of these thoughts rushed through the Saxon's mind. But even then, Hengist knew that there now could be no outcome but combat. He had taken the risk to get into the camp unnoticed, and it would have been brilliantly cunning, if it had worked out, but now it left him alone in a deadly position. His eyes steadily watching his opponent, Hengist emerged fully from the tent. His eyes were fierce, but Uther could see his wrinkled hands shaking. He was older than Uther had thought, just under sixty, he imagined, with a tight and lithe body, all of which made him fearsome, and venerable, but also a bit desperate and slightly pathetic.

"Oh!" Uther laughed, and his hand came up to cover his mouth as he saw that Hengist was not wearing armor. The Saxon's face grimly withstood the humiliation as his opponent gloated over his dawning great fortune. Uther thought quickly on what might be the most satisfying insult to taunt the invader with, and finally said; "Look at you, slipping nearly naked into my pavilion!"

The Saxon bared his teeth. "I have brought a gift," he said, and raised his dagger. Uther also saw another one tucked into his belt. Hengist crouched in place and put his most fearsome face on.

Uther didn't flinch. "A rather wee gift," he said, "is it not?"

Hengist leapt. His knife point made a dull thud as it hit the rings of the knight's hauberk. Uther watched the blade stop directly above his chest, unable to go further, and while that happened, his arm came forward and pushed the dagger into Hengist's stomach. At the first feeling of it, the Saxon leapt back, and as he retreated, Uther wrenched his wrist around in a tight circle, causing the sharp blade to arc within Hengist's guts.

The invader gasped. He stepped back, mouth hanging open, as the blade slipped out of him. The quiet, rain-like sound of blood hitting the grass and fallen leaves was heard. He backed away silently, the hand covering his stomach now wet and red, as Uther stepped forward, matching him step for step. Hengist's eyes searched side to side frantically, looking for any means of escape. He once more glanced at the advancing knight, and a small moan of unexpectedly high pitch issued from him.

"Did you come here, Hengist," said Uther, voice now low and steady, "because you want to be sure to be killed by me?"

The Saxon's lips curled up over his teeth in hatred. His eyes traveled all over the advancing knight's body, looking for anywhere he could strike with his knife, but it would mean getting close enough to do it without being wounded yet again. A sharp pain, deep within him, made him wince and a wave of dizziness and nausea washed over him. He was losing blood.

With this thought, he gripped the handle of his blade in clenched fist, and threw himself forward. There was no time for strategy, nor did he have the energy for anything but ruthless attack. He slashed the air left, as Uther stepped back, then slashed right. Uther simply stepped to the side, but as Hengist stumbled past, he turned his blade within his hands and directed a jab back toward Uther's abdomen.

It felt like a punch, the blade stopped entirely by his armor. Uther barely felt it, but, with a strange calmness and clarity of mind, he saw Hengist's bent-over body passing by him, examined it for weakness, and was able to hook his dagger under the far side of the Saxon's throat, letting the man's forward movement sink it into his flesh as Uther pulled it back toward him.

Hengist continued by, body propelled by the momentum of his leap, but his head snapped back, blue eyes shining livid, as his hand came up to touch his neck. His fingertips were met with the gentle touch of a spurt of blood. His daring plan had failed, his glorious military career—and dreams of ruling the Saxon state of Britain—would come to an abrupt end here, in this encampment. After his bold assault! He had to admit to himself now that, while he knew his plan was audacious and had good chance of failure, he had never actually considered that it would fail. His mouth came open and face took on a child's open expression of frustration, knowing full well this new wound meant that he would not be leaving that camp.

Off balance and not looking where he was going, Hengist tripped and fell forward, landing roughly on his face and shoulder.

Uther's blade hung downward and swung left and right at the end of his fingers, a drop of blood flying off with each arc. He moved slowly and with patience, his mind suffused with the strange calm of combat, and the certain knowledge that his enemy had been destroyed.

Hengist pulled his face up out of the dirt and lifted himself half up with a forearm, making a high-pitched strangled groan that sounded rather like a pig. He looked back, seeing Uther following close behind him, regarding him with an expression of curiosity, and at once turned his eyes down before a desperate gasp, but whiny, like a sob, issued from him. Within a few short moments he had transformed from stealthy warlord to wounded animal, and the cruelty of his situation, plus the sadistic gloating of Uther just behind him, was too awful to bear. Not to mention that his limbs were no longer able to support him as waves of lightheadedness swept through his brain, and a metallic taste spread throughout his mouth. He fell forward once more onto his face, rolling his eyes downward, where he saw Uther crouch to take a seat upon a stone behind him.

"Don't," Hengist said, but had to swallow to contain the blood that filled his mouth. He was so tired. It cost great effort to speak. He watched as Uther wiped the end of his blade across his leg, then flicked the weapon downward, sending it to stick upward out of the ground at his feet. The large knight leaned forward, placing an elbow on his knee and resting head in his hand, as his eyes stayed steadily trained on the weakening man before him.

"Don't just watch me die," said Hengist through ragged breaths. Uther shrugged. "Why not?"

-23-

Blaise had settled in nicely and had made his room up very comfortably so that he could relax there and also work with Merlin on his book. He enjoyed taking daily walks around the lands that surrounded the cottage in which they lived. The surrounding forest and valley was fantastically wild and beautiful, although one could not help but be aware that it was also replete with dangers, and if one were injured far from their home, one might never be found.

One day Merlin knocked on the door while he was engaged in reading, and entered. "Blaise, I am glad to find you here," Merlin said, "I want you to feel something."

Merlin sat down opposite him as the holy man simply looked back with his plain blue eyes, waiting.

The seer held out a dull round black stone to him, and placed it in his hand. Blaise looked at it in his palms, then let his fingers run over it to feel it.

"A rock," he said.

"Yes," replied Merlin. "Now, in your other hand..." and he placed another stone there. This one was blacker and more shiny.

Blaise looked at it, felt it, and said, "Another rock."

"Quite right," said Merlin. "Do they both feel the same?"

Blaise worked each with his fingers, and lightly bounced them on his palms. "This one is smoother," he said.

"Um-hm," Merlin said. "Hold them quietly. Anything else?"

Blaise closed his eyes and held the two stones in his hand and remained still for a moment.

"No," he said afterward.

"Think on the feeling you get when handling saint's relics," said Merlin, watching the old man eagerly. "Think about that feeling when you hold these stones."

Blaise remained looking at Merlin for a moment, as he thought, then looked down to the stones in his hand. He watched them for a minute in silence, as Merlin remained motionless and quiet, and then there was a moment when Blaise was exceptionally still. Then he shifted in place.

"But honestly," Blaise said, his tone vaguely apologetic, "I'm never sure, really, if I do feel that feeling or if I'm just imagining it."

"Say you weren't imagining it," said Merlin. "Could you go further into the feeling that the thing you held was," he drew the word out, "significant, somehow?"

The old man held on quietly. His face seemed slightly emotional, and he said, "I could try."

Merlin said nothing, and Blaise looked at the stones for a while, with a sympathy growing in his eyes, and then he closed them. His fingers shifted and began to caress the stones.

"Would you say, if you were to go along with this feeling," Merlin said, "that one of these stones is more powerful than the other?"

Blaise felt them both, and weighed them in his palms again, then reached forward with the shinier one.

"That's right," Merlin said, reaching forward to take them both back from Blaise's hands. "You're exactly right. Now stretch both your palms out," he said, and the hermit did so silently, as he seemed not in the mood to talk, and held them open to the air. "Now," Merlin said, "Take this one again," and he handed him the dull stone, "and take this one."

"Oh!" Blaise exclaimed. He looked at his hands, then brought the shiny stone up near his face. "What are these?"

"Resonant stones," said Merlin, taking the dull one. "Although this one isn't, this is just a rock." He tossed it aside. "Now keep that one," he said, "and take this one." He handed Blaise a larger stone, about the size of an orange, which was a deep blue and somewhat translucent, with a stripe of whitish band that ran through it.

Blaise looked at it eagerly as it sat in his hand. "Hmmm," he said, with pleasure. "Different. It's different, isn't it?" he asked. He looked at it again as he rolled it in his hand.

"Yes, it is," said Merlin. "Cool and tranquil, no? That one is from a pool of the cool and clearest water among the wet trunks and leaves very far from where people have ever been," he said. "They are like waters," Merlin said, "they contain the essence of what is around them, and when you taste them," he closed his eyes with the thought, "it's as though you are taken to that place."

Blaise opened his eyes. "And these have been here the whole time?" he asked.

Merlin nodded. Blaise shook his head in wonder and looked from one stone to the other.

"Give me that one," Merlin took the darker stone, "and now take this," and he handed him a flat stone of rich burgundy.

"Ah," said Blaise, his eyes closing as though he felt an aching sweetness. "Oh, now," he said.

Merlin smiled. "I want you to start looking for these stones, on your walks," he said. "You will be able to feel them, when you do a bit more work to become familiar with their different tones and characters." He took the blue stone now, and handed Blaise a cloudy egg-shaped white one, about the size of a fist.

"Oh, woah-ho now!" uttered Blaise, who seemed to have a moment where he lost his composure. Some strands of wispy white hair fell into his face. "Some of these are," he breathed, "quite something."

Merlin smiled, and looked gladly up at his companion. "Collect them with your pockets," Merlin said. "If there are any that you particularly like, you can keep them. If you find some that are too large, or that you cannot get to safely, remember where they are and I will come collect them later."

Blaise held up the white rock and looked with humility at it. "This will add quite some new flavor to my walks."

Merlin grasped his wrist warmly. "I would not ask you to do it if I didn't know that it will lead you to experience wondrous things, and see places of the most agonizing beauty, which I know you will be able to

132

appreciate" he said. "And know, Blaise, that there are few people I could ask to do this," he said, "who are as pure of heart as they would need to be."

Blaise lowered the stones and looked on Merlin with kind eyes, blinking silently at him.

"But Blaise," Merlin said, hand still tenderly on his arm, "pay heed to the feeling that tells you to stay away, and always trust it, for there are places, now that you are so attuned, that could be quite dangerous for you." Merlin looked him in the eye. "And let me know where those places are, too."

Blaise nodded, and sat back in his chair, putting the burgundy stone down and holding only the cloudy white one, clasping it in both hands and bringing it near him to rest on his belly. He looked into the distance and seemed to fall into a state of placid thought, remaining motionless for some time.

"Can I keep this one?" he asked of the milky white translucent rock.

"Sorry no," replied Merlin, "That one is appointed to a very special purpose," he said. "But that won't be for a year or so, and you can keep it until that time, if you like."

Blaise nodded serenely. "Thank you for showing me this, Merlin," he said after a moment.

-24-

So the king lodged in the town Merlin suggested, where many of the inhabitants made joyful welcome of him, gave thanks that he had returned and declared themselves loyal and unwavering. The king had a few days of making himself known in the town, meeting several people but no one that he was seeking, until one day, weary of handshakes and commending of children, he found a highborn man in very fine dress striding directly to him across the town square.

"Sir," he said, "Merlin bid me to come to you. And he wants you to know that he was the woodsman who addressed your messengers in the tavern, and also the herdsman with whom you spoke in the woods. I give you proof in that he said he would come to you only of his own will."

The king's eyes searched those of the regal man eagerly, for he was curious to know if this, too, was Merlin, and in his eagerness he forgot to say anything.

"Merlin told you the truth that day," said the man and stepped back, making a gesture toward the king, "but you still do not need anything from him. And Merlin has never wanted to see any king unless there was something great for him to accomplish."

"Dear friend," spoke the king, "I would see him very happily now, and I have great need of his help to assure our success in," he thought quickly, "driving the remaining Saxons out and reclaiming Britain for its people." The king thought he should say something noble, since it didn't seem right to simply say he sought Merlin so that he would win.

The man smiled cleverly. "Because you say so," he said, "Merlin sends you some wonderful news. Hengist is dead," he said. "Killed by your brother, Uther."

The king gasped at the news. Merlin, he thought... this Merlin is wonderful! His mind thought on the implications, all of them of indicating great advantage to him, and he uttered "Is this true?"

"You would be unwise to believe me before you prove it for yourself," the nobleman said. "Stay in this town and send messengers to your brother to see if what I have said is true." He cocked his head curiously. "And if it is, believe even more in the worth of Merlin's counsel." With this, the man turned, some people passed very close between them, and when they drew away, the man could not be found. Pendragon stood amazed for a moment, dazed by the news.

The king sent his messengers at first light to seek news of Hengist, but they had not ridden more than a day before they met Uther's messengers, come to tell him how Hengist had been killed.

134

When the king heard this, he was very excited, for it had seemed almost too good to hope, that this great seer would give such an immense advantage to him. He already had, for it was a great advance to have Hengist dead, and his men leaderless. And they could have the advantage of Merlin's vision and advice on everything from now on? With that power behind him, all of the challenges he anticipated being so arduous could melt away almost effortlessly.

After this the king made himself widely available and visible in town, which brought him in constant contact with the townsfolk, and had him meeting a great deal of people. One of these was a hermit of regal bearing who appeared older and more wizened than the king, middle-aged, his head bald and beard full and gray, but not seeming frail or weak. He projected a firm masculine strength, and his eyes gazed directly at the king with immense confidence.

"Sir," asked this man of the king, "are you waiting for someone in this town?"

The king's eyes sharpened as he took in the regal man. "I wait here for Merlin to come to speak with me."

The man chuckled gently and laid a firm hand on the king's shoulder. He was of such steady assurance he was able to make the young king feel like a child. "King, you are very great," said the man, "but you are not so wise that you can recognize the one you seek when he is talking to you. Now, if you call those who would know Merlin to a private place, you can ask them if I could ever be this Merlin that you seek."

They returned to the lodging where the king was staying, which was not in any way fit for a king, although Pendragon understood the value in loyalty of allowing the common people to host him and his retinue. When the king entered the common area with the strange man following behind, he found those men who had known Merlin when he was advisor to Vortiger.

"My lords," said the king, with the older man standing beside him, "I am waiting for Merlin, but I do not know what he looks like. You have seen him when he made predictions to Vortiger." He found it hard to contain a slight smile, tickled by the situation. "If you see him, I beg you would tell me."

"Yes sir," said Brantius. "His impression is so," he appeared to be choosing among several unpleasant words, "singular, it would be impossible for us not to recognize him if we saw him."

This brought a smile to the face of the man the king had brought, who looked at Brantius and asked "How can one who does not recognize himself recognize another?"

Brantius was unsure how to respond to that, so he said "I would definitely recognize him—he's only seven years old, perhaps eight by now—but I do not see him here."

The hermit put his hand on the king's shoulder. "Let us find a room where we can speak alone," he said, "and I will show him to you."

The king led him back to his own chamber, and had the advisors stand outside. The strange man entered the room with hands on his hips, and his eyes took in the manner in which the king kept his private chamber and found it quite orderly, which pleased him. He turned as the king shut the door behind him, eyes expectantly looking to the stranger with great eagerness, for he dared not believe he had finally come into the presence of the great seer.

"Sir," said the man, "I would like very much to make friendship with you and your brother Uther. And you should know verily that I am the Merlin you have been seeking, but those who believe they know me do not know me at all. You will see this quite soon."

The king trembled in reverence and awe as he had not done in a long time, and he hesitated to speak for fear of harming the fragile union as it was just beginning to form. "It is great to meet you, Merlin," he said. "I have heard much of your talents."

"But still not so much that you would know how powerful I actually am," the old man said. "Go now and bring those who say they know me, as well as the men you trust the most. They will tell you with certainty that you have found me," and he pointed at the king, "but know that, had I willed it, you never would have found me."

The king nodded. He was unsure what that was supposed to mean, or what he was supposed to take from it, but he wasn't going to argue. "I will do anything you say," he said.

He fetched the men and when they opened the door again, there was the boy Merlin that they had seen advise King Vortiger, and they said "Sir, it is true you have found Merlin. This is the boy we saw inform King Vortiger of his death long before it happened."

"Be sure you know who this is," said the king.

"We know that this is Merlin," said Brantius.

"Sir, they tell you the truth," said Merlin, and when the king turned to him, he was once more the impressive bearded hermit who had appeared to him, for this was the form that he wished for most people to know him, and would make it easier for them to believe the things he said. "In that guise, as a boy, was how I appeared to them then," he said, "but this will be known as my true appearance now. So, king," said Merlin, and he turned full to Pendragon and reared up royally, hands on his hips, and spreading out the great emerald cloak he wore. "Tell me. What is your will?"

The king's eyes looked at Merlin as though he were a delicate gift, which is what he was. They gleamed with promise as his hands rubbed each other greedily, weighing his words with the greatest delicacy. "I beg you humbly, Merlin, if it is possible, to be my loyal friend and use your incredible foresight to advise me on how to serve this country most successfully," he said. "And let me be faithful to you in return, for every man has told me that you are most powerful and wise."

Merlin stood proudly before him as the king said these words. Then he said, "Sir, I will gladly accept your friendship, and be certain, you will never ask me for anything that I will not plainly tell you, if it is something I know about."

"Would you please tell me," said the king, "whether I spoke to you after I came here looking for you?"

"I am the old man you found tending the livestock," said Merlin, "and I am the man who told you that Hengist had been killed."

The king smiled to Roldan and Brantius. "You knew him badly before," he said jokingly.

"Sir, we never saw him change his appearance in this way," said Roldan. "Nor did we even know that it was even possible. But it is plain that he can say and do things no one else can."

The king turned back to Merlin. On his face was the most curious smile. He paced a wide circle around him, hands on hips, unable to decide what to ask first. "How did you have knowledge of Hengist's death?"

Merlin told him the story of how he had visited Uther in the encampment and warned him of the attempt on his life. He watched the face of the king as the ruler realized that Merlin had not only turned the entire war their way, but had saved his brother's life.

"It is a wonder that he believed you," said Pendragon. "In what form did you appear to him?"

"I took the shape of a withered old man, and I found him standing by himself," Merlin said. "I told him outright that he must be very watchful that night, for if not he would have to die."

"Did you reveal yourself to him?"

"He does not know who I was, or who warned him," said Merlin, "and will not know until you yourself make it known. These are steps I take to ensure that the both of you will believe for yourselves in what I tell you."

"You have told me enough, and done enough," said the king, "if all that you have said is true—and you saved the life of my brother—I could never disbelieve a word you said."

"Go and tell your brother what I have said to you and if he tells you that this is exactly what happened, never disbelieve me on any subject. I will tell you how to recognize me when I approach your brother. I will appear as the old wretch who warned him of Hengist's attack."

"And when will you speak to my brother?"

"I will happily tell you," said Merlin, and then he pointed a firm finger toward Pendragon. "But be careful, if you truly want my friendship, that you never tell anyone else, for if I learn that ever you have betrayed my trust, you would lose my faith in you forever, which will hurt you far more greatly than me."

"If I lie to you, ever," said the king, with a great sweeping gesture, "trust me never again. But I will question you extensively," he said, "and I tell you this openly."

"Question me in any way that will help you believe," said Merlin, "but lie to me or insult me with tests of doubt and you will find yourself sore mischieved. And you should know that I will speak to both you and your brother on the eleventh day after you once more are with him."

Then Merlin and the king shook hands, and soon after, Merlin returned to Blaise. The king sat out in the hall with his advisors and knights, who chatted away aimlessly while his gaze remained focused on the middle distance, transfixed by thoughts of this Merlin, with a faint, delighted smile on his face.

-25-

Merlin waited on the roof of their cottage. It was about three hours after midnight, and from this place he had a lovely view down a valley whose rolling hills were lined with grass and trees, dotted here and again with exposed rocks. At the end of the valley was a waterfall that filled the air with a distant rushing sound, and appeared a misty light blue in the cool moonlight that illuminated the scene.

Merlin thought on what he was about to do with a leaden heart. His eyes had cast his vision deep into the future, and he had found the woman he sought, without doubt it was her, but he also saw how it would leave her. What the rest of her life would be like afterward, when she could never again be so innocent. Yet he could see no one else but her, for only she in all the land, with the depth of her wish to be good and remain virtuous, could create the person he needed. With a sigh, he rose to his feet, stepped down toward the edge of the roof, and, turning his head as he heard an owl's cry from the direction of the forest, stepped down in her chamber.

She lay there, body entangled with the duke's, her face pressed against the skin of his neck, a look of complete contentment on her face. It's true, she was absolutely lovely, even more so, and more overwhelmingly, than he had seen in his mind. Her skin was utterly unblemished and looked as soft and pure as cream, and he saw her breasts rise and fall slightly with her quiet, even breath. They lay nude together. The sight of them together made him think on a symbolic painting meant to show the perfect example of man, rough and masculine, and woman, beautiful and strong, entangled together, complete and completing each other.

Merlin found a chemise, the undergarment that hung closest to her body, lifted it quickly and tucked it into his robe. His feet stepped delicately around the sleeping forms of the lovers, then he moved off to find a seat against the wall, separated by the sleeping couple by a hanging skein of veils and pelts. Merlin spent a moment thinking pensively, his eyes sunken and distant, then he touched one finger to his other palm, made a circular motion above with his fingers, and the woman awoke.

She did not find anything amiss, nor did she feel anything but comfort and security, close there, pressed against the strong, firm body of the duke. She kissed him lightly twice on the neck. Then she turned her head to look out into the room, her face showing a mild curiosity, as though she had heard something. The fire still burnt and filled the quiet room with a lovely flickering glow. She stepped to the window and looked down at the stone walls of the castle, all a cool gray-blue in the moonlight, set against the blackness of the sea just beyond. The night was quiet and filled with peace, save for the distant crashing of the waves against the rocks below, and her room with the duke felt absolutely safe and comfortable.

Her head turned to the side suddenly, and she saw someone sitting there, perfectly still, against the wall. He was in a robe with a hood pulled up, and she could not see his face. Curious, not at all threatened, she went over and stood before him. She was still nude, her full breasts and lovely curves and dips shining beautifully in the flickering firelight, but she did not feel intruded upon or abashed,

140

because the feeling of the moment was so calm. The man sat against the wall in peace and completely without an air of violence, and at the same time, she had the strange sense that he wasn't actually there at all, or if any of this were actually happening. If it was not a dream, it was something very much like it.

The man raised his hand and offered his open palm in homage. "Fair Igraine," he said, "blessed mother. I come to begin making penance for all that will befall you."

She smiled and cocked her head in curiosity, rather than feel threatened, as the entire mood of the visit was one of wonder. "What will befall me?" she asked.

The man in the robe indicated four garlands of gold, laid out next to where he sat, with the most delicate fringe of golden threads, here and there enclosing tiny lustrous stones and richly-colored shards of gems. "Accept these garlands as a small part of my offering," he said.

His fingers moved above the first. "This one," he said, "will help your eldest daughter with her studies. The second will help your middle daughter bear many worthy sons." He looked up at her. "This one," he said, indicating the third, "will help your younger daughter in her practice of the healing arts. And this, largest one," he said, running his fingers over the most ornate of the garlands, "is for you, and will strengthen your innate goodness and help you remain virtuous."

She leaned in and examined the mixture of gold and stones that made up the garlands, and when she leaned back the man was no longer there, because he was once more in Northumberland. We will not meet Igraine again in this book, but as we read on we will know that she is out there, living the last of her carefree days with a husband she loves truly, the Duke of Tintagel.

Merlin returned home and hung Igraine's chemise in a small closet in his room, somewhere he was sure Blaise would not find it. He hung the garment below a sprig of wolfsbane mixed with roots of nightshade, from which the human oils contained in the garment would be naturally repelled. These would, over the next few days, drip onto a pan he placed below the garment, and be gathered in a small cup beneath the center of that. Over flame, Merlin would turn this dense, sticky fluid into a fine white powder, which he would then funnel into a small bottle of blue glass.

-26-

Pendragon rode for many days until he came to the encampment where Uther and his men were chipping away at the remnants of the Saxons when they dared emerge from the stronghold where Hengist had remained with them. When the brothers saw each other, Uther came running at once to embrace him, and Pendragon swung his leg over and slid down off his horse, throwing his arms open as he ran at his brother. Their chests met with a hearty thud as they held each other a great while.

Pulling back, Uther said "Pendragon! You will not believe what great things I have to tell you!"

Pendragon raised a hand. "Don't tell me," he said, "and I will tell *you* things even more amazing. And introduce you to someone who promises to give us great advantage in this war. But first— congratulations in ridding us of Hengist!" He gripped his younger brother's shoulders as Uther puffed up proudly. "All of our efforts will be much easier now."

"The country is virtually ours!" said Uther, still amazed. "The Saxons are leaderless. But you would not believe—"

Pendragon once more raised his hand. "Don't!" he said. "But let us find somewhere to speak privately."

They made a few more hellos and managed some business, then repaired to the royal pavilion at the center of the camp. Pendragon changed out of his traveling clothes, and, once comfortable, Uther said "I am dying to tell you my news! Whatever you have to tell me first," he said, "let's have it."

142

Pendragon smiled mischievously and almost found it hard to begin, the moment was too delicious. "My news," he said, voice booming in his excitement, "is to tell you *your* news!" He enjoyed the moment of his brother's confusion, then said "An old wretch appeared to you in the middle of the night at this camp," he said. "He informed you that Hengist was coming just then to kill you, and that you should arm and defend yourself, for he would not be wearing armor."

Uther was dumbfounded. "How did you know?" he asked at last. "I never told anyone about the old man."

Pendragon laughed heartily. "Because I have met the man who told you this. He is a great seer—perhaps the best that has ever lived." And here he grabbed Uther by the shoulders and stared in delighted wonder at him. "And he wants to be *our friend!* And use his powers to offer us advantage. Great advantage!" he said. "He will help us drive out the Saxons completely and settle the wars over this land!"

"Who is he?" asked Uther. "Why does he want to help us?"

"He wants to help us," said Pendragon, "primarily because, well, we're *us.*"

Uther laughed and spread his arms, hands pointing in to indicate himself. "And we are, by all accounts, wondrous and formidable."

"And in every shape and form the better of every living man," continued Pendragon, eyes laughing. "But also, he knows of our birthright, and he is keen to have Britain ruled by the British, which obviously…" and here he once more indicated himself. "His name is Merlin, and he is the son of a demon, from whence he gains his powers, which far exceed those of any man now living."

Uther's face clouded. "Can we trust someone born of the devil?"

Pendragon raised his finger. "Yes, because he was turned to God by his mother, who had him baptized at the moment of his birth. Thus he retained the devil's advantages, while also attaining the blessings and advantages of God. He works on earth to bring about the will of God and, brother," Pendragon turned to Uther and once more gripped his shoulders in both hands, "he wants to help *us.*"

Uther blinked as the import of the words settled over his mind. "You're saying he knows the will of God, and wants to work the will of

143

God," he said, staring back seriously into Pendragon's eyes "and to him, that means helping *us?*" he said.

Pendragon nodded, eyes wide with amazement and cheeks pulled up into an unstoppable grin, and he could only shrug and open his arms in a gesture of grateful incredulity, saying "Yes!" and once again, "Yes!" He shook his head in wonderment and the two brothers embraced each other. They held their large bodies close as the excitement, wonder and thrill of a thousand different thoughts coursed through their heads. Having returned from Brittany unsure what they would face, most probably years of grinding war, they now faced the prospect of securing the reign much more quickly, and having to move onto the next phase—governing the stable country— much sooner than they expected. Which was good... except that they had planned for, and been trained mostly for war, violent, bloody war, with stability a vague and illusory goal—that they had barely planned for at all.

At last they pulled apart, and gazed upon each other, dumbfounded in wonderment. Uther's gaze lingered on the crown atop his brother's head, and thought excellent, Pendragon will receive invaluable advantages that will secure his place as king for several decades, and he, Uther, will gain all the advantages of being the brother of the king, and second in command. "You will be unstoppable," said Uther.

"*We*, brother," said Pendragon. "This old man who spoke to you," he said, "would you recognize him if you saw him again?"

Uther nodded with certainty. "Of course, I can still see his face before me."

"Because, and you may know this as fact, he will speak to us eleven days from now," said Pendragon. "Let's do all we can to be ever together on that day, until he comes, so I can see whether or not I will recognize him."

They clasped their hands in agreement. "Congratulations to us," said Uther. "We thought we would face years of nothing but fighting," It still seemed almost too amazing to talk about. "With the knowledge and advantages this Merlin offers us...."

144

"We can rule," finished Pendragon, "instead of merely fighting for our rightful place. We can use that time to create the country that we want." He paused. "And which Merlin wants."

"Yes," said Uther, nodding his head in a goofy way. "As long as we want what Merlin wants," he said jokingly, and they both laughed together, acknowledging the strangeness of the situation.

Neither could think of anything else for the next few days. Merlin was stuck deep in their heads, like a song.

-27-

Merlin and Blaise were involved in a game of chess. They peered over the board, eyes moving from piece to piece, plotting out the possible scenarios for each, as both men stroked their gray beards. Merlin had promised not to use his knowledge of the future to influence the game, which was the only condition under which Blaise would consent to play. No, Merlin assured him, he wanted to test and train his own strategic abilities and skills of guessing potential future outcomes without resorting to his second sight. Although, when he found himself cornered, it was very difficult not to give the future just the tiniest once-over.

Merlin had showed Blaise his middle-aged hermit appearance, and said it would become known as his primary appearance from that time, and this was how they should know him. That is the guise in which he sat with Blaise then.

Blaise studied the layout of the pieces. "How are you finding the brothers?" he asked.

Merlin sighed. "They are quite…" he thought, then said, "sweet. Pendragon has great nobility in him, and is genuine in his wish to help his people, so that is excellent, and I think I might help him in making great strides for the country, before Arthur comes." He reached forward and his hand covered a rook, but he chose not to move it. "Uther," he said. "Uther is a robust warrior, and yearns with great heart to be a good and respected leader, but thinks so little of himself that he is afraid he doesn't have it in him. Honestly, they are both quite young and changeable, and I still have much to learn about them."

Blaise's eyes stayed on the board. "But if you can see the future..." he said, and let his upturned open palms complete the sentence for him.

"I know," sighed Merlin, "but it is still quite vague. The future is not like the past. It is undecided. And uncertain. And unfocused. And while I can sometimes see an event quite strongly, the path to get to that event is often obscure." He reached out and, after all that deliberation, moved a pawn one space. "I can move things around, and sometimes the path reveals itself quite clearly. And sometimes people— like these brothers and their friends—do unforeseen things that alter my plans. Or they don't take my advice," he said. "Or they think that yes, I have access to all of the knowledge that has ever existed in the world, but *they're smart too*, and they want to make their own decisions," Merlin sat back in his chair, "and that alters the future. You know how changeable people can be."

Blaise merely grunted. He leaned forward and was closely examining the board.

"These brothers are particularly headstrong," said Merlin. "Perhaps they have too much faith in the claim of their birthright. Well, honestly, I need to know them better, and I will need to know that they believe in me absolutely, which they will need to do. This is the point of all this appearing in this guise and that; that they come to believe in me completely, even more than their own senses."

Blaise looked up momentarily. "By coming to them as all sorts of different people?"

"Not just that, but people who predict things, and other people who confirm those predictions. And with these brothers, who are very confident in themselves—at this stage, overconfident—I will need to tell them a great deal of what they most want to hear, for that most wins favor with boys of this type. And with that in mind," Merlin reached

146

behind him and brought forward a piece of parchment, a pen and vial of ink, "I will have you write a letter for me, if you don't mind. Uther has his mind very much on a lady friend of his, and if I can bring him a letter from her, telling him what would make him happiest to hear, he would have great trust in me."

Blaise sat back. "You want me to write a letter from a young woman?"

Merlin nodded. "I will dictate."

Blaise pointed a finger at the young wizard. "You're not involving me in any deceit of which I would disapprove, are you?"

Merlin threw his outstretched hand innocently over his heart. "How can you imagine such a thing?" asked the seer. "It is only positive tidings for the young man, who is actually quite a romantic, although he possesses the technique of a boar. It will make him positively disposed toward me, which will make it easier for him to accept me as a friend."

Blaise still peered at him suspiciously.

"So that I may better guide them in drawing our country toward God," said Merlin.

Blaise nodded, then reached out and, with a swift move of his bishop, eliminated the pawn that Merlin had just brought forward. "Okay," he said. "Let us do it now."

Merlin stared at the board. That pawn was the beginning of a long series of moves he had planned. "It's not fair," he said.

"How is that?" Blaise asked.

"I have natural gifts," Merlin said. "They were not my asking, yet I am punished for it in play."

Blaise rolled his eyes. "You're saying it's not fair that you aren't allowed to use your unfair advantage," he said.

"Let us begin this letter," said Merlin, "while we are at this natural pause in play."

Blaise took up the pen and paper and set down the words as Merlin said them, which we will spare you now, as you are to hear them later, and only once did Blaise put down his pen and look askance at Merlin.

"He should ignore the will of her husband and ravish her in private?" asked Blaise.

Merlin shrugged. "These are young people," he said. "They... well, you know what gets these young bucks going today."

Blaise went back to the writing. "No, I certainly do not," he grumbled.

Soon enough the letter was finished, and while the ink was still wet, Merlin removed a small blue glass vial from his robe, dumped out a white powder onto his palm, and blew it onto the letter, where it sent a pale cloud billowing across the table.

"What is that?" asked Blaise.

"Just a perfume of sorts," said Merlin.

"It doesn't smell very flowery," said Blaise.

"I don't pretend to know what these kids might like," said Merlin, taking up the letter and tucking it away. "Now," he said, regarding the chess board once more, "shall we finish this ludicrous game you have involved me in?"

-28-

It was already past the hour of nones, and no sign of Merlin. Pendragon and Uther had spent the entire day together, sitting, talking, conducting business and receiving visitors on carpets laid down between their pavilions. In the morning it was kind of fun, and each was eager to make the acquaintance and earn the friendship of the seer, but as the hours went on, the thrill started to fade away, and it just became kind of annoying. Uther, who normally would go forth with his great friend Ulfius and the other knights to train with swords and exercise his skills of battle—as well as have a few drinks and maybe befriend a few comely maidens of the nearby towns—was now stuck at his brother's side as he met with advisors, looked at maps and planned out strategies, mediated disputes between men... it was growing quite dull, and he looked longingly toward the creek that ran beside their campground, for it was also rather hot in the sun, and the idea of running over for a dip sounded wondrously refreshing.

"How long do you have to wait?" asked Ulfius. He was the same age as Uther, twenty, and the both of them had known, grown and fought alongside each other all their lives. He was a large, imposing strong man, like Uther, but where Uther had long hair and a beard that came down to the middle of his chest, Ulfius sported a great, thick mustache that curved down to his chin beside his mouth, and was matched in rich darkness by his deeply-set eyes and thick black eyebrows. He also always sought fun and adventure, like Uther, and loved drink, women, and a good laugh, which made them excellent merry companions.

Uther opened his hands and shrugged. His eyes indicated that he found the wait tedious, but he didn't want to let on too much in front of his brother, who was always a bit more able to focus on tasks of little amusement. They both blew their cheeks out in frustration, and Uther drummed his fingers on the arm of his chair.

Ulfius cocked his thumb toward the creek. "Can't we just go have a splash in the creek? It's so beastly hot," he said. "We could be back in five minutes."

"Let me ask my brother," Uther said, and made a face indicating, between friends, that he found it a drag to have to ask his brother for permission. Ulfius pursed his lips and nodded, his arms folded before him, legs stretched straight out, almost too big for the chair in which he sat.

Pendragon was involved in poring over a map that showed the nearby Saxon encampments, and seemed slightly peeved to have to take time away from his work, and to once more be the serious, disapproving one, telling his brother no. "I would very much like you to be here when Merlin comes," he said.

Uther nodded, but indicated the creek. "Five minutes," he said.

"I know it is hot," said Pendragon. "I'm sorry, but I have these obligations. If you could wait an…" and then he looked over all he had to do, "two hours, I could go with you."

Uther huffed. "I know he's coming, but," and here he indicated their pavilions, "all day?"

"You could occupy yourself by helping me," said Pendragon. "This strategy will involve you, too."

"I do help you," said Uther, turning away.

At that moment one of their guards brought a small, skinny boy messenger forward. "This boy brings a message for Uther," the guard said.

"Great tidings from your lady," said the boy, a knowing gleam in his eye, as he waved the letter in his hand.

"See?" said Pendragon. "That will help you pass the time."

Uther's eyes snapped to alertness and he gazed on the letter greedily. "Can I listen to it in my pavilion?" he asked his brother. "You can see if anyone goes in or out. It's just there."

Pendragon looked up from his maps and leaned to the side to examine the entrance of Uther's pavilion. He could clearly see it, not more than twenty feet away. "Post a guard," he said.

"Of course," said Uther, indicating with a finger that the boy follow him. As he passed Ulfius, who was still in the same, desultory pose, he said with a wink. "A message from my lady."

The messenger boy was eagerly eyeing Ulfius, taking note of his size, demeanor and appearance.

The knight sprang up immediately. "A-ha!" he said. "This brightens the day considerably. Let's hope she allows herself to be a bit saucy." He made to follow Uther and the boy into the tent.

Uther put up a hand. "Let me hear it first in private," he said.

Ulfius was pulled up short, then rolled his eyes. "Ugh," he said, "young lovers." He pointed a finger at his friend. "I will expect a faithful report, leaving out no detail, no matter how salacious."

Uther laughed. "Oh, you will hear all about it, as usual."

The knight tossed his head as though he didn't care. "Fine," he said, "you go in that hot pavilion there, I am going to check out the creek."

"Ah, you bastard," Uther said. "Have at it, and if I'm ever set at liberty, I will find you there." Then he looked down at the boy, who was watching them both carefully, absorbing every detail, and tapped him on the shoulder, indicating that they go in. The knight went his way, while Uther and the boy entered the quiet, dark confines of the tent.

The boy stood patiently while Uther fastened the tent's flaps, then turned to face him. The boy held the letter out toward him. "Blissful tidings from your lady!" said he. "She greets you and wishes you the utmost strength and speed in your campaign."

"Read it to me," said Uther.

"First, look on her hand," said the boy. "Smell her perfume. Her greeting is much more than the words she says."

Uther took the letter and broke the seal. As he unfolded the letter, he jumped with a quickly uttered "Ah!" and put his finger into his mouth. The paper had given him a small cut on his index finger. He looked at her graceful hand as he sucked on his finger, then put his nose to the paper and inhaled, smelling a slight trace of womanly scent, which intoxicated his nostrils and caused him to close his eyes. He quickly handed the letter back to the boy, careful to keep his finger away, as it was bleeding slightly.

"Now read it," he said.

Uther sat down on some of the pillows arranged in his sleeping space, while the boy stood standing in front of him. He leaned back against the wooden support of the tent. "You were with my lady when she wrote this?" he asked.

"Yes," said the boy. "She spoke very highly of you and said she missed you greatly, but admired the adventure you are on and knows that you will be brave and heroic."

"Okay, enough," said Uther. "Read it."

The messenger boy read it out, stopping to embellish details, based on his own memory, or to commend Uther for having won the true love of so fair and noble a lady, even though she were married to another man.

"And she says," went on the boy, "'when my husband is present I may not respond, may even scorn you, or scorn the gifts that you offer me, but know with certainty that my heart beats for no one but you, and that my husband will never again command both my thoughts and my emotions as you can. For this reason I tell you to never believe that I do not love you, no matter how much I may make it seem like it is the opposite, for that is what it means to have won the undying love of one who is wedded to another.'" The boy paused and watched the effect of these words on the young knight. "'Always believe in my love, no matter how much I turn away from you, and know with great certainty that when we are once more in private, I will repay your patience, and your faithfulness.'"

Uther had the boy read the letter several times over, and kept him around for hours in conversation, where he asked for news of his lady and how she was doing, and feeling, and how she spoke of him. Then Uther took the letter himself and discharged the boy, and finally, when he felt ready, emerged from the pavilion, just as night was falling.

As time passed, darkness enveloped the camp, the king and his brother ate, Ulfius sat with them and drank and made merry talk, and they each heard the contents of Uther's letter—or at least as much as he would have them know—and they spent their night in this way until it was almost midnight, by which time Ulfius had retired, leaving the brothers alone, sitting around the small fire.

"Well," Pendragon said, "the day is almost over, and no Merlin," he said, eyes lowered in disappointment. "I guess he lied to us."

Both shook their heads, for each had entertained his own thoughts of all the success they might achieve with the seer's favor, and now... well, they were almost too tired to work through all the implications. "That is a great disappointment, and I—but wait!" Here Uther leapt to his feet, eyes scanning the darkness, then abruptly he turned to his brother. "Stay here, and I will introduce you to someone almost as wondrous."

He ran off after someone he had seen, and a moment later returned, guiding a small, wizened old man in a worn cloak, almost pushing the old man forward in his excitement to introduce him to his brother. "Pendragon!" Uther said, "Look, this is the man who warned me of Hengist's attack, and he who saved my life!"

When Pendragon's eyes alighted on the little man, he could not prevent a warm, knowing smirk from forming on his lips, for he knew exactly who it was. "Very pleased to meet you," he said, reaching forth his hand.

The old man took it and smiled knowingly, but Uther was too excited to wait. "Hengist attacked me just as you said," he told the man. "How did you know he was in the camp? And unarmed? Who are you, anyway? Do you live in these parts?"

The old man smiled at all the questions, and he glanced over at Pendragon with a conspiratorial look. "I will be happy to explain everything to you," he said.

"My brother knew of Hengist's attempt on my life," said Uther, "and that you came to me before to warn me, although he was halfway across the country at the time."

The old man nodded. "He could not have known if someone hadn't told him," he said. "Come into your pavilion and I will show you some wonders of which I know about," and he led them to the opening of the pavilion.

The old man went in first and bid them stay outside, and when, a second later, he called for him to enter, they came in and saw the young boy who had brought the letter to Uther that morning. Uther was astonished, for he had seen no one enter or leave, and could not find the old man anywhere. He even asked the messenger boy if he had seen the old man, which made both the boy and Pendragon laugh. Then the boy had them go outside again, and when he bid them enter once more, Uther found Merlin in a form he had never seen before, that in which he had spoken to Pendragon, and the form which he had decided would be his primary appearance, the bearded hermit in his forties. And he had them once more go outside, and when he called for them to enter again, Uther now found the wizened old man once more. This man called

Pendragon to him and whispered in his ear, then bid them to step out once more, and as they did, Pendragon repeated what the old man had said, which were details of the letter he had received earlier, that Uther had kept secret. Uther was thoroughly bewildered, and astonished (and a bit embarrassed), but when they entered once more, and found the bearded man in his forties, while no one had been seen entering or leaving the tent. At last, Pendragon said to Merlin "Sir, are you ready for me to tell my brother your name?"

Merlin smiled with great mischief. "Yes, please," he said.

"Uther," said the king, "this man is the old man who appeared to you, and the young boy who brought you the letter, and a great many different people whom I have seen. This is Merlin," the king gestured with an open hand, "whom I travelled to Northumberland to seek. And this man has knowledge of every single thing that has ever happened, as well as of everything that is yet to come."

Uther looked at the man before him for a long while, as numerous calculations went through his head. "Thank you for saving my life," he said to Merlin, "let me say that first." Merlin bowed and made a gesture of welcome. "And king," he said, turning to his brother, a smile growing on his face, "this man could be of great use to us."

Merlin addressed them as one. "I want both of you to understand that there is nothing I wish to know that I cannot know. And king," he addressed Pendragon, "do you have any doubt that the things I have said to you are true?"

"You have never lied to me so far," said Pendragon.

"And Uther," Merlin said, "did I not tell you the truth about the love of your lady, and the plotting of Hengist?"

"I could never disbelieve you, after all you have told me" he said. "And because you are so wise and worthy, I ask you to always be about my brother and offer him your knowledge and protection." He put his arm about Pendragon's shoulder.

Merlin bowed to the brothers. "I will gladly remain by your side, and I wish very greatly to be friends with you two, worthy and noble brothers, and to help you to drive out the Saxons and reclaim Britain for its rightful people. To this end, I will offer you all of my knowledge and every great advantage that you could ever wish."

Uther and Pendragon were both so excited by this they could say nothing, and only looked at each other, chests puffed up with tickled anticipation, smiles they could barely contain. In their eyes, each other saw many thoughts swirling of all that could be accomplished with the help of a peerless seer such as this. Pendragon, as king, would be all but unstoppable, and Uther would be right there, second to the king but without his obligations and responsibilities.

"There are some things you must know, however," said Merlin, and he bid the two brothers to sit on the pillows arrayed across one side of the room, while he remained standing before them. "I want you to know, and I tell you this because you must understand my ways if we are to be friends, and allies. You know that I am the son of the devil. And because of this I must, by the force of my nature, be away from all people at certain times. But I promise you that, wherever I am, I will be more aware of both of you, and everything that you do, than anyone else. And as soon as I know that either of you are in any kind of difficulty, I will come straightaway to help you and offer my advice."

The brothers found themselves choked up by the plain and unadorned offer of devotion, and both of them simply nodded in response and gratitude.

"And if you wish to keep me on friendly terms," said Merlin, "you will not grumble when I go away, and whenever I come, you will show all people under your leadership how grateful and glad you are to have me back, so that all the worthy people will follow your example and be glad to see me as well. There will be, and are, evildoers among those you call your men, those who hate you and will hate me, but if you always show me cheerful face, they will not dare expose themselves by doing otherwise."

The brothers nodded gravely, and shared a glance, wondering who among their men might the wizard be speaking.

"Also be assured that I will not come to you in any shape other than this, or appear in any other guise without your knowledge. I will make your advisors and close liegemen aware of who I am, such that,

155

when I return to you, they will be happy too, and tell you how lucky you are to have such a great seer on your side."

Both brothers agreed heartily.

"Then, in our unshakable trust, you may ask me any question that comes into your mind, and I will counsel you with the best information it is possible for anyone to give. But I tell you plainly," and here he pointed at one brother, then the other, "it is in your best interest to honor this trust between us, and never damage it, for if you ever lie to me, I will know it instantly, and this will hurt you greatly, but me, it will harm not a bit." He looked at each of them gravely to let this warning sink in. "Ask of me anything you must to believe in the words that I tell you, but do not toy with me frivolously, or disrespect and dishonor our trust by lying to me."

Both brothers nodded. "I will test the truth of everything that you say," said Pendragon, "but I will never lie to you or test you frivolously."

Merlin nodded, smiled, then clapped his hands. "Then gather your closest advisors and the liegemen that you trust the most, and in three days I will show you how clever I am, and what great advantage you enjoy with me!" He held his arms out wide, striding back and forth before them like a great and eager showman, and both brothers could not help but grin eagerly and bounce in their seats with excitement.

"On that day, you and your men will hear how you may drive the Saxons out in great numbers, and enjoy a singular military triumph, yet without the loss of a single man on either side." He pointed at both brothers. "Gather your men, and hear it predicted. Then, when you accomplish it, all of your men, and all of those people of this land who follow you, will see your achievement and know without doubt," and here he opened his hands in a wide and sweeping gesture, "that the sons of Constance have returned, and are truly the worthy and rightful rulers of this land!"

Three days later, the king had gathered all his trusted advisors and the men he held closest to him and introduced them to Merlin. For those advisors who had known him during Vortiger's time, he did as he had done with Uther, and showed them his true guise as a seven year old boy, then showed them the guise of the hermit in his forties, which they of course assumed to be his real appearance, as it accorded more with what they thought a wise seer should look like.

When this happened, Sir Brantius felt something akin to anger begin to stir in him. He had not spent all of his years toiling in education and enduring the humiliations of the court while spiraling ever-closer to the king just to be shunted aside by a lucky brat with a few runes to cast. The boy could take on any appearance, and now took on the sympathetic look of a wise and weary adult man, when Brantius knew him to be an inexperienced child—and he would show the king that, as soon as he could.

His pique rose even further as Merlin took the floor, immediately in front of the king and Uther, seated slightly to his right, while Roldan, Ulfius and all the others sat around him in a worshipful circle. "Now," said Merlin, "the Saxons who followed Hengist remain in the castle that you have been besieging, but you are unable to make any progress there. What do your advisors say about how to be rid of them?"

"Just keep at them," said Uther. "They're surrounded. It's only a matter of time before we break in, and then they'll have it."

"A good plan," said Merlin, "but you lose more men every day, and you cannot move forward to make progress in this country until they are bested." Merlin turned to look around the faces of the gathered advisors. "Is there another way?"

"Rain on them with flaming arrows and flung balls of fire, and burn them in their castle until they come out," said another.

"Another path to take," said Merlin, pointing at the man. "You continue to lose men, it's true, and the outlook is not at all certain, but it might work," he said, "eventually. Are there any other ideas?"

Brantius stepped forward, cleared his throat and kept his gaze down modestly. "I have always felt," he began, "that we lose much in simply killing these Saxon men, who are very fearsome and skilled in battle. Instead," he lifted his hands, held still, as though in the birth of a great thought, and let his palms fall forward, "if they surrender, or are defeated in battle, let them join us." He then shook his head as though overwhelmed by the simple humanity of it all. "Induce them to offer their allegiance to us and we only become stronger."

Merlin harrumphed. "And grow further away from the spirit of the British people, while also inviting future saboteurs into your ranks," he said, walking right by Brantius with a dismissive wave. "No, that is not it."

Brantius stood, still in his attitude of great wisdom, while all eyes were once again on the wizard, his words forgotten. His face burned, and he vowed then and there that he would eliminate that little prick.

"I want you all to know," said Merlin, raising his open hand, "that since the Saxons lost Hengist, all they want to do is give up your land and flee."

All the gathered men, including Brantius, gasped. No one had thought of that.

"They have no leader," Merlin continued. "Their food is running out. They are tired, and weary of fighting, and they miss the sight of their home, and have come to despise the sight of yours. All this you will find out tomorrow, when you have your best man," and here he pointed at Ulfius, who straightened up in surprise, "ride to them and offer them a truce."

"A truce!" Brantius could not help but exclaim.

Indeed, the word had never entered their minds.

"You will offer them a truce," continued Merlin, "for three months. The Saxons do not have enough food to last three months," the wizard added confidentially, then made a gesture of wiping his hands.

"You will offer them safe passage to the sea, and the ships to return home in."

"Give them the ships!" Roldan repeated in admiration.

"Ships don't grow on trees," said Brantius.

"They cost less in the long sum than the constant loss of good men," said Merlin, pointing directly to Brantius. Then he turned once more to address the king. "Call on them to leave you the land that belonged to your father, offer them safe passage out, and give them the means to get back to the land they love. You can do this without the loss of a single one of your good men, and they will both be grateful to your wisdom and wary of your power."

King Pendragon could barely suppress his beaming smile, for he could see what a brilliant, unexpected plan the seer had presented him with. Uther looked at him, amazed smile on his face, and shook his head in wonderment. Pendragon took Uther's outstretched hand and they held for a moment in triumph, then the king stood to his feet. "You have spoken well, Merlin," said the king. "I will do exactly as you say."

Merlin nodded, and in the next moment, he and a crowd of fawning admirers were following him out of the room. Brantius stood, astounded and bewildered as men gathered around the king, patting him on the back in congratulation.

"Rid of the Saxons without so much as a fight!" said one of the advisors. "This Merlin could be an unimaginable advantage to our kingdom!"

The king, still beaming, nodded. "If this works out as he says," Pendragon added, "Merlin will never leave my court!"

The words chilled Brantius as he felt a tingling anxiety spread across his wrinkled forehead. His eyes watched after the shuffling form of the seer as he left, surrounded by the excitedly chattering close advisors to the king.

30

Merlin had been scanning all though the land, and had come upon a few woodworkers who produced works of great intricacy, narrowed those down to those who believed in the creed and the faith, and started visiting them in disguise. Over time, he came down to one who had a small workshop on the outskirts of Carduel. Merlin showed up one day, in his chosen daily, middle-aged appearance, and approached the man, who was sitting outside his workshop, smoking a pipe.

"Good day, sir," said Merlin. "I understand that you do very fine work with wood."

"I do indeed," said the man. "Have you work for me?"

"I do," said Merlin. "I have a small job, which will require great skill and dexterity, and if you perform it well, I may have a much larger commission for you."

The man nodded, and slowly rose, requiring a great deal of effort and time to bring his elderly body into a standing position. "Let's go in and see what you've got," he said. "Is that part of what you'd like me to work with?" he asked, pointing to a large branch that Merlin held in one hand, and the canvas bag held in his other.

Merlin nodded, and they entered the dark of the woodshop, which was warm and smelled of sawdust. In the center was a large table, and lining the walls were various benches and pegs which held several woodworking tools of every description. It was a welcoming place, and the more time Merlin spent there, the more convinced he was that he had found the right man.

The man, who introduced himself as Upton, patted the table and indicated for Merlin to place his materials there. He put the branch on the table, and put the canvas bag down, which landed with a heavy thud.

"I would like you to make me a staff out of this branch," said Merlin. "My intention is that it serve me the rest of my life."

"That's how I make them," said Upton. "That looks like a nice sturdy piece of wood."

Merlin smiled, and nodded. "It is from a immensely great tree in a very wild forest in the Orkneys."

"Ah-ha," said the man, and reached out to caress the bark of the branch.

Merlin watched him, and liked his manner and way of touching his materials quite well. He then removed a large, flattish stone of about two feet in length, which had been broken off from the massive stone that covered the white dragon. He then removed several other, smaller stones, some of which Blaise had found, and some of which he had collected himself. Before he could continue, the woodworker's eyes focused on these stones, and he reached forward to grab one.

"Ah," Upton said, and his eyes raised swiftly to look at Merlin, and he let his gaze sweep the wizard up and down, before fixing him in the eyes once more. Merlin was surprised and delighted, tickled by the man's behavior.

"Mmm-hmmm," the man said, feeling the stone in his hand, then reaching out to grasp another. "Oh ho!" he said, and put them both down. "You are some sort of... cleric?" he asked.

Cleric, " Merlin spat. "No. You might call me more of a," he searched for the word, "mystic. Independent mystic."

"An independent mystic," Upton repeated. He let his fingers poke amongst the stones that Merlin had brought. "And you need the right tool," he added.

"Exactly," Merlin said.

And they both passed a moment in comfortable silence.

"I would like a staff of about this height," Merlin motioned with his hand. "I would like a shaft from this stone," he indicated the white dragon stone, "in the upper core of the stick, exposed on the top. I want a piece of it exposed at the bottom end as well, where it will touch the earth."

The man remained looking at him for some time, rhythmically puffing away at his pipe. "I get you," he said at last.

"I would like some of these smaller stones cut into small shafts, and inlaid in the wood going down to about a foot from the top," Merlin said. The man nodded. "They must penetrate into the wood from the outside, and touch the shaft of the central stone within."

The man nodded, and raised his eyes to Merlin, a knowing, and impressed, smile on his face. "My, my, my" he said. "What a staff this will be."

"Indeed," said Merlin. "There must be greatly skilled workmanship amongst the wood and stones within," he said. "They must lock together with great precision, without the slightest hollow within."

Upton crossed his arms. "I could cut the stones," he said, "but if you really want them cut the best they could possibly be—"

"I do," said Merlin.

"Then I would recommend that you also engage the services of my friend Lanford, who is a stonemason of great skill and," he reached out his hand and wiggled his fingers above the stones, "sensitivity," he finished. "To stones. I could arrange it all for you."

"That sounds quite nice," said Merlin.

"We work together quite well," said Upton. "We discovered that years ago." He picked up the branch with his arm and held it, turning it this way and that.

"I have great hopes for the finished result," said Merlin. "As I said, we will consider this somewhat of a test," he said. "If you complete this to the level of artfulness that I require, then I shall return in a year or so with a much larger, far more intricate commission." He regarded the man with smiling eyes, for he liked him greatly. "One that will bring you much renown and acclaim."

The man came around the table, and stepped close to Merlin, all the while holding him with his steady, reverent gaze. He took Merlin's hand, and held it with great tenderness and care.

"It is a great honor to meet you, sir," Upton said, lowering his head.

162

31

So the king went with Merlin, Uther, Ulfius and a few other of his men and advisors, and camped near the castle that the Saxons occupied. Ulfius was sent with a group of knights to ride to the gate of the stronghold, and when the Saxons saw them, they sent out a small contingent to meet them.

Ulfius told them that the king sought a truce, and would allow them safe passage out of the country as well as give them the ships to leave on if they agreed to depart without further warfare. The Saxons took the news back and conferred amongst themselves. They had little food left to feed themselves, and so some of them, who were wearied by their endless war in that land, argued that they should take the offer and leave right away. But others spoke louder and said that they had come all that way, made all that effort, and all of that would be lost if they gave up now. They prevailed, and so the messengers were sent back to Ulfius' group to tell them that they would agree to a truce if the king lifted the siege but left them the castle. In return they would give him, each year, ten knights, ten maidens, and a hundred each greyhounds, warhorses and palfreys.

Ulfius took the news and told it to the king, who sat down, considering it thoughtfully. It would certainly end the useless loss of men and expenses that were going down the drain in the protracted siege, and allow him to use those resources in repairing the newly-secured parts of the country. He would have taken the deal, but Merlin would not hear of it.

"No," the wizard said, "they must leave. Becoming entangled in such an affair will only make things worse, and lengthen your problems with these invaders. Besides," he continued, "they want to leave, for they have nothing to eat. They are just trying to retain their honor, but they have gone too far for that now."

Then Merlin strode right by the king and issued these orders to Ulfius. "Tell them they will have no truce if they do not depart, but each of them will be taken prisoner and die a shameful death, for we have no need of their people in this country. But if they go," Merlin raised a finger, "they will have their lives, and safe passage to the sea, where we will hand over the ships they will need to return to their country."

Now Merlin turned to the king. "I promise you that they will take this proposal and go of their own will, for what they hide from you is that they have nothing to eat, and will be starving here within a month if they stay."

Then the king looked strange, and felt strange, for Merlin had clearly already given the order, and what now was left to him—to repeat it? He stood, and did exactly that, sending Ulfius back with the message. And when the Saxons heard that they could leave without further trouble, they agreed with stern faces, but in their hearts they were overjoyed.

So the king and his party returned, each in wonder that the siege that had, a day ago, seemed endlessly violent and intractable, would end without another loss of life on either side. Many stepped up to congratulate the king on his triumph, and his unique, nonviolent solution to the matter—one which none of them had ever even considered, or thought possible—and the king took these accolades smilingly but remained quiet, for in his heart he knew clearly that this achievement had little, or nothing, to do with him.

-32-

Then it was the day the Saxons who had held with Hengist were to leave. King Pendragon, Uther, Ulfius, all of the advisors and Merlin, as well as countless of Pendragon's men were to gather to see them out. The ceremony to mark their leaving was to be a complicated construction composed of interleaved layers of honor and humiliation. On the one hand, they were leaving in defeat from a country they had intended to invade and colonize. On the other, they had made a pragmatic decision to leave peacefully, especially once their leader, who had pushed for the invasion, was dead, leaving only his followers, who weren't entirely sure why they were there in the first place. And this pragmatic decision allowed them to leave without further loss of men— who were gradually being decreased every day that they held out pointlessly and Britain kept them constantly besieged—and allowed them to walk out with honor. Only, on a further level, with the Britons lining a path that the Saxon troops would take out of their castle stronghold, forcing them to march past their victors as they went, it was an honorable defeat with a subtle but clear level of humiliation. They could walk out honorably, but not without marching under the firm gaze of those who were ordering them out.

Merlin had advised, and Pendragon had issued firm orders, that his troops were not to make any contemptuous or mocking expressions to the Saxons as they left, each knowing full well that certain of his men would go ahead anyway, especially after engaging in close battle with the enemy for so long. But it was an occasion in which the fact of the official orders mattered, even more than the reality of how they were enforced. Merlin told Pendragon to convey to his men how a nonviolent victory with honor could be even more satisfying than a simplistic killing of a foe, an idea which ran counter to the ideals the troops had ever been exposed to, although they were willing to try it out and see how it felt.

On certain occasions such as this, a king is aware that the events of that day will be recorded and become part of history. As Pendragon dressed for the day—or more accurately, was dressed, although he was getting used to being "alone" while several servants hovered about him—his mind was both blank, as he knew there would be a certain amount of simply walking through the events of the day, and at a high awareness that numerous eyes would be on him, and his every movement and facial expression would be observed and parsed for any shades of meaning they might contain. It was to be a historic day, one that would alter the course of the country, and it would forever be known as one that he presided over as king. It was, even before it happened, to be one of the most significant events in the reign of King Pendragon. Because of that, Pendragon almost couldn't allow his thoughts to stray too far, or he feared he would go down a path that could find it all unraveling, collapsing under the weight of its tremendous importance. There would be a great deal of simply staring forward, not thinking anything, just allowing the day to pass without incident, and that, he told himself, was really the best thing he could do. When he thought about all the eyes that would be on him, or the incredible significance of the day, he started to quail inside, and the thought of sitting atop his horse for hours as the Saxons trudged past seemed like an onerous obligation he would have preferred not to endure. No, a large part of being king is merely being a symbol, he thought, and today was the day to be nothing but a symbol, to empty himself and simply be seen there, solid and strong and blank, for all watching to project their own thoughts onto. He hadn't thought that he would ever become such a person—he honestly hadn't really thought that being a king would be composed of so many of these absolutely bizarre moments—but he found himself there, at that time, preparing to make his big achievement for the day simply sitting regally atop a horse.

Of course, his real achievement was the truce, and the departure of the Saxons. That is what people would remember, and that is what history would record about that day. It would be Pendragon's achievement! Although it was Merlin's idea. Here was another area of thought that was best given a wide berth. Whose achievement was it? It would go down as Pendragon's, and all he had to do was keep quiet. It's not even like he was denying anyone rightful credit. That was the deal—Merlin had the brilliant idea, Pendragon carried it out, and got to accept credit for it. Those were, apparently, the terms of the "advantage" that he enjoyed with Merlin at his side. It was a great advantage—one that could not be refused. With it, he looked forward to a long, successful—perhaps, it was not too wild to think, an incredibly successful kingship.

He could go forward with his own ideas, but half of them, or more, would probably fail. Getting the Saxons to leave without a further life lost on either side—that idea never would have originated with him. He simply never, ever would have thought about it, so trained had he been, his entire life, for war. So, score one for Merlin. Pendragon had to know that if he had followed his own wisdom, they would have been locked in endless war for all of the future that could be foreseen. He had won, by enacting Merlin's plan. This was how Pendragon's first great victory was also a bit of a private defeat.

Not to mention that, in all the years he had dreamed of returning home to claim his birthright, and all the time he looked forward to facing, and surmounting, the challenges that kingship would throw at him, he never once imagined that he would never have to do any of that, because his role would primarily be as executor of someone else's ideas.

Still, who could knowingly turn away from assured success?

It was all too much to think about just then. Uther might tell him not to think about it at all. His younger brother was always exhorting him to think less, and act more, for he did have a tendency to get mired in the intricacies of complex situations. Perhaps it didn't matter at all, who really was running the country. And he did recognize it as the kind of thing that might drive him crazy. He put it out of his mind, and a few hours later, was at the front of a line of his troops, sitting atop his horse, just beside Uther and Ulfius, each on their own horses. Across from them, about thirty feet away, was another line of his own men, and in between, an open path for the Saxons to begin their trek toward the sea, to take their departure from the country.

They were in the wide valley near where Hengist had commandeered a large, heavily fortified castle and made it his stronghold. The castle loomed large and dark in the king's vision to the left. Straight ahead, a line of mountains that were topped in black rock, with a bright, vivid line of green grass that began a few hundred feet down from the ridge, and extended all through the valley in which the king and his men found themselves. Armies of Pendragon's men created a corridor leading from the castle on the left, extending to the king and past him, off about four hundred feet to the right, toward Winchester, and the sea. The day was cloudy but not cold, although wet, so much that the green of the grass shone bright under the lowering skies, as though lit from beneath.

There was a horn, and Pendragon could see some of his own men on horseback begin the procession from the castle. As the horses came slowly forward, behind them marched orderly lines of Saxon troops, in battalion after battalion about ten men across and twenty long, moving slowly down the open corridor toward the king. They would march past him, and continue, both led and followed by his men until they reached the port. They had no need to fear any Saxon rebellion on the way, since they were not allowing the enemy to leave with their weapons or armor. When they reached the sea, they would board the very ships that Pendragon and his men had arrived on, and take them back to Saxony.

The first Saxon troops trudged by the king. He was interested to see how they would react, and saw that most of them kept their eyes directed downward and stepped forward mechanically as they walked out in defeat. He could see some of them looking up to scan the faces of the men lined up alongside their procession, and a few of them gazed openly at the king as he passed. He sometimes returned their glances, seeing them angry, or proudly defiant, or merely curious and exhausted by fighting. But for the most part they kept their eyes down, and the king offered them the dignity of keeping his own face blank and expressionless, ensuring their departure, but trying not to shame or embarrass them any more than they already would be.

Then, at the front of the line of his own troops that faced him, he saw Merlin. He was directly across from him, and he stared at Pendragon so intently, with such a queer smile on his face, that it made the king very uncomfortable. He straightened to rigidity atop his steed, and looked away immediately, made very self conscious. Then he thought that might seem odd, he was friends with Merlin after all, and he turned his eyes back, expecting to wave hello at him—or maybe just nod? A wave seemed somehow undignified—but the wizard's eyes were trained on him with such an intense gaze, and at the same time, seeming somehow not to see him, that Pendragon's eyes instinctively jumped away.

He watched the lines of passing men as they approached, keeping his head angled a bit to the left to watch them, although he was still aware of Merlin out of the corner of his eye. Did the wizard mean to make him uncomfortable? Did he mean to—well, was he here, and so obvious, to hammer home that none of this was Pendragon's doing? No one had said that, obviously. No one but the king himself. But the presence of the wizard seemed to have some meaning, and it brought the king's mind right back to his line of thinking that morning; could any of this be credited to him? When he could stand it no more, for he felt the gaze of the seer like a nagging, uncomfortable presence, like an insect on his arm, his eyes darted back to him, and found him looking nearby—at Uther.

But his eyes returned to the king at once, in such a way that it seemed that he heard the king's thoughts, and Pendragon had to realize, in a way that he hadn't before, that Merlin was probably aware of every one of his thoughts. This made his skin crawl, to be honest. He remained absolutely motionless atop his horse, holding himself rigid in sudden nervousness, and his eyes looked immediately away, feeling suddenly naked, exposed, and he wanted nothing more than to be away from Merlin. This was followed by the immediate, and peerlessly unnerving, realization that Merlin probably knew that thought, too, and with it came a simple, singular impulse to flee. It took all his strength to simply sit in place, maintaining a placid expression as the Saxons continued to troop by.

He felt at once that Merlin must have been privy to his entire thought process of that morning, on whether this truce was really his own doing, and whether anything he might do during his own kingship would, in fact, be to his own credit. Was he to be a puppet king? Was he a puppet to this wizard? His eyes turned boldly to the wizard across from him at this, as though demanding an answer. He found the wizard looking at him, as though studying him, watching him as he went through all of these thoughts, and while he was able to share his gaze for a short time, once more he was forced to lower his eyes. Was he an object of study to the seer? Were they all? Or—was Merlin not thinking any of this at all? Was Merlin across from him right now to deliberately make him uncomfortable, so that he might be studied? That was definitely how it felt, and at once a wave of defiance hardened within him, and he could feel his jaw setting. He felt that this, this moment, was his triumph as king, and it made him angry that the wizard was there, distorting it all around him. Then it followed hard after that it wasn't even his triumph! It was true, Pendragon had done what was best for the country, but it was Merlin's doing, which....

Would be a great boon and advantage for the country. With this thought, the anger and tension dropped out of Pendragon, and he saw that this is what he needed to keep his eyes on. What was best for the country. That was where he and Merlin agreed, and when it came down to it, it didn't matter who did what, as long as the country succeeded. Pendragon then felt a little childish for being so petty. Maybe he was just a puppet for the wizard—maybe that made him lucky. He had been handed an advantage that no king on earth had ever had, and he would be a fool not to use it over a little matter of whether it was his own idea or someone else's. Besides, all of the glory would accrue to him. Everyone in the country would believe that it was his genius that led them, and Merlin was happy for him to take all the credit. Then Pendragon thought on how Merlin must feel; using his own knowledge and power to put the kingdom on the right path, while arranging for all the credit to go somewhere else. To him, in fact. Pendragon decided that if he had to be a wildly successful king, and it remained his little secret that someone else handed him all his best ideas, well, there were far worse fates.

And then he had what seems should be an obvious thought for a king, but wasn't: that when he became troubled, or confused, his first thought should be for the good of not himself, but the country. He was, after all, its king, which meant not that he was owed all the glory, but that he was entrusted to be the guardian of the lives of all within his realm. Looking at it that way, of course he would be blessed to receive the best advice he could get in order to live up to that trust.

Then his eyes turned once more to Merlin across from him, no longer with anger or fear, and he met the gaze of the wizard with confidence. Then he found that the expression of the seer had changed entirely, and regarded him with an overwhelming air of warmth and affection. Merlin smiled at him, not one of his creepy smiles, but a genuine expression of fond regard, and he nodded knowingly. One of the wizard's hands came up and gestured toward the king in a motion of reverence, and a moment later he slipped backward into the crowd and was lost from sight.

Pendragon breathed easier and simply sat, collecting his thoughts for a long while as he let the tension he had created in himself run out—something today's big kingly goal of "sit quietly on your horse and maintain a noble face" made blessedly possible. All of his worries of that morning now seemed, from a different perspective, to be nothing more substantial than pointless problems that he had worked up in his mind, and he could see that, if he allowed it, these illusions could easily get the better of him and perhaps even derail his kingship. That in addition to controlling the country, he also faced the challenge of controlling his own mind.

A movement nearby distracted him from his thoughts, and when he looked up, he saw the smiling Uther bring his horse a bit closer to him. The end of the line of Saxon troops had now emerged from the castle, and soon the entire group of invaders would be past them, continuing their procession to the sea, and out of the Briton's country. Pendragon was knocked forward by the impact of Uther's strong hand clapping him on the back.

"Well, brother," Uther said proudly, "you've done it."

Pendragon lifted his head up and looked back at him, mouth drawing into a half-smile while opening to respond, trying to think of something clever, mind thrown back on the irony of whether he had done anything at all, and while he was caught up in his thoughts, the moment passed and it seemed ridiculous to make any reply. He nodded warmly at his brother, smiled graciously, then turned his head away.

Part Three
THE THREEFOLD DEATH

Once the Saxon armies who had held with Hengist had departed, leaving only a few, unorganized strongholds scattered here and there throughout the realm, the country enjoyed a period of great peace, and Pendragon went about building new castles and repairing the towns and villages that had been damaged in the years of fighting. Acting on Merlin's advice, he gave generously to the people of the country and made visible improvements to their towns and cities, such that all knew him to be a good king, and the realm in good hands. Merlin advised him that it is always best for a king to be as generous as possible with his riches and attentions, for when many in his kingdom have personal and tangible reasons to be grateful to their leader, they all speak well of him and hold solid and lasting loyalty. About two years passed in this period of peace and growth.

During this time Pendragon earned much love and devotion from his people, but one who was not happy was Sir Brantius. He had seen Merlin barge in and take his place between him and Vortiger, and then he had seen him do the same to Pendragon, taking his place as foremost among the king's closest advisors, and pushing all others, who had won the king's confidence through years of toil and loyalty, that much further out. After Merlin's ingenious plan to have the Saxons merely walk out of their land—which could easily have been the result of a few well-placed spies or a very good guess—Brantius waited to see how things would settle out. But the king had no eyes, and certainly no ears, for anyone but Merlin, even though the seer spent long weeks away from the king's side. Soon it seemed that any hope of seeing the wizard permanently sent away, and Brantius claiming a place closer to the king's side—which anyone could understand the advantages of, both in honor and monetary gain—was not within the realm of possibility. Then Brantius began to seek a way to drive a wedge of doubt into the king's mind, and perhaps even have the purported wizard sent packing, or at least demoted to a place where latecomers to the king's party more rightly belonged.

Brantius had started to make a show of being troubled by the advice Merlin gave, or the degree of trust that the king showed in him, but neither the king nor his brother Uther took any heed of him, a fact that galled Brantius all the more. Then one day after Merlin had just left the room, and Pendragon was there alone, poring over maps, Brantius made a casual comment.

"He certainly is the most wise man now alive," he said. "Anyone could see why he has claimed complete rule over this kingdom."

The king said nothing, made no reaction, as Brantius stood to the side, observing while appearing to gaze at some papers in his hands. Pendragon rocked a little bit in his chair, stroked his beard, cleared his throat a bit, and finally, in a straightforward voice, said "Be assured, Sir Brantius, I retain complete rule over this kingdom."

"Oh!" Brantius threw his hand over his chest, as though he had misspoken. "Of course, sire! I just, oh, I'm so sorry!" He laughed. "I guess it's just, you know," he smiled intimately, "how it appears, or—what people say."

He went right back to examination of his papers and allowed the king to stew.

Pendragon said nothing, continued with his work, but Brantius could see him begin to tap his foot, scan over all the maps, reshuffle them, and examine one he had just looked at again. He was clearly distracted. Brantius said nothing, just stood back, pacing around the king, watching him closely from behind but appearing to look at his papers when he could be seen from the front. The king sighed, put down his maps and raised his eyes to the advisor, who was then looking away, pretending not to notice.

"Have you heard people say this?" said the king.

"Hm?" Brantius looked up from his work. "Oh, that Merlin is actually..." he paused, "the one in charge? Oh, no. I mean, not directly. But no," he said firmly. "Everyone knows," he said. "Everyone knows that you make all the important decisions. Yourself, that is."

He smiled at the king, who had put down his work and regarded him with a not unpleasant, but wearied expression. But Brantius knew how to read the subdued expressions of kings, who learned quickly to keep their most violent emotions in check, and chose that moment to seat himself beside the ruler and speak to him confidentially.

"But," he said, "do you ever wonder if you can—or should—give this man so much power? I would hate to see any harm come to you or the people under your rule."

The king raised his head. He thought about it for a moment, then said "No. I trust Merlin implicitly."

"You do," Brantius said, and lowered his head, staring at the maps spread across the table as he made show with furrowed brow of great troubling thoughts passing through his mind. At last he sighed. "Then I will say no more," he said, and rose to leave.

The king watched him as he went, and opened the door to go, slowly, and just as he was turning back to give the king one last, remorseful look, the king said "In what way might Merlin harm me?" he asked. "Or this country?"

Brantius closed the door immediately. "It is just—" he said, "well, it is widely known that all of the intelligence he gives you, and all of the powers that he has, are those given to him by the devil." He sat down once more at the same table as the king, and on his face an expression of concern verging on intense physical pain. "I know that your aims are the same as those shared by our Lord above. Is it not at least prudent to wonder if the advice he gives you is," and here he cringed, "in line with what the Lord wants? And would we even be able to know?" He shook his head. "Before it is too late."

The king returned to poring over his maps. "Merlin was baptized at birth," he said, "which allowed him to keep the devil's powers, but to use them to perform God's will."

"Yes, I have heard that," said Brantius. "Most wondrous. And we know that because…?"

Pendragon replied without a pause. "Because he told us."

Brantius said nothing, but looked at the king with concerned eyes, and waited for the import of the words to sink in, and the king to raise his eyes to meet his. Then he saw it there; the tiniest touch of doubt.

"And what with these periods in which he must flee from people, because he feels the devil's nature coming out in him," he picked up a paperweight from atop the maps and toyed with it absently as he made show that the thoughts were coming unbidden into his mind, "periods when he is in such a state, as he admits openly, he fears that he might do harm to people."

The king said nothing.

"Since it is the devil's everlasting nature to bring harm to people."

The king once more raised the map he was looking at, and cleared his throat. "We have had no reason whatsoever to distrust the advice that Merlin gives us."

Brantius shook his head to show that there was no doubt. "Well said. I'm sure it's nothing to be concerned over," he said. "And it's true that he had brought you nothing but advantage and excellent advice, so far, and won this lasting peace for you," he said. "So I suppose if there was any deceit behind it...." and his voice trailed off.

The king dropped his gaze to the maps before him, but Brantius could see that he was not looking at them. He quickly lowered his own eyes, looked at his fingernails, and gave the king's mind time to turn in its own rotation.

"I suppose it is for us to simply trust," said the advisor, "and believe that he has our best interests at heart," he said. "I just wish that more people in this land could see the great part that is your glory, and what you have accomplished by being the worthy leader that *you* are," he said as he put the paperweight down once more, and rolled it over with his fingers. "And not just believe that all of your achievements can be laid down to the advice of this seer."

The king remained with head lowered to the maps before him, and made no outward show of upset, or any reaction at all, but Brantius' words had now hit him where he was most tender. Because much as he had resolved to keep his mind only on what was best for the country, it was impossible to quell the nagging matter that nearly all of the

176

advantages he had gained could be traced back, directly or indirectly, to Merlin's advice and influence, and he wondered, exactly as Brantius had said, to what extent his people knew that his accomplishments were his own.

Worse, the seer had grown so close over the past few years, and been so inextricably involved with his own strategy and conquests, that he himself did not know any more which was his own part in the good things that he had brought about, and what was entirely to be laid down to the influence of the wizard.

It had been there, growing over time, especially in the past few months, this wish to do something that might be known widely as his own initiative. And a growing—slight, but growing—resistance to following Merlin's plans in favor of enacting a plan that was purely his own. To make his own decision. Would he ever get to do that?

Or would he have a glorious, successful rule, that would be spoken of as the work of his advisor the wizard?

What *was* best for the country, even… to have a king who brought prosperity, but was the lapdog of a seer? Or to be a leader of integrity, whose strengths were from within him, not without?

And, as Brantius mentioned, how did they even know that Merlin worked for God's aims? They knew that only because he told them so himself. Then an ugly image came into Pendragon's head, of himself in the same room he was now, sitting helpless, learning that Merlin had betrayed them and was now gone, the country in some sort of awful state. This would leave him to fix it alone, forcing him to rule by his own decision—which he had no experience of, since Merlin had told him everything he was to do up until that point. And all of the blame for whatever calamity was to happen would then accrue at his feet—for trusting the wizard, and handing over control of the state to him.

It's true that everything the wizard had said up until that point had been accurate. But if one started to wonder if he was just setting up for a grand deception, somehow even all that accuracy could seem diabolical.

"What would you do?" the king asked of Brantius. "I would not do anything that would have Merlin upset."

"Oh, I would never dare dream upset him," said Brantius, standing up once more and beginning to pace as he talked, "nor touch him in any way."

The king shook his head, but his eyes would not meet the other's. "I think you should leave this," he said.

"And for you never to know if he can be trusted?" he asked. "Until it is too late. I would only arrange to test his foreknowledge in a way that will cause no harm to anyone, but will reveal whether the powers he commands are his own, or the devil's." Brantius was careful to keep his eyes lowered and not appear overeager, for he did not want the king to think that this was a matter of any importance to him. "You would not appear to be involved at all."

He thought on his plan, and was pleased at his own intelligence, for it would not only shunt Merlin aside, but frame himself most prominently in the king's favor, as sole savior of the kingdom.

The king had not yet raised his eyes from the table, and he seemed to deliberate with great heaviness on what was being asked of him. He drew in a long breath, and his shoulders raised, then he slowly let it out in a sigh that seemed to go on a full minute. "If you can contrive a way to test him without any trace that he is being deceived," said the king, "I will allow it. But wit you well," he said, and raised his finger while lifting his eyes to stare with gravity at his loyal advisor, "you must be prepared to drop this matter entirely if there is any hint whatsoever that he suspects, or if there is any indication that your actions might lose his trust and the favor he has bestowed."

The thrill Brantius felt caused him to draw up quickly where he stood, and he had to tamp down his excitement so as not to betray his larger intentions. He could not wait to tell his wife of his plans, and to hear her dream aloud of their great advantages when he became closer, and even more trusted and respected of the king.

"You will see tomorrow, my lord," said he. "It will be, I think, nothing more than a question. He will have no idea at all that his wisdom and sight is being tested." Then he leaned forward and placed a warm hand on the king's forearm. "And you will be confirmed in your trust of him," he said, "or have warning that he is untrue, but at least

178

you won't have to go on just," and he lowered his voice to deliver the final jab, "blindly trusting."

The king nodded, pulled his hand back out from under the advisor's, and went back to studying his maps.

Brantius left the room at once, as there was no need to stay, and he knew when it was time to get out. Once the door was closed, and he saw that there was no one else within sight, he allowed himself three short jumps in place for sheer excitement.

-34-

The next day, the king and his advisors, including Brantius among many others, were sitting and poring over a list of proposed improvements to varying towns vying for royal funds, and which roads between towns to put effort toward making more stable, and safer, for such were the tasks of peacetime. Uther and Ulfius were, at that time, off in other towns.

Merlin sat quietly, elbow on table, head resting in his hand, drumming his fingers on the edge of the wood.

He watched Pendragon. He watched Brantius. And he waited, face carrying a grim and joyless expression. Drumming his fingers and waiting.

At last there was a break in the task, and Brantius contrived to come over to where Merlin was sitting. Placing his hands with familiarity on the seer's shoulders, he said to no one in particular "How lucky we are to have the service of the wisest man in the world and by far the most able to be trusted, for I was there as he told Vortiger exactly how he would die in the fire, the one set by you, my king," and here he looked down at Merlin, who did not return his gaze, in a show of approval, "which is exactly what happened."

Several of the other men nodded in appreciation.

"I wonder then, seer, if you might tell me what my death will be," Brantius said. "I would be most curious to know, and then I might guard against it and we will see, in time, if you are right."

Merlin, whose weary head was supported by his hand, said "I could tell you what your death will be with no effort at all." He raised a finger and pointed. "But you should be sure that you wish to know, Sir Brantius. Most people want to remain ignorant about the manner of their death."

Brantius claimed a brave pose in front of the king. "Why would they not?" he asked pensively.

"Because the knowledge is more than they can comfortably handle," said Merlin, "and it poisons their ability to enjoy days that should be carefree and blissful, because the rest of their lives are consumed with thoughts of how it will end."

The king sat at table, watching this exchange with keen interest, but saying nothing.

Brantius put one leg up on a chair, rakishly. "We in the king's service all understand that our lives may be cut short at any time, in noble battle or on business of the king, and all have made peace with danger," he said, then put his hand on his chin and appeared to be thinking. "I would very much like to know the manner in which you say that I will die."

Merlin stood up abruptly and clapped his hands, once. "Then you shall have your desire," he said. "You have asked me to tell you of your death and I am ready to say it."

Brantius stood, leg raised, proudly facing the wizard. "Say on," he said boldly.

"You should know with certainty that on the day of your death, you will fall from a horse and your neck will snap," he said. "This is how you will depart from life on that day."

Brantius' eyebrows raised in an expression of triumph, and he turned to regard all of the assembled men at table, who had all heard very clearly, including the king. "We have all heard well what this man has said," he spoke. "Now, God keep me, we will see in time if it is true."

Merlin turned to the king, and fixed him with an eye that held no affection. "Sir, I am weary," he shook his head, making as though he were about to say more, but nothing came. "I will join you later if it is your will," he said.

"Of course," granted the king.

Merlin let his gaze linger on the king's face, with an expression of bitterness and disappointment. Then he left the room without another word, closing the door behind him.

Brantius waited a moment to be sure that the seer had shuffled off, and closed the door behind him, then turned to the king with bright eyes. "You heard well what he said, my lord," he spoke excitedly. "Now tomorrow, we will test him further."

"You are testing Merlin?" asked one of the other advisors.

The king had not meant this scheme to become known, had ideally wanted it only between he and Brantius, and it seemed reckless and pushy for Brantius to make public mention of it in this way. "Let us keep it among ourselves," he said, now that the man had made reference to it.

The other advisors were now all clearly thinking about it, and wondering how Merlin might be tested.

"And wit you well that I will not have Merlin toyed with or insulted," said the king, pointing with authority. "So be careful, for I would never have him angry with me, or lose his trust."

Brantius threw his hand over his chest, as though the very suggestion was an offense to him. "Of course not, my king. And nevertheless, it is for you, so that you may be sure to surround yourself with the best advisors. Here is what I propose. Tomorrow, contrive to bring Merlin by my house, and I will disguise myself as another man, lying on my deathbed, and my wife will also help us in this illusion."

"And what will this prove?" asked one of the advisors.

"Then I will ask Merlin once more to predict my death," he said, throwing his hand out cleverly. "He should say the same thing, but we will see," and Brantius lowered his face and made show of deference to the king, "and we will know if he is indeed worthy of placing the whole trust of the kingdom in him."

The king's advisers nodded at the wisdom of the plan, and looked at the king for approval, for many of them, in their own way, also had something to gain if Merlin were pried away from the king's side.

The assent of the other advisors helped to quash the annoyance the king felt over having the plan suddenly made known, despite Brantius' assurances to the contrary. Their additional questioning of Merlin, now revealed, reinforced the seed of doubt that had been planted in the king's mind, and he too longed to be sure of the seer's sight. In the quiet hours of the night he had thought long on how closely, and quickly, he had aligned himself with the wizard's wishes, and followed his directions almost without question—much as he tried to drive these thoughts from his mind. He looked around the room at his advisors, some of whom had been with him much longer than Merlin. Some of them had been around since the days of Constance, his father, and he knew them to be the most devoted and knowledgeable of men, whereas he had known Merlin... how long? And now he thought of how it must seem to them, who had toiled away in good faith for so long, to see the king place all his trust in this one seer, who had come in with several advantageous strategies and predictions, but... how well did he know Merlin? How much was it possible to know Merlin at all?

The king sat silently, eyes lowered to the table, as he remained in thought for a long series of minutes. Then he said "What time should we arrive?"

-35-

The next day, the king was dressed and ready to go out, with all of his necessary attendants, and he stopped by Merlin, affecting a jaunty air. "Merlin," he said, "we are going into town, where I will visit a sick man who has requested my presence, and blessing. If you would like," the king said, "please come along."

Merlin looked at the king with a grim countenance, and sighed. "No," he said. "I would prefer not to go with you."

The king made a mincing grin. He had not anticipated this. "Well," he said, wringing his hands, "actually, I apologize, but I already promised that I would bring you. The man's wife is quite distraught at his condition, and I said that you would be able to offer some words of advice."

Merlin looked at the king so long, and so directly, that the monarch eventually had to lower his eyes. "Well," said Merlin at last, "a king is only as good as his promises."

A pained smile played over Pendragon's lips, and he could not bear to raise his eyes to meet the wizard's. "Let us go then," he said, gathering the rest of his men, and leading the way to their carriage.

On the way, Merlin remained silent and kept his gaze directed out the window, making quite plain to everyone that he was not at all pleased. Some of the king's men directed questions to him, but he answered them with one word, or not at all. The king felt a queasy tingling in his stomach as he beheld this, and he had the sinking feeling that he was displeasing Merlin, which he never wanted to do, but at the same time, a thought came with a flash of angry defiance. Did he not have the right to know this man, in whom he had placed so much trust? The moodiness of the wizard only made him more confirmed that he was doing something that displeased him, which also affirmed the king's right to test him. He could hardly be expected to place the path of the kingdom in the hands of this relative stranger without assurance, could he? He was allowed to make *some* decisions on his own, was he not?

When they arrived outside the man's house, his wife ran out to greet the carriage. She was crying, and made great show of being distraught, her eyes settling on Merlin quite often, eager to get a look at him, to see how he acted, to see what he wore, to see how he reacted to the news of her husband, who she claimed was just inside, teetering on the brink of death.

The king embraced her and led her inside, his hand around her back. "Let us go see him at once," he said, "and perhaps my seer may bring you some good news," he said, "or at least bring you such counsel that can set your mind at ease."

Merlin watched them with an appraising expression, but followed them quietly into the house, and upstairs, where they were led into a room where a man lay in bed.

The room was fresh as spring, not close and stuffy, as a room where a man who had been lying on his sick bed for days would be. The linens he was surrounded by were fresh, crisp and fair-smelling. The man lay under layers of blankets and sheets, only his face showing, which was pale as death—owing to the insultingly obvious layer of powder that covered his visage. The woman made great show of falling at the side of the bed where her husband lay, weeping as she clutched at his hand—which was a few shades pinker and more robust than his face—and reached for the hand of the king, who had come around to her side of the bed.

"Come, Merlin," said the king. "Look at this man and advise on his state of health and what his wife can expect."

Merlin came around to stand next to the king, but he kept his eyes trained on the king's face, his judgmental gaze burning into him to the point where it made the king quite uncomfortable and caused him to lower his eyes, as all the time he smiled, trying to act confident and natural.

"Tell me, king," said Merlin, "how long have you known this man?"

The king stammered. "Well, I have met him once or twice before," he said, "at celebrations, um," and he paused, while his eyes searched back and forth, "and, I think, that is all."

Merlin nodded slowly, deliberately. "I see," he said. "And have I ever met this man before?"

The king was able to look at Merlin for just a moment before shame made him drop his gaze to the sick man. "No, I don't believe so," he said.

"Please, sir," said the man's wife, falling at the king's feet, "have your seer say on my husband here, whom I have cared for so long in this illness. Will he die in this bed?"

184

Pendragon let his hand rest comfortingly on the back of the woman's head, and turned with sympathetic face to Merlin. "Is there anything you can say on this man's death? And whether or not he will get well, or die in his bed?" the king asked.

Merlin crossed his arms. "I will have you know with absolute certainty that this man will not die in this bed, nor from this illness."

There was a moment of silence, charged with the many hidden expectations all the different parties came into the ruse with.

Then the man in bed made a great show of gathering his strength to speak, which was quite overdramatic and insulted Merlin quite grievously, and he finally whispered out, in his weakest voice, "Please tell me then," he said, "what my death will be, if it is not to be in this bed?"

Merlin stood at the foot of the bed, his eyes looking directly at him with great judgment and annoyance, such that it was difficult for him to maintain the wizard's gaze. Merlin leaned forward, placing his angry face even closer, and he spoke in a tone thick with enmity.

"On the day of your death," said Merlin, "you will hang, and you will die in the place where you are found hanging."

A palpable silent gasp came over all except the wizard.

Then Merlin lowered his gaze and looked very upset, and sighed out in great annoyance, and shuffled a bit backwards. "I will leave you now," he said to the king, fixing him with a gaze of extreme disappointment, and left the room quickly. By the time he hit the bottom stair, he was miles away.

One of the advisors made sure he was gone, then closed the door firmly behind him. "What death did he predict yesterday?" he asked.

Brantius sat right up in his bed, removing the hat and scarf he had worn over his face. "He said yesterday that I would be thrown from a horse and break my neck!" he said triumphantly. "Now he says that I will be found hanging!"

"Well, those deaths are so different," said the advisor, "they couldn't possibly go together."

Pendragon was pacing wildly, eyes lowered to the floor beneath him. "It is very troubling," said the king.

"Troubling, indeed!" said Brantius, leaping up spryly from the bed. "That such an obvious fraud should have gotten so close to the king!" he said. "My God! Sir," he said to the king, shaking his head in disbelief as the thrill of a gambit expertly executed ran through him, "if you know anything at all, you must realize that he has deceived you!" He puffed out his chest and rose to his full height, as his wife swanned around in violent demonstrations of hysteria. "We can only hope that he has not led you too far down the path toward his own unholy ends!"

"Breaking your neck in a fall and hanging," the king said, looking up suddenly with reddened eyes, showing livid on a pale face. "Both could not possibly happen to the same man."

"Of course not," Brantius said. "He's a fraud at best, an evil trickster at worst."

"The very act of falling precludes the possibility of hanging!" said the king.

"How lucky you are that my husband exposed this so-called seer to you," said Brantius' wife, wishing to further cement the king's notice of her husband.

Pendragon was clearly very troubled, and he had begun pacing, his hands interlocked before his lips, gaze trained on the floor, as his mind reeled. "I trusted him so," he said. "That is what disturbs me the most. All that he has advised us toward was in our best interests—I mean, so far."

"So far," echoed Brantius.

"Thank God you know who you can trust now," said Brantius' wife.

"This must be very troubling to you," said Brantius, moving around to place a comforting hand on the king's arm. "But continue to trust in me, and we will clear your court of this deceiver, and any others," he said. "Tomorrow we will test him a third and final time, and if he once more tells a falsehood, we will eject him from your court!" he boomed. "Then surround you only with people who have the interests of the king and kingdom truly at heart!"

The king nodded weakly. "I will do whatever you say," he said.

"Tomorrow, come to the abbey a few hour's ride west of here," he said. "I will once more play the sick man, and the abbot will tell you that I am one of his monks, that I am in a dreadful state, and he is very worried that I will die." Brantius put out a hand to indicate a clever aside. "That way the request will come from somewhere else, which will further throw off suspicion," he said. "The abbot will beseech you to come and bring your seer, and for him to say on my fate, and thus we will test this all-seeing, all knowing fraud even harder than today, and if he lies once more, we will expose him then and there," he said, raising a triumphant fist, "and be rid of him at once."

The king nodded. "I will be there," he said. "And I will bring my brother, so that neither of us may be deceived again."

-36-

A young woman was just leaving the room when a sudden gust of wind swept through the enclosed space, and a towheaded young boy, who had not been there a second before, stomped past her out the door, shouting "Mother!" The young girl stood, hand over her heaving chest, as he continued right past her, stomping out into the main hall, and began climbing the stairs.

"Mother!" he yelled.

Meylinde stepped out of where she had been leading a set of girls in study, and met him at the top of the stairs. "Merlin!" she exclaimed. "Has something happened?"

He climbed quickly, arms swinging side to side as he trudged up methodically. "They have made me angry, mother!"

She turned immediately and went to the end of the hallway to open the door of Merlin's room. In the corner was a large cage with iron bars and a sturdy lock. There was a fair-sized log in the middle of the space.

She stood back and watched him coming, seeing his brow beginning to bulge forward over dulled eyes, and knew he was just barely holding onto consciousness. His cheeks bulged out to the sides as his teeth grew large, extending out of his mouth as he drew once more into his devilish state. His arms also extended, knuckles dragging on the floor, as his nails rapidly grew out into long claws.

The misshapen child trudged past her where she held the door open, his eyes staring straight ahead, now barely able to recognize his own mother. He went directly into the cage, running as he got closer, and leapt onto the log. His claws dug into the bark as his wide-open mouth bit, viciously, several times at the log, exactly in the manner of a cat.

His mother closed and locked the bars of the cage behind him, then stepped quietly out, closing the door of the room behind her. She lit a lamp so that he would have the protection of light.

She expected to see her son Merlin, a child once more, the next morning.

-37-

That night, after he had dined and retired to his private chamber, Pendragon told Uther, who had just returned that day, all that had transpired, and that Merlin had been, with certainty, exposed as a fraud, and liar.

"I can hardly believe it," said Uther, "but I guess to imagine someone like that is as wondrous as he says he is," he shook his head, "it's just too good to imagine."

"And to be caught out so easily!" said Pendragon. "I'm ashamed, honestly. How could I have let him get so close to us, and to take his advice so readily, without really knowing who he is?" he said. "Or whom he truly serves."

188

"No need to be tough on yourself," said Uther. "He gave us great intelligence—he did, in fact, save my life," he said, "and help us kill Hengist, and capture his castle. Those are real, tangible benefits, and they are not inconsiderable."

"I know," said Pendragon. "But one has to wonder... did he just tell us a few correct things in order to win our trust, hoping only to deceive us later?"

"He also helped us achieve what we returned for," said Uther. "We thought we would be several years in bloody war, trying to reclaim our rightful place as leaders of this country, and because of Merlin, we walked in and did it," he snapped his fingers, "in a heartbeat."

"Of course I know that," Pendragon said, "but when I learn that he is not infallible—and honestly," and he turned and looked at Uther square on, "how could we ever believe that anyone is infallible? And knows things that no one else on earth could know? He helped us achieve our goal, but... maybe because it somehow aligns with *his* goal. And we don't really know what his ultimate goal may be."

Uther paced back and forth, clearly troubled. "I don't know," he said. "He seems so trustworthy, and the advantages he offers us," he opened his hands, "well, they are advantages no one else can offer."

"And perhaps," Pendragon said, "too good to be true."

"But he showed us all of those different guises," Uther said. "And he knew so many things that no one else could know."

"Many different guises," said Pendragon, "but what does that really prove? He showed us what he wanted to show us in order to get us to believe. When I think back on it, it's just a blur of numerous disguises and reveals. But... maybe it was *meant* to be a blur. When he is tested on matters on which he is not prepared beforehand, he gives incorrect answers."

"Are they incorrect?" Uther said. "We have not seen yet."

Pendragon stopped in place and looked seriously at his brother. "How can the same man both break his neck in a fall and hang in place?" he asked. "And who knows what more he will say tomorrow?"

Uther crossed his arms, and pursed his lips as he thought, staring downward at the rugs on the floor. "I don't know," he said. "It seems unlikely, but…" and he shook his head in wonderment, "I am loath to give up such an obvious advantage so quickly."

"He tells us himself that his powers come from the devil," said Pendragon.

"Exactly," replied Uther. "Why would he tell us that so openly if he meant to deceive us?"

Pendragon took a break from pacing to take in a long breath, and let it out in confusion. "I don't know," he said. "But he is deceiving us, I saw that plainly. You will see it tomorrow, and we can see how you feel then." The king's face was clouded with the dark thoughts that were whirling in his brain. "Thinking you can trust this person, then learning that you can't, thinking you can trust that person," Pendragon said to Uther, "one can never know for sure, and it is so wearying."

"Well, you know that you may trust in me," said Uther, "if no one else."

"I do, and I am so glad to have you," said the king, placing his hand on his brother's shoulder. "I didn't realize, being king…." He shook his head and let the thought go. "Having at least one person I can trust—"

But at that moment a corridor opened in the space beside them, extending much further back than the stone wall of the room that they were in, accompanied by a low moaning wind as the air was sucked violently back into the newly-opened space. The eerie sound made the small hairs on each brother's arms stand straight in place, and when the corridor was opened fully, Merlin stepped down into their room, at which point it closed behind him. The low keening of sucking wind stopped the moment the opening closed and disappeared into the air.

The wizard's appraising eye rested first on one brother, then the other, with gaze that held no affection, or pity. For their part, he had appeared so suddenly, and precisely when they were talking about him, that they had trouble meeting his gaze, and shuffled bashfully, eyes lowered to the floor.

"King Pendragon," Merlin said, "and brother Uther. I am glad to find you both together, for I would speak to you before you lead me into this farce tomorrow."

190

"Farce, Merlin?" asked Pendragon.

"You be silent," said the wizard sharply, "lest you make me more angry than I am." He directed an extremely severe glance toward Pendragon that made him drop his eyes at once. "You brothers," he shook his head in amazement. "The more I get to know you, the more insane I truly think that you are."

Both of them swallowed and stood quietly in place like two schoolboys facing a scolding.

"Do you believe that I do not know that this man is testing me?" he said, voice low and laced with contempt. "And do you think that I do not see directly through his scheme?" he said. "He wants to discredit me in order to advance his own place in your court, king. And you are on the verge of letting him do it because of his simplistic tricks."

Pendragon tried to shore up his courage, and lift his eyes to face the gaze of the wizard, but when he saw the fury in Merlin's eyes, he could no longer keep his gaze steady there.

"And you, Pendragon," he said, "do you believe that I am unaware of the many and varied ways in which you have lied to me?"

Pendragon swallowed.

Merlin balled his hands into fists, and set his shoulders, and his eyes looked to the side of the room as he stood, body trembling, for a long moment before he spoke again. When he did, his voice was low and desolate of affection.

"Do you think, for one second, that I do not know how this fool who you are allowing to test me will die? Yes, in fact I do know. And tomorrow," he said, pointing a damning finger at the brothers, "I will tell him still another death than the ones I have told him already."

Pendragon's shoulders dropped when he heard this. "Truly?" he asked, whirling on the wizard in amazement. "Can a man really die in all the ways that you have said?"

"If he does not," said Merlin, "then you truly are deceived, and you should have me buried alive at night. But if he does," and he strode before them with hands on hips, "then believe me forevermore. I see perfectly well what this man's death will be."

Then Merlin snapped his fingers, causing the two brothers to raise their eyes to meet his fiery gaze, and pointed finger.

"And I see *yours*, too," he said. "And when you see how this man dies, you will come to me and ask me about your own death."

Both men stood cringing, like punished schoolboys, but Pendragon had it much the worse, for he knew that he had lied to Merlin repeatedly—stupid, insulting lies, too, he now saw clearly—which caused him to fear the wizard greatly, and repent of his own stupid foolishness. And now, as Merlin spoke to them about their own deaths, he felt a nauseating quaking in his own stomach, which was the knowledge that he had done something really, really wrong, and thus opened himself to consequences far beyond any he was ready to deal with.

Then suddenly, in a very clear and vivid memory, returned the wizard's words that lying to him would hurt the liar much worse than it would him.

There Merlin stood before them, hands on hips, causing his shoulders to stand tall and wide, and his robes to hang straight off of him, making him appear huge and fearsome, which was not even to mention the sneer of contempt that made his face tight and vindictive, eyes flashing with undisguised fury. Pendragon's lip began to tremble as he realized he was indeed terrified of the angry wizard.

Merlin pointed at Uther, but his eyes remained fixed with a terrible steadiness right on Pendragon. "And I say now to Uther only this; that I will see *him* rule as king before ever I leave this realm."

Pendragon gasped in sharp astonishment, then collapsed forward as though punched in the gut. Uther's eyes widened and went unfocused as his head fell forward into his hands. Then the wind rose with a loud screaming wail as the hole in space opened up behind the wizard. He stepped backward, it closed a moment later, and he was gone, leaving silence in his wake.

38

The next day, bright and early, Brantius and his wife were arranging his bed at a room deep within the abbey, with the abbot they had entreated to help them. Brantius lay abed, as his wife dabbed white makeup on his face, which was difficult as he was trying to speak with the abbot.

"Now, you recall," said the abbot, "that you will not forget to laud my place in the exposing of this fraudulent advisor. Our humble abbey could certainly use an infusion of fresh funds, such as the king has been handing out to anyone who gains his ear."

"Well now," said Brantius' wife, "my husband will be on the very right hand of the king forevermore after this, you'll see," she said.

"Remember the honor you owe to me," said Brantius, "and I will remember you often to the king." He looked around the vast stone chamber. "There is no reason this could not be known as my primary place of spiritual retreat."

"Oh," said the abbot. "It would be most fortuitous if men came to be in the habit of finding you here."

"You stick with us," said the wife, nodding officiously.

"I'll be so happy not to spend another day looking at the insipid face of that child of the devil," Brantius said. "His manner is so insulting."

"You are doing a noble thing by driving that abomination away from the king's side," said the abbot.

"And don't you forget to mention how cramped and small our house is getting," his wife said, arranging the bedclothes around her husband's body.

"We'll come to that in time," Brantius said. "Cannot shove everything through at once."

"There's only so much longer I can stand to be there," the woman said.

A monk poked his head in the door. "The king and his party have arrived."

"I will come to greet them," said the abbot, and left with the monk.

The wife arranged a few final sheets around the bed and draped some cloths over Brantius' head. "Should we make some of these damp," she asked, "like you've been sweating through the night?"

"It's fine," said Brantius, "no one will notice. Now get yourself hidden, I want to have a chance to relax before they come in."

She squeezed his hand warmly. "My righteous husband," she said. "I would kiss you, but I don't want to mar your makeup."

"Get hidden," he said. "They cannot find you here."

She squeezed his hand once more, shaking it in excitement, uttered "good luck!" and scuttled away to stand behind a wooden door at the back of the room.

Brantius looked over his outfit, made a few last arrangements of his heavy bedclothes, then lay back, staring at the ceiling. Unsure what to do, he began moaning in mock agony, and moving his head slowly from side to side, to get into his role more completely.

His wife stuck her head back in. "Did you need me?" she asked.

"No, get gone!" he said. "The king will be here momentarily."

"Oh," she put a hand over her mouth. "But I heard you moaning."

"I am acting!" he said. "Go out and do not come back in for any reason, until the king and his men have left."

Her head vanished and she pulled the door closed behind her without a word.

Brantius lay his head back and resumed his quiet moaning.

A few minutes later, the main door at the far end of the room was opened, and King Pendragon was shown in by the abbot, followed by his brother and Merlin. Brantius did not raise his head, so he did not see the grim expressions on the face of Uther and especially the king, but when they came close, he could see that the king's face was ashen and pale, and was avoiding making eye contact with him as best he could.

Merlin, by contrast, came right up to the man lying as sick with an expression of frank annoyance. He stood at the man's bedside and his eyes wandered over all of the excessive bedclothes and bandages, and the obvious powder makeup that covered his face.

"This is he," said the abbot. "Oh, he has lingered like this for several days now, and we are terribly worried. Please king, for God's sake," he said, "have your seer pronounce on whether this worthy man will ever rise again from this bed." He reached forward to place his hand on the sick man's arm, affecting a troubled face and shaking his head with great sorrow.

Merlin watched his face as he did this, for it provided him grim amusement to watch people as they were lying. "Would you like me to say on this matter, king?" he asked Pendragon.

"Yes," the king said, without raising his eyes from the floor.

"Then I will say that this man certainly will rise again from this bed," he said, "for he isn't sick at all. This is Sir Brantius in disguise, who is testing me uselessly, hoping that by discrediting me he can worm his way closer to the king."

Brantius lay still in place, unsure what to do. His eyes stared at the ceiling, not daring to move them to take in the seer, or the king, and break the ruse, confirming that what Merlin said was true.

"Umm," the abbot said lowly, hands making useless gestures around the bedclothes of the prone man. "How can you say that so heartlessly?" he asked. "Clearly this man is in the greatest suffering imaginable."

"And Brantius," said Merlin, leaning in over the prostrate man with a smile of the most sinister sharpness, and speaking with relish in his voice, "all of your efforts will amount to nothing, for indeed you will die in both manners that I have told you, and now I will tell you a third way, even stranger than the first two."

Brantius dared to lower his eyes to see the wizard, king and his brother gathered there at the foot of his bed. Uther stood back a few feet, face an expression of stony impatience, but it was Pendragon's expression that shocked him the most, for there disappointment was mixed with the most loveless anger, blaming the lying man for drawing him into the scheme, and driving a wedge between he and his closest and most precious advisor.

The shock hit him suddenly, and he quickly sat up on his elbows, the bedclothes covering his neck and upper chest falling away.

"You should know without doubt," said Merlin, "that on the day on which you die, you will fall from a horse and break your neck, you will hang and be found hanging in the place where you die," the wizard counted on his fingers, "and what's more," he said, "you will drown."

The wooden door at the rear of the room opened abruptly, and Brantius' wife burst into the room, saying nothing, but staring at Merlin with an expression of shock and simple-minded amazement.

The eyes of Brantius himself darted frantically between Merlin, the king, and all those around. He could not understand how his scheme had collapsed so suddenly, but what's more, how the seer could now pronounce a third death, one even more ludicrous, and yet no one was reacting with amazement or scorn.

"Whoever is with you then will see your death and see all of these things happen, and then," Merlin turned to the king, "you can certainly judge for yourself whether or not I tell you the truth! And as for you, Brantius," said Merlin, turning back to the prostrate man, "you can drop your pretense now, for I see your ill will toward me quite clearly, and I know quite well how your simple mind thinks."

"Yes, Brantius," said the king, shaking his head wearily but not deigning to look at the knight, "drop this pretense. It has gone too far."

Brantius now sat up fully. "My lord!" he exclaimed. "Now you can obviously recognize the madness of this man you call advisor."

"No one could die all like that," his wife blurted. "Three different ways!"

"Sir," Brantius stood up full, threw off the covering robes and came around to where the king stood, but found the king drawing his arms in and retreating from him. "How can you trust him when he plainly does not know what he is saying?" He perceived the vastly changed manner of the king, and his voice rose a bit higher in pitch. "You can—obviously—anyone, any child, would know that it is not possible for one man to die in all of those ways. To hang, and drown,

196

and break my neck, all at once? Now king," and here he tried to place his hand comfortingly on the king's shoulder, but the man moved swiftly out of his grasp, "think on how wise you are to believe such a man."

As he saw the king and his brother retreating even further from him, his eyes searched around desperately, and he felt an uncomfortable tickle in this throat. "How wise is it, indeed, to make him, he who draws his power from the devil, the lord over you, one so wise, and install him as the head of your council!"

He stood, pathetically, with his arms outstretched, as he saw his passionate plea draw no response at all from the king.

Brantius' wife strode even further into the room. "You would choose a son of the devil himself over my husband!" she said. "Who served at the side of King Vortiger while you were still a frightened child on the run!"

Brantius turned on her with a look at said, if we interpret it most charitably, that her comments were not welcome.

King Pendragon's gaze fell on Sir Brantius, but all affection had left his eye, and his manner was regal, pitiless, and unfeeling. His arms were folded firmly before his chest. He spoke. "I will never forsake Merlin for anything you have said," he announced, then pointed, "and certainly not before I have seen the manner in which you die."

Brantius froze, and felt as though the blood in his body had stilled in place. His face went ghastly pale, and his hand came up involuntarily to cover his chest. His mouth had fallen open in amazement, and he could think of nothing more.

The king, seeing nothing more required, turned and swiftly left the room, followed by Uther, Merlin, and the unctuous abbot, who beseeched him to stay and discuss the affairs of the abbey.

39

A king can never be alone. Everywhere he goes, armed guards, knights, carriage drivers trained in combat, advisors. And the people who want something from you. All of the many, many people who want something from you, now that you are the king. People sucking up, and pretending to like you. It was hard not to be nauseated by it, to come to despise people. For Pendragon, there were times lately, many, many times lately, where the only people he really liked—aside from his brother—were "his people." That is, the people he ruled over. The people he represented. The important distinction being that he did not personally know them. They were an idea, a concept, a group of people out there. There were times when, well, he couldn't really think too deeply on them, or imagine them individually, because what he would imagine is them asking for something from him, and then he would start to resent them.

He had tried to clear the afternoon after their visit to the abbey, but that wasn't really possible for a king, either. There were things to plan, people who had to be seen, briefings to be had on where the Saxon were holding out, which cities or castles were being besieged, or which needed infusions of money or supplies. And all that time, it was nearly impossible to focus. He could not get what Merlin had said out of his mind. Several of his afternoon appointments went on long and became almost interminable, as his mind kept being drawn back to the wizard's words—and the tone in which he had said them—and what they meant. For God's sake, what they meant.

He didn't want to have to feign illness and cancel appointments just to get some time to himself, and perhaps even generate more people coming to see him, hoping to ensure that he was all right, or see if he needed anything, if he needed a doctor, if some hot wine wasn't exactly what he needed. It was honestly not hard to start to hate people, well-intentioned as they were. He had to laugh at the irony of how he used to be the introspective one; the one who craved time alone or to go walking alone. How he loved walking alone along the cliff tops in Brittany where they had sheltered and hidden after Vortiger had killed their brother. It was so quiet and peaceful, but for the crashing of the waves against the cliffs of rock. How clear everything was in those days. He was fired up to kill the man who had assassinated their brother and usurped their birthright. Those walks along the beautiful green grasses atop those cliffs, during almost all of which he had imagined returning to Britain, vanquishing Vortiger, and becoming king! And how wonderful it would be!

The problem, as you may have guessed, is that comment Merlin made, about seeing Uther king before he parted from the realm. That part was not the problem—by all means, let Uther be king—the problem was the implication that Pendragon would die. Die soon? Die in twenty years? Die gloriously? Die horribly—or ignobly? Or not die at all, but have to abdicate through illness or, who knows, maybe just not feeling like it anymore. The comment was very vague. And that was the other problem.

Merlin knew all things, Pendragon was indeed assured of that, and he knew precisely what he was doing when he flung that comment out. It was, plain and simple, revenge. The most clever, diabolical revenge he could ever have thought of—well, in fact, Pendragon could never have actually thought of such a thing—because it had thrown his mind into complete turmoil and, honestly, Pendragon had no way of imagining how he might ever calm the questioning that it had started.

That was the other thing. The nastiness of it. It was breathtaking. It was true, he had allowed himself to be tempted, to disbelieve Merlin, and to lie to Merlin. Pendragon involuntarily cringed now, when he thought of all the little lies—stupid, obvious lies—like even that Merlin had not met the man before, and getting worse from there—and he also remembered Merlin giving him those long, disappointed, increasingly irritated looks, which should have let him know. He knew now that the wizard was seeing right through him all that time, and those glances were meant to alert him. But he had been blind, and blinded, by the threat of being caught out, deceived, and—he had to admit—the excitement and pride of being savvy to deception, exposing it. And doing something for his own kingdom—something that would be unquestionably his own doing. He would then, also, reclaim his own kingdom and know without doubt that *he* was its ruler. He had allowed himself to get carried away by these thoughts. It was hubris, he knew. And the fact that Merlin was simply too good to be true. It was all incredibly difficult to believe, especially when there was no other being like him, ever on earth. Ever even *heard* of on earth.

Still, no matter how you looked at it, the fact was, Merlin told him never to lie, and he had lied.

But the reason Merlin wasn't like anyone else on earth is that he was half-devil, and told Pendragon plainly that he still suffered to overcome traces of the devil's influence and, for God's sake, the *cruelty* of it was not something that could be expected from even his most vicious of enemies. That was almost more enduring than the actual prediction. If he had read the same prediction in a book, it would have disturbed him, but good lord, the vicious, hateful way the wizard had fixed him with a merciless eye when he said it. And the knowledge that the seer had known full well the torment that comment would throw him into. Merlin knew exactly what he was doing, that much was certain, weighed his words—and their ambiguity—to cause maximum anguish. And now he was supposed to just go on and work with him? Mend ways and keep him as part of his court?

How could he possibly work with Merlin ever again, knowing that he carried that much spite and rage within him? How could he ever believe that he would be on good terms with the seer again?

Then that final thought; that he had been handed, without any work or effort of his own, the greatest gift that a king could have, and ruined it. He could blame Brantius—and he did, you may be sure—but ultimately the fault lay directly in him. Oh, how could he have done it?

The king began to tear up, right in an assembly of his advisors, and had to be brought back to attention with a touch on his shoulder. They had been repeatedly calling his name, for he knew not how long. The king made light of it, but that's when he decided he had to clear off his schedule and, no matter what it took, get some time alone, retreat

200

from all company, and spend the night in solitude. He told his minders that he was not feeling well, that he would take his supper alone, and from then on he did not want to be disturbed, did not even want anyone to knock on the door. And then, within a few minutes, there he was, alone in his chamber. Or as alone as you can be with guards a few feet outside your door, constantly listening to be sure everything is all right.

Perhaps you know that feeling of wanting to be alone for a long while, wishing for it and yearning for it, then finally taking the necessary measures, and then there you are; alone, like you wanted, and unsure what to do with it or how to enjoy it. The king paced around his chamber, eyes not focusing on anything in particular, his thoughts undirected. Then he thought; okay, I should put my efforts into trying to find a way out of this situation. How to resolve it, put it behind him, and move on. Okay, so—how?

This confusion is what was left by the viciousness of the emotional slap that Merlin had given him—slap? Or, more like a burn? A scalding?—because it was just so hard to see beyond. And the king's mind drifted to how it might have been had he never met Merlin. He might have had a normal kingship. Best not to forget that hundreds of kings—not many of the entire British realm, but still, numerous smaller ones—had done just fine without divine (or was it devilish?) help. He had jumped at the promise of immense advantages that the thought of a seer like Merlin offered, without thinking of the reality of what that might mean, or any negative downside whatsoever. They might not have been so successful, but they would not now also be living in cringing terror, and any triumphs and mistakes they made would be their own.

And that brought back the particularly galling thought, one that, no matter what turn of mind he made, was inescapable: His triumphs were not his, not really. There were Merlin's. What did Pendragon really have to do with it? He executed Merlin's instructions. Yes, yes, he had to go through with it, he had to actually make it happen in the fact, and there was some glory in that, but he was just doing what Merlin said.

So now… what? Kick Merlin out? It couldn't happen; the advantages he offered were too great. Even in all this round of thought, it was clear that Uther would be dead, right now, were it not for Merlin. And what would he do without his brother, who had been with him since he could remember? Hengist would be alive. They would not have captured his castle. They would never have had the idea to simply offer to let the Saxons leave, and to supply them the boats with which to do so. If Pendragon thought about it honestly, his natural impulse would have been to attack them. Then lord knows how many losses of men he would have had, how long the conflict would have raged on, and at what great expense. They would still be fighting right now. Instead they were building new churches and bridges and roads, during this time of peace, and the scarred and damaged land was only now bouncing back from the constant ravages of destructive warfare.

No, there was no way to ever separate from Merlin. And Pendragon would simply have to get used to his place as the king who was, essentially, second in command. He had gotten a small taste of what happened when he tried to act on his own council, and had been slapped back sharply for it. So—how to proceed?

Pendragon stood in the center of his room, still wearing his robes and all trappings of his kingship, all alone.

Now he wanted company. Now he would have to go out and say he felt better, or that he had done his thinking or—well, who knows what. He was the king, he could do any damn thing he wanted, and yet he was in a position of constantly needing to explain himself.

It came to him with the clarity of a vision that he would have to apologize to Merlin. Just flat-out acknowledge for his trespass, give evidence that he had thought it through and humbly ask for forgiveness. If he was to be Merlin's lap dog—and here he sighed deeply and felt his brow grow heavy and his head weary—it was time to beg to be allowed back onto his lap.

He would make an offering. And at once he thought; honor him. Apologize, and make a big show of honoring him. After all, the entire court knew that he had tested Merlin, regardless of how he had wished to hide it. (Now the entire court was abuzz with Merlin's wild predictions over Brantius' death.) He would offer Merlin a staff of scribes to write down all that he said, and leave it up to him, he could write down anything that he would. Whatever he decided, and Pendragon would make sure he knew that he had free reign to design the project in exactly the manner that he saw fit.

Okay, that was it. And now the king would make ready to speak to Merlin. Of course, the irony was—and this was one of those challenges of dealing with the wizard that, honestly, a person really just couldn't think about in any depth, lest he go mad—that he knew full well that Merlin was fully aware of the entire train of thought such as you have just read.

The king drew a deep breath, sighed, placed his hands on his hips, took a moment, and finally lifted his head to say out loud; "Merlin, I would speak with you."

His voice sounded loudly in the empty room.

Nothing happened.

Then, thinking that perhaps that was all a bit too commanding, not humble enough, he said "Merlin, I would very much like to speak with you."

Thirty minutes passed, then an hour, before the king knew with certainty that Merlin would not come.

-40-

Upton was sitting, smoking his pipe outside of his small workshop, engaged in conversation with another man, about his age, but wider in the shoulders and the shape of his head, and shorter, with dark, smart eyes that lay beneath heavy black eyebrows. Merlin came around the corner, and Upton raised his eyebrows and moved to nudge his friend Lanford, who was that minute in the long last third of an elaborate joke involving a maiden and a dwarf. "Mister Merlin," he said, leaning forward and taking a great deal of time to stand. He nudged his friend. "This is Merlin, who I told you about, and whose staff you worked on."

"Ah!" the man said, turning his bright eyes upward to the wizard. "A pleasure," he said, reaching out his hand. "I was hoping to be here to meet you."

"He wanted to meet the man who demanded a work of such precision," said Upton, laughing gently. "This is the stonemason I told you that I work well with."

"I can see that you both share a great rapport," said Merlin, smiling. He was able to scan their histories and futures in a moment, and could see that they were both very fine men, and he liked them both very much. "I hope that you have the staff I commissioned from you ready."

"We sure do," said Lanford, "and a pleasure it was to work on, too." He ran inside the dark workshop to get the piece.

"He loves a good challenge, that one," Upton laughed. "He wanted to meet you," he said again. "See the man who asked for such an intricate piece."

Merlin smiled warmly. He was hoping they would have exactly that reaction.

Lanford came walking jauntily out of the workshop, holding a long package wrapped in a covering of burlap. He undid the end, showing a lovely head to the staff, rounded and with inlaid stones in octagon shapes that, through their translucent nature, showed them to descend straight into the core of the wood to some depth.

"Ah!" said Merlin with delight, and took hold of it, drawing its length out of the cloth. The inlaid stones started at the black octagon on the upper tip, which had been buffed to a lovely shine, and continued down to where Merlin's hand would normally hold the shaft, whereupon they started diminishing, in a lovely and artful way, until they ceased, and the rest of the rod, down to the foot, was a lovely finished wood. They had left some of the burls and sanded down the nubs of small branches off of it, but had left indications of where they were, leaving the whole thing looking beautifully natural.

"This is a very fine piece of craft you have created here," Merlin said, and both of the men shuffled happily in place, like two good dogs who had just received praise. "Why, you boys have known each other your whole lives," Merlin said.

The men smiled at one another, and Lanford placed his hand affectionately on his friend's shoulder.

"Now, I had enough of the black stone," Lanford said, pointing along the length of the staff, "so I took the liberty of extending it the full length of the staff," he said, "inside. From top to bottom."

Merlin looked at the foot of the staff, and found a black hexagon there that matched the one at the head, and knew that they formed a core of the stone connected all the way to the head, and branching off into the smaller crystals that came out to where his hand would normally hold the staff. He then lowered it, and looked at Lanford as though very impressed, which the old stonemason lapped up with great bursting pride.

In fact, Merlin had been hoping that they would do that, and whether they thought to do it on their own was part of his test.

Merlin then wrapped his hand around the neck of it, over the translucent stones, and brought it upright, then touched it to the earth. He felt the surging energy immediately, right into his hand, and could not keep a smile from spreading across his face. "Very fine work," he said, nodding warmly. "Very fine."

"That work for you?" asked Upton.

"Yes," Merlin said, "it does exactly what it is supposed to. Which you knew." Upton smiled bashfully. "You have also done excellent woodwork here," he added. "It is exactly what I would have wanted."

Both men couldn't contain their smiles, and cast happy, sidelong glances toward each other.

"You have done excellent work, and as I told Upton," Merlin said, "in the future I will have a very large commission for both of you, which will require exactly this level of understanding, care and precision, on a much grander scale."

Both men's face grew almost comically earnest, as they both nodded eagerly. They really were like a couple of eager, happy dogs. "Just give us a bit of warning and we'll clear our schedules," Upton said.

"It will take you almost a full month of continued labor."

Both men were stilled for a moment, with the thought of such a large job, but then they recovered and nodded in agreement like seasoned pros.

Merlin paid them, and gave them both handsome tips, then, because they were just so likable, and he had great pleasure from the work they had done on his staff, he hugged them both. What good men, he thought. What a pleasure to meet such fine men.

He took his staff and made his way to leave, but then he stopped in place. He thought, and considered, and he ran his hand through his beard, while the men stood, waiting on him. "Lanford," he said at last. "I'm not sure... ah, oh well." Merlin finally made up his mind to tell him. "If you can persuade your daughter to give up the knight she is in love with," he held out a hand, "which will take a very gentle, caring touch," he said, "then she will end up marrying a fine duke within two years."

Lanford looked at him for a moment with a blank face, then his face lit up with excitement, and he all but knocked his friend over with the sidelong knock he gave him in the chest. "You see, Upton? I told you! I told you ever since she met that fellow! Not a bad man, but—"

But when he once again turned, Merlin had gone.

-41-

Uther had actually been avoiding his brother. After they returned from the abbey, Pendragon had to go directly into his numerous responsibilities, any of which Uther was always welcome to be at, but he had slipped away soon after the carriage returned, and Pendragon hadn't seemed to miss him. In fact, the carriage ride back

206

was one of their most awkward ever. A stranger observing them wouldn't have even known that they were brothers. No one spoke the entire way home.

And there, sitting across from them, Merlin, silent, severe and unperturbed. He said nothing the entire way, looking out at the passing countryside the whole time. Still, even through his silence, he was able to let them all know that at that moment, at least, he considered Pendragon as beneath even his contempt.

How could Uther feel, except happy that it wasn't him?

And then there was the matter of that little comment. That Merlin would see Uther king before he parted from the realm. He knew full well that Pendragon had heard it in every possible nuance of meaning, and so had he. It hit them both like a flaming ball from a catapult, and sent both reeling.

You might think it sounded like positive news for Uther—and it did—but it was also inextricably linked to the fact that his brother would die. And it couldn't help but excite his own hidden hopes and ambitions to be king—as well as his terrified anxiety at the thought of being king, but all of the expense of his brother's death. It was as simple as that.

How could Uther not have spent the entire night after that comment without dreaming of what it would be like when he was king? How could he not walk through the castle, and recall all of the different towns and villages in the realm, and even those that he had never seen as of yet, and not imagine what it would be like when they were all his? And with every one of those thoughts, immediately after, that wishing to be king was, in fact, wishing that his brother would die.

He was as supportive a brother to the king as there could possibly be, and Pendragon was incredibly generous and open with his command, such that the people understood that, in effect, they benefitted from two worthy leaders, but... it was simple human nature, when Pendragon made a decision, for Uther to question if that was the course that he would have taken. Thus far that had all been perfectly fine, because Pendragon was unquestionably the king, and Uther's thoughts were just idle speculations, like thought exercises, like daydreams; what would it be like if I were king? Would I have made that decision? With one single little comment, Merlin had put a reality to those speculations. They suddenly became real. Not a someday thing—although another troubling aspect was the lack of specific detail—but *when* Uther became king. When Pendragon died.

Uther found his thumb rubbing anxiously over the paper cut on his index finger as he thought. Rubbing it had become a nervous habit, to the point where the two sides of the cut were beginning to grow calloused.

The other troubling aspect, which Uther had never spoken of to anyone except Pendragon and Ulfius—and even then, as a distant hypothetical—was that Uther had very little confidence in himself as king. There were many more times that he was happy he was *not* king as that he wished that he was. He was too enamored of the attentions of the maidens—all of that would be severely curtailed—and he was bored by long, complicated, multi-step political strategies. Plus, he just didn't really like people. The people he liked, he liked very much, but the pompous advisors and unctuous hangers-on that fluttered around Pendragon, he could not stand—and he knew that was not even the smallest fraction of the people that all wanted something of the king. Plus, he had seen up close how Pendragon had to conceal his emotions and maintain an equanimous demeanor around even people he could not stand. Uther, if he couldn't stand someone, he couldn't stand them. How would that work out as king?

Need we also mention that a lot of the daily routine of the king tended to be really, really boring? Uther liked constant movement, constant excitement. No, the arrangement as it was, brother to the king, was the ideal one.

Uther noticed himself rubbing the calloused cut and ceased. He had to stop doing that or it would never heal.

He had to find Ulfius. As soon as the carriage from the abbey alighted, he went to find his friend where he knew he would be, training less experienced knights in combat. Ulfius saw him, set a few students up to practice a move, then came directly to him. "Uther!" he said. "How did it go? Is Merlin cast out?"

Uther shook his head and widened his eyes in such a way that indicated that there was much, much to tell. "Would you like to go get a drink?"

"It is not yet the hour of sext," said Ulfius, then finished, "Yes. Yes, indeed I would." He turned to the assembled knights in his class. "I must leave," he said.

"Official business of the king," offered Uther.

"King's business!" Ulfius said, waving his hand. "Continue practicing among yourselves and I'll see you…" he turned to study Uther's face, "tomorrow," he finished.

Then they were gone. As you can imagine, the knights in training practiced for a few minutes more, until both leaders had enough time to get away, then started making excuses to leave.

Uther and Ulfius repaired to a tavern in which, due to Uther's status, they could command an alcove near the back where they would not be disturbed. When both of them had an ale in front of them, Uther told Ulfius about Merlin's visit the night before, and his overwhelming blast of anger—which Uther said he was glad was not directed at him—and their visit to the abbey that morning, during which Merlin called out Sir Brantius and told him yet another seemingly incompatible death, and assured him that it would play out just that way.

"Really?" Ulfius said. He looked away, eyes searching the dark corners of the mostly-empty tavern as he thought, then took a swig of his ale, wiping the foam from his large mustache, then turned back to Uther. "Do you really think that's possible?"

Uther looked upward and gestured with his upturned palms in a way that indicated his bewilderment. "No, it seems impossible. But," he said, "Merlin has not been wrong in one word he has ever said. Ever." He fixed his friend's eyes over the top of his drink. "So if anyone else had said it, I would never believe. Since Merlin said it," he raised his cup, "I will wait and see." He drank, then dropped the cup once more to the table. "And I will not be surprised when it happens."

Ulfius shook his head and blew out a breath in amazement. "What a circumstance. What a—" he once more shook his head in wonder. "How bizarre to have this man among us," he said.

"Oh, it gets yet more strange," said Uther. "But first, just a little something to remember; do not ever, ever, ever, *ever* make Merlin angry."

Ulfius raised his drink. "Noted."

"He said something, in his anger," said Uther, "which was..." he was running out of ways to express his amazement. "Let's just say that we might say mean things," he nodded and raised his eyebrows, "right? Get angry and say something to hurt someone? But Merlin has weapons in his arsenal such as we cannot conceive."

Ulfius nodded again, and lowered his gaze to the table.

"And he said something that I have not been able to get out of my mind, and," Uther grimaced, "I am loath to tell anyone, but at the same time—it very well might make me crazy."

"Is that why you begged off of drinking last night?" asked Ulfius.

"Yes," Uther replied, unconsciously rubbing his finger again. "I'm being driven mad by this thing and," he shook his head ruefully, "I could not be around anyone."

"Let's have it," his friend said eagerly.

"I must ask you, I must pretty much demand," he said, "that you never mention this to a living soul." He sighed in confusion. "Or a dead one."

Ulfius pulled at one end of his tremendous mustache. "Must be pretty good."

Uther chuckled ruefully. "And spreading it might incur Merlin's wrath."

"My lips are like the tomb," said the knight.

Uther's eyes grew reflective for a moment, he lowered a finger to toy around the top of his cup, then he said, "When Merlin was yelling at Pendragon about lying to him—he doesn't care if you disbelieve him," he said, "or test him honestly, but, well, I was there when he demanded that we never lie to him, and," he paused, "he said that if we did, it would be very damaging for us, but wouldn't hurt him at all." He raised his cup, took a swig while looking into the eyes of his friend, and slowly replaced it on the table. "Last night I got a taste of what he meant."

Ulfius said nothing, but waited.

"After screaming at Pendragon, with a fearsome wrath, just as he's about to leave," Uther waved his hand to communicate the dismissiveness of the comment, "he points to me and says he will see me king before he is parted from this realm."

Ulfius' eyes widened, looked away briefly as he thought, then he said "But that's great!"

Uther smiled painfully. "Well, yes," he said. "I mean, maybe." Then he raised his shoulders in a cringing gesture. "But what does that mean," he asked, "happens to Pendragon?"

"Oh," Uther said, looking sharply away.

They both passed a moment in quiet, each thinking.

"This requires more ale," said Ulfius. It was speedily arranged.

"So," continued Uther, "I couldn't get it out of my mind. Last night, or all this morning." He shook his head. "I couldn't be around Pendragon last night, and it was extremely awkward travelling this morning, I can tell you."

"And what does Pendragon think?" asked Ulfius.

"I haven't spoken to him about it," Uther said. "I have to. But—" and he raised his open hands, "how could I not be excited about being king?"

Ulfius raised his eyebrows and nodded. "I understand," he said.

"And terrified," Uther added.

"I can understand that, too," Ulfius said. "But this comment. Do you think Pendragon even noticed it?"

"Ha!" Uther chortled.

"Okay," Ulfius said. "So it's safe to assume it is weighing on his mind as well."

"If it hasn't all but destroyed him," Uther said. "I know my brother. He hears things very sensitively, and thinks on them very deeply. Which is why he is such a good king," he said, and took a drink. "Surely a much better king than I could ever be."

"Now," said Ulfius, "let's not go down that road before it even happens."

"I get what you're saying," Uther said. "But the fact is, it's true."

Ulfius looked at his drink and nodded pensively. "But with this warning, you have time to absorb what you need to know."

Uther laughed grimly. "I think I would need to know how to be a completely different person," he said.

Ulfius wagged his head in half agreement. "There are many different temperaments that can make a king," he said.

"And," Uther continued, "should I just hang around my brother and pick it all up, and all the while he knows that he will die?"

"Now," Ulfius said, "Merlin never said anything about Pendragon dying." Then he raised his eyes and saw Uther staring at him with knowing eyes. "But, yes," he added, "it does pretty much add up to that. Or something terrible happening to him."

Uther nodded gravely. "At the same time," he shrugged, "how can I not be eager to be king?"

"No," Ulfius said, "I completely understand." He sat back and shook his head woefully. "You are in a real bind."

They both sat in silence for a few minutes, each sipping his drink and thinking. "And every time I imagine being king," Uther said, "and get excited about what that might mean..." he put his head forward into his hands, "the next thought that comes is for that to happen," and he raised his eyes to look at his friend, "my brother will die. And then comes a horrible feeling—and not just because he'll be dead."

Ulfius nodded and they both sank once more into pensive silence. A minute passed without either of them speaking.

"Well," said Ulfius at last, "here's what you have to do. I don't see how there's any other choice."

Uther, head still forward, supported on his elbows, thumb rubbing over his callous, lifted his face to gaze on that of his friend.

"You have to talk of it openly with Pendragon." He shrugged. "That is what it comes down to. If you know he heard it and has thought on it, then you just have to breach the topic with him." He leaned forward and took up his cup. "I know Pendragon, and he's not a fool. He knows you heard it, and he knows you know." The knight raised his eyebrows and scrunched one cheek. "And I'm sure he also understands why you, why, some part of you," he said, "would be excited."

Uther looked him right in the face for a long while, then lowered his eyes. "Yes," he said at last, "I know you are right."

"And I wouldn't wait too much longer, either," said Ulfius. "Especially if you know that he is in great anguish over it. Don't let this come between you," he said. "That may be what the wizard wants."

"Or he is..." and Uther hunched his shoulders as though the creeps had come over him, "waiting and watching to see what we will do. There's something about him that..." he shook his head, lost for words, "it's as though we're some *experiment* to him. Pawns in *his* plan. And if we do not perform the role he has set out...." Uther widened his eyes and shook his head gravely, to indicate dire, although unknowable, consequences.

His friend took it in. "How bizarre to have this person step into our lives," he said.

Uther raised an open hand. "He's not a person," he said. "Not like you or me. He's not even, really, a human being."

Uther once more took up his cup. "What a..." he had thought to say 'curse,' then thought it over and considered saying 'blessing,' but he finally just finished, "strange circumstance."

"It's important to remember that," said Uther, "should you have dealings with him." Then he raised his own drink, "Say, for example," he said, "when I am king."

His friend raised his own cup and tapped it against Uther's. "Still," he said, "all the more reason for you and Pendragon to be united, together, and," his hand curled in the air as he searched for words, "not have any division between you as you go into what you have to face. Especially if you really are to be king," he said, "it would be far more beneficial to go toward that with," he shrugged, knowing it would be awkward, "well, with his blessing, if that's possible."

Uther nodded, and his eyes grew a little wet and shiny. He had to clear his throat before he spoke. "I believe it is possible," he said quietly. "My brother is a very, very gentle and fair man." His eyes lowered and he waited a while before speaking again. "It is not diminishing myself to say, in truth, that he is a much, much better king than I could ever be."

Ulfius looked at him square on, sighed and shrugged. "So it is," he said. "But if you have to be king, you will do it." He placed a hand on his friend's arm. "And I will help you."

They regarded each other and smiled grimly. After a long moment, Uther raised his cup. "To Pendragon," he said.

Ulfius clinked his drink against his, and said "To Uther and Pendragon," he said. "Brothers united, and worthy kings of Britain."

Tears came to Uther's eyes rapidly, so quickly that he could not wipe them away, especially with glass in hand. This make Ulfius smile warmly, so he didn't even try. They both drank heartily.

It wasn't long before Uther had to go, so Ulfius, never one to let alcohol go to waste, stayed a few minutes behind and finished his ale. And Uther's. When he emerged once more into the daylight—surprisingly bright after having been in the close darkness of the tavern—an old beggar poked Ulfius in the leg with a cane and demanded some money for a meal. Ulfius reached within his tunic, felt into his purse, and gave the beggar a coin. Seeing how pleased the old man was, he gave another.

"Ulfius," said the old man.

Ulfius was surprised to hear that the beggar knew his name.

"He who serves his master, serves himself," said the beggar. "Take care to always offer the best advice to your lord, and you will find great rewards!" He raised an open hand in a gesture of tribute to the knight.

Ulfius nodded thanks to the man, but then there was a loud noise from down the street, and when Ulfius looked back, the old beggar must have wandered off, for he was gone. Ulfius looked about, stroking his mustache thoughtfully, before turning back to his quarters for a nap.

Sir Brantius was so upset by what had happened that he begged to stay at the abbey for two more days. He then made clear to his wife that he wanted to slip back home quietly, which she replied to with an "uh-ha," that sounded just the least little bit patronizing. After the king had left, so abruptly, she had helped him off with his disguise, and wiped the makeup from his face while clucking about how unfair it all was and how appalling it was that Pendragon could give that grumpy, grizzled little charlatan so much power over him, but as the night wore on, and they had both spent time in silence, her answers to his comments became shorter, and sharper, and tinged with just the tiniest amount of ironic distance. And, where she once replied to his points on how unfair the entire situation was, and how sorely abused and grievously tested he was—not to mention insulted to the very core—with hearty assent, wiping of his brow and outraged clucking, she soon started to come back with perfunctory agreements, and even rejoinders of the "what did you expect?" variety. When he, at the close of the second day, made mention of how he might stay away from court a few days after they had returned to town, in order that they should have time to miss him, she had actually emitted a short chuckle, and when he looked over, she was caught at the tail end of suppressing a smile. She never did end up replying.

When they did return, the carriage pulling up in front of their house, the first thing he saw was children running away, into their various houses, and, not long after being inside, the windows opening up with their mothers leaning out, seemingly just to take in the fine day, but eyes glancing quickly over to look at him as he entered his home. Suddenly others appeared on the street, men and teen boys, stepping out from doors or alleys, with an urgent need just then to be there, apparently, leaning casually against the houses, eyes darting downward, faces turning around the moment he looked toward them. It was quite obvious—it was rather ridiculous how crowded the street had suddenly become—and he didn't wait for his bags to be unloaded before he ducked quickly into the house.

There, in the quiet darkness, he put his hand over his chest and felt the first tinges of a creeping sensation of his skin, a tingling climbing up his spine. What did they know? Why did they want to see him?

He turned and peered out the window. They were still there, maybe even more of them now. He saw his wife, standing to the front of the horses, looking away down the street, and when her face turned to look toward him and he could plainly see it, there was panic there. She moved as quickly as she could without appearing to run, paid to have the bags brought in, and was suddenly in the door, back against the wall on the other side from him, fear on her face.

"What is going on?" he asked.

Her cheeks balled up in a flash of anger and her teeth were exposed before she quashed it and spoke to him in a low and even voice. "Obviously your little stunt has been heard about in town." A moment later there was a knock, she opened the door for the bags, followed the men upstairs, and didn't come back down.

Even the porters gave Brantius a special eye as they descended the stairs and came in the room specially to ask if there was anything more he wanted. Maybe they had been looking at him funny at the beginning of the trip, but he hadn't seen enough to notice then.

"Plan to go out riding today?" one of them asked upon leaving. The other poked him in the ribs and they both controlled their laughter until they were out the door.

Brantius went to the window and pulled back the curtain, slightly. When he did, two people standing just outside walked quickly away. There were other people standing in the street, talking, gossiping. Some of them looked directly at his house. Some pointed. Some he looked at and thought, 'oh, that's just everyday street life,' until one of them would abruptly look over, or point to his house.

Had they all heard?

He went and sat in the room at the back of the house, resting his head in his hands, and thought for about an hour. Or tried to think. In

216

his body he felt a heightened anxiety that kept the muscles on edge, like when there is a loud high-pitched sound ringing. Something was going on. He knew that the town was interested in Merlin, in the wonder of him as a person, and whether or not the things he said could possibly be true. In fact, the whole kingdom was interested in this. They had all heard of the wizard, but no, they couldn't all have heard of *him*. His story… it wasn't that interesting, was it? It had come to nothing, after all. He tried, and failed. Why would they care?

He heard a noise, and when he turned his head, there was a young boy, face and hands pressed up against the window, watching him. Brantius started up slightly, and the boy ran away.

He went immediately upstairs, while his wife was coming down. "I am going out," she said.

"I am weary from travel," he said, his voice sounding unconvincing, even to him. "I will stay in." It was only a short time before the hour of sext, and the sun was bright and high in the sky. His wife was past him, down the stairs, and she did not reply.

He lay on the bed, facing up, eyes examining the lines and whorls of the wood grain of the ceiling beams. It was what he often did, unconsciously, in the hours before sleep, as he thought on how to advance himself at court. Who had to be moved out of his way, whom to give this information to but not that, who had to be told something false because he knew they would tell it to someone else. He was always careful, he thought to be sure that nothing he said or did could ever come back on him. And thus far, it had all worked out beautifully. To the extent that he considered himself somewhat of a master of the art.

Soon the rectangle of sunlight had moved from the wall and was a narrow line of reddish illumination against the floor wood when he heard the door downstairs. He lay back on the bed and waited for his wife to come up. The room grew gloomy and still as a tomb as he heard, after the initial sound of creaks and steps when she entered, nothing more. No sound of her climbing the stairs, as usually happened. Brantius finally raised his head, listening but hearing nothing, then swung his legs around to hang off the side of the bed.

He crept downstairs slowly. The stairway and halls were dim outlines in the dying light. His wife had not lit any lamps or candles. He heard a slight sniffling sound, and came back into the room where he had been. His wife was in the chair he had vacated, bent at the waist, with her head in her hands. Her back bobbed slightly with the movement of her elevated breathing. And there was the child, peering in the window again, watching her. It was so dusky, he did not see Brantius until he was right there, at the window, knocking harshly from within.

The child looked up, the image of his astonished face freezing in Brantius' brain before he bolted away and out of their yard. When he turned, his wife had also raised her head, and he saw her face confused and startled, with skin pale and eyes rimmed with red. He moved over immediately and knelt down in front of her.

He took her hand in his. It was wet. "My dear," he asked tenderly, "whatever is so wrong?" He kissed her hand.

She looked him right in the face, her visage a taut mixture of confusion, bewilderment and pain as her eyes searched his for a long moment before speaking.

"Every single person in this town, or—in this kingdom," she said, and looked at his hand where it clutched hers, "is waiting to see how you will die."

-43-

It's not always easy to find a time to talk with the king, especially privately. Uther entered the hall where the king was seated at table, surrounded by advisors, leaning forward and closely studying the documents they presented. No one looked up at him, and, overcome by a sudden shyness, he just closed the door and retreated. Later, he saw his brother walking across the courtyard, again surrounded, and this time he caught his brother's eye, and they nodded across the distance, but it was obviously not the right time to ask him for a moment alone. Not to mention that Uther felt odd about approaching him with all of those other people around—as if somehow they knew what he wanted, and what Merlin had said. The way the king showed a trace of anxiety when he saw Uther, and looked quickly away, told him that his brother was also ruminating. Turning on himself as he often did, and imagining that others could see the guilt that he felt, Uther assumed that his brother knew that he was thinking about being king himself, when Pendragon was out of the way.

This thought, wrong as it was, made him even more shy to be around his brother, a new and unpleasant feeling, but he finally forced a word to him as they sat near each other at dinner, and asked if they might speak alone soon. It could not be done that evening, so Uther spent the whole next day outright avoiding Pendragon, trying to drive anxious predictions about their talk from his mind, until it was time for him to appear at his chamber door that evening. His brother also appeared to be nervous, and they made small talk as drinks were served, everyone made comfortable, and the servants sent outside. Uther spoke first.

"We haven't had a chance to talk since," Uther lowered his eyes and winced, "Merlin," he found himself pausing again, "Uh, said… what he did."

Pendragon chuckled bitterly. "Yes," he said, "what did you think about that?"

Uther looked up. "What did *you* think about it?"

His brother stopped pacing and rubbed his forehead. "Well," he asked, "what do you think it meant?"

Uther gave a frustrated laugh, and threw up his hands. "Fine," he said, "I will go first!" When Pendragon smiled and shook his head at the strangeness of it all, he continued. "He said I would be king one day. I mean… it made me have all kinds of thoughts. Confusing thoughts." He lowered his eyes once again. "I don't really sit here, wishing that I were king," he said, "but at the same time…."

"It sounds appealing," Pendragon finished.

219

"Yes."

The king began pacing again. "That's normal, Uther," he said. "Any normal, ambitious person, such as we are, would want to be king."

He turned and looked plainly at his brother with a nonjudgmental look that comforted him.

"And I'll just bring out," continued Pendragon, "that there is the strong implication that I will die."

Uther sighed in relief and his shoulders slumped. "Yes," he said.

"I heard it, too," said Pendragon. "Believe me."

"It was shocking, and," Uther shook his head, "well, it's all I have been able to think about since."

"Me too!" Pendragon exclaimed, and suddenly all the new awkwardness that had grown up between them was gone, and they were the close brothers, infinitely comfortable in each other's presence again. Pendragon sat down next to Uther. "One thing, well, aside from how shocking it is to think about, is how… how *cruel* Merlin was in saying it."

"Yes!" Uther exclaimed, eyes wide. "It was clearly his punishment for you."

"And it's enough to make you think…." Pendragon simply shook his head.

"How did we let ourselves in for this kind of punishment," Uther finished.

"That is exactly it, brother. What have we…" the king's voice drifted off. "And *who*, exactly, have we entered into this endeavor with?"

"And is there any way to get out of it now?" asked Uther. "If we wanted to."

"I am so glad you came to me," said Pendragon, leaning his arm and head onto his brother's shoulder. "All of this has been weighing so heavily on my mind. And as you can imagine, for me…" he shook his head and shrugged. "Well, it's the implication that I will die."

"I know," said Uther, who sat back to look full on his brother. "I can't imagine how that must be for you."

Pendragon widened his eyes. "And are we talking about weeks from now? Years from now?" He shook his head in confusion. "Days? How am I supposed to react?"

"I think the main point is that you are to fear Merlin," replied Uther. "He just dropped it out there. Well, clearly he uses his foresight as a weapon."

Pendragon had to laugh. "And a powerful weapon it is!" he said. "That's really what got to me—the viciousness of it. That's what made me question who we have gotten ourselves involved with. And do we have any choice to get out of it?"

Uther raised his open palms to show that he had no answers. "On the other hand," he said, "had it not been for him, Hengist would have killed me, and we never would have driven his followers out. We thought it would take years to come back here and establish your rule, and…." He snapped his fingers.

Pendragon leaned back against the wall and shook his head. They agreed, he knew—there was nothing more to say. "He does seem to want Britain to be claimed for the Britons," he said.

"So we are lucky that we fit his purpose," said Uther, then added; "Which once again places *him* in charge."

"Well, that's what an ally is," Pendragon said. "You both share a similar aim. Even though you might not want to be linked to anyone at all. That's what you'll realize when you become king, well—here we are talking about it!"

Uther 's face darkened and he leaned forward onto his knees. "It's incredibly uncomfortable."

Pendragon placed a firm hand on his shoulder. "I want you to relax about it," he said. "It is something he said, not anything you did." He stood once more, and began pacing in front of his brother. "And it is out of our control."

"I am glad to hear you say so," Uther said, "and, of course, having heard him say that, I have thought about being king. And of course I am excited about that," he spoke frankly, "but… for that to happen," he shook his head and sighed, "something would have to happen to you. Something pretty bad."

"Like that I would die."

"Exactly," Uther said, unable to meet his brother's eyes, "and... well, it makes me feel awful."

Pendragon smiled gently as he gazed down on his brother. "Don't," he said. "As I said, it is normal to want to be king... although I don't think you—or anyone— could fully realize the less pleasant aspects that come along with it."

"Like?"

The king began pacing again. "Well, the weight of all the responsibility, and having to make decisions for everyone in the whole kingdom. Everyone wanting something from you all the time. Never being able to relax, never knowing who you can trust. Barely ever having even a second alone." He caught himself, then put on a more composed face. "If you wish, we can begin to talk about what it is like," he faced his brother, "with the expectation that you will soon be king."

Uther winced. "Pendragon! I don't..." he lowered his gaze again. "Well, we needn't be morbid."

The king chuckled affectionately. "If we trust Merlin, then we must accept that it will probably be true. No need to be overly sentimental about it. You're not saying that you want me to die, I hear that clearly, but..." he shrugged, "we should be prepared, as best we can. And, one thing we can never forget—we're not just talking about our own fates, but that of the entire country."

Uther's hands came up at once to hold his head. "That's exactly why I cannot be king."

Pendragon laughed out loud, and stepped over to pat his brother's back. "You will rise to the challenge, I know it," he said. "And because we have this time to prepare you... we should be happy, and make the most of it."

Uther raised an eyebrow ironically. "Another advantage so great we have no choice but to accept it."

The king threw up his hands to express the frustration, and lack of freedom, the situation demanded.

"I like it with you as king," Uther said, "and me as your right hand."

Pendragon nodded. "It works," he agreed. Then his face clouded. "One only wishes for a little more time to," he paused reflectively, "let it work." He shook his head and snapped out of it. "But," he said, "we know what is coming, and we have the advantage of preparation, therefore, without announcing it to anyone," he stopped short and regarded his brother where he sat, "we will begin preparing you to face what you will as the king."

Uther blew out a big breath of apprehension, then acquiesced. "Agreed," he said. "We will proceed and I will make myself more available to be educated and trained."

Pendragon nodded in approval. "Now," he asked, "as for Merlin, I wanted to ask your advice. How should I proceed from here? He seems very angry with me." He crossed his arms.

Uther thought about it for a moment, but only had one answer. "I think the only thing you can do is apologize."

"I have thought of that," Pendragon said. "But he is very, very clever—he is probably hearing this conversation even as we have it— and I feel whatever I do must be done with a true and open heart." His face grimaced as many thoughts crossed his mind. "Which is difficult to do, when one is allowed no mental privacy, but," he sighed, "I thought, perhaps, to also offer him something. As a gift, and also a gesture of trust."

Uther looked at him. "A specially-engraved goblet."

Pendragon laughed. "Or an artfully-stitched robe that reads 'king of the wizards!'" he joked. "No, I was thinking... what if we offer to write his every utterance down in a book? That would show how much we value him and his wisdom."

"Ah, good suggestion," Uther said, pointing in agreement. "I do think that he is very susceptible to flattery. And then we would have this book," he added, "to draw on in the future."

"Or *you* would," said Pendragon. "It's just a gesture to apologize and to, well, hopefully to win back his favor."

Uther nodded, stood, and said he thought it was a good idea, and that the wizard was sure to agree to it. As for him forgiving Pendragon... well, they would have to see how he reacted. They took the opportunity the quiet evening together offered and talked further, until deep into the night, and when it was time to part, the brothers embraced each other, and Pendragon said, "Do not ever be afraid to come to me with anything that might be bothering you, even if it's grim or unpleasant," he said. "We must never allow ourselves to be drawn apart," he let go of his brother, and his gaze was trained on the floor. "Especially if we have only little time left."

-44-

Merlin showed up at his mother's in the early evening. He was once more a boy, now aged ten, and he took care, this time, to appear outside and enter through the door, so as not to disturb anyone. His mother was busy teaching one of her young girls, so he spent an hour chatting amiably with Rossa, finding out how she had been and how things had been going in their shelter. When his mother walked in later, she was delighted to see him, and ran to embrace him directly. Rossa asked whether he would stay to dinner, and he agreed, and they all ate at the large table, Merlin, the two women, and the six young maidens who were staying there.

After dinner, Rossa went home, the girls went to their rooms to talk or read, and Meylinde and Merlin were left alone in the large hall. She took her seat in her rocking chair in front of the fire that burned in the great stone fireplace. She asked Merlin how he was, and he told her that there would be much for him to catch her up on, and plus there was something he particularly wanted her advice on.

But first, he wanted to know how she had been and what had been happening with her. It was a bit of a farce, what they went through, because both of them knew that Merlin was already familiar with everything that had happened with his mother, because of course he kept special tabs on her, but he knew that it was important to sit with her, in person, and hear her tell him of her life from her own mouth.

She then asked him how he was, and he told her of all the adventures he had had, and how Blaise was—things he had not been able to tell her during his quick, anger-fueled overnight visit—and described both Pendragon and Uther, and how they were very worthy young men, although a bit rash and impetuous, which was something he wanted to talk to her about, but first:

"I have settled on a basic general appearance, that most people will come to know me in," he said, "and I would like to show it to you." He then became the likeness of the middle-aged, bearded man that was his common appearance when he appeared to Uther and Pendragon.

His mother smiled sweetly, the lines around her eyes crinkling as she looked on the appearance of her boy, and her mirth grew such that she had to suppress a laugh. "Well," she said at last, "that look does," she shook her head, her gaze roaming over his body, "conform with what people might think that a great, mystic wise man might look like."

Merlin nodded. "Therefore, it is in this form that you will most know me from now on," he said. "I can't very well advise kings from the guise of a young boy," he said. "Well, I can, but it adds a whole additional layer of—" and he shook his head and hands to indicate the bizarre awkwardness. "Appearing like this will make things go more smoothly, and—oh no, what's wrong?" he asked, for she had stopped smiling, and her face had taken on the slightest hint of distance.

She looked at him in his adult guise for a long moment, as though trying to think of how best to say what she wanted, and finally she said, "Merlin, could you, with me," and her lips pressed together with emotion and hoping she wasn't just being silly, but she asked, "appear as you really are, at your real age, with me?"

He was again his ten-year-old self by the time she had finished her sentence. He came at once to her side and took her hand. "Of course, mother," he said. "I just, I thought...."

She stroked his head and smiled. "Maybe I'm just being silly," she said. "I know other mothers have no problem accepting whichever incarnations their sons choose to appear in."

He looked her in the eyes for a moment, confused, then he realized that she was joking and ribbing him for being special, and the strange situation she was in, being his mother. He smiled warmly and ran his hand up and down her soft arm.

"Then it shall be just that way, mother," he said, "and I will always appear in my unadorned appearance with you, since you ask."

"Thank you," she said. "You'll be grown up too fast as it is," she added, "and I don't want to miss any of your development. Certainly not have you be a grown man before you're even eleven years old," she said, smiling.

"Then this will be the only place, from now on, in which anyone will see me as I really am," he declared.

"Oh no, don't say that," she said pleasantly, and gave him an affectionate appraisal for a moment. "Maybe one day," she said, "you'll want to show someone else your true appearance."

"Why would I do that?"

She burst out laughing. It took her a moment of chuckling before she could get words out to tell him. "Because maybe you might *like* someone, Merlin," she said, "and want to them to see you as you truly are."

His eyes took on that same brow-nettled, furiously focused gaze he had shown even in the cradle. Then his head moved slightly to the side, a thought having hit him, and he nodded.

"I see," he said. "That would be quite a powerful incentive to inspire intimacy."

Meylinde cackled. "True!" she said, her other hand banging the arm of her chair. "Or," she added, as another suggestion, "you could show it for no other reason that you want to be open with that person."

"I will think on this," he said. "But there is another matter which I very much want to discuss with you."

Then he told her of Pendragon, and how he liked the king very much, and thought that he was an excellent Briton, even an exemplary one, but he was young, and didn't know when to reign in his arrogance. And the king looked at him, Merlin, like he was some lucky bonus advantage one king has over another, like a well-positioned castle,

226

instead of a poorly-defended one. So he told her how the king accepted all the advantages Merlin gave him, but when he was questioned, the king proved to be suspicious, but not only that, he thought that perhaps he knew better than Merlin.

Merlin knelt beside his mother and leaned forward on her thigh, his head on his folded arms, continuing to speak as her left hand came down to caress the back of his head and neck as he talked. "Now," he said, "I had told the king, do not lie to me. I said it twice, the second time more firmly than the first. And I told him in plain language that if he lied, it would hurt him far more than it did me." He looked up at her and opened his hand, to say that he could not have been clearer with Pendragon.

"And then he did it. Treated me like I was a complete idiot. You should have seen the makeup of this man pretending to be sick—it was preposterous. And I have Pendragon, staring me right in the face, thinking I'm falling for it. And I looked at him like," and he showed her his face, "are you honestly going to stand right there in front of me and pretend that I don't know what's going on? And he did, despite, again, my giving him numerous indications that I was displeased." Merlin raised and shook his hands at his ears. "So anyway, I," he paused, and his face looked like a boy, one who didn't want to confess to being bad, "told him I was angry—"

"Oh no," his mother said.

"And I *was*," Merlin said, "I had never—" he stopped himself, "it was unexpected," he said.

"Oh my," she said. "That's quite a claim."

"Indeed," he said, and they both thought on it for a while. "And," he continued, "I said something, that meant very little to me, but Pendragon and his brother seem to be taking it very hard, and considering it to be their punishment..."

"And is it?" Meylinde asked.

"Well," the child reared up straight, "I *told* them, if you lie to me, it will hurt you and not me." He put up his hands in defeat. "There it is, right there," he said. "I told them. I don't know what more I could say."

She looked down upon him, and before she gave a reaction, she asked him, "What did you say?"

Merlin looked down. "Something about, well, hinting at, you know, that he might die soon."

"Oh!" she said, leaning her head back. "Merlin, Merlin, Merlin," she said.

The child shook his head, half in real frustration. "I haven't had this role before, either, should anyone be curious. It's not like I have a set of instructions to go by. I didn't know that he was going to have such a strong reaction. And then, now—this is the actual issue I want to discuss with you."

"Oh," she was surprised, then leaned back in the chair and reassembled her attention.

"Now, *now*," Merlin emphasized, tapping with his finger, "that he feels the pain he was oblivious to the possibility of, because he was so sure of what he knew, and now that he knows he's not back home playing with wooden swords, but on the level of kings...." He noticed his mother waiting patiently. "Now he wants to beg forgiveness of me."

Meylinde regarded him with a look that showed she understood, even why he was angry, and she began once more stroking his head, and he settled forward on his crossed arms, atop her thigh.

"So then what is the question?" his mother asked.

Merlin shifted in his position and thought. "How do you," he shook his head, "forgive someone?" He shook his head again. "I clearly told him; he would get hurt. So, I feel blameless. And forgive him, I mean," he made a dismissive gesture, "we all know the famous importance the Lord gives to forgiveness, but... am I supposed to just pretend that I don't know he treated me this way?"

Meylinde raised a hand. "First, you have to admit that some of the things that mean nothing to you, because you see across generations, can have a devastating effect on someone to whom it affects," she said. "And people, most people," she said, "find it almost impossible to see beyond anything but their own lives."

"I know," Merlin agreed sadly.

"Secondly," she went on, "people can hear something, like that he would get hurt by lying to you, and… somehow it isn't real. Somehow, especially over time, it begins to seem like," she held her hands in the air, "it couldn't really be as bad as all that." And then her manner changed, and became more thoughtful, and she went on, "And you have to know that the people you come upon have no way of truly knowing what you are, because of your part-devil side, and have no way to even conceive of what that might mean for them. Especially on the level of what simply happens… in a day."

Merlin leaned forward across her legs, and thought about what she said.

"And so you told Pendragon that if he lied to you it would hurt him," she said, looking down from where she sat above him, "but there's no way he could have understood what that might really mean. And so he was shocked, and hurt, in a way he had never been before, and maybe never even thought could be."

"I'm quite sure it was the latter," said Merlin.

"But consider this, Merlin," she said, and she ran her hand over his face until he looked up at her from where he rested in her lap. "Perhaps he learned from this. Perhaps now, because of this happening, he is wiser. He has matured." And her gentle fingers stroked his hair, and his face grew pouty as he thought, and he thought for a long while.

"And perhaps this is exactly what he needed to happen in order to become the king who can truly trust you," she said, and placed her fingers under his chin and lifted his face. "And that's why it's wonderful that you were the one to show him that. Perhaps that's a way in which you affect history—"

"Oh, I affect history," the child said.

"Not just in the things that you do directly, or the things that you advise others to do," she pinched his nose affectionately with this, "but also through the insight you bring to the people you touch," she said, and, as though the thought had never struck her, she had to sit up in her chair and look at her child.

He just knelt, his head resting on her leg, and looked up at her while they shared a quiet moment.

"And as for how to forgive someone, that it something you have to discover for yourself, in your heart," she said. "Which I think will be very good for you," she added, "and something you will learn by. But you know, you have often said that you are committed to work for the Lord, and the Lord says one thing only: *forgive*." She raised her eyebrows. "So there really is no question."

He turned his head downward, so that he was resting on his forehead, and grumbled "I know." Then he looked out to stare across the room. "But it is difficult. He knowingly deceived me."

"I know," she said.

"After I told him, with... astonishing clarity...."

"I know," she said, chuckling. "It is difficult. You just have to say you forgive him, and then," she said, "get over it in your heart as best you can. And think about this, also," she raised a finger. "If you do not forgive him, neither of you can move on. You'll just be angry, and he'll be sorry, and you'll both be stuck there. And then nothing else, none of your grand plans, can happen."

He let his head rest on its side, and gazed up at her. "You are right, mother."

She looked down on him with loving eyes, and let her hand run gently through his hair. This ten-year-old boy, son of a demon, advisor to kings, designer of the future, dealer of rough existential justice to anyone who would dare to go against him or his wishes. She sighed.

"My sweet boy," she said.

-45-

Pendragon paced nervously in his room. His mind had been half taken over all day with rehearsals of his talk with Merlin that night. Now it was time for the wizard to appear, and Pendragon was still nervous, but glad the time was finally arriving. He would know something, at least, within the hour. He kept coming back to the question of what would happen if Merlin never forgave him, then had to tell himself that there was no point in pursuing those thoughts until it was a reality. But it wasn't easy. Thankfully, there was soon a knock at the door, and there he was.

"Merlin," he said, inviting him in. "Using the door," he said.

"Sometimes the traditional ways are best," the wizard said, stepping in and turning to face the king. Pendragon regarded him, wrung his hands before him, and sighed.

"Merlin," said Pendragon, "I am glad that you have come to me. Thank you."

"I am your friend and adviser," said Merlin. "Of course I will always be glad to speak with you."

Pendragon looked at him ruefully, unsure what to say in response. He didn't want to call Merlin a liar in the midst of his own apology. At last he lowered his head and opened his hands. "Let us be truthful with each other, Merlin. I have felt very keenly that you are angry at me for lying to you. I wanted to apologize to you, for it is my fondest hope that things can be as they once were between us."

"That was my hope as well," said Merlin. "Before you played such an active part in your friend's deception."

"I regret that very deeply," said Pendragon. "You should know that your punishment has caused me unimaginable pain and sorrow."

"My punishment?" asked Merlin.

Pendragon was again unsure what to think. He decided the best way forward was with no confrontation or contradiction. "You gave me a hint of my future," he said. "Or rather, you gave Uther a hint of a his, which had implications for me."

Merlin appeared confused. "And that was... punishment?" he asked

Pendragon looked at him with widened eyes, his shoulders now setting back in a tight and defensive posture. What was he to make of this man? He finally decided that trickery or insincerity of any kind was not the answer, he had to go forward as honestly as he could. "You told my brother, in front of me," he said, "that you would see him king before you were parted from him."

"Yes," said Merlin.

Pendragon again could only stare at him with widened eyes. At last he threw up his hands in frustration. "And since then," he said, "I have been obsessed with thoughts of my own death!"

Merlin's brow winkled. "But I did not say when you would die. Or how you would die." The wizard seemed genuinely confused.

The king's shoulders lost their tension and he fell forward in astonished bewilderment. He almost laughed. "Merlin," he said, "truly you are not human for, it seems to me, you show little appreciation for the kind of thoughts that might go through a man's head, having heard a comment like that." Then Pendragon looked up swiftly, in moment of fear that even a small contradiction like that could anger the wizard.

"My mother has often said so," said Merlin.

The king shook his head. "Yet you seem as though every word that comes out of your mouth has been weighed with the importance of..." he searched to find the appropriate reference, "scripture."

Merlin then stared at him for a long silent moment with half-narrowed and appraising eyes. "Yet still you did not listen to me," he said at last.

"That is a human failing," said the king. "Or, let me be clear, that is *my* failing."

"You know that I am half devil," said Merlin. "Because of that, I have found that I am very swift to anger, and once it has started," he pressed his hands together and sighed, "it is a very hard for me to quell the anger within myself."

"I see," said Pendragon.

"And you know also that my head is filled with knowledge of all things past and future," the wizard continued. "And for that reason, I have been told, and have had to realize, that while I see the movement of all people across history," he stretched out a hand in a sweeping gesture, "it is difficult for me to see the plight and feelings of any one particular man or woman."

"I see," said Pendragon, and lowered his head in thought. He began to pace in the chamber, and brought his hand up to press against his beard under his chin.

Merlin watched him as he walked back and forth, and one could see the affection returning to his eyes, driving out the coldness toward Pendragon that had taken residence there.

"I can imagine something else that may be of use to you," said Pendragon. When Merlin's silence indicated curiosity, he continued. "It sounds as though, from what you are describing, that your brain is constantly full of knowledge of the past, and possibilities for the future."

When the wizard nodded, he continued.

"Men, on the other hand, have brains that are not constantly full," Pendragon said, "and sometimes that emptiness works against us." Once more the king put his hand under his chin and began to pace. "And we fill that emptiness sometimes—some people are not troubled by this at all—but some people fill their brains with thoughts, trying to figure everything out, and we can make the slightest incidents, or facial expressions, or," and he gestured to Merlin, "*comments* into something we can think on for hours and days, even for unending amounts of time."

"I see," said Merlin, tilting back his head, and his eyes drifted off as he thought of the implications of what he had heard.

"And I would think that would be a great weapon in your arsenal against mankind," said Pendragon. "For if a person is prone to introspection, the slightest carefully aimed word," he shook his head and chuckled, "can near-well drive them completely mad."

The wizard nodded, his eyes remaining fixed on the floor. But it was only for a moment, then his eyes raised to smilingly appraise the king.

"Pendragon," he said, "I have no arsenal of weapons against mankind."

The king swiftly lifted his eyes to lock with Merlin's, and they both stood still in silence for a moment.

Then they simultaneously exploded in laughter. Pendragon let himself get close enough, and seeing no resistance, he let a hand come out to affectionately pat the shoulder of the wizard. Then he moved to stand just before him.

"There is something I must do," said Pendragon, and he knelt down first on one knee, then the both.

"Oh, don't do that," said Merlin.

"Merlin," said Pendragon, and reached out to take the wizard's hand, even as he kept his head lowered and gazed on the man's feet. "Let me formally apologize. You warned me not to lie to you, yet I did. I have been humbled, and I am sorry for my trespass. I apologize for what I have done, and humbly ask to be your friend and confidante once more."

Merlin's face grew red and warm, and he felt sheepish, a curious reaction he didn't know that he could have. "Oh come, stand up," he said.

"I ask that you accept my apology," said Pendragon.

"I..." and for a moment Merlin hung confused, and thought on his recent conversation with his mother, because, well, he didn't know what it meant to accept an apology and move on, or have a relationship strengthened by it. "Pendragon," he said, "you disappointed me. I was sorry to see that." He paused, lowered his eyes for a moment as the king nodded, then continued. "I accept your apology, and we are indeed friends, Pendragon," he said, placing his other hand atop theirs where they were joined. "Now please stand. A king should kneel to no one, including me," he said.

Pendragon took longer than expected to rise once more to his feet—the premature aging and stiffness of body that came from being king was starting to settle over him, even at his youngish age—and when he stood and raised his head, he was pleased to see Merlin returning his gaze with the familiar warmth and gleam of mischief.

The seer patted their joined hands, and said "I am sorry, Pendragon, that I spoke to you out of anger, and wielded my knowledge of the future thoughtlessly. My only excuse could be that—well, actually, I have two."

And the two men laughed together.

"One is that I am half devil," he said.

"That one works for every occasion," said Pendragon.

Merlin nodded, smiling. "The other, is that," and he gestured to himself, "I am only ten years old," he said, "and, while wiser than any other man on earth, am still learning." He paused. "Especially about interacting with humans."

Pendragon's eyes widened. "You are," he scoffed, "ten years old?"

Merlin nodded. "I was born ten years ago," he said. "But of course, I'm a special case."

The king laughed, raised his eyebrows, and simply shook his head in wonder. "Well, my young friend," he said, "I should also like to honor you, by providing scribes that will record your every utterance in a book that we will preserve for the benefit of those to come."

"Ugh!" Merlin scoffed, waving his hands in disgust. "Scribes around me all the time! Never!"

Pendragon's face fell. "Well," he said weakly, "um, you could… make this book in any manner that you choose."

"I have thought on this," said Merlin, "for I am aware of your book idea." He folded his arms and raised a finger. "How about if I record a number of prophecies that would be helpful to people in the future? That way I could meet with scribes at proscribed times, and you would be left with a book that would benefit the people of your land for many centuries."

The king thought on it. "That sounds perfect," he said. "Exactly as you would like, I would be happy to have it."

Merlin nodded, shook the king's hand, but then kept it within his own. "Pendragon," he said, and gripped their clasped hands, "I spoke rashly with you before. But if you will allow me, I will tell you more of your future, such that you will have no doubt of your purpose, and importance—lasting importance—to this great land that you command."

Pendragon's eyes began to gleam with lust to know the future, and then he broke, and thought darkly, for a moment, but then returned, even more interested, and finally could stand no more. He said, "Yes, Merlin, tell me."

Merlin released their hands, and opened his arms in a gesture, palms turning upward, indicating worship of Pendragon and his fortune. "Pendragon," Merlin said, with the warm tone of a proud parent, "you are the blood of Britain. There is coming a great king—the greatest this land will ever know—in the years that will come after you have left the earth, and he will win this country for its natural people, drive out all invaders, and assemble a fellowship of the most worthy men found in this realm to protect the weak and right wrongs where they find them. In this way, he will create the first lasting peace and order this land has ever known, and he will lay the basis for everything that this country will ever become."

Pendragon's eyes widened as he saw into the possibilities.

"Pendragon," Merlin said, gazing proudly on him, "this king will be of your lineage. You will not be his father, but you will be the blood that runs through his veins, as well as the blood that saturates this land," Merlin gestured toward the earth, "from which he draws his power. The king, and the land, will be one!" Merlin yelled, then saw that he might have gotten a little abstract. "In a way that perhaps humans cannot understand, but can *feel*. And this king's name will be known as long as the world lasts, and your name will endure with him—for all time."

A shininess had come into Pendragon's eyes, so moved was he by the words that the wise man told him. His brow had wrinkled with emotion, and his lips were pressed tightly together in order to contain the powerful feelings he felt.

Merlin used one hand to gesture toward Pendragon. "At that time when you enter the circle of blood—and you will know it without question," said Merlin, "then you will know it is time for your blood to enter the earth, and for you to leave this world." Merlin once more gripped his hand, hard, and stared him in the eye. "And after you have gone, I will use the utmost of my powerful craft to practice the most impressive magic I have ever brought about—as of yet," he said, "and unite your blood with the spirits that animate this land, then channel that power into this king to come, and it will be *you*, Pendragon," he said, "who provide that power, and birthright, and connection to this land that he will use to wrench this country from nothing, and create a kingdom," and Merlin made a sweeping gesture with his hands, then failed for words, "such as you could never even imagine."

Then he finished, and stared with smiling eyes at the dazed and dazzled king, who stood before him, blinking tearful eyes.

"I wish I could see it!" Pendragon said at last, the words coming out as a whisper. "Thank you, Merlin," he finally added.

"Ha!" laughed the seer. "I, and all who walk in this country, should thank you!" he boomed. "But you must tell no one of what I have told you," he said, "not even your brother. This is for you, and you alone, in penance for the uncertainty you have gone through on account of me."

Pendragon nodded silently. "I will tell no one," he said.

Merlin nodded. "I know," he said. "Now," he waved his hand, turning away, "when shall we get started on this book?"

-46-

When Sir Brantius stepped outside, there was a noose drawn in the dirt. He looked at it for a long moment with disappointed eyes, and sighed. It was always the noose. Drowning or breaking one's neck after being thrown from a horse were simply not as easy to draw or express in one, simple image, so the noose was always it. He raised his head to look up the street. Sometimes the person who had drawn it—often a young boy of squire's age—was somewhere visible, waiting. In this case, nothing, but then, about five doors down, the front door opened and a boy came out, turned, saw him there, and froze. Then he went right back in, and, a few moments later, re-emerged, followed by his brother and father. They all turned to gape, and, seeing Brantius there, turned their heads away immediately. Trying to act casual. When they found excuse to look back, Brantius waved at them, wearing a curdled smile on his face. The father simply stepped back inside, as though he hadn't seen, while his two sons pretended to be playing in the street. For a moment, a young daughter stuck her head out, looked at him, and stayed looking, until the hand of a parent reached out and pulled her back.

It had only gotten worse since they had returned from the abbey, just under a week ago, as more and more people heard about his testing of Merlin, and the seer's predictions about his death. Everyone in town was curious about Merlin—he was a bit of a celebrity, and sightings of him were news, although he mostly kept himself away from places where ordinary people might question him. Sir Brantius was now, also, somewhat of an unwilling celebrity, although of the wrong kind. People were fascinated by him, but not in such a way that they wanted to know him.

Brantius locked his door and began trundling down the street. He could feel the eyes on him as he walked, following him. He could hear the conversations stop as he approached, and begin again, louder and more heated, when he had walked a few paces by. The merchants he frequented were slightly friendlier, more curious, while the other patrons might stand a little further away. He caught the women who visited his wife watching him from the corners of their eyes, and saw how they listened with keen interest after asking how he was, or after his health.

At this point, he was still bewildered by it. His feelings were all over the place, sometimes angry, sometimes wounded to the point of crying, sometimes bitter, sometimes remorseful and overcome with sorrow. Often he felt his forehead tingling and lips trembling, and he felt like a little boy who had been unjustly punished. Blamed for something he had not done, but bravely taking it and waiting stoically until his virtue was revealed and he was vindicated.

Only there was no reason to think that he would ever be vindicated.

No reason, except for how very unjust it all was. He had only been trying to help the king! And advance his own position, sure, but to the king's benefit, and to drive away that madman. You would think that

Pendragon would at least appreciate his effort, even if it hadn't worked out. And now, he had, as we might say nowadays, lost control of the narrative. When, by all reason, the story should be that there was a preposterous prediction made about the manner in which he would die, which was ridiculous and showed Merlin to be dangerously insane, the story actually was that there was a preposterous prediction made about the manner in which he would die, and, against all odds and reason, it would probably work out to be true.

It should be "How could anyone possibly believe that?" Instead, it was "You'll see, it'll go just that way."

In any case, it was the whiplash of feeling that still left him bewildered. Last week he had been confidently plotting to expose the charlatan and readying to finally take his place at the right hand of the king. Now he was a marked man, and the only notable event in his future was the extravagant way in which he would die.

Every aspect of his life was now shadowed by death. And he had brought it all on himself.

By the time he had reached court, and entered the chamber where the king sat, his mood had darkened to anger and a tight, vicious bitterness. He felt that dangerous trap of feeling in which he wanted to be welcomed as a trusted and loved member of the king's close circle, yet in his heart he was furious and enraged with all of them. He tried to keep the sarcasm out of his voice as he spoke, first to ask what issues were being debated, then to offer his opinions. The particular look in the others' eyes as he spoke, a weary tolerance, allowing him to speak without comment, but not listening—or did he just imagine it all?—was what he saw. Others avoided looking him in the eye entirely. And even as he spoke, he heard the new tone of desperation in his own voice, begging to be heard, where once he had been bold and respected.

He hated himself, as he saw himself in the eyes of the others; pathetic and despised. A hanger-on. A necessary annoyance, to be tolerated.

He found himself growing angry, about to say something, to lash out—which would be disastrous. He simply moved away from the group around the king. He found that no one asked him to stay. No one looked up to see where he was going. Pendragon himself had never once looked at him the entire time.

Finding another group of the king's retinue standing on the other side of the room, he stood near them at first, listening to the conversation, placing a hand on the shoulders of Roldan, and eventually speaking up himself. Then... well, have you had that experience of being at a party, and finding the group you are speaking with gradually breaking up, until at last you are left alone?

And you go over to another little group of people? And before you know it, they have all drifted away, too? Leaving you all alone once more?

Sir Brantius looked at them all, some of them his friends of many years, too, with lowering brows and a jaw set with growing hatred. What small, disloyal, common people they were. But just a thin layer below, that hatred was focused on himself. He had done this to himself. Him and that cursed little twisted old half-devil—

The door opened and Merlin walked in. He entered without fanfare—although the assembled company straightened their shoulders and stepped back as though *he* were the king. Brantius knew he probably shouldn't say anything... but it seemed too good a point to pass up.

"You'd think that *he* were the king," he said to the man next to him.

That man looked at him, then walked over to where a group was gathering around Merlin and the king, who now stood to place his hand on the wizard's shoulder.

"Everyone," said the king, "please listen." He waited for the group to gather around, and to quiet. "We have decided that we will assign scribes to Merlin, to write down everything that he says, and to create a book of prophecies."

The idea was met with great acclaim and all present—except for one—made noises and words of assent and agreement.

"This will be a great help to us and," Pendragon lowered his eyes to the table in front of him, "those kings that come after me in the future."

It was done, agreed, and everyone loved it. Merlin left soon after, his eyes locking with Brantius' for one moment as he scanned the room upon leaving, and then he was gone, while Brantius' face burned with heat, and limbs coursed with nervous, explosive energy. He thought about it, decided not to, clenched his fists and thought he could not stand it, turned swiftly to the king—realized it would be wisest to say nothing, to lay low, and slink away—but no, not him! A moment later he was kneeling at the king's side.

Pendragon turned his head to see who had sat down so swiftly beside him, then turned away quickly, almost with embarrassment, when he saw who it was.

"My lord," said Brantius, "despite my history with this court, and experience at others," he was already sounding imperious—and whiny—and tried to adjust his tone, "it would seem that my presence here is no longer…" he was going to say 'valued,' but it sounded too emotional, "necessary." He waited for it to have impact. It had none.

"There is another king," he said, "one of your liegemen, at a town near here, and he has offered me a place in his court, and invited me to reside in his town," said Brantius. "It is not far from here."

"Oh, ah," said the king, "I see."

Sir Brantius looked at the king, his own eyes growing scratchy, as the king looked away, studying the papers before him.

"And I thought that I might take him up on it," he said. The king did not react. "Since I am no longer," he gestured to the room, "serving any useful purpose here."

"Mmm," said the king, and nodded. "Yes," he said, without looking back, "that sounds like it might be a good idea."

Brantius felt his face grow suddenly heavy and his eyelids sag, as though he might cry. He wanted to stare boldly at the king, but he found himself pressing down to quell a suddenly trembling lip. He felt like a child. He couldn't believe it.

"I am happy to issue a recommendation for you, if you like," said the king, absently. He had gone back to poring over his map. He didn't look at Brantius again, and Brantius got the feeling that the king did not want to look at him.

He kept staring at the man, then lowered his eyes, and sat for a long moment with a crashing tumult of feeling going on inside him, of falling, weakness, helplessness, until he suddenly became aware that he was sitting too close, too long. He would have loved to tell the king to shove his recommendation, but he was the king. And this, Brantius thought, is now my lot. "I will accept that gratefully, my lord," he said, and stood.

Seeing no one looking to him, no one beckoning him—and nothing more to do in that large chamber—a sudden chill overtook him and he moved swiftly toward the door. He paused, hand on the handle, and not wanting to, took a look back.

The king was surrounded by advisors, all closely poring over their maps. None took notice when he left.

-47-

"So," Blaise said, eyeing Merlin warily, "this new book," he paused, "will be the same as the book we are working on?"

"No," Merlin replied, "that would be inefficient, and you know that I have no time on earth to waste. The book I will dictate for Pendragon will be entirely different from your book, for it will be filled with things that cannot be understood until after they have happened."

"Ah," said the holy man. "That's a relief."

"I would not have you toil for no purpose," replied Merlin. "Speaking of toil," he asked, eyeing a large pile of multicolored stones sitting in the sunlight on the windowsill behind the hermit, "how is your stone-collecting coming?"

"Oh, quite well," said Blaise, opening a drawer in his desk and pulling out a small canvas sack. He emptied the contents onto the desk in front of him, creating a pile of small stones of every color, some striped with lines of mineral, others translucent or nearly clear. "Here is what I have found. There are some quite nice ones."

Merlin looked at them, a rather unimpressed expression on his face, and poked among them with his fingers. "Yes, quite nice," he said. "What are those ones over there?" he pointed.

Blaise looked at him, then turned around in his chair, making no hurry, regarded the pile of stones there, looking quite attractive in the sunlight, and turned back to face the seer. "Those are mine," he said.

Merlin's eyes widened. "Yours?" he asked.

"You said I could keep any ones that I particularly like," said the old man, drawing up defensively.

"And you need," he calculated for a moment, "all sixty-seven of those?"

"I don't need them," said the hermit, voice cautious. "I like them."

Merlin sighed. "I am very glad," he said, "that you have found affinity with them. But the project that I have in mind is very important and..." he gestured to the meager pile in front of him, "I will need, roughly, four times as many as this. And I need ones," his fingers poked in a desultory way among the rocks piled before him, "that are very strong." He then let his eyes rest on the pile behind the old man.

"Well then you should have said so," Blaise said, and leaned back, folding his arms before him.

Merlin stared at him, then some more, but the hermit did not flinch.

"That is my failing," Merlin said at last. "But I didn't think that you—"

"I thought you could see all things," Blaise remarked.

The magicians eyes narrowed. "Well," he huffed, "you might be surprised that I allow people—people I particularly *like*—a bit of privacy in regards to what they do and the workings of their minds."

Blaise nodded slowly. "Uh-huh," he said flatly.

"Regardless," Merlin said, "I need more stones than this."

Blaise remained with arms crossed before him. "Then I will get more," he said.

Merlin's mouth fell open and he had extended his hand toward the larger pile before he thought better, drew back his hand, and sat back, crossing his own arms. "Excellent," he said.

"Excellent," repeated Blaise.

"Thank you most kindly for collecting these ones," said Merlin, opening the sack and beginning to scoop the stones in.

"You've very welcome," replied Blaise.

The stones collected, they sat in still silence, looking at each other, before Merlin finally hopped off his stool, headed for the door and, with a last look at the pile on the windowsill—which Blaise still sat in front of, face firm, arms crossed—nodded, smiled and left the room.

-48-

In the next weeks, Merlin spent a few hours each day with a number of scribes that had been selected by him for the purpose, and dictated the *Book of Prophecies,* which you can still read today, as part of Geoffery of Monmouth's *History of the Kings of Britain.* After the book was completed, and Pendragon had it immediately copied in several iterations, he placed the original where it might be safest and best preserved, and made sure Merlin knew of the efforts he made, for he wanted him to know how highly he valued it. Merlin accepted the honor without a word, and then told Pendragon to gather Uther and prepare a time when they could be alone to speak, for he had news that would hold great importance for the king and the future of his kingdom.

Pendragon made the arrangements for that night, and within a few hours, he, Merlin and Uther were alone in his chamber. After all were made comfortable, he bid Merlin, "Please tell us what news you have and spare us nothing."

The seer stood before the brothers, both of whom were too nervous and eager to hear his news to sit in the two chairs arranged for them. "Pendragon," he said, indicating the king, "and Uther," he continued, gesturing to the brother. "I have been very happy with both of you and the great progress this realm has made under your reign. And you should know that the news that I bring you now is given because of the great affection I have for you, and my wish to honor you and to do what is best for you, and this country."

Both brothers bowed to him reverently. "Merlin, we also bear great love for you, and trust implicitly that you will always do what is best for the kingdom. Please say all that you are willing to, and hold back nothing that pertains to us or the security of this realm."

Merlin smiled warmly. "I will never hide anything from you that pertains to the strength of your kingdom. And now I will tell something of great importance," he said, and raised a finger. "Do you remember," he asked, "those Saxons whom you gave leave to vacate your land after Hengist's death?"

Both brothers stood up straighter, expressions of concern coming onto their faces. "We do indeed," said Uther.

"They are back in Saxony, telling the news of Hengist's death," said Merlin. "He was of very noble stock, and much loved by his people there. And Hengist's kinsmen, as well as the fellow knights of those who have returned, are telling them that they fled in weakness, and should have remained and fought strongly to avenge their leader, even if they should have died."

Pendragon and Uther shared a look. "I knew it couldn't have been that easy," said Uther, dragging his chair noisily forward and letting his weight fall heavily into it.

"Those people are saying now that they will never again be able to feel honor in themselves unless they avenge Hengist's death upon you and your land." Merlin turned and began slowly pacing as he spoke. "They believe that they can overpower you, this kingdom," his arms spread out as he gestured, "and even this entire island." He pointed to Pendragon. "And they're right."

Pendragon was frozen, his eyes searching the floor as he considered. Uther, after a second of thought, sprang from the chair he had just taken and uttered, "Could they possibly have such a great army that they can withstand ours?"

"For every man that you have," Merlin said, turning, "they will have two. In men, you are vastly overmatched. So if you do not apply your force with great wisdom, and most judiciously, they will destroy you," he clasped his hands and lowered them, "and take away your kingdom, just like that!" He snapped his fingers.

Uther whirled, turning to face the rear wall with a great movement of frustration. Pendragon was still, and joined his hands before his bowed head, thinking. Then his hands rose up and his fingers threaded through his thick hair, as his eyes remained focused on a spot in the air before him. Uther turned once more, seeming about to say something, but he looked at the still figure of his brother, then he closed his mouth and looked away. They passed a moment in silence, Merlin's eyes eagerly taking in the behavior of both, until Pendragon raised his head, drew a breath, and spoke in an even tone.

"Merlin, please tell us what we can do to keep the country for ourselves," he said. "We will follow your advice exactly, and never fail to execute any order that you give us. And," he stepped forward, and his pained eyes implored the wizard, "we humble ourselves to your guidance if you will help us preserve this country for ourselves."

"Yes," said Uther loudly, then calmed, and gestured toward his brother. "Yes, we will do as you say."

Merlin nodded gravely. "You should know that the enemy horde will land on this island on the eleventh day of June. None in your kingdom will know about it, unless you tell them, and I forbid either of you to make word of it," he said sharply, pointing to first Pendragon, then Uther. "Not even Ulfius," he said to Uther, who had a moment where he was struck still, for he had just been thinking that very thing.

"Say not a word, for there are indeed spies among you, but do as I tell you," continued Merlin. "In the weeks beforehand, send for all of your liegemen, and all of your knights, both rich and poor, and show them great feasts and fantastic generousity of gifts, for it cannot be underestimated how much generosity toward those under you can ensure their faithfulness and good will for you when you need them."

246

Pendragon nodded. "We will do as you say."

"It is always a wise thing to be mindful of a man's well being, and showing concern for them can do much to keep them near you. Now," Merlin went on, "when you have done this, and fed them and bestowed gifts for weeks, then you call them all together, and bid them, for the great love that they bear to you, to be with you on the plain of Salisbury during the last week of June."

"Salisbury?" Pendragon asked.

"What—you said the Saxons will land the eleventh!" Uther uttered, eyes flashing. "By that time..." he looked at the wizard, "Should we let them even come ashore?"

That gleam appeared in Merlin's eye, and he raised a finger as one eyebrow went up as he spoke with cleverness. "Indeed you should," he said, as he began pacing back and forth before them. "You will not only let them come ashore, you will let them get inland, a long way inland." His chest leaned forward and he used his hands with great fingering gestures as he laid out his plans with relish. "Meanwhile, you will let them see that you have come between them and their ships, and they will have way to escape your country. You will take away their option of retreat, should they have wanted it. And when they see this," he smiled a greedy, vicious smile, "they will become very disheartened."

Pendragon's hand came up to his mouth, arms folded before him, as he thought. But his posture had changed, and where a moment ago was shock and fear, now his mind had locked into military mode, and was turning to the ways in which they could win, and how they could ingeniously array their smaller forces to get the better of the invaders.

"Then," Merlin went on, making a curve through the air with extended finger, "one of you will go to the river near Salisbury with your army, and you will move near the enemy in such a way that you will force them to camp with no access to the river."

Uther gasped at the simplicity of it.

"When they have set up their encampment, but cannot get access to any water," Merlin reached forward his hand as though grasping the very enemy with it, "I tell you, even the boldest among them will be very distraught. And there you will hold, weakening them," he said.

"Weakening them for two days. And, on the third day," he raised a fist, "you will fight!"

Pendragon folded his arms, and raised his face, which held a fresh resolve, to look at Merlin.

"And if you do this exactly as I have said," Merlin pointed, then opened his hands wide, "You may know in truth that the people of your kingdom will have the victory."

As they stood before Merlin, Uther and Pendragon shared a glance of rich understanding, and yearning, as though the answer they were seeking had come.

-49-

The air hung thick with a deep fog. It gave the day the still feeling of a silent morning, although it was late afternoon. The tree trunks and their twisting branches were various shades of gray, coming into form as they drew nearer, growing fainter as they receded further behind, making it seem as though Sir Brantius and his small retinue were riding along in a moving bubble, progressing at a horse's trot through the forest.

The men made faint banter, but Brantius shared none of it. In fact, it irritated him, their chatter. But he dared not reprimand them, or appear cross, if he didn't want to be the recipient of their belittling, condescending looks. They were notably less reverent of late, that was for sure. His men with better prospects had found other positions. He had found only one man to replace those three, and this one seemed to be watching him even as he served, bringing him his horse with a certain relish in his eye, as if to say "Is this the horse? The one that will throw you to your death? Is this the day, do you think?" And Brantius said nothing. He would not be a servant to his servant, although he was afraid that he already was. Thus he stayed quiet and rode ahead, eyes

248

watching the tangled trees as they faded into visibility, or kept his eyes to the wet ground as it passed beneath him.

He was on his way from the small kingdom of Fenstock, whose king, Baginor, had made gestures to accept him as an advisor, and take him into his court. Brantius had allowed himself to think positively of the change; one could get lost in a court the size of Pendragon's. Yes, he would no longer be at the side of the king of all the realm, but perhaps the wiser man seeks a smaller arena in which he could command greater attention. And Fenstock was nice. In its way. For a small kingdom, which could have its charms. Brantius' wife had refused to come and look at it, although her life would be affected by their move as much as his.

King Baginor was a true and honorable gentleman, of greater nobility than many, who showed a keen understanding of the things that truly mattered to a king, thus demonstrating that the opulent riches and displays of might that most kings might traffic in were not his way. Who needs comfortable chairs? Perhaps some of the king's advisors had become a bit too comfortable. Brantius let fall into his conversation, like graceful sprinkles, bits of fact such as that he had been a member of the court of Constance, although he was not made an advisor until the short reign of Maine. Serving then at the side of Vortiger—had to be a bit twisty here, and make it sound like he served Vortiger in a trusted capacity while inside his heart broke for Britain to be once more governed by its true nobility—but in any case, he was there at the battle of the two dragons, such a momentous occasion! And he served Pendragon faithfully, which the Merlin incident only proved. He had decided that it was foolish to pretend the issue did not exist. He continued by bewailing that Pendragon did not heed his advice, and was being misled by magicians, making his continued tenure there impossible for any man with a true heart. "And as anyone can see," he ended with a flourish, "I am as alive and well as ever on this day."

The king laughed, and his men laughed, but then—that look. Did Brantius imagine it? Alive, 'on this day.' Why had he said that? Foolish to give them ammunition. That slight added gleam in their eye, their being just a little bit too eager for friendship, and examining him, as though they might report back to their friends what he was like. It seemed always there, now, or—did he imagine it? He calmed himself and told himself, he even spoke it aloud, that not everyone was watching him and awaiting his death. Many people probably didn't even know about it. He repeated this, and he could keep it so present in the front of his mind that he could continue blithely—there was, in fact, no other choice—and pretend that there was nothing whatsoever the matter, no pall hanging over him. It was all just silliness. But he knew people, and had seen people, all his life, be easier and far less circumspect around him. His good friends, the people he truly respected, could no longer bear to be around him. His wife was still close with many of them. They looked at him with eyes of sadness now. Leaving him with... well, King Baginor would hardly be the worst of all possible lords he could swear service to.

And if Baginor's men, his companions in this new court, looked at him, watched him, asked him if he had any accidents lately, or—and this was really the lowest, something that sprang from pure, stupid immaturity—asked him what Merlin was like, it would simply be his burden to prove his worth to them. To shake off their expectations and win them over through day after day of insightful, faithful, worthy service to the king. Until he became just another advisor, one of the better ones, who had put in many years of tireless service to his leader.

The trees cleared out now and soon all that lay ahead of them was a grey wall of fog. Gradually a meadow appeared before them, and Brantius led his men on their following horses down into a valley which seemed to be crossed by a thin river. The path wound down, and surely the dark shape emerging from the mist was a bridge.

Brantius thought about making this journey again, bringing all of his things. Bringing his wife. It could be turned around. He could succeed in Fenstock. He had already picked out a few handsome members of Baginor's court, and had adroitly picked out which ones might be the most influential, the ones he might win as friends, and who might help him worm his way into place as one of the king's most-esteemed staff. There was one, whom Brantius thought to be worthy of the highest esteem, and even honorable, but when his horses were

250

being delivered to him, he saw this man across the courtyard, passing money to another man. They both laughed and looked over at him, then quickly turned away when they saw him looking, and Brantius reddened. His skin burned, and he was glad that his horse raised its neck just then, hiding him from the men, for he wasn't sure what his face looked like just at that moment. He thought if they had seen, they might have watched his face show a hopeless despondency, as it came over him, with a dreadful certainty, that the men had placed some kind of bet on him.

He kept his head down and led his horse out, mounting only once outside the castle, and he had been able to compose himself accordingly. He was sure his men had seen nothing. This was to be his life now. Fortune favors the bold, they say. It had been Brantius' motto, he repeated it loudly and often. It gave him character. It led him to make his bold move to unseat Merlin at Pendragon's side. He was bold—that was Brantius! He saw an opportunity to pry that wretched son of the devil away from the king, and insert himself right in that place, and by god, it was bold! No one could say it wasn't bold. And fortune favors the bold.

Brantius' horse stepped up on the wet wood of the bridge, the sound of hooves echoing hollowly through the tranquil afternoon, whose light was fading, before the sun had even come out. At the next step, its leg went right through one of the boards, old and saturated with water, and the beast lurched forward, launching Brantius to land on the back of his head, the weight of his body crushing it under soon after, with a snap not audible, but felt in the knight's neck. He saw the heavy horse struggling just behind him, for he had been thrown above the head of the beast, and he sprang to get his body out of the way— only he could not move. The head and neck of the horse thrashed this side and that, its foreleg almost completely through the bridge, and as it did, it started yanking Brantius' heavy leg, which had become entangled in the animal's bridle. Brantius could not feel the movement of the leg, but the movement of the struggling horse shoved him, and his eyes searched wildly as his body was pushed partly off the bridge. He thought he saw the water beneath him, but could not crane his head to look. Slowly he tilted, and he watched the horizon begin to upend with a slowness he was unable to stop.

He fell off the bridge, and the weight of his fall forced the horse's head down to the wood of the bridge, pulled by its bridle. The animal's eye looked wildly at the sky above as it was held roughly in this uncomfortable position, while Brantius hung upside-down off the side of the bridge, his head and arms submerged in the water.

Part Four
THE THIRD KING

The plain at Salisbury was a deep green expanse of shimmering, undulating grass. The blades were all wet with the just-passed rain, and the gray clouds were still low and moving slowly away, toward the distant sea. There was not a soul around that morning, and the scene was one of solitude and peace; a carpet of lush green, punctuated here and there by tight copses of trees, under a silent canopy of heavy gray clouds, sliding by just overhead.

On one gentle rise in the vast green field lay two large, flat stones, side by side. They were wet and covered by the growth of moss and the first touch of lichen that had gathered in the few years that they had been there. Near them, a corridor opened up in the air and a man stepped out onto the grass.

Merlin looked about, holding his staff as he slowly turned this way and that, taking in the scene. It was his first time seeing it in person, not just in his mind. His eyes could only see about a half mile in any direction, because of the clouds and morning mist, but his senses could see the subtle hills and slopes of the land for infinite miles in any direction.

He walked up the gentle rise to where the two stones lay, side by side. These were the stones that had covered the two sleeping dragons, which Merlin had sent here from Dinas Emrys. He walked all around them, looking what could be seen from each point around them, and also what was in the earth beneath the site, and which channels and deep rock formations were below.

When he was satisfied, he turned to face the rocks, and opened his arms. The stones moved gracefully, as though they had no weight at all, out to the side, away from each other. Then, when he turned his palms downward and moved his hands back together, the rocks slid, with just the quietest sound of grinding earth, under the grass, as though they were diving beneath water. Then you could see a low

254

mound, not over three inches, created by the stones as they moved beneath the grass, and they came back together, leaving about three feet between them. They were like two rectangles placed next to each other, under the ground, with only a slight depression in the land between then, like a very shallow trench. Merlin left the long slits on the grass where the rocks had slid underground, because that would be healed seamlessly in time.

When he had placed them just so, and was pleased, Merlin turned and walked to a place straight out from where the trench between them pointed, and began walking at a right angle to it. After a few feet, he started to drag his staff behind him, and in the place where it touched, the earth sank into a depression. Merlin walked around the entire area in a curving movement, lifting it once, and was able to make a geometrically-perfect circle. He came back almost to the point at which he had started, leaving an opening at that end, in line with the trench between the two underground stones. Now there was a circular ditch around the site, open in two places. And now, across from Merlin, at the beginning of the trench, there were twenty-four urns that he had brought there while he was walking.

He stood by the urns and admired his handiwork. It was all quite symmetrical, and that helped make him calm inside. Satisfied, but not finished with his work yet, he overturned one of the urns and let the water it held flow out into the ditch. He did this with each of the urns, which contained the water from the underground pool that had covered the dragons for so many years.

The water coursed around the circle, and by the time he had emptied the last urn, and sent it back to Northumberland so as not to clog the pristine landscape, it filled the entire ditch with about a foot of water. Merlin sat on the mound around the ditch and, using his mind, examined it from different angles, seeing if it produced the effect that he wanted, which it did. He removed an apple from his cloak and ate it as he waited to see how long the water would remain in the ditch until all of it was absorbed into the earth. He cracked into the crisp fruit with relish, and looked all about here and there, extremely pleased with his work. He waited until all of the water that had held the dragons was absorbed into the earth there, until no more could be seen. Then he vanished.

-51-

Pendragon hosted all of his liegemen and all the knights of the realm of Logres, which included all of the country south of Cambria and Cumbria, and had its capitol in the city of Logres, which we now refer to as London. He sent the invitation out so wide that all knew they were welcome, even if they had never met the king in person before. He promised that he, and his brother Uther, would make the acquaintance of all that made the effort to come before him, and planned to give each rich gifts, in the hopes that any and all would bear allegiance to him, and vow to be with him when he would need their assistance. He made funds available for the rebuilding of churches and courts and any buildings that had been destroyed in the wars his men had fought, and he gave gifts to farmers whose fields had been ravaged by the clashes his men had with the Saxons across their land. He feasted all of them, and their wives, with such generosity as they had never seen, and did all he could to win their affection, just as Merlin had suggested.

News of Brantius' death reached Pendragon just prior to the feasts. He remembered the moment he heard it, for his ears seemed to pop at the news, and for a moment he heard a ringing that hushed all the sounds around him, until they gradually returned and he was able to make a polite response. It caused the prick of a certain nagging feeling; something he could not place, but which remained in the background of every moment from that time on. He talked about it with Uther. Not the feeling, but the news, that Merlin had been right, even in his most outlandish prediction, and both agreed that they were lucky to have gotten Merlin back on their side. Very true, said Pendragon, but something more... something about what Merlin had said to him. But there was little time to think on it, with the feasts, although the king could never quite drive it entirely from his mind.

The death became the talk of the feasts, repeated everywhere, and certain parties even made an effort to go see the dead man's house, while others asked all who had known him if they could have suspected anything. Pendragon found discussion of it wearying, and turned the conversation to how his realm was blessed with the incredibly accurate foresight of the wizard, the wisest man who ever lived, as another selling point to rally the support of the people around him. Merlin himself was greatly celebrated, but cleverly deflected conversation away from Brantius' attempt to test him, and showed himself upset when people persisted. He was also uniquely able to make himself scarce from anyone he did not wish to see, an ability Pendragon sorely envied.

Uther was clearly put upon by the endless need to socialize, to bear up with a constant show of happiness and be responsible for embodying the security of the kingdom, but he made little mention of it. It was just something that Pendragon would see, as his brother, when Uther took time between talking to visiting liegemen to collapse for a quiet moment, leaning against a wall, or close his eyes and allow himself a pause to rest while at table. Pendragon saw him do it even right while someone was talking to him. But he smiled at his brother. He was shoring up, and making an effort, that was for sure. He wanted to learn what was involved with being king. Pendragon knew that he wouldn't like it, his brother was far too fun-loving, and hated placing his own pleasure second to official business, but perhaps he would learn. He would find out quickly how much was involved with being king, and how some pleasure can be deferred, or done without, when such great responsibility rested on him.

After the guests had left, and Pendragon had requested that they bring their forces to join him on the plain of Salisbury at the last week of June, then the weight of that nagging thought came once more with renewed vigor. He found himself nervous around Merlin, eager to ask, afraid to offend, and always on edge, until one day, while the wizard was alone with he and Uther, and they were poring over maps, moving pieces that represented their armies around, and discussing the battle to come, Pendragon could stand it no more and simply spoke out loud.

"Merlin," he said, "for God's sake, please tell us if we will die in this battle."

Uther looked up quickly. It seemed this question had not been on his mind, and he understood that the comment Merlin had made so long ago still wormed its way incessantly through his brother's mind. He then turned to Merlin.

The wizard took his time in drawing up straight, and placed the pieces he had been holding carefully on the table before he spoke. "King," he said, "surely you know that everything that is begun must, in time, come to an end, and that no one may escape death, but all of us must accept it as we have to. Every person who is alive will die, and both of you know without doubt that you too will die one day, and no amount of power or wealth can change that."

Then Pendragon stepped forward, around the table, and came to stand close to the wizard. His brown eyes searched Merlin's, for he was no longer afraid to show his vulnerability to the seer. "You told me that you knew my death the same as you saw that of the man who was testing you, and you said that when I heard of his death, I would come asking about mine." Then he smiled in a painful grimace of acquiescence. "Once more, you were telling the truth, and since I have learned of his death, I can think of almost nothing else but whether, in this battle, I will die. That's why I ask you," and he reached out to grasp Merlin's arm gently, "please tell me if I will die."

Merlin looked him in the eyes, then turned away. He thought for a moment, then turned his face to Uther. "Do you want this as well?" he asked.

Uther's eyes had a plaintive expression as they looked at the seer. He did not, actually, want to know, but, as his eyes darted over to glance at Pendragon, whose pensive, haunted eyes held his for a moment, he knew his brother wanted this very badly, and he said "Yes."

"I want you both to swear on the most powerful holy relics that you own," said Merlin, "and promise to the saints that you will do everything I advise you, for your own benefit and for your honor. When

258

you have done this," he said, "then I will tell you in the greatest trust the things you ask of me."

They had the relics brought out, and repaired to Pendragon's private chamber, where they could all be alone and not heard. And both of them placed their hands on the relics and swore an oath, just as Merlin had laid out.

"Do you know what it is you have sworn?" the wizard asked them, speaking to them solemnly. "I will tell you. You have sworn that when the day of the battle is come, you will be the worthiest men you can be and have faith to yourself and to God, for no one can be faithful to himself if he is not first to God. This will help you in battle. There is something else you must do. Both of you," he pointed to each brother, "will confess to a priest. And before this battle, you will have every one of your men confess as well, and forgive each other of all anger and ill will, and resolve every dispute that is between them, for if they do not, they will not be able to fight for what they know is right with unburdened and true hearts."

He stood back for a moment, and let his blazing eyes do the work of transfixing the brothers as he unloaded his words. "If you do this, and ensure that all of your men are clean and confessed, the Saxons will be beaten, for they do not believe in the Holy Trinity, and you will be defending what is yours by birthright, what belongs to you by both law and religion." Then Merlin stopped speaking, drew his hands in, and allowed his eyes to pass from one brother to the other.

"I want you to know," he said lowly, reaching out an open hand, "that since Christianity was brought to this island, there has never been, nor will there be ever again in this land, such a great battle as that which is upon us."

The declaration brought tears of reverence and intimidation to Pendragon's eyes, and with a quick sidelong glance, he could see that Uther was listening with intent fascination as well. The battle loomed before them, it was coming, implacable, and it was hard not to feel that their lives would be forever altered by the time it passed.

"Each of you will commit your utmost to the other's honor and welfare, and that of your men, and now I will have you know something that I will tell you without hiding." He clasped his hands before him, and looked at the brothers gravely. "One of you will depart from the world in this battle. And the one who comes back will create, in the place where the battle will happen, the most beautiful and sacred burial ground, with my help. And I tell you," Merlin said, raising a bony finger in promise, "I will labor so diligently that what I build there will remain as long as the world lasts."

Each of the brothers looked stonily ahead, but each was having very different thoughts. For Pendragon the news calmed him, touched the little place where he was itching, and then it seemed as though he were foolish to even ask. Merlin had, in effect, told him before. His shoulders remained full and strong, but he felt a slight slipping of energy within him, and realized it was relief. He thought of knowing there were only a few weeks ahead. It seemed pleasant, and beautiful too, and there were other thoughts, but he ignored them for now. His hand went out without thinking and he clapped his palm down on Uther's shoulder.

The touch made Uther grimace with emotion, as he was hurting very smartly. Pendragon had been at his side all of his life. It was impossible to imagine him not there—and then, the possibility that he would be king? Merlin could be wrong, he supposed? Maybe it was he who would die. Merlin said only one of them, but there was what he had said before. Why did he play these games with them? And inside, Uther's innards shrank slightly, as the thought of the court without his brother, and everyone looking to him, suddenly seemed very big, and immensely scary.

Merlin watched the thoughts play across the brother's minds with great relish. He had taken a step back and stood, hands still clasped before him, as he let the two men have their moment. Then he opened his hands and spoke again.

"Now you strive with your utmost to be worthy men who can carry through what I have said with all your heart and body, so that each of you may be garlanded with the greatest honor when you come before the Lord. One of you will come back," he said, "but I will not say who, because I want both of you to be brave and bold, and give your all to attain the most honor that you can."

Both of the brothers raised their heads to him, and he saw their bravest faces and ones stricken.

-52-

Now everything was changed. Neither spoke openly about it, but Uther, without bidding, began to hang about Pendragon nearly all day, and rearranged all of his activities to be constantly at his brother's side. They didn't mention it, but the tenor of their talk began to carry the understanding that Pendragon was passing on what he knew to Uther, in his final few weeks, and helping his brother to understand what it would mean to be king. Things that he should know, and things that he would have to contend with, but might not have expected. Not long into it, Uther asked if he could have Ulfius remain close during this time, too.

"Because he will be around me always, and I trust in his wisdom and allegiance, so perhaps he should hear all that you are saying to me, too," Uther suggested.

"I understand what you are saying," said Pendragon, and then thought a little bit before he spoke further. "And I wish I had a friend like that," he said pensively. "That certainly would have made my days of ruling more...." and his voice drifted off. "But I think that you should, well, I should be free to tell you anything openly as the man who will be the next king. With Ulfius here, that wouldn't be quite the same. And even, I would say," and Pendragon lowered his gaze, and sighed for a moment, "one of the hardest things I had to learn as king is that one is alone. You can have advisors, and brothers," he clapped his brother on the shoulder, "but when it comes down to it, there is only you, and everyone is looking to you," he said.

Uther nodded. "Of course," he said, "as you say."

"Besides," continued Pendragon, "we can never know when even the most beloved of our friends might be killed."

Uther said nothing, but one observing could notice how his face went somewhat ashen, and he swallowed hard. After a moment of silence, they continued their discussions, and Pendragon told him of how his day would come to be filled with briefings of things that were going on around the country, little towns that needed road repairs or bridges built, or large cities growing overcome with human waste, and disease, and that soon Uther would find that his thoughts, even in private times, would soon come to be occupied with the fates of others, and the welfare of towns, and the successful interlocking of various smaller kingdoms, such that they might all function in harmony to support the larger realm.

"Luckily, as we know," said Uther, "I have much available mind space."

Pendragon smiled wryly. "And you should know that you will have far less free time to engage with the maidens," he said. "You should take note of that, and perhaps choose one that you can rely on and will be there to support you," he said. "It will be hard, when you are king," said Pendragon, "to know who around you that you can trust, and you may find your circle actually shrinking, rather than growing larger, as friendships and allegiances come with obligations." His eyes stared off to a place past Uther. "And you will start to decide which people it is worth investing your personal interest in." His eyes returned to his brother. "Which may be difficult for one as naturally gregarious as yourself."

Uther smiled understandingly, but said nothing.

"And Uther," Pendragon said, and put a hand on his brother's shoulder as he looked on him with resigned, sad eyes, "I suspect you will find difficulty in the slow turning of your personal sphere into one of…" and his voice trailed off, as he made a gesture indicating the wide world. Then his eyes snapped to Uther. "Don't dismiss this, or think 'Oh, I'll handle it when the time comes.'" Pendragon said. "Prepare for it. That's the wisest way." He let his hand drop now. "And know that it will be up to you to demand any private time you wish to have, for if you don't, your every moment will be swallowed up by the affairs of your kingdom."

Uther nodded. "You're making it sound really fun," he said.

Pendragon smiled warmly. "It has its advantages, which I will not need to prepare you for. And I know you will enjoy them. I wish, Uther," and he chuckled mirthlessly, "that I would be here to see it. I know you will be a fine king."

Uther's eyes abruptly grew misty, and he had to rub them to see clearly. "I think," he said, "well, I know... that I will not be as great a king as you."

"Yes, and," Pendragon seemed suddenly somewhat annoyed. "Why don't you just drop that talk, eh?" he asked.

Uther glanced up suddenly to see if he was kidding. No, he was actually quite annoyed.

"It's not helping you, it's not amusing me, or anyone—" Pendragon broke off suddenly and turned away, but Uther remembered the intense look of his focused brown eyes. "It's a baby move. Do you think someone will say 'Oh no, we were wrong about Uther, he can't be king because he's just not suited to it?'" Pendragon glared at him. "You *will* be king. You can focus on your faults, and cry, but I am telling you, you will need every second of your time to shore up your strengths— which you have," he jabbed a finger at his brother, "considerable of."

Pendragon put his hand on his hip and turned away, huffing out. Uther sat stock still, not processing, only feeling his brother's rebuke.

Pendragon turned, and his face and tone had changed. "Uther," he said, "the man you are here, now," he gestured to his brother, "is not the same one who will be king. The very act of becoming king will change you, and the things that you go through, and you will change and grow into the position in ways that you can't begin to imagine," he sighed. "Nor could I prepare you for. You just have to allow yourself to let those changes happen. Don't keep saying you can't. You will rise to it," he said. "You will see." And he shook his head, smiled and said once more, "I wish I could see you."

Uther nodded as he and his brother shared a long look. Then Uther looked away, and wrung his hands together. "What about Merlin?" he asked at last.

"Merlin," Pendragon said. "Merlin. We are blessed to have Merlin on our side," he said plainly. "He gives us advantages we could never dream of, and the knowledge he brings us has made every difference in our fortunes. And I truly believe," Pendragon raised his head, "that we would not have been able to regain control of this country if it had not been for him."

Uther nodded in silent agreement.

"You will have to come to an understanding, within yourself," continued his brother, "of how much of that is you," he placed a pointed finger above Uther's heart, "and how much of it is owing to him. And whether or not it even matters, after a certain point. Merlin is a condition of our kingships, and," he sighed, "it is better to consider him one of the advantages of one's situation, just like, say, a location that is close to fresh water. Don't turn away from the advantages Merlin offers, just because you want to exert your own will," advised Pendragon.

Uther thought for a moment. "I could see where that could become an issue," he said.

Pendragon nodded. "We have," and he took a heavy breath, and sighed, "kingships unique in the history of our country, for we, neither of us, will ever know—" and he broke off suddenly, and coughed, and had to clear his throat, his eyes growing wet and red. "We will never know, truly, what we could have accomplished for ourselves." Then they both passed a moment in silence, and thought on this.

"But Merlin is here," he said, "and we could never turn away from his advantages. So they are," he shrugged, "inextricable with our kingships, and one should not go too far down the path of pondering with much depth what credit goes to him, and what credit is yours alone. They are the same."

Uther nodded. It was something that he knew, given his personality, might begin to chafe most sorely.

"Remember, even when you are most frustrated—and angry," Pendragon went on, "that Merlin offers you advantages no other man could, and do everything, no matter how much it may gall you—and I say all of this knowing full well that he hears my thoughts and knows we are having this conversation—do everything you can to maintain his good will and allegiance. And listen and believe in everything he says," Pendragon finished.

Uther widened his eyes and leaned back. "We learned that," he said.

"Even so," Pendragon said, "even from your position, it might be hard for you to understand the," and here his forehead wrinkled in pain, "tyranny of his power, when it is turned on you. Do not test him," he said, raising a finger, "or allow others to test him. Where you think, 'but I am safe, because it is these *others* testing him, not me.' Because your lie, and deceit, is in allowing them to do so, and..." his voice trailed off as he shook his head in exasperation. "Just do not rankle him at all, in any way, for he has ways of throwing us about... that we have no way to conceive of."

Uther nodded, and they both regarded each other with expressions that were tinged with hope, and fear, and wonderment at all that had befallen them, and what was still to come. They talked of a few more things, and made arrangements to talk more in the future, and Pendragon even arranged a session with Ulfius and Uther both, to tell Ulfius how he could best support Uther and how they could take advantage of the benefits their close trusting relationship would offer when in the office of king. Then they spoke of other things, until Uther grew tired, and Pendragon had more matters of leadership to return to, and they both stood and embraced prior to parting.

Lately they had moved, without either making comment on it, from simple waves upon parting, to warm and long embraces. And they had noticed a new pressure in their hugs, as if trying to dig in and feel it, feel their brother at their side, while they still could.

"Don't be afraid, Uther," Pendragon said, as he held his brother close, "I know you can be a great king."

Uther's body shivered and his eyes grew wet, and he was glad his face was pressed into his brother's chest, where it could not be seen. "It's just that," he said. "I'm scared because... I *want* to be a good king."

265

"I know," Pendragon said, and his large, brown eyes looked on his brother with great affection.

And after another moment, and another long, hard squeeze, they separated, and then it was time for Pendragon to return to his business. Uther lingered in the doorway, as the advisors and knights who had gathered outside streamed into the room to address their matters with the king, and he took another long glance at his brother, head down and already engaged in matters of the realm, before closing the door.

-53-

Soon enough the it was the time that Pendragon had summoned all who owed him allegiance in his realm, and they came to the Whitsuntide court he held that year along the riverside. Again, he gave out much wealth and gifts—and good armor—and made himself readily visible and available to meet with friends as well as those who had not yet met him personally, and there were many good times and cheerful faces, as well as hearty promises to be faithful to him and do all possible to drive the invaders out of their land. Uther was, as he had been for the past weeks, almost always at his brother's side, and Pendragon took pains to introduce him to everyone he met. They made no special point of it, and certainly didn't reveal the design behind why they were making him more widely known—the fact that he was the king's brother and next in line for the throne was reason enough—but they made sure that he was seen and known by all those who would likely become his liegemen in future days.

Soon enough, word reached Pendragon that the Saxons had landed, and when he learned that it was on the eleventh day of June, he knew with certainty that he could not doubt anything that Merlin ever said. This brought with it a strange calmness that he had not anticipated, and instead of darkening his spirits, it lightened them, and brought with it a new, bittersweet and sublime appreciation of the things around him; the trees, the undulating countryside of grass and, funnily enough, the sheep—who knew the sight of white sheep dotting a green hill could be so heartbreaking? He now drank in sunsets and took great pleasure in the good men of his company, and the women who selflessly gave themselves in support of all matters, and even the children that here and there ran about the festivities caused new wonder in him, although tinged with sadness, for he had hoped one day to find a companionable woman and have children of his own. But in the main, his mood was suffused with aching love for his people and country, and the perfection of God's gift. He even, while strolling by the river one day with some people from a small town he had never visited, was momentarily stunned by the bejeweled emerald beauty of a frog he saw sunning itself. He had been young—he still was young—and he had never before thought of the close of life, and only during these last days did its precious, elusive quality seem beautiful, tragic and perfect.

Pendragon sent word for all his bishops and other leaders of the church to come, and all men who were to go into fighting—and anyone else who wished to—were ordered into confession. Small tents were set up in which men could meet with the churchmen in private, and soon lines were forming outside of them—something Pendragon never thought that he would see. Orders were also given that all conflicts were to be resolved, under threat of punishment, and if there was anything that belonged to someone else and had become a source of strife between them, it was to be returned to its rightful owner and peace to be made between both parties.

It was amazing the effect this had. Both Uther and Pendragon never would have believed it if they hadn't seen it with their own eyes. The first night, there was a perceptible lightness of tone at the evening feasts and entertainments. The second night, the amount of people with their arms around each other, laughing and sharing drinks, was unmistakably increased. By the third night, for it took that many days to get through the thousands of men gathered with them, the mood was electric with fond feeling and fellowship, to an extent that was simply astounding. Almost unceasing laughter was heard, and singing, or the affectionate bellowing of a group of drunken men, to the point where Uther actually tried to find anyone unhappy—and could not. He made a point of noting this for any future battles, for he could see now plainly that these men could go into war with clean hearts, and focus squarely on the goal they shared.

Merlin himself was scarce during these celebrations, for many people had great curiosity about him, and sought to ask him for their own futures, or to solve personal problems for them, or of Sir Brantius, the news of which had reached all corners of the country. You can imagine how this wouldn't appeal to him as it was, but worse, the flippant or irreverent way in which people asked for his advice was enough to push him into anger, and it was much better for all if he stayed to himself. Still, on the morning before the armies were to ride out to be arrayed against the enemy, he let the brothers know that he would speak to them alone that night, and tell them what they could expect in the battle to come.

He met with them, that night, in a tent out amongst the celebrations, the air thick with the foggy smoke and flickering light of the hanging lamps. The brothers sat, side by side on their rug-covered chairs, while the wizard strode and gestured before them.

"The day after tomorrow the Saxons break camp and ride out, away from the sea," he said. "Uther," he pointed, "you will ride forth with a great many men-at-arms. Send Ulfius and his men to get between the Saxons and their ships, and make sure they see that they are there, and that any retreat from this country is impossible. You, separately, will follow the enemy until they have ridden far away from the river and the sea, and have come close to the middle of the plain."

Merlin's right hand was raised, palm forward, and his eyes blazed with a fire that neither of the brothers were sure that they had seen before. His shoulders could be seen to be rising and falling swiftly as his breathing became shallow.

"When they do, you will ride close to them and keep them until you force them to halt and make camp. Once they have, draw back," Merlin said, stepping back himself, and bowing. "When they want to ride out the next morning, hold them there," he said. "When they want

268

to move, stay so densely arrayed and close upon them that they cannot, and must make camp again." He smiled deviously. "Show them without question that you are their masters."

Both Pendragon and Uther were lightheaded. There was no question about it, they were dizzy. Perhaps it was the close, smoke-filled air of the tent with its lamps, and the anticipation of the battle, and what they had drunk that night—or the fact that Merlin had previously said that this would be the greatest battle that would ever occur in that country. The force of it came on so strong that the main impression was not of the battle to come, but of Merlin and these little, tossed-off comments of his. Does he do it purposely to send their minds spinning beyond madness?

The wizard faced them with great grandeur, both palms now held forward, as though pushing at an imperceptible weight, teeth visible as he breathed heavily.

"When they have gone two days with dwindling water, and alone on a plain in a strange country," he said, "you can be assured that not even one among them will not wish to be back in the land where he came from."

Uther could see it happening in his mind. It seemed so simple.

"Then, Pendragon," Merlin said, pointing with bony arm protruding from his cloak, "you will bring your men close along the farther side from them, and in the first morning's light you will move in very close to them on the other side, so that they may see you." He brought his hands together. "Then, I tell you, every man on the Saxon side will be stricken with fear, and quail in his heart, and they will then all wish that they had never set foot in your land."

Pendragon could see it in his mind, and feel the fear that would seize them at that moment.

"And on the morning of that third day," Merlin said, leaning back and opening his arms wide, "you will see a red dragon blazing in the air, and it will be made of flame and filling all the sky. There will be no mistaking it," the wizard held up an open hand, eyes blazing fiercely, then pointed at Pendragon. "And when you see the embodiment of your own name in the sky, you will know that then it is the time to charge, and fight, for you can then be assured that the victory will belong to you on that day."

A long moment passed where none of them could speak. First, both brothers sat, hunched with shoulders rounded roughly forward, staring at Merlin with wide eyes, and mouths slack, like panting dogs, caught up in a lust for victory, and the promise of wielding great power. It enchanted them, and they let it, for once the battle had begun, no let-up in their forward fury could be allowed. They knew enough from battle to let the lightheadedness, and the exhilaration, take them over until they could once again relax.

Then Uther looked to Pendragon, who immediately turned, and they shared a pregnant gaze for several moments, riding together through several states of emotion. The confessions that day had worked on them too, and they gazed on each other with the complete trust and openness that can only come from a weightless heart, and a lifetime spent at the other's side. Pendragon let out his hand, and Uther took it immediately. Each had his part, and understood it, and knew that the other would fulfill his place without doubt. They turned forward once more to find Merlin beaming with pride at them.

"Thank you for your invaluable assistance, Merlin," said Pendragon, "is the least I can say."

The wizard brought his hands together and bowed. "I am at your service, my king," he said. "And I would have you know one other thing."

Pendragon indicated his interest.

"The fiery dragon that you will see in the sky on the third day," he said, brow lowering to look at Pendragon quite significantly. "That is not my craft."

Pendragon squeezed Uther's hand very hard, to the point where the brother thought he might have to wrench it away, and he took in a quick, stuttering breath. His eyes were suddenly awash in tears, and they flowed over.

The king had lost all pretense of dignity, as only Merlin and his brother were there. He stood and walked with naked emotion at Merlin, and put one arm around him and crushed him close with clumsy force, whether the advisor wanted it or not. Merlin was overcome to see his

270

words and knowledge bring such effect to the young king. A moment later, Uther was also part of the clutching group, and all three held to each other and gave in to the terrible, exhilarating feeling the moment had, without thought of holding anything back.

-54-

The next morning dawned wonderfully warm and clear. Uther's men were all arrayed on horseback and ready to ride out. Ulfius would be at his side during the long ride, then separate with his own battalions when the time came closer to action. It was almost time to go. He could see that some of the men were getting antsy and wondering what the holdup was, and he was wondering if he might have to go rouse Pendragon from his pavilion, when there he was.

He stood, at the head of his small group of attendants, hands on hips and looking at Uther with satisfaction. Uther left his horse with a squire, and stepped over to where the king was. They stood in front of each other, the morning sun shining brightly on Pendragon, making him glow with a colorful brilliance against the receding blue of the night's dark.

Many thoughts played across the brothers' faces, but none of them seemed worthy of speaking out loud—they were, for the most part, understood—and they simply looked at each other, half smiles, wrinkled brows of concern, raised eyebrows, and long stares of affection and the pain of loss all coming and passing without comment, as the brothers took their last looks at each other.

At last Pendragon simply opened his arms, and Uther stepped forward, and they gripped each other strongly. There were no tears. They had each gone through every extreme of emotion in the days and hours leading to that moment, but their hands held each other, pushing forward, chest to chest, heads resting on the other's shoulders, eyes pressed tightly closed. They remained like this, silently, for a long moment, then still longer.

At last they separated, but still held hands. Uther tried to speak, but his voice was froggy, and he had to clear his throat. "Fight well, brother," he said at last.

"Fight well," Pendragon said to him.

Then neither moved. They just stood, hands clasped tightly, looking each other in the eyes. At last a tortured smile came over Pendragon's face, and he let his hand drop. Uther stepped back, heaved a breath and slowly blew it out, then finally turned and walked back to his horse. His men were summoned to attention, and once Uther gave the signal, they turned to ride.

Uther turned his head to see his brother watching him, and there seemed nothing to do but give an exaggerated, joking wave, acknowledging the oddity of the situation, and he saw Pendragon's smile. It was then that a violent sob came on him with shocking suddenness, and he pulled his bridle to turn his horse away. His eyes remained on the ground, not that he could see it, just blurry green, and a moment later he felt Ulfius' hand land on his shoulder, pat it, then slide off. They rode on.

They had made it to the foot of the hill two bow-shots from the encampment, when Uther could no longer stand the thought that he might have taken his last look at his brother, and his head whipped around.

Pendragon was still there, standing apart, watching after him.

Uther did not stare long, but there was that aching. Trying to etch that image into his mind, to somehow see it in a more intense way, to see it with greater feeling, or vividness, when there was nothing that could be done to make it more than an image. He turned away once more.

At the crest of the hill Uther could not contain himself, for a sudden void had seemed to open up in his chest, and he once more threw his head back, but Pendragon could not be seen.

Ulfius led the troops for the next few hours, as Uther rode a horse's-length ahead, head bowed forward, shoulders rhythmically jumping up and down. The wind was high then so nothing could be heard.

Ulfius led his men straight to the sea, then they turned their horses east to follow the shoreline, receiving reports all the while of the Saxon's movements. They had to wait out of sight for the timing to be just right, for Uther and Pendragon had briefed him completely on the importance of the Saxons being able to see his men, cutting off any means of their escape. It was war on their psyches, and Ulfius loved it; so long as a good battle followed, too.

They received word, and rode in once the Saxons had gone about six bow-shots up the rise away from the ocean and into the heart of the country. As Ulfius rode around the side of the hill, slowly the retreating lines of Saxon men came into view, marching slowly upward. The wet and misty air rendered them a dull line against the green of the hill, and they were far enough away, and it was windy and wet enough, that the sound of the British knights moving in behind them went unnoticed. Soon the horses and their riders had filed behind Ulfius, spread out all along the beach, and he looked once more at the retreating Saxons. They still seemed not to notice the Britons. Ulfius smiled beneath his grand mustache, and shook his head, exchanging a look with the knight next to him. Some warriors were just not very aware of their surroundings.

He thought about what he might use, for the Saxons were in danger of moving out of sight, so he asked the knight next to him if he might see his helmet for a moment. The knight undid his, and Ulfius removed his own, and he held them by the straps and banged them together, three times. The sound echoed throughout the wet air, filled then only with the sound of the wind.

It took a moment, then one of the retreating troops, one at the back, turned around. He stopped in place, and the angle of his legs and the way his body slumped displayed unpleasant surprise, even from that distance. Then the others near him noticed he wasn't with them, and turned to see. They also stopped when they saw the British knights arrayed all along the beach behind them. Soon after, the entire group of marching troops stopped, and turned. Their figures were only small blots on the landscape, but it was close enough to see the postures of their bodies, which hung motionless as they beheld the army behind them, sitting, waiting.

The knight next to Ulfius smiled and bumped his arm against his. "Now they're thinking how wise they were to come where they're not invited," he said.

Ulfius smiled, nodded and turned his head back. Some shift had come over the retreating troops' bodies, and although they hadn't moved, the fact of their very stillness showed their minds in fear. He could imagine their thoughts, as they saw that their element of surprise was spoiled, lost and gone, and if matters went so poorly as to come to retreat, well, that would no longer be possible. What this meant now, as surely every one of those Saxons knew, was that they would have to engage in battle, at a distinct disadvantage. They stood in place, staring grimly back.

In a moment, men in a smaller group could be seen walking around from the sides, the leaders coming back to see. Their walking stopped as they perceived the Britons arrayed behind them, and stood in stunned poses, until they straightened a bit, but even then stayed to regard the enemy a bit longer, arms hanging at sides. Then the leader turned, made a gesture forward, and a few moments later, the troops turned once more, and began marching steadily away until they were lost into the mist.

Ulfius sat on his horse, watched the men, then, with a smile and a shrug, nodded to his fellow knight on the right, then on the left. "Feels pretty good," he said, a satisfied smile on his face. The men beside him could only shake their heads in agreement.

"As long as we also get a proper battle," said the knight on his right.

"Fear not," Ulfius said, "we are assured of that." He spurred his horse to step gently forward. "Come, let's follow behind, that we not lose sight of them."

"This strategy of Merlin's is certainly uncommon," the man on his left said, "and ingenious."

Ulfius slowed his horse a bit then, and when he came next to this man, kicked his leg gently. "It is the strategy of our king, Pendragon," said Ulfius, with a firm but smiling face, "and his bold and worthy brother, Uther, acting on the knowledge of Merlin," he said. The man grew stiff, and he opened his mouth, but then said nothing, smiled and nodded agreeably.

The knights rode on.

Leaving some men to guard approach to the Saxon ships, they shadowed the moving Saxons for most of the day, keeping between them and the river, and letting themselves be seen there, until they met up with Uther's battalions of men, protecting access to the river close to the plain of Salisbury. Ulfius met Uther there, and reported how the Saxons reacted when they saw retreat cut off.

"Oh," said Uther, smiling and shaking his head in amazement, "I wish I'd been there to see that."

"I believe that it represented man's nature laid bare," said Ulfius jokingly. "How was it when they came over that rise and saw you here? Must have been about the same."

Uther nodded and a wise smirk came across his face. "It was good! They stopped right there on that hilltop and just held," Uther said, smiling broadly. "They just—" he imitated the freeze, then laughed. "And one of them fell over."

Ulfius laughed out. "Careless!" he said.

They chuckled together. "I don't think they feel very welcome here at all," said Uther.

"Which is in every ways a shame," replied Ulfius. "I hate to see them having a rough time of it, after all the trouble they took to get here."

They chatted for a bit as their men took water and rest, then Ulfius was to lead his men around to continue barring any retreat the enemy might try to make. He had his orders to merely keep them in place that night and all through the next day and night, then after he saw something wondrous in the sky on the morning of the third day, he was to lead his men in attack. Uther purposely wouldn't tell him what it was to be expected, as he wanted to leave it as a surprise.

"I just hope they give us a good fight," said Ulfius, departing. "No honor in cutting down men with no fire in them." He raised one cheek in an unimpressed look. "Starving them of water and keeping them from their ships is less fun."

"It may allow us to defeat an army twice our size," Uther said, and cocked his head at the trade-off. "If you don't get enough battle, you and I can go a round or two when we return."

Ulfius raised his eyebrows. "You said *you*, correct?" He waved a goodbye as he rode away, and within a few minutes, he and his men were on their way to guard the uncovered edge of the invading troops.

They rode for most of the day, and mid-afternoon, they came upon a group of peasants, mostly men and older boys but also a few women and teen girls, moving in the opposite direction, carrying not only swords in varying states of quality and repair, but hoes, shovels, and even a few kitchen knives. One woman, much older than Ulfius thought should be anywhere near there, held only a rock. Their eyes looked up and regarded the knights, and especially Ulfius, with nervous eyes as they drew close.

"And where are you lot going?" asked Ulfius, looking on them in amused wonder.

"We are going to the fighting," said a man in front firmly, keeping his eyes down and moving ahead. He seemed extremely stubborn.

One side of Ulfius' mustache came up as he pulled his horse up short, and stopped. His cheeks grew into little balls as he could not keep himself from smiling.

"And what is it you intend to do there, then?" he asked slyly.

The old man who had spoken said nothing, but his eyes darted up to meet Ulfius', before setting his jaw and moving steadily forward.

276

His son, for it was unmistakably his child, a man of thirty or so, growled fiercely. "We're making war," he said, looked up at the knight with his father's same expression, and added "and you won't stop us."

The knight fell back in his saddle, head rising up, and he began to issue a bellowing laugh, such that the knights who followed him, and had also stopped when he pulled up, began to laugh as well, and look with kind eyes toward the common people. Ulfius' head came down, and his eyes crinkled with goodwill towards the people, hanging just above his grand mustache, which was drawn up straight across like an iron bar. "Well," he said, "I doubt there is anything a simple knight such as myself could possibly do to stop you."

There was a visible expression of relief in the crowded line of the peasants, their yellowed and dirty shifts and rough fabrics that covered them in sharp contrast to the bright heraldry and shining mail armor of the knights. They wanted to fight. It's not that the common people wanted to stay home and be protected by the nation's knights—the ones who felt like that *were* at home—the ones who were here were those who wanted to fight with their own hands. They took a personal issue with the Saxons in their lands, and wanted to be there to give them a bit back, their own selves. They would not be held back, and Ulfius would never have them be so.

"I hate the Saxons," said a portly boy of about fourteen, with a round pink face, holding a pitchfork.

"As do I," Ulfius responded, nodding quite rightly.

"I'm going to take one of theirs eyes out," said a young woman with a fierce and strong body.

"That's very wise," replied the knight.

"They've got grabby hands," she continued.

"Why don't you take a few of them off, then?" Ulfius suggested. "You can throw them in the trough for the pigs. Now however," he said, leaning back in his saddle and raising his finger, "I should inform you that there won't be any fighting until the morning after tomorrow."

A bulky woman of about forty-some, in very simple and worn clothes, stopped right in place, and the people behind came still forward, until there was a tumble of about seven people before they

277

could steady themselves, and Ulfius had to get down and make sure that all were all right, and help the people to their feet. The woman who stopped had been cut in the back by a young man carrying a hoe. Ulfius apologized for their upset, and reminded them that they were very tender, and unarmed, and to take the day tomorrow to think hard on whether they really wanted to put themselves in the middle of a deadly melee. Before the stubborn man from earlier could gear up, as he seemed meaning to do, however, Ulfius added "But if you do decide to return, before first light of the morning after tomorrow, we won't send you away."

He came up from his knee to stand, and took the bridle of his horse. "We can benefit each other most if you stay behind us and collect weapons and armor, and ensure that those who have fallen do not rise again." He mounted once more. "Take care of yourselves, and each other," he said, and fixed certain people in the crowd, old and young, whom he judged to show the hint of recklessness. "Remember, there is no honor in killing yourself foolishly," he said. "No honor."

Then he bid them well and walked a few paces forward, at which point he slowed again, and called out, to any who would listen, "And we'll be camping just two hour's ride more from here, with naught but camp rations and what we may hunt." He licked his lips. "Therefore, anyone over the next two nights who might come by with any savory pies would be received most readily."

-56-

Herwyg had woken before light and stepped out of his tent within the Saxon encampment to piss, but he had almost nothing in him. The fluid was dark and almost reddish. God, it was hard to wake up. He stood now near the front of the Saxon lines, the clouds growing light but still a stony blue gray, broken in a few places through to open sky, and

278

his mail weighed on him heavily. He was exhausted... and then the lack of water. It had only been yesterday afternoon that they had run out completely, and that after severe rationing since the evening before. Soon the last drop from the last waterskin was gone, and the meat they could catch (thankfully rabbits were plentiful on that plain) was dry and sinewy. Still, much as they would have liked to have something to wash it down with, they were forced instead to pull what moisture they could from the meat.

Since the intention of the Saxons was to conquer there, and settle there, when Herwyg came on shore, and ascended with his brother troops toward the fields and hills, he thought he was looking at his new home. He had no choice, it was the campaign of his master, but it seemed fertile and generous land, and certainly better than the harsh and endless winter he had just come through. He did not have the perspective to consider that he saw it on a tenderly warm June morning. Hopes were high then; they had not yet realized that the Britons had come between them and their ships.

Then later, they learned that they could not get access to water. And all of this added to the grim disappointment that had set in after they spied the first of the enemy knights, for their landing was supposed to take the Britons by surprise.

Then that beautiful land began to turn into a particular kind of nightmare setting. The vast fields of unbroken, undulating grass, with its bright, vivid green—and nothing else, for they were huge empty spaces—seemed a peaceful rest at first, but soon turned into a kind of existential test. There was nothing there, *nothing*. Just empty blankets of vibrant green blades, so much so that it became uncanny, and looked like it could not be real. Then the day before, when the first sigh that indicates the weariness of dehydration came, the sky had been such a vivid blue, endlessly rich and deep, with clouds of such unsurpassing whiteness, unbelievably fluffy, to the point that it seemed it was a wondrous sight to behold. But then, with time and thirst, it became just a bit too wondrous, it begin to seem unreal, at which point a terror began to curdle in his heart. The sight was so heartrendingly beautiful, it could kill him. The vivid blues and whites, the greens, could be poisonous.

The dehydration began to take hold, and came in waves. The moment when thirsty turns into parched, when weariness takes on a heaviness the muscles don't normally have, and the vision momentarily becomes cloudy. That was last night. This morning, Herwyg's brother soldiers seemed to stand by sheer balancing of flesh, not by any energy with which they were holding their bodies ready for battle. A man a few rows behind was actually moaning. The sound came invisibly though the perfectly lovely June morning, where the scent of the tiny flowers and luscious grass blades was beginning to fill the air, and the lines of men stood like motionless tree trunks. Herwyg looked, and focused on the man next to him, whose face was sallow and cheeks seemed to sag, his head bowed down, as though scarcely awake, eyes barely-open slits.

But then his eyes gradually opened, and his head came back, mouth expanding open, staring at a bright fiery light that had begun spreading within the sky. Herwyg turned his gaze upward, to see what was enthralling the man so. The sun was being freed from its shadow, and its brilliant morning rays came racing toward them in a brightening wave that spread its glow behind the clouds.

Then, when the light hit the breaks in the layer of cloud color, these blazed brilliantly, the intensity rising as the tint evolved through a golden orange and toward scarlet. A stillness spread through all the men, lined up in rows extending ten rows in front of Herwyg, and countless behind, as they all beheld the incredible sight, like a generous gift of nature. It caught all the Saxon's hearts with the aching knowledge that they were witnessing something incredible.

But the blaze along the holes in the blanket of clouds began to array into a shape, which was at first unbelievable, but then became unmistakable. It was the shape of a dragon. There was no denying that one saw it—and no denying that there was nothing, in any way, natural about it. Things like that did not happen. The realization seemed to come over the mass of men at once, and from some direction, for there were close men all around, was heard a low wailing of dread. Then the color grew more intense, and more vivid, so much that it passed out of

280

the realm of the natural and into the realm of the supernatural. It began taking on a red of the deepest hue. This was not something where they saw a beautiful sunrise and mistook it for a crimson dragon. This was dark, unmistakable *red*—the red of blood. The sky opened up like a bloody wound above them, and when a ray of sun illuminated the clouds in such a way it appeared to be a torrent of fire spewing from the dragon's mouth, then some men began to scream.

The sound became intense all at once, along with a low rumbling, and Herwyg could not be sure what the sound was. He saw the line of British troops that had been waiting for them all these last days on the plain with them, just outside their camp, and the mass of men now seemed to vibrate with a strange movement. It occurred to him that they were charging just as the sound of approaching hail turned out to be a wave of arrows that washed over and beyond him, and Herwyg would have been amazed and dumbfounded at the incredible chain of astounding events happening in such a short span of time, but he was dead.

-57-

Uther kept his horse close to the wall of shields the Saxons had arrayed themselves behind, and stabbed downward, repeatedly, with his spear. He did it mindlessly, not even seeing the enemy as men, just a moving mass of chain mail and helmets, and himself playing a game of looking for vulnerable spots. See one; stab it. A new one opens; stab it. There was blood, the odd flash of eye within a helmet, the sudden sight of teeth in a screaming mouth, and swords coming out from within the shields to stab at his horse, but his steed was armored and inured to battle.

He had finally managed to get his mind together in the dark pre-dawn hour before the dragon appeared, as he stood in the morning twilight, awaiting the sign. He had filled the ride there, as best he could, with chat and banter with his fellow knights as he rode, for in the moments between conversations, the thoughts came in hard, and relentlessly. That his brother would be dead after this battle was over. That he would be made king. That he would be a horrible failure as king. That everyone would see him for what he was—a waste. That they would say he was a big, dumb warrior, and big, dumb warriors were always welcome—in the king's army. Not as the king. He once again thought about how perfect it was with Pendragon as the king, and he next to the throne. Why couldn't it stay like that? Yes, it's useless to dwell on the past. On what couldn't be. But that didn't pull the thoughts from his mind, or prevent the aching return of those sudden moments, when his stomach dropped out and he said once more; why couldn't Pendragon just... *live?*

But he had done it; he had driven the thoughts from his brain, and sat astride his horse, letting his mind fall into that calmness that precedes a battle, the simultaneous excitement of all the nerves with the accompanying distant calm that sees everything as happening a bow-shot away. He had told himself to put all thoughts away for now, to just get through the battle, and every time a sudden swoon into emotion came over him, he would tell himself that again. A brother's death—that he could discuss with no one, for no one else could know—and the promotion to king, either of these things would be enough to send most men into nervous hysterics on a peaceful summer's day. On the morning of a battle of major importance, the stress was so extreme it rose to the level of the laughable. What more could you do but laugh? And say to himself, as he did, that he would forgive any thought that came into his mind that day, and not dwell on it or make it another reason he was unfit to lead. He would let the thoughts come in, and just go right out again. Like clouds.

So there he was, mind finally calm and serene, blank and full, in the cold wet air before the sun made its fist appearance. Then he felt a hand on his ankle, he looked down, and—Merlin.

"Do your all to prove your most worth, Uther," the wizard said, eyes burning upward into him. "For you have no need to fear death in this battle." He moved swiftly behind Uther, and was gone.

The feelings hit Uther as roughly as a punch in the face, first a rush of gladness—he would not die!—then, like a proportional wave coming back, horrible guilt and shame. He slumped forward and gripped the reins in his clenched hands, feeling the calloused cut on his finger pressed hard, opening again. He crushed his eyes closed and drew all of his body into tightness, making his shoulders dense, hard boulders of muscle, as his mind was sent haywire, until it all came spinning back with one thought—God damn Merlin!—*Why does he say these things to him?*

The sudden burst of anger he felt at the magician made him whirl to look behind him, furious sneer on his face and hatred in his eyes, but of course Merlin was gone. Not like confronting him would do any good, anyway. He could picture Merlin in his mind, placing his hand innocently on his chest and asking "What?" in that faux-naïve voice. "I only told you that you're not going to die."

Then Uther was thrown right back into having to try to calm his mind, trying to tell himself to let the thoughts come and go. To let them be clouds, coming, going. But the shock to his senses remained, and he could not shove his unruly thoughts back into the mental containers he had devised for them.

Thankfully, it was not long before the dragon appeared in the sky, and the charge into battle. And as he sat, waiting for vulnerable places to open, and then stabbing them, the image of the dragon stayed in his mind. He had been able to keep his mind from dwelling on the dragon the night Merlin had told them about it, and all the days after, he was able to keep from dwelling on it, and when it did cross his mind, he thought how wonderful it was for Pendragon. How just, and right, and fitting it was as a tribute for his excellent brother, the king. But now, as he began to think on—and try not to think on—his future reign, one thought could not help but start to appear, and reappear, in a nagging way, in his brain.

Will I get a dragon?

That was the question, but he didn't really ask it, because he knew.

There was no way anything this spectacular would ever happen for him. That, actually, was fine. Uther wouldn't be upset with a smooth and unremarkable kingship, he would actually welcome it. Less chance for everyone to discover all of his inadequacies. Maybe he would have a kingship of reduced tumult, one more suited to his leadership abilities—and that is where something stuck. Was he just to accept that his kingship would be known primarily as the one *after* his brother's? A sort of placeholder, a void place, the empty years after King Pendragon had ruled so illustriously, and when so many incredible marvels were seen. Was that just—it?

Then, he would have to remind himself, he was not yet king, had not yet experienced one day of rulership, and as anyone would know, he had no idea whatsoever of what might come. Still, the idea that his kingship might ultimately be a bit of a disappointment, that he wouldn't measure up, that the best he could hope for was to rise to competence, seemed somehow already established. But then he reminded himself that, today of all days, he would have no control over the thoughts that stormed across his mind—and that bastard wizard wasn't helping—and that he would forgive himself for any of his thoughts. And if he were to blame for them, he would accept all of it.

Thus he fought, feeling so many emotions that he was unable to process them, and yet so many that they whirled into a blur, leaving his mind paradoxically empty. With Pendragon's death coming, and his ascension to king, he didn't have any idea when he might actually feel again. So he continued stabbing, stabbing, and killing, killing, killing, and several Saxon lives ended while Uther continued on mechanically, mind elsewhere.

58

The fighting continued straight until just before nightfall. The mist of morning had burned off early, leaving an absolutely beautiful, warm and sunny June day, somewhat incongruous with the scenes of battle and slaughter taking place on that lovely field. Now the sun was lowering in the sky and taking on a reddish hue, glinting off the helmets and armor of the few men remaining. The air was filled with the sound of the banging, and grinding, and scraping of steel, undergirded by the grunting, bellowing and moaning of men, as they fought man after man after man, or lay wounded or dying on the ground. The sound came from everywhere at once, and became a dull roar as it filled the air, as now-sparse armies were clashing as far as the eye could see in every direction. For us people of today, having seen so many depictions of these grand battles, it is almost impossible for us not to hear it happening to the accompaniment of a loud, bombastic and grandiose musical soundtrack. But in reality the evening rang only with an unorganized cacophony of clanging steel and the utterances of men in various states of anger, terror, pain, agony or lamentation.

The air was permeated with the smell of blood.

There was little way to tell how the battle was going during the middle of it, except that Pendragon would receive reports from different parts of the battleground when he was able to speak with a messenger or anyone who had come from other parts. By all accounts it was all but won, and his own eyes could see it for himself. The battleground was now sparse of men still standing, and those who remained fought in a desultory—or outright exhausted—way, knowing that those who were able to would soon depart the battlefield for the fall of night. The scattered Saxons that Pendragon now encountered were weary, and it was plainly perceptible in their eyes that they had no lust for battle. Now any ferocity they were able to muster came from the fact that they simply had no choice but to fight, although everything in their perception told them it was useless. It would be hard for any of us to comprehend the effect of physical exhaustion combined with overwhelming fear, plain and simple, on the morale and motivation of any one soldier, and the struggle to lift a heavy sword when he knew that no matter how hard he fought, only death awaited.

The hooves of the king's horse sunk a half-inch with every step into earth that had become mud with human blood. The grass covering of the gentle rise he slowly rode up, stabbing downward at struggling Saxons as they came forward along the way, had been pummeled into bare earth by the constant trudging of men's feet and horse's hooves, and saturated with the blood of both Saxon and British as it spurted and seeped from wounds, until it was a wet paste, sprinkled through with the ripped-out leaves. His horse's feet found purchase with difficulty, stepping among the splayed limbs and torsos of the fallen men of both sides, and even the bodies of fallen horses killed or wounded in the melee. He was exhausted by the day of fighting, although also somewhat exhilarated by the overwhelming sense that the Britons were everywhere giving the Saxons a proper rout, and that they had probably already won. This exhilaration was no doubt added to by the blood he had lost through the several small wounds he had received throughout the day, although his spirits were buoyed up by the cheers and acclaim he received from the men, especially the peasants, as they found him there, fighting alongside them.

Pendragon was fighting a Saxon, holding his spear and stabbing it down into the space below the enemy's helmet and into his shoulders, when the man directed his sword into his horse's flank just behind the foreleg. The animal reared in pain, and its hooves slipped in the wet side of an unexpected trench in the ground. Horse, king and Saxon all fell, and in a moment Pendragon was suddenly immersed in a sticky pool of warm fluid. It got into his mouth and filled it with a metallic taste, and for a moment he dared not open his eyes, but felt the warm wetness saturate his hauberk and underclothes.

He pressed his hands down instinctively and lifted his head, whereupon a sheet of the fluid ran down across the slit of his helmet, and he could see its scarlet color as the sunlight shone through the thin liquid, until it drained off to become a few viscous trickles. It was blood. He, his horse, and the Saxon had fallen into a wide ditch filled about a foot deep with it. When his vision cleared enough, he saw the Saxon standing over him, wet armor highlighted by the reddening sun, raising his arms above him, sword held between them. He brought it straight down, into Pendragon's side.

He felt the punch on his abdomen for a moment, as the rings of his mail held for a second, before bursting and allowing the blade to enter deeply, where he felt its movement in his guts. His horse had fallen next to him, onto its back in the trench of blood, and it writhed there in pain, legs flailing out wildly. One of the hooves struck the Saxon about the chest and flung him down, and Pendragon used that moment to try to push himself, using his legs, up onto the other side. As he did, he arched his left arm behind his back and used it to pull the sword out of his side. He could feel it slide out of the organs deep within him. Then one of the horse's hooves caught him on the helmet and bashed him face down into the wet earth.

The king rolled away, out of range of the horse's flailing legs, turned on his side and, seeing no immediate threat, allowed himself to simply rest for a moment. He could see his men, the ones assigned to stick by the king during the press, and—well, actually he could only see two of them, and they were both involved in heavy combat. Then one of them was slain before his eyes. Pendragon barely had the strength to react, but it was hard to see, as that man had been known to the king since even before he and Uther had returned. Beyond where that man once was, he could see the man on horseback who carried the king's pennant. He was being besieged by two enemy knights slashing at him, and as Pendragon watched, his horse's hooves began to slip in the wet mud, and horse and rider could be seen to start to slide slowly backward, even as the pennant-holder was slashing away at his assailants with his free hand.

He saw the horse lose its balance, and, amid the din of the clashing of steel of metal and men's cries and moans, the beast's eyes widened wildly, showing their whites. It slipped backwards and finally fell over, tossing its rider, with the king's pennant, to the ground.

Now no one would be able to tell where the king was.

Pendragon fell onto his back. He allowed himself to simply lie and stare upward for a moment, seeing only orange-tinged clouds in the sky above him through the thin slit of his helmet, as he gave in to the exhaustion he felt. He knew blood was leaking out of the wound in his side, as well as some of the other, smaller cuts he had received in the battle. Oddly, what he felt was the beginnings of a sense of relief. Knowing that no one could tell where he was… to his surprise, that was a huge relief. Here I am, he thought, finally a free moment from the burden of being king. And he thought how the battle was going well, how the British were all but assured of winning, especially after what he knew Merlin had said, and without even thinking about it, reached up to undo the straps holding his helmet in place.

He sat up on his haunches, then fully upright. Ten feet away on this side, and twenty on that, men raged in battle, yet for the moment, he was able to sit among them quietly. He removed the helmet that covered his head, exposing the mail beneath, feeling the cooling air where it reached his head, and took in a great, deep breath of air. He looked down the endlessly unfurling field, which was shiny and wet, reflecting the sun like metal as it grew larger and its color more livid. What he saw before him was a vision composed primarily in scarlet and black, as the range of colors started to drain in the lowering light, and the red sun and sky of fantastically fiery clouds shone brightly off the shining waves of land saturated with blood. The few standing men, fighting here and there, seemed as black silhouettes in the harsh light, except for the glint of the burning sun on their helmets and blades. Threading through them, an a endless stream of men and horses clomping off toward their encampment, leaving the battle at the close of day. It was an inspiring sight, and Pendragon was all but sure that their side had won. It had also been, at the same time as the unceasing slaughter was going on, a fantastically clear and beautiful June day, and the warm breeze that now threaded through the legs of the knights and horses, and over the bodies and separated limbs—yet completely indifferent to it all—was so sweet as to make the heart break. How beautiful and clean it seemed! He wished he could just sit there quietly,

288

and take in the superb sight. Pendragon shook his head in amazement. Merlin was right, there would never be a battle like this, and not just because of the clash of men, but this day, this fiery sky—he had almost forgotten the dragon of fire in the sky that morning!—and it seemed one could only wonder and feel thankful that one was alive on that day.

He turned onto his chest, and, with struggle, raised himself to stand. He wobbled on his feet slightly, and felt a brief moment of lightheadedness pass over him, but he was able to center himself. The place around him seemed to hold few enemies. Still, he was not more than a moment on his feet before one ran at him, axe upraised.

Pendragon stepped out of the way of the blow, and got the man a good nick in the flank. After a few more blows, bashing down on the rings of chain mail on his arm and neck, he left the man fallen and maimed. Thankfully, there were few men left who wished to fight, and the majority of those were so sparse now they left twenty or forty paces between them as they strode off the field, stepping over the bodies and fallen animals. His own men went past him toward the camp, and although he carried his crowned helmet in his hand, any one of them could have recognized him for the king simply by looking at the heraldry on his surcoat. But it was dark with blood, and besides, exhaustion and hours of violence on their bodies kept their heads downward and gazes forward. He caught the eye of a certain Saxon walking lifelessly off in the other direction, unchallenged, and he regarded the king with a deadened, rueful gaze as he walked stonily past. The king continued walking, in a third direction from any of the men, and he made his way up a gentle rise. He didn't really even know why. His boots slipped under him as he tried to step upward on the bloody grass.

By the time he had reached a position higher up, the lightheadedness was no longer going away, but was blending into a general numbness, not unlike a euphoria, that settled over his brain. He knew that he was losing large amounts of blood. And no one knew where he was. Pendragon smiled, and his brow grew heavy, and it seemed like he could just take a moment of rest. By now there was no one around him, though numerous distant men were still visible, and the land was dim now, just a dark brown, the air having deepened into a thick red you felt you could almost touch, while the blasting sun shone through clouds that arched above and below it. A wave of weariness passed over him, a serious one, and he knew he should push on, identify himself to some group of knights who would take him and be sure that he made it back to camp. But there was no one around him now and he could not deny that he was so glad for it. The night was so beautiful and rare that he just wanted to enjoy it alone—and praise to God, it somehow seemed like he could. Then he turned to examine the valleys below the hill, and what he saw stunned him.

There, on the plain where he had just climbed up from, the bright red sun and sky shone on the surface of the liquid in the ditch he had fallen into, which was now tickled with shining ripples by the cool evening breeze that wafted over the saturated battlefield. He could see now that the ditch formed an almost-complete circle, with the opening aligned exactly to him, and which blazed out with reflected sunlight against the dark brown surrounding field and low hills, creating a ring of light hovering in the space below him. Pendragon's mouth fell open, and an involuntary laugh, coming out more like a desperate bark, issued from his aching abdomen. He couldn't believe it—that Merlin! There it was, just as he had said. The circle of blood.

His shoulders relaxed and he almost let his sword slip from his hand. The giddy lightheadedness that was tingling in his brain became sharper in a wave, and he realized that he wasn't just exhausted, he was dying. The wounds, and simple loss of blood, were on the verge of overcoming him and that's what he was feeling.

Should he try to find his minders? Put up his pennant once more? A good king would, he guessed. Continue on. But Merlin told him that when he saw what he saw—and there could be no mistaking it—that it would be time for him to die. And Merlin, he knew now with certainty, would never say untruth. And with that, a surging wave of relief, and following wave of euphoria, passed over his body from head down to toe, relaxing his muscles through shoulders to legs, and he looked down at the crowned helmet still held in his hand, grasped it harder, and hurled it across the battlefield. It banged down distantly and rolled across the wet grass.

He breathed in the crisp air as it streamed across the land, and it seemed to fill his lungs with an incredible purity. He peeled the mail off his head and let the cool wind chill and tighten his wet scalp—it was so invigorating! He turned around to once more behold the bright circle, already fading, where it glowed within the field beneath him. It was as clear as the dragon that had appeared in the sky, and just as clearly not something from nature. It made Pendragon's brow grow weak and he felt that he might weep, for he knew that he was witnessing a great marvel. His legs grew weak and he stumbled, but he took a step forward, and after that another, and soon he was running toward the circle.

The cool evening wind entering him seemed like the purest water, and his giddiness increased, until he felt that he was laughing as he ran, his heart pounding and lungs bursting. But he was not laughing, because he was too eager simply to get there. He ran and ran to the circle, and with each pounding step he grew lighter. His head was no longer full of thoughts, just the wish to get into that circle. Pendragon couldn't help but smile, and tears streamed suddenly from his eyes as he ran, his lips opening in a sweetly pained smile that showed his bank of white teeth. Merlin said that this would be the greatest battle that would ever take place in that country. Even with the might of this great king to come, and who knows what else in the future, he thought, *this* was it. The greatest battle. The thought made his chest cringe in pride, and hot tears come anew. With rushing legs, he entered the circle.

He made his way to the center of it, where he attempted to step on the chest of a fallen Saxon, but his foot slipped on the bloody mail, sending him hurtling forward to the earth. He hit with his upraised arms and shoulders, then rolled on his back down a slight valley between two low mounds in the earth, where he lay cradled on his back. By that time the last light was leaving the sky, and the field was all but empty. He heard someone in the far distance, calling out for the king, but he knew he had gone too far with his loss of blood, and what's more—he didn't want to be found. Let him rest at last. The voice was

291

heard father away, and he was glad. The evening breeze was so sweet, just growing from cool to cold, and he wanted nothing more than to be alone out there.

The earth there was saturated with blood, and Pendragon thought about the ring of blood that surrounded him, and the incredible sight he had seen, the circle shining brightly against the hill. Honestly, the day had begun with a wonder and ended with one. He remembered how Merlin had told him that he would be the blood of Britain, and how the land would absorb his blood, and that of the other Britons, and the Saxons. And it had proved true, that field was soaked in blood, and he thought on how incredible it was, the land absorbing their blood—his actual blood. He would be in that land always. And he thought on the king to come, and with a whimpering laugh, he wished that he could meet him, and know him.

With the thought of this new king commanding his brain, for also his thinking was growing fuzzy, and his vision cloudy, he lifted up the mail on one side and, turning his sword upward in his hand, sliced open his own flank. Once that was done, and the blood was gushing out of him and into the earth, he threw the sword, as best he could, and lay his head back on the ground. A satisfied smile now came over his face, breathing now in shallow pants, as he thought over how wonderful it all was. He had brought the country from here to there, displaced Vortiger and Hengist, now routing this wave of Saxons... he knew that Uther would have more to do, and this new king, the man to come, would also have much to do, but he had done enough, and suddenly it all seemed quite enough, and quite gratifying.

The blood coming out his flank was both hot and cool, where the night air touched it on his skin, and as he looked heavenward, he could see the stars appearing in the darkening blue of the clear sky. The field had almost entirely emptied now, and the coming night became quiet, save for the sounds of birds indifferent to the fighting, and Pendragon reached his arms up until he saw his blood-covered fingers outstretched against the stars beyond.

He was laughing, giddy and lightheaded, and his mind was suffused with a tingling fog as he shouted "Take it!" The sound was so

292

hoarse and weak it made him laugh even more, and reach out further, toward that new king, and he yelled, "Take it!"

59

Thus ended the battle of Salisbury. Many of Uther's knights were killed there, while many others walked away, unscathed or wounded to varying degrees, but every one of the Saxons was killed, or found dead as they tried to make their way back to the sea.

Pendragon's body was discovered, and Uther stood above it for long minutes, staring down with grim eyes, as though willing it to move. But it did not. The plain the day after was resolutely drained of any atmosphere or magic it might have had, and the gray light that made it through the heavy clouds rendered the fallen men as still shapes strewn everywhere about against the dull color of the grass, which was already returning to green. He felt it for the first time there, as he stood above his brother; the mortifying sense that everyone was now looking at him, waiting for him to tell them what to do. Or waiting, just a second longer than before, to observe his reactions. He ordered his brother to be buried where he was, and all of the other men to be gathered up and buried there, within and around the unexplained circular ditch they found there. The hole for Pendragon had to be dug straight down from where his body fell, for there were discovered under the ground two great stones on either side, and Uther ordered that his name not be written above him, for no one could see the placement of his grave there, in the center and slightly above, and not know that he was the lord of all that surrounded him.

Then Uther journeyed to the city of Logres, where he gathered all of his chief vassals and the prelates of the Holy Church who were under him, and had himself crowned and anointed king. When all of this was done, Merlin once more came to him, and Uther was greatly happy to receive him. Merlin advised that Uther now make known to everyone how he had put his power behind the brothers, and given them foreknowledge of everything that had happened, such that all understood Uther to be unquestionably aligned with Merlin, and their combined might and wisdom would make their realm all but unshakable. Then Merlin stepped up so that all could see him, and know him, and he told the meaning of the dragon's appearance in the sky, and how it signaled the death of Pendragon and the transition of kingship to Uther, and because of this, Uther made known to all that he would be adopting his brother's name in tribute, and that from then on, all would refer to him as Uther Pendragon.

Merlin stayed around him for quite a while then, for which Uther was desperately glad, for the rest of the time seemed to be mostly filled with him walking around the castle, aware that he could move Pendragon's things out, and arrange the chambers and living quarters exactly as he liked, only he wasn't sure what he liked, and couldn't bear to touch his brother's things. It wasn't true, of course, although it seemed like it. He actually spent most of his time in meetings and conferences. Nor was he constantly at a loss for what he was supposed to do, as he feared, for that was taken care of by the constant stream of people coming to him with different tasks, or needing direction or approvals. He found that he was more able to supply those who looked to him with advice than he expected, and as the days, and then weeks, went on, his confidence grew as well. And as there seemed to be no war or looming crisis on the horizon, the continuance of which he began to include in his prayers, he started to feel like, at least during times of relative peace, he could hold it together, and maybe even do so admirably.

After a few weeks had passed, and the kingdom was coming together and moving on with greater stability, Merlin came to him and said "Are you ready to honor your brother, who lies on the plain of Salisbury?"

"What would you have me do?" Uther replied. "I will do anything that you ask."

Merlin pointed at him. "You made a promise to do what I wish, and I said that I would create a monument such as has never been seen, that will stand in place as long as the world lasts," he said. "And now it is the time to do that. Keep your word, and I will do as I promised."

Uther once more said that he would do anything Merlin requested, and the wizard told him of some great stones, of immense size and power, that lay in Ireland, and would require many ships to transport to Britain and bring to Salisbury. Even in that moment, Uther suspected that if these stones were so great, their ships could hardly transport them, and if Merlin was offering to build a monument from them, he must have some way to bring them there... but he would not disagree, and he acquiesced to every one of Merlin's demands.

Many men and ships went to Ireland, and when they saw the stones, they knew immediately that they were so enormous and heavy that they would never be budged, so they all trudged back to their ships, sailed across the sea, and told the king the news. Merlin came not far behind them, saying that the men could not do what they were tasked with, and so he would have to do it all himself. Uther looked at him with quiet confusion, almost amused, and said that Merlin should certainly do whatever he thought right. But in bed that night he lay awake, with a comely and fresh new maiden at his side, and wondered why Merlin went through these things. What did he get out of them? Was it making everyone go all the way there (thankfully Uther himself was not required to go), only to acknowledge, in front of him, that they couldn't do it, and he could? Sending a fleet of ships across the ocean and back for no reason cost money, significant money, but... he was pretty much never, ever going to say no to Merlin. Maybe it was for him to outlay money in order to place a value on Merlin's worth? He honestly could not figure what the wizard got out of these little games.

And by the way, his fears of never having time, or ability, to engage with the maidens as he used to? That didn't turn out to be a problem after all. In fact, quite the contrary, and he was surprised to learn that there were some, not many, but some, who considered his brother somewhat of a moral stiff.

But back to the story, Merlin huffed and sighed and said, "Well, since they have all disappointed me, I suppose that I must do all that I promised by myself." And Uther shook his head, and agreed that this was verging on tragedy, and revealed a serious breach in the might of his kingdom—which he was eternally glad to the magician for exposing—and that, since there was no other but Merlin, except God, that could accomplish it, he knew that all who loved his brother, and all of those who visited the site in centuries to come, would be cheered by the sight of whatever he saw fit to erect on than plain in the memory of the king.

"Then that is what I shall do," Merlin said, perhaps on the verge of wondering if Uther were mocking him, "for then I would have fulfilled what I pledged to Pendragon. If not," and he fixed Uther with a serious gaze, "then I would have started something that can never be brought to an end."

-60-

Merlin asked that the king and a considerable retinue travel to Salisbury to see the stones he had brought there, and later, the monument he had built. The hillock where his brother was interred was now covered with massive gray stones of a roughly rectangular shape, balanced all over each other at strange angles, and a riot of smaller stones that were long rectangles. The king looked up at the green hill to see the pile of dark gray stones under a misty gray sky, and even in disarray, the sheer weight of it looked like something wondrous and amazing. He knew that whatever Merlin constructed there would be spectacular.

His people, many specifically requested by Merlin, came and marveled as they walked around the stones, and all agreed that no one else could have brought them there. Uther assumed that this was all

296

thought through by the seer, picking the right people who would go back and make wide report of the incredible feats he was capable of, for he was a marvel at shifting and controlling opinion. You can be sure that Uther had already experienced several moments where he wondered which of them was actually in charge, but he remembered his brother's advice, and knew that Merlin wanted what was best for the kingdom, so he never let those thoughts stick in his mind.

Merlin asked Uther to meet him alone at the site the next day, saying he wanted to show him something that he would never forget as long as he lived. Of course Uther agreed. The day was cloudy and cool, with the threat of misty rain, and a light but steady wind traveled constantly across the plain as he could see Merlin, in his deep blue robe, holding his staff, standing and waiting for him among the huge stones at the top of the rise.

Uther stepped up, leaving his nearest men, a small group, far enough away to be far outside the circular ditch, and nodded to his advisor. They said nothing, but Uther once again marveled at the stones, some of which were about thirty feet in length, and must have weighed several tons each. To be around them was even a bit uncanny, in that Merlin way, for you felt how impossible they would be for anyone else to move. He walked among them, running his hand over the surfaces, sometimes rough and some smooth. "I am still amazed and impressed by your ability to get these stones here, Merlin. How did you do it?"

"Through my great craft," said Merlin. "And soon you will see how I arrange them. These stones will stand for the power of your brother, and all that he has given to this country."

"Let us all always remember all that my brother gave for this country," said Uther, who had become almost rote in his unvarying praise for his brother.

"Indeed we should," said Merlin. "Your brother was a good king because he always ruled with the good of his people, and the country they lived in, foremost in his heart," he said, walking slowly amongst the stones, clutching his staff near its head. Then he looked sharply at Uther. "Do you think that you will also be a good king in that way?" he asked.

They were alone within that circle, the nearest person about a bow-shot away. Uther was not sure he had ever been so completely alone with Merlin, with other people so far away, not across the room or at least next door, and he knew that the sorcerer had brought him there for a very special purpose, so they might have this moment, alone in the mist and wind, on that spot. If he were honest, he would have guessed that the reason for the request was probably so that they could tighten their bond and increase their trust, so that they might rule more successfully together.

"I will strive to always put my people first," said Uther confidently, "so that I may be a good king, as my brother was."

Merlin cocked his head, and narrowed his eyes. "You have heard that the gifts I possess come from the devil, but my wisdom to use them for the good of this country comes from God," said Merlin. "And you have seen that I have knowledge far exceeding that of any human being, and gave you the foreknowledge of Hengist's attack, and the Saxons coming to this land."

Uther wasn't quite sure what he was getting at, but everything he said was true, and he would have no trouble to admit it. "Yes Merlin," he said, "you are trusted by me above all men in the world." The seer looked at him with eyes that seemed to find him wanting, as if this answer was unacceptable. Uther stood up straighter. If Merlin wanted to be stern and officious now, it was for him to comply. "And I will always try above all never to lose your favor, or fail to recognize the great advantage that you offer me," he added.

Merlin continued to gaze into his eyes, and his two hands made a twisting and lifting gesture. There was a deep thud, several, actually, all around Uther, and he jumped quickly in an alarmed way as there was movement and sound all about him. Certain of the rocks, that were long and thin, were moving everywhere at once, and they arrayed themselves, in just a short moment, into a long semi circle, and the sound of the knocks and thuds was stilled abruptly as they hung silently above the ground. Then they went down into the ground, the earth opening up to receive them, and a moment later, were standing quietly, sticking straight up out of the ground.

Uther had never seen the magician perform anything like this, and stared at him, frozen, with gaping eyes. Everything Merlin had done so far were quiet things like telling facts no one could know, or appearing in different guises, so to see him now throwing around massive objects without use of physical effort was something new and honestly a bit frightening.

The morning fell silent again, as the activity ceased. Uther still held his body stiff, as he had just been at the center of a movement of large rocks, any of which could have broken his foot or leg. He remained very still, arms raised and tense, and looked at Merlin, who held him with great focused attention in his unwavering gaze.

"I told you and your brother, and I tell you again now," said the wizard, his voice low and velvety, "if you lie to me, or if you disrespect the great secrets and wonders that I offer you, you will be hurt far more than it will hurt me." He paced a bit in place, then turned his head to gaze thoughtfully at Uther. "Do you believe that?"

Uther nodded eagerly. "Yes, ahh—" he said, for suddenly just above his head a great stone, weighing tons, blocked the light, and his word trailed off into a muffled scream as it seemed that he would be crushed. His head whirled over to look at Merlin with enlarged eyes, to find that the seer regarded him with a distant, pitiless gaze. Uther's breath quickened into shallow pants, and he turned once more, in time to see the enormous stones lift and whirl into place, as though light as foam, to create five boxy arcs of three stones each, in a larger semicircle just outside the semicircle of long rocks. It took Uther a moment of silence, after the last stone had fallen into place, balanced on top, before he realized that he was no longer in immediate danger.

Fear, deep fear, came into his body, freezing him, and when he turned and saw Merlin there, he dropped immediately to his knees.

"No, Merlin," he said breathlessly, "I will never lie to you or try to deceive you," his words came out in barks with each breath. "Or disrespect the advice and knowledge that you offer me," he said, bending forward at the waist, and looked up once more at Merlin, who towered over him. "I want to..." he started, but swallowed his words, so plaintively he knew they would come out. "I want to be a good king," he forced out.

But he was not sure he could. And so, as he admitted his wish, and tears came to his eyes, he knew now why Merlin had arranged this time where he could be alone, and away from everyone, away from the threat of men of his retinue who would report that the king had been seen crying, or seen bowing to Merlin. That was Merlin—in time, you saw what his reasoning had been, but as it was unfolding, it could be incomprehensible, or unnerving, or outright scary. Whatever you thought, he was already there, having thought through to every end point, down every possible alley. Inescapable, and a touch suffocating— and perhaps cruel. Then Uther realized that the responsibilities of kingship weren't the only thing Pendragon's presence had shielded him from.

Now he was just a few feet before the wizard, and had to bend back on his haunches to look up at him. "Do you think you have the ability to be a good king, Uther?" Merlin asked.

Uther had to lower his eyes. "I hope so," he cried.

"We're all *hoping* so, Uther" said Merlin, and gave the king a long, extended glance through worried eyes that made the king's heart shrink. "Stand, please," said the wizard, turning away with a grimace. "No king should kneel to anyone."

He said it with a slight tone of disgust, or annoyance, in his voice, and Uther was stung through, his feelings once more back in a childhood moment, when his father, the illustrious Constance, had called him out for cowardice. Then he was unsure, does he stand just because Merlin says so? Or does he remain kneeling to show that he is able to think on his own—even if his thought may be wrong—or idiotic?

He rose to standing, with unsure motions, and could barely raise his eyes to meet Merlin's for a moment before he had to lower them again. In the last few minutes, without his noticing, a ring of numerous long and thin stones, like the ones forming the inner semicircle, had been placed standing in a circle outside the semicircle of large rocks.

Merlin waited, silently, until Uther found the strength to stand before him, and could force himself to meet the sorcerer's gaze. Uther did, but it was tremendously hard not to look away, and he felt that Merlin was terrorizing him, as a hard father might do. For his own good, maybe, but terrorizing him nonetheless. Every impulse in him told him to lower his eyes, look down, but he divorced himself from his feelings, and forced himself to look back at Merlin no matter how hard it was.

When Uther had steadied himself, Merlin spoke lowly. "Can you put the good of your people before yourself, Uther?" he asked. "Like a good king must?"

"Yes, I can," yelled Uther.

"Do you think that I can help you become a good king, Uther?" Merlin asked in a pointed tone. "Or do you think that I will lead you astray?"

"You will help me become a good king, Merlin," Uther said. He was breathing through clenched teeth.

"Your brother was worried that all of his accomplishments were actually mine," said Merlin, entwining his hands behind his back as he began to pace. "Is that something you worry about also, Uther?"

"No, Merlin," Uther pushed the words out.

"Do not lie!" Merlin hissed.

"I—" the king whimpered, "I think about it. I don't know what the answer is." He hung his head and said nothing more.

"That is honest," said Merlin. His eyes were afire and he would not move them off the new king as he paced in a circle around him. "Do you have any cause to doubt my word or to think that I would ever mislead you in any way?"

"No Merlin," shouted Uther, "everything you have said has come true, and you have never lied to me in anything."

The wizard walked around him slowly, tapping a finger against his lips. "What happened to your brother when he doubted my word and went along with that man in trying to deceive me?"

"He suffered greatly," said Uther, and the hot tears spilled over his cheeks. "He suffered greatly and it haunted him, I know, until his last day."

"And do you think I suffered too, Uther? When your brother tried to deceive me?"

301

The wizard stopped in front of the king and his eyes bore into him with a relentless steadiness.

"No, you did not suffer, Merlin," yelled Uther. "Pendragon brought great suffering upon himself, and I was also," his breath caught as his throat choked closed, "thrown into turmoil," he said. "But you did not suffer."

Merlin nodded and resumed pacing around him. "You are wrong, Uther, I did suffer," said Merlin. "I suffered because I trusted in Pendragon and I offered my gift to him, and you, and he lied to me and treated my craft with the reverence of a carnival magician." He all but spat out the last words.

"And," he continued, in new, confidential tone, "I begin to hate mankind when they lie to me, and devalue my gift. And I do not want that, because it pushes me toward my devilish state," his eyes snapped to Uther's, "and that is something I do not like."

Uther eyes grew even wilder and his emotions confused. "He did not—" he stammered, afraid of saying the wrong thing, "Pendragon learned quickly, Merlin, as have I. To respect and honor you. No one," it was hard for him to find words, quaking as he was, and his voice began to crack with emotion, "no one has had dealing with anyone like you, Merlin. No one, ever, on earth! Pendragon… he didn't know."

"But *you* know now, don't you, Uther?" Merlin said.

"Yes I do, Merlin!" shouted the king.

"And do you believe that you know more than me, Uther?"

"No!"

"And what will happen to you if you ever lie to me, or deceive me, Uther?"

The king pulled his arms in and involuntarily shuddered. "I will be hurt very badly!"

At this, Merlin's arm gave a sudden jerk upward, and his hand popped open to expose his outstretched fingers, and the far stones, huge things that weighed several tons each, lifted light as a feather in a circle around the site, whirled silently in the air and came down simultaneously, causing the earth to heave, and a sound like thunder to blast out, then echo and recede into a distant rumbling that passed for miles across the countryside.

Now the entire center arrangement, where the two men stood, was surrounded by thirty tall stones standing on end. Uther's weak stance had been upset by the heaving jerk the ground gave when the stones fell, and he had fallen to his knees, leaning forward on one hand. Merlin stood a few feet before him, and Uther didn't want to get up. He wanted to cower down.

"Pendragon lied to me and deceived me," Merlin said, "yet I built this magnificent monument to him so that all can think on his memory. Why do you think I did that, Uther?"

Uther remained staring at the grass. "Because he was a good king!"

"He was a good king, and he did much to bring this land together for its rightful people, and to drive out the invaders, and *that* is what I care about," said the seer. "That is all that I care about, Uther."

And I don't care about you, Uther heard. He cowered beneath the wizard and took in the meaning of his words.

There was a sound of knocking stones all around, and when Uther looked around, he saw smaller boulders rolling up the sides of the standing stones, and settling into place along the top, until there was a continuous circle atop the outer ring. It seemed only a moment before the movement was complete, the sound once again died away, and there were no more loose stones lying on the ground. Each of them had been used.

Uther saw Merlin's hand in his field of vision, and looked up to see the wizard leaning over him. He took the accepted hand and was helped to his feet. He turned away almost immediately, to wipe away his tears and compose himself. He tried to appear as though he were taking in the completed monument, which was, indeed, beyond impressive. It is still there, by the way, on the plain of Salisbury, and you can go see it even now.

"You have created an incredible monument," Uther said, turning at last to look at Merlin, who seemed like a harmless middle-aged man. His chest was still trembling within his shirt, and he knew his eyes were red. "I wish Pendragon were able to see it, but I know all who look on it will think of him, and the battle of Salisbury," he said. "Thank you, Merlin."

The wizard bowed and nodded. "When I see you again, back home, I will tell you how to gather together all of the great leaders of this country, all of those who do not hold with the Saxons, and bring them into lasting allegiance with you," he said, and then he stepped forward and gripped Uther's arm. "And this, *your* kingdom, will be the first unified, organized kingdom to rule the entire realm of Logres."

Merlin stepped back, and smiled, and held out his hand, indicating the king. And Uther, so frightened a moment ago, recalled how he could be charming, even sweet, and trembling with such excitement that his enthusiasm was infectious, and beguiling, especially when one was the recipient of all of his attention. But Uther had been too terrified of him to return his enthusiasm with a genuine smile. He forced one on. "That is marvelous, Merlin," he said.

He wondered if that tone was incomprehensible, or invisible, to the wizard; when people were agreeable because they are scared.

"You will rule for many years, Uther," said Merlin with satisfaction, "and during that time, great and marvelous changes will come to this country. You will see." And Merlin smiled warmly, and stepped backward. "I will see you in a few days, and I will tell you what you must do to begin consolidating your realm." He bowed and made a gesture of regard to Uther. "King," he said.

Uther nodded, and a portal opened in the air behind Merlin, which he stepped backward into. It closed and he was gone. Then could Uther finally breathe. He gasped.

He stepped through the arrangement of stones—that was strange enough, to suddenly be within this strange sanctuary, where a moment ago there had been a pile of disorganized stones. Uther looked, discreetly, to be sure that none of his men were coming near. He could see them, down there at the foot of the rise, gazing upward at the new monument, which was only to be expected. But he ducked back when he saw them, not wanting to be seen. They had orders not to approach, but he had to be sure that he was alone.

Uther walked into the center of the monument, where he was sure his men could not spot him, and hunched down. He was careful not to lean against any of the stones—he could just see knocking one of them over, and the chat he would have with Merlin then. His face was warming to red, and his vision started to swim, as he realized that he was truly alone and could let his feelings out.

Having kneeled in the grass, alone, he threw his head forward into his hands and let the crying and terror come, and the loss—no one to protect him now, and everyone looking to him to know what to do, and no one, anymore, who knew what to do, and no brother there, and as he cried, the lonely abyss seemed to open before him, with nothing to grab onto.

-61-

Upton wended his way down the path through the meadow, whistling a jaunty morning tune and carrying his lunch in a sack. He stopped in his tracks when he saw the enormous flat slice of tree trunk held up on wooden horses in the middle of the field behind his workshop. It was about eight inches thick, and roughly twenty feet in diameter. It obviously couldn't fit into his workshop. His eyes grew wide as he immediately began to calculate what he would have to do to work it. This must be the commission that Merlin had warned them was coming—and here was Merlin, standing up from where he had been resting on the far side of the table.

"Excellent morning, Upton," he said. "I have brought you the commission I mentioned to you."

"Yes, and you were not joking about it being large," the old man said, running his hands over the surface of the wood. "This is some piece of tree," he said. "Where did you get it?"

"It's from a great tree that grew in Cumbria," Merlin said. "It is over a thousand years old," he added, looking on it with great satisfaction. "I did not cut it down," he hastened to add. "It fell over naturally, and this piece is from its stump."

Upton looked at it, and then, following an impulse, put both hands flat on the surface of the wood. "That is some piece of wood," he said.

"It is going to become, through your best work, and that of your friend Lanford, the most renowned table in the world."

Upton raised his head to look at him, then once more lowered his eyes to look at the wood, with its beautiful waves of concentric lines, and ran his fingers over its rough wooden surface. "My," he said, just above a whisper, as he looked at the richly colored wood. "I ought to get Lanford," he said then, raising his head. "He should hear what it is that you want." He looked back at the magnificent wood. "And what exactly we are called on to make."

Merlin nodded, and the man went off to fetch his friend and colleague. Merlin amused himself by looking around the meadow as he waited, and exalted in the variety of plants and insects he found there, marveling at their variety and perfection. Soon he heard the excited voices of good men, and he knew his friends had returned.

"Oh, my, my, my," Lanford said as he laid eyes on the piece of wood, involuntarily coming forward to place both hands on it. "What a slice of tree! Good day, Merlin," he said.

"Good day, Lanford," said Merlin. "I hope you are ready to do some of your finest work."

"He said that this," Upton tapped on the surface of the wood, "will become the most famous table in the world."

"How do you know that?" Lanford asked.

Merlin smiled. "I heard an old lady tell me," he said. "And she knows all things."

Lanford gave him a wry look, knowing he was being cagey, but asked no more. "Are we going to work on it out here?"

"Well, we certainly can't get it inside, can we?" Upton asked.

"I have brought you a tarp that you can throw over it when you are done working for the evening," Merlin said. "But I am fairly certain that we are in for a long stretch of pleasant weather." He then motioned toward some other stones and materials he had brought. "Would you like me to tell you what I would like done with it?"

The men nodded and came around to where he stood, and followed him to where a series of stone wedges lay leaning against the side of Upton's workshop. Merlin had taken flat sections, not more than a quarter inch thick, from the stones that covered the dragons at Dinas Emrys, and also from twenty-two of the stones from Pendragon's monument at Salisbury.

"I have split the table lengthwise right down the center," said Merlin.

"How did you do that?" blurted Lanford.

Merlin had to laugh. "With my teeth," he said.

"Let the man talk!" Upton said.

Merlin motioned to the stones. "I would like these stones to be arrayed inside the table, fitting very closely, in fact, perfectly into carved spaces within the wood, so that there is no space left whatsoever."

Lanford looked at Upton, eyebrows upraised.

"We can do that," Upton said.

I would like this one," and Merlin pointed to the stone from the white dragon, "to go at one end, and this one," he pointed to the stone from the red dragon, "to go opposite it. The rest of these wedges you may array around the center. I would like these stones," and he reached down to pick up a leather sack, and emptied the contents, consisting of several rocks that Blaise had collected on his wanderings, on the wood.

"This table is going to be incredibly heavy," said Upton.

"How are you going to get it where it's going?" Lanford asked.

Merlin laughed at his simple and straightforward curiosity. "I'm going to roll it," he said. "Obviously."

Both of the old men leaned back and sighed, wondering at the huge amount of work this commission would entail.

"I would like these stones to be inlaid, just as you did with my staff," he said. "Cut into octagons, just the same," and he held out his staff to show them. "They should be inlaid around the outer edge of the surface, so they are right where a man's hands would happen to fall when seated here," he said. "And they must make contact, inside the table, with the great gray stone wedges within."

Lanford sorted among the smaller stones with his fingers, some of which were opaque, but some translucent, or almost completely clear, and some opaque but with depths of reflected color that seemed to come from within.

Then Merlin removed an egg-shaped stone just slightly larger than a man's fist, that had been split right down the middle, so it created an elongated half-sphere, and was of an engaging rich milky white of incredible depth. You could see deep into it, yet at the same time, it was completely white. "And this stone will be at the center of the table, completely enclosed, where it will touch the points of all of the wedge stones."

The two men looked at each other, and Lanford whistled.

"As for the surface," Merlin reached into his cloak, took out a piece of paper and laid it out. There was a round drawing on it, the table, with concentric circles, and lines radiating out from the center, creating twenty-four places. "The stones will be inlaid around here," he showed them. "Then a flat surface, for eating and doing work," and he showed them the outer ring of the table. "In here," and he pointed to an inner ring, "you may decorate with a work of intertwining vines, as on the crosses you see in the graveyard," he said. "Across that pattern," he pointed to a thin circle within the pattern, should be a flat surface suitable for carving in a name to whom that place belongs."

"What happens when you have to change the name?" asked Lanford.

Merlin just looked at the man and smiled.

"He'll handle it!" Upton shouted.

"The center, here," and Merlin pointed to the large circle at the center of the table, then placed his hand on Upton's back. "I want you do to your most subtle work, and create the semblance of waves spreading and returning from a drop of water in a circular pool. Do you see what I mean?"

308

"Like…" Upton tried to picture it in his mind, "the rings that spread from a drop of water?"

"And the rings that come back," Merlin said. "Use your most subtle craft, and suggest as many expanding and contracting rings as you can."

Upton looked intimidated, and stared at the drawing, then looked up at the great disc of wood that sat before them.

"Ah, you can do it," said Lanford, clapping him on the back. "It'll be lovely."

"And that is all," said Merlin. "I trust you both to do an excellent job, and if you have any other suggestions, I encourage you to follow them through on your own, as I trust your eye and craftsmanship."

Both men looked bashful at this comment. Lanford tried to lift the wood, and ran his fingers over the bark that was still along the edge. "What kind of room will have space for a table such as this?" he asked.

Merlin's eyes began to shine with pride. "This table will belong to the king of all the realm," he said, "and the most important people of our time will sit at it."

The men said nothing, but turned to Merlin with faces that were absolutely open, and hung without guile as they listened to his words.

"And after serving the current king, and his worthy knights, this table will remain hidden for many years," said Merlin, "but then it will become the beloved table of the greatest king this land will ever know, and it will host the most worthy men that will ever walk in this country, men who will be talked about until the world ends," said Merlin. "And your work," he placed his hand flat on the wood, "will become the most celebrated table the world has ever known, and will serve as the model for countless tables that will all strive to be like this one. And this table will be known around the world, and will still be talked about thousands of years from now."

Both men stared at him, silent.

"I hope I am alive to see the great king sit at it," said Upton quietly. And Merlin smiled gently, but said nothing, because he knew that he wouldn't.

The first few months went well, and Uther grew in confidence. The reality was that there were many people invested in the success of the king, and willing to help him learn what he needed to do in order to run the realm in an orderly way. When it happened, he thought; 'Of course, a successful reign benefits them as much as me," but before that, he had imagined himself completely alone, and, although he often fell back into this loneliness and anxiety, he was learning to calm it, or put it out of his mind completely. He had Ulfius move closer to his own quarters within the castle, and they spent much time together, as well as with various maidens, for one of Ulfius' unofficial duties had become finding the most energetic and beautiful women who showed eagerness to meet the king. Uther realized that in large part, he was free to create the kingship in the image that he wanted it, and he lost no time in doing so.

He did have moments in which he wondered if his accomplishments were his, or Merlin's, but it didn't get to him. It wasn't difficult, since there were no large conflicts—what Saxon enclaves were left in the country remained quiet for now—and his duties mostly consisted of meetings, greetings, feasts, celebrations, and the resolution of small conflicts, most of which he didn't need Merlin for anyway.

Then, as the time came to almost a year after he assumed the throne, Merlin came to Uther, and said to him, "King, I must speak to you privately about a simple thing you can do to please God and secure the stability of your kingdom."

"I will make time to speak with you," said Uther, and arranged for them to have time in private that night, in his chamber.

That night, Merlin said, "King, I see plainly that control of all this land is yours, and it is not possible that anyone could rule it better."

Uther bowed to Merlin and thanked him for his generous words.

"And now I come to you with a suggestion about what you could do to unite your kingdom in fellowship and allegiance, and also to please God. In fact, there is nothing you could do that would so easily earn you the love of God."

"Tell me, Merlin," said Uther.

Merlin nodded and began to pace before him. "What I say to you may sound very strange, but I bid you to keep it hidden, and do not tell your knights or courtiers, for I want all of the worth, honor and good will that is generated from it to be attributed to you."

"That is very thoughtful, Merlin," said Uther. "I will do exactly as you advise, since you have worked it out to be so beneficial to me."

"Sir, you know that our Lord's son came to earth to save mankind, and while He was here, He sat down to the Last Supper with His disciples, and He said 'there is one of you here who will betray me,' and everything went just as He said, and eventually that one was forced to leave his fellowship, just as He predicted."

Uther nodded. "Yes, Merlin, everything you say is true."

"Now," continued Merlin, "there was a knight that knew Christ when he was on earth, and he took Him down from the cross, and was in the wilderness with Him after he was raised from the dead, and he inherited the cup that held Christ's blood, and which served wine at the Last Supper, and that cup is called the sangrail."

Uther nodded, but said nothing.

"That knight brought the sangrail to this country, where it currently resides," continued Merlin. "And as he was traveling with his disciples, they experienced great famine, and he asked God for an indication of why he wanted them to suffer. And the Lord instructed him to make a table, in the name of the table that was at the Last Supper, and to cover the table with white samite, and to put the grail on the table, also covered with white samite."

Uther was thoroughly engrossed.

"Anyone who sat at that table could have his heart's desires fulfilled in every way, and the Lord used that table to divide the good from the wicked, which is why there is always one seat left empty, which stands for the place where Judas sat at the Last Supper. This seat will always be left empty, until it is the will of our Lord to put another man, of his choice, there and complete the fellowship. And thus this table, and the one from the Last Supper, are very much alike, although God uses the second table to perfect the hearts of those who are graced to sit there, and no one can sit at that table and not be wholly changed for the better."

"This is an incredible wonder, Merlin."

"And I will tell you something yet more wondrous, and how you can see, and create, wonders in your own time, that will last much longer than you are here on earth."

Uther nodded and leaned forward.

"If you will do as I advise," Merlin said, "you will set up a third table, in the name of the Trinity, and by these three tables will the Trinity be signified in its three persons, the Father, the Son, and the Holy Ghost." Merlin stood back, and straightened, holding his hand up. "I promise that if you do this, great good will come to your kingdom, and country, and also great honor to your body and soul, and in your time will happen the formation of a magnificent fellowship that will ever amaze you, for this table will have the ability to draw all who sit at it into lasting friendship, and love, and devotion to each other that they have never known. And I promise that if you do this, it will be one of the most talked-about things ever to happen in your kingdom."

"Well, Merlin, I could hardly fail to do anything that would so easily please the Lord," he said. "I will do anything that you advise."

"And would you want to oversee the creation of this table?" asked Merlin. "Or should I see to it?"

"Sir, I wish to do everything exactly according to the Lord's wishes, which is why I entrust it to you, who are better able to know what the Lord would want. And I will give you as much silver and men to carry out your wishes, so you can have it done as you like."

"Excellent sire, I will do so," said Merlin, quite pleased. "And now look to the place where you would like most to do what you must."

"I would have it done in the place that you suggest," said the king immediately.

Merlin smiled, for this is the answer he wanted. "I would suggest that it be done at Carduel, in Wales. Arrange to have all of your people gather to meet you there on Whitsunday, and be ready to give out great gifts and be of excellent cheer. And I will go ahead and have the table built, and it will be ready when you arrive for your high court."

Uther nodded, and he was getting excited, imagining the gathering in his mind. Also, because he knew by now that when Merlin got this excited, and had that certain gleam in his eye and tone in his voice, that he had something wondrous and unbelievable planned.

"When you have gathered the great people of your realm, I will go among them and tell you which ones are worthy to be seated at the table, and who will become the first fellowship of your land. And we will leave a void place, where no one may be seated, to signify the place where Judas sat. And you, king," he pointed at Uther, "you will serve these men from your own hand, and greet them with the humility that you wish them to have unto you."

Uther stood, and placed his hands on his hips, much in the pose that his brother used to naturally take. "I'll do it!" he declared.

"Good!" said Merlin. "Then let me go devise this table, and I will see you, with those people who will form the first great unified kingdom of Logres, in Carduel a week before Whitsunday!" Then he left the room, by the door.

Then Uther sat down once more, and put his head forward onto his hand, and his eyes gleamed as he thought on this court, and the solidification of his kingdom, and how Merlin said he would rule for many years.

-63-

The king arrived in Carduel a day before all of the other knights and ladies of his kingdom were set to arrive, and took residence in the castle there that was to host his Whitsuntide court. That afternoon Merlin came to him, and said that he would now show him the great table that the king had ordered, and tell him how he was to hold his feast there in such a way that would solidify the unity of his kingdom.

Merlin led him into a great room at the base of the castle's grand tower, a vast octagonal space that was filled with a massive table that took up the entire center. Merlin led the king in, then stood back as Uther's eyes took in the result of the labors that Merlin had put in for him.

The table was huge, such that the king had never seen before. Along its rounded edge was a beautiful array of inlaid stones in octagonal shapes of various sizes and colors, some of which were merely shiny, others of which caught the light with their translucent qualities, in which you could see how they penetrated deeply into the wood itself. The king was compelled to reach out and run his hand over these stones, so rich and beautifully colored were they, like an array of stars surrounding the outer edge. There was then a smooth surface, shiny with varnish but making visible the natural circles of the wood, and within that, about an arm's reach closer to the center, was a large circle with a pattern of stylized vines, adorned with delicately carved leaves and flowers, appearing to be densely interwoven but ordered. Within that, forming the center of the table, far beyond the reach of anyone sitting at it, was a section of raised circular ridges, like a pattern of waves spreading on water, that was enhanced by the natural concentric circles of the wood grain, such that when the king walked around the table, it gave the uncanny appearance of movement.

"Merlin," the king said at last, leaning down on the table with open hands, for the beauty and craft of the table compelled one to touch it, "you have done what you said and created the most beautiful table that exists in the world, and I am..." the king gazed on the table as he searched for the right words, "I am humbled that you should have chosen to grace my kingdom with it."

"This is what you have done, my lord," said Merlin, "with your adherence to my advice and your generous funding, with which I was able to secure the work of the finest craftsmen in our land. And I know that you have pleased God by completing a representation of the Holy Trinity with the other tables that have served Christ and his disciples."

"Thank you for helping me to win the favor of God."

"Now," said Merlin, "if you will listen to me, I will tell you how to use the power of this table to bring the worthiest men into your allegiance, such that you will bring your entire realm into alignment, and create a structure of rule that this country has never known, and will secure your place as the honored and worthy king for many years to come."

"I will do as you advise," the king said.

"Tomorrow, all the kings, knights and barons of your kingdom, and their worthy ladies, will arrive for your celebrations. You will be generous with your gifts, and give away all of the wealth that you accumulated during the battle of Salisbury, honoring the sacrifice of your brother and all the worthy Britons who perished there by spreading the fruit of their accomplishment among the people of your land," he said. "A king cannot be too generous, and there is little he can do to secure the allegiance of those who have less than by distributing your wealth to those who will support you and bring your plans for this island to fruition."

"You have taught me that well, and I believe it," said the king.

"You will also be generous with your time, and make yourself available to meet and get to know all the worthy gentlemen and ladies that will gather here with you, for there is little of such value in creating fellowship like letting the people of your kingdom meet you and see into your eyes, and feel the confidence, honor and wisdom that resides there. And this will do incalculable work to ensure trust in your leadership, for they will display their confidence in you to the people that they encounter, but you will never meet, such that even the lowliest peasant may feel secure that their land is overseen by the wisest and most gracious lord they could ask for."

"I will do so Merlin," said the king, "and I look forward to it."

"You should, for your land contains many people quite worthy of your trust and friendship. Conduct yourself as I have advised for the week leading up to Whitsunday, and on the final night of your court I will go among the people and choose the worthiest men of your kingdom, and you will invite them to join you for a feast at this table. This room will be closed off so that you will not have servants and sundry folk coming and going."

Merlin placed his hand on the king's arm. "I want you to serve your guests with your own hand, and humble yourself before them and make them know that you want them in your fellowship. And I will, through my craft and the power of this table, make it so that the men who are at this feast will never, once they have sat there, want to leave this place and go back to their lands and domains. And thus you will create a kingdom filled with worthy men and ladies who will all support you in your efforts and make ruling everyone on this island far easier than it would be otherwise."

Uther nodded, and said that he would do exactly as Merlin advised. Anything he could do to make his rule run smoothly, and avoid any conflicts that might expose his inadequacies, he would do. Uther's mind was often filled with images of the greatness he could accomplish as king, but also often preoccupied with scenarios in which he lost control of his kingdom, and saw it slipping gradually out of his grasp.

All of which Merlin well knew.

"This is your seat," Merlin said, pointing to a place slightly larger and more grand than the others. Merlin then led the king around the table to the place directly opposite, which was also a bit larger than the rest, and also clearly a bit more special. "This seat is the one that stands for the place Judas had at the Last Supper, and is always to remain empty," said Merlin. "Do not let anyone sit there, and indeed they will ask you, because once they see that only the worthiest men are allowed to sit with you, they will want to sit with you also, and they will point to this seat and ask that they be seated there."

The king gazed on the enormous expanse of the incredible table. "It seems a pity that each place of this table cannot be filled," he said. "And that it could achieve perfect fellowship by being complete."

"It is complete, and perfect, as it is, including the void place," said Merlin. "This empty seat will keep the image of Judas ever in your mind, and remind you that betrayal and disloyalty are something that every

316

king must always be on guard against," Merlin said, touching the table there. "And I can tell you that this seat will not always remain empty, but will not be filled in your time, for the person that will sit there has not yet been conceived. In fact," Merlin added, "his father, who will also sit at this table, has not yet been conceived."

Uther nodded, and said nothing, for Merlin's words had brought an ugly awareness to him, which ran contrary to the warmth and confidence he had been feeling, that he was just one in a line of kings, and that this table would go on to serve others after his time.

"The one who will take this place is the knight who will fulfill the adventures of the grail. This will signal the end of the era in which we now live, and the time when the rule of Christ will drive out the numerous Gods and spirits that now hold sway in this land. This will not happen in your time," Merlin said, "but during the reign of a great king who will rule after you."

"I see," said Uther. That king, in the age to come, Merlin inferred, would be a "great" king. But he, in his age.... Uther hid his feelings, and remained impassive, but could not feel joy for what that other king would achieve.

"I bid you," continued Merlin, seeming to sense his thoughts, "hold all of your gatherings and high courts in this town, and stay and hold your court here three times a year. And for ever, when people speak of this table, they will say that the Round Table was founded by Uther Pendragon in his time."

Uther nodded. He knew that he should be happy at this gift, but it was hard to ignore that the true greatness of this table would be achieved by a king after him. His thumb began to rub again at the calloused cut in the flesh of his finger.

Merlin noted his silence. "As I have said, this table completes the symbolic Trinity with the tables that have served God himself, and the power of this table is not to be underestimated." He looked at Uther, and waited for the king to meet his gaze. "Do your utmost to always respect this table, and do not dishonor it, or disrespect my advice to you, by letting anyone sit in the void place." Merlin pointed at the place with a steady, unwavering finger. "Doing so will not hurt the table, or me, or God, but will bring great consequences to you, and destroy any unworthy man who thinks so highly of himself that he will dare to sit there. Do you understand?"

"Yes," said Uther, but his mind was elsewhere.

"Once I have selected the good and honorable men who will join you at this table," said Merlin, "I will be gone from you for two years."

"Gah—" choked the king. "Two years? Then you will not be in this town for all the feast days that I hold here?"

"No, I will not," said Merlin. "For I want all of the honor of this table, and these feasts, to accrue to you, and let no one say that I was responsible for your successes, or any of your accomplishments that will be achieved during that time."

The king swallowed, and tried to relax the tightening he had felt come to his brow. "Thank you, Merlin," he said.

Merlin once more placed his hand on the king's arm, and looked at him, smiling, in the eyes. "Trust when I tell you that you will face no great crisis during that time, or have need to enter into grand battle, and while that happens, you will see your own abilities grow, until you are comfortable wearing the mantle of the king." Merlin nodded, smiled at Uther, who could only force a smile but whose eyes had widened with intimidation. "And also, by my being away, you will be forced to trust in your own abilities, and I know that when I rejoin you," he used both hands to indicate the greatness of the king, "you will have fully grown into your power, and have ruled by your own decisions, such that the extent of your own wisdom and abilities will be clear to you."

Uther nodded, and his eyes dropped once more to the table. He knew he must say something, so he forced his eyes up to meet Merlin's long enough to say "Thank you," once more. But his hand, kept down to his side, continued to nervously rub his thumb against the callous on his forefinger.

The guests arrived and Uther feted them just as Merlin advised he should, giving away lavish gifts of armor, money and land, and making sure that everyone present was well fed, well attended to and happy. He went among them and visited with those whom he knew, and was sure to spend time getting to know those he hadn't met previously. Merlin also made himself available, though not nearly as much as Uther, since the package of King Uther that they were attempting to instill confidence in included that he had the advantage of the world's greatest seer on his side, whose foreknowledge would make the king well-neigh invincible. Merlin enjoyed meeting the people of the kingdom, and browsed their histories and futures as he walked among them or talked and got to know them, and there were several men and women that he liked very much, and felt were very devoted and decent people. One of them was the knight Sir Ector, whom he spent one evening talking to at length about the state of the country, what direction he would like to see it go in, and what he felt was most important in the stable prosperity of a kingdom. There were also some people that he took an immediate dislike to, for he could see at once into their hearts, and he made note of them as well.

He also found Mark, now lead of Uther's messengers, and made sure that he and his family, and the other messengers he had met, were well and in secure positions.

The week passed quickly in mirth and fun, and on the last night, Merlin went among the men and picked twenty-two of the most worthy that would sit with Uther at the Round Table that night. He chose Ulfius, of course, and Duke Gorlois of Tintagel—who unfortunately could not be joined by his wife—and the duke's esteemed knight, Bretel. Ulfius and Bretel took an immediate liking to each other, and were often found together in lively chat, drinking or practice swordplay when they were not otherwise called to gatherings with the king. King Pellinore was also selected, as were Kings Lot, Uriens and Nentres. King Lot made it plain that he supported Uther all the way, and spoke to him about the importance of royal lineage to the making of a true leader. Sir Baudwin was chosen, as was the King with the Hundred Knights, and King Leodegrance.

This left several men and women not selected to sit at the table, and Merlin was right that several of them seemed to take it hard, as they judged themselves to be quite worthy and overlooked unfairly. One of them, Sir Riger, found his eyes narrowing in dislike of the little wizard, and vowed that one day, he would indeed sit at that table— especially since there was an empty seat left over just for him.

When the men were chosen, Merlin shared a glance with Uther from across the room, nodded, and stepped out.

All marveled at the beauty of the Round Table, commended Uther for his wisdom in having it built, and ran their hands over it as they stood around it, feeling its wondrous, cool smoothness. When Uther bid them all to take their seats, they asked about the empty place, of course, and sat in lively conversation, many letting their hands run over the table, especially over the lovely, colorful inlaid stones, for there was something about the alluring surface of the table that made one want to touch it. The room was filled with lively, friendly voices, and the atmosphere was one of warm friendship and promise.

Uther then wheeled a cart around and served a broth to everyone with his own hand. No one made light of it, or made jokes about it, saying 'oh, are your servants so lazy?' or the suchlike, because the gesture was plain to everyone. They looked on him with great warmth and admiration as he humbled himself to serve them, and even Uther could feel the power of his gesture, and understand Merlin's brilliance in suggesting it. Several of the men reached out and ran a hand over the king's back or along his arm as he served, and as they did he felt any trace of the fears he had draining away, as he could see clearly now that Merlin was right—this week of feasts, and this particular, special repast, would go astonishingly far in cementing the allegiance of these, most worthy of men, and assuring the smooth running of his kingship. He wished he could tell Merlin about it

320

tomorrow. But increasingly, when he thought of the two years to come without seeing the wizard, the dread he had felt lessened dramatically, and he began to see that perhaps he could do it alone. Perhaps the next two years would be the biggest surprise of his life, and he would find himself the noble king he always wished he could be, but never thought he could rise to. Pendragon said he could grow into it. Maybe he was right.

All of the men were strangely taken by the broth, marveling at its rich but pure flavor. Merlin had shown up in the kitchen the day before with twenty-four urns of water, and insisted that the cooks use that to make the broth, and for any other cooking needs they had for that night's dinner.

When that course was done the servants took the bowls away—Uther was not to cast himself as the kitchen slave—and Uther went around the table again, placing each man's meal before him and telling him personally that he wished for them to enjoy their dinner. The men inhaled and were intoxicated by the wonderful smells of the meal before him, and each thought that he had never seen anything quite so delicious.

When he was done, Uther took his seat at the head of the table. The men dug into their meals, and conversation was quick and lively, each finding their company witty and wonderful, and sorry they hadn't made the acquaintance of such honorable men earlier. And they thanked Uther, in their minds, for bringing them together with such a fine group of illustrious leaders.

After they had finished, and all present were warm, sleepy-eyed and well fed, the servants came among them and removed the plates and filled the glasses once more, leaving wine on the table should anyone want more. Then the doors were quietly closed, leaving the men inside alone together. The servants had instructions not to enter again until the king himself opened the door from within.

At that moment, far across the country, Merlin was at Pendragon's monument and burial place on the plain of Salisbury, which was silent and magnificent, the powerful stones standing like great guardians against the light carpet of moonlit grass. The full moon was directly overhead—Merlin knew that, on this night, at this time, it would be aligned absolutely straight overhead, which is part of why he told Uther to hold his feast on that night. Even he felt special and privileged to be in such a magical place at such a quiet, serene moment. Then he reminded himself that he had built it, and felt even more tickled.

He had work to do. He had a number of milky, almost-clear stones, carved into crescent moon shapes, and he was busy hanging them in the spaces within the outer ring of standing stones. They were such that one could put them into the space sideways, then turn them, at which point they could be let go, and would hang between the two standing stones, connecting them. By the time he was done, it was as though a string of garlands created a complete circle amongst the outer standing stones, and the moonlight shone through the milky rock in such a way that illuminated them with its lovely light. Then Merlin had chanting to do, and gestures to make, and even dancing, nude dancing, around the inside of the outermost group of stones. Then, all this done, he removed a milky white stone from his bag, with a lovely opalescent quality that showed pale colors within interior of the solid half-egg shape, and placed it directly in the dead center of the monument. Then he removed himself quickly, and sat under the bright moonlight in the grass just outside the circular ditch.

Back at the Round Table, King Lot felt his shoulders relax, his tension leave, and—there was no doubt that a wholesale change of affect washed over him. He found himself silently looking at his new companions, a slight but solid smile on his face. As he looked around, these truly seemed like the most worthy men he could ever know, and his heart surged with admiration for them. He placed his hands forward on the table, where they naturally landed over the cool inset stones, and allowed his gaze to wander from face to face, where he saw bravery, and wisdom, and humility and perseverance in the face of adversity. Gradually all in the room fell quiet, not with any tension or need to speak, but in the ease that comes with complete comfort. Sir Ector was also letting his eyes wander across the faces of his companions, the expression of aching affection on his face touchingly unrestrained. They

322

noticed that all of the men had fallen silent, and were doing nothing but looking at each other. Each had never seen such a fine collection of men, and with each face, their hearts surged anew with an overwhelming need to know that person, to be his friend, and always offer him help when he needed it.

King Uriens was seated next to Duke Gorlois, and as they regarded each other with smiling faces, they found their hands clutching to one another without their even noticing, for it seemed so natural, they were not self-conscious about it at all. Ulfius, next to the king, patted his friend's hand, then left it there, atop his, and a moment later, they too held each other's hands in an easy, affectionate manner, as Ulfius looked across at Bretel, and thought that he had never seen so fine a knight. The gaze in Bretel's eyes did not judge him for it, simply took it in and returned open respect, they could simply stare at each other without either feeling the need to turn away, and in time, streaks of tears came downward from Bretel's eyes.

King Leodegrance's mouth came open, and his breath became labored as he was overcome with love for the men that surrounded him. It was not just them, it was a feeling of the country, that these men were of their land, and he felt the incredible strength that was apparent when all of them were together—and he never wanted to be parted from them. Looking around the table, all of the men had, without bidding, taken each other's hands, and most of their faces were wet with silent tears as their faces showed the ache of unguarded affection for everyone that surrounded them. And although it seemed like only a few minutes to those that were in attendance, they were actually in there, hands clutched in complete silence, for three hours.

"Is it moving?" said King Uriens, breaking the silence and seen looking with keen eyes toward the center of the table.

"I know, I thought it was moving, too!" responded Gorlois.

"Perhaps it is the light playing tricks with its shadows," added Nentres, for the flickering torchlight, along with the round circles of wood grain, created moving shadows of the ridges that were carved into the center of the table.

By then King Pellinore had removed his hands from his companions, and used them to wipe the wetness from his face. "I have no wish to ever leave this place," he said.

The admission made King Lot breathe out wetly. "I feel that way, too," he said. "Many of you I know only slightly. Many I have never met before at all. And now," he said, also wiping at his face, "I am thinking of asking my wife and children to move to this place, so I can be near all of you, and..." his hand ran over the smooth surface of the wood and stones, "this table."

"I want to be at this table every day at the hour of terce," said Uriens. "And live in this town, and..." he shook his head in wonder, "this is what my heart is telling me to do."

No one felt embarrassed or ashamed to tell his thoughts, because the feeling of trust and intimacy among their fellowship was that great.

"It is this table," said Bretel, who could not contain his tears, which he smeared over the table's surface as his hand ran over it.

"I have no bonds with most of you," said Ulfius. "And yet," he continued, eyes wide, "I feel the love for you that a son should have for his father," he said. "Or more."

Pellinore spoke again. "And it seems that we should never be parted from one another," he said, "unless it is by death."

And Uther, who was also overcome with these feelings of intense fellowship and love from these kings and knights of his kingdom, found tears streaming down his own cheeks, but he cared not to wipe them away, and he asked "Do all of you feel this way?" And each man seated there agreed that he did.

"Then let us take hands once more, and swear to love, believe and honor each other, just as you would your own self," he said, "and swear that we will do all that we can so this fellowship is never broken."

Then the men all cried in assent, and saw no need to unclasp hands when they were done. And they were the first Knights of the Round Table.

And Uther, as the king who all of this goodwill and feeling of allegiance centered around, could find no more trace of the fears or insecurity he had felt earlier, nothing but the high of the gathered love he felt flowing from all of his men—the first solid bond of knights from across all the lands of his new kingdom—and the knowledge, now solid as rock and firmly lodged within him, that he could vanquish his weakness, and if not extinguish it utterly, defeat it, as in combat, and kill it, so that he could rule confidently with great justice and honor.

When the king finally opened the door once more, and all the men filed out, they were shocked to be greeted by the bright light of morning. Each had thought he had been inside only a few hours! The brilliant sun warmed their faces and they stood, silently, their arms around each other's shoulders, feeling the wonderful exhaustion that comes from a night of exhilarating emotion. Uther looked down, across the wives and maidens who had been wondering where their husbands had been, and the squires who were readying their lord's horses to depart, and past them, to the castle and the houses within, the scurrying activity of peasants and busy merchants, and beyond that, to the red-orange sun that shone powerfully, silently down across the morning mists that touched the green grasses and gathered clumps of trees in the far distance, and he knew, with the unshakable truth of something his parents had told him, that he could, and would, be a good king.

In the Next Book

In **The Swithen Book 3: The Void Place** (*available now*), King Uther is struggling with the feeling that he is merely Merlin's puppet. Igraine is happily married with two daughters and has a great husband, who is also Uther's friend. Uther fixates on his friend's wife and has to possess her. Merlin steps in to help, but wants something out of the deal, too—a child of noble lineage—and may have been manipulating them all to get it. By the end, two lives are destroyed, but one is created—Arthur—and a sword appears in a stone in the kingdom of Logres, unable to be drawn by anyone but the future king.

Stay updated on future releases at theswithen.com.

Please share your opinion of this book with others

Please take the time to share your honest opinions about this book in a review online, to your friends and family, and on social media. I am an independent author, without the support that other authors receive, and your honest review or comment is tremendously influential, incredibly helpful, and greatly appreciated. Thank you for taking the time to share your honest opinions.

Website: https://theswithen.com
Facebook: https://www.facebook.com/TheSwithen/
Instagram: theswithen
Twitter: @TheSwithen
Email: TheSwithen@gmail.com

Made in the USA
Coppell, TX
08 November 2021